Bath Night...

Lady Maccon opened the closet door wide and took in the sorry sight of the gentleman before her. Lord Akeldama's drones were men of fashion and social standing. They set the mode for all of London with regards to collar points and spats. The handsome young man who stood before her represented the best London society had to offer—a beautiful plum tailcoat, a high-tied waterfall of white about his neck, his hair curled just so about the ears— except that he was dripping with soap suds, his neck cloth was coming untied, and one collar point drooped sadly.

"Oh, dear, what has she done now?"

"Far too much to explain, my lady. I think you had better come at once."

Alexia looked down at her beautiful new dress. "But I do so like this gown."

Praise for

The Parasol Protectorate Series

"Carriger debuts brilliantly with a blend of Victorian romance, screwball comedy of manners and alternate history.... This intoxicatingly witty parody will appeal to a wide cross-section of romance, fantasy and steampunk fans." —*Publishers Weekly* (Starred Review)

"Spectacular debut novel...a real page-turner."
—*Romantic Times*

"*Soulless* is a character-driven romp with great world-building and delicious rapier wit that recalls Austen and P. G. Wodehouse." —io9.com

"A delightfully fun supernatural comedy of manners, with a refreshing romance thrown in—and a highly promising first novel." —*Locus*

"*Soulless* has all the delicate charm of a Victorian parasol, and all the wicked force of a Victorian parasol secretly weighted with brass shot and expertly wielded. Ravishing."
—Lev Grossman, *New York Times*
Bestselling Author of *The Magicians*

BY GAIL CARRIGER

TIMELESS

The Parasol Protectorate: Book the Fifth

GAIL CARRIGER

www.orbitbooks.net

Copyright © 2012 by Tofa Borregaard
Excerpt from *Blood Rights* copyright © 2011 by Kristen Painter
All rights reserved. In accordance with the U.S. Copyright Act of 1976, the scanning, uploading, and electronic sharing of any part of this book without the permission of the publisher is unlawful piracy and theft of the author's intellectual property. If you would like to use material from the book (other than for review purposes), prior written permission must be obtained by contacting the publisher at permissions@hbgusa.com. Thank you for your support of the author's rights.

Orbit
Hachette Book Group
237 Park Avenue
New York, NY 10017
www.orbitbooks.net

Orbit is an imprint of Hachette Book Group. The Orbit name and logo are trademarks of Little, Brown Book Group Limited.

The Hachette Speakers Bureau provides a wide range of authors for speaking events. To find out more, go to www.hachettespeakersbureau.com or call (866) 376-6591.

The publisher is not responsible for websites (or their content) that are not owned by the publisher.

Printed in the United States of America

First edition: March 2012

10 9 8 7 6 5 4

Acknowledgments

Phrannish read this last book during the middle of production. Rach read it a week after giving birth. Iz did her rounds ill, having just returned from Israel and in the process of buying a house. So for all my girls, with lives more grown-up than mine, this writer beast is eternally grateful that you put said lives on hold...one final time. My personal parasol protectorate, thank you. We must do it again sometime.

TIMELESS

CHAPTER ONE

———

In Which There Is Almost a Bath and Definitely a Trip to the Theater

I said no such thing," grumbled Lord Maccon, allowing himself, begrudgingly, to be trussed in a new evening jacket. He twisted his head around, annoyed by the height of the collar and the tightness of the cravat. Floote patiently waited for him to stop twitching before continuing with the jacket. Werewolf or not, Lord Maccon would look his best or Floote's given name wasn't Algernon—which it was.

"Yes, you did, my dear." Lady Alexia Maccon was one of the few people in London who dared contradict Lord Maccon. Being his wife, it might be said that she rather specialized in doing so. Alexia was already dressed, her statuesque form resplendent in a maroon silk and black lace evening gown with mandarin collar and Asian sleeves, newly arrived from Paris. "I remember it quite distinctly." She pretended distraction in transferring her necessaries into a black beaded reticule. "I said we should show our patronage and support on opening night, and you *grunted* at me."

"Well, there, that explains everything. That was a grunt of displeasure." Lord Maccon wrinkled his nose like a petulant child while Floote skirted about him, puffing away nonexistent crumbs with the latest in steam-controlled air-puffing dewrinklers.

"No, dear, no. It was definitely one of your affirmative grunts."

Conall Maccon paused at that and gave his wife a startled look. "God's teeth, woman, how could you possibly tell?"

"Three years of marriage, dear. Regardless, I've replied in the affirmative that we will be in attendance at the Adelphi at nine sharp in time to take our box. We are *both* expected. There is no way out of it."

Lord Maccon sighed, giving in. Which was a good thing, as his wife and Floote had managed to strap him into full evening dress and there was no way to escape that.

In a show of solidarity, he grabbed his wife, pulling her against him and snuffling her neck. Alexia suppressed a smile and, in deference to Floote's austere presence, pretended not to enjoy herself immensely.

"Lovely dress, my love, very flattering."

Alexia gave her husband a little ear nibble for this compliment. "Thank you, my heart. However, you ought to know that the most interesting thing about this dress is how remarkably easy it is to get into and out of."

Floote cleared his throat to remind them of his presence.

"Wife, I intend to test the veracity of that statement when we return from this outing of yours."

Alexia pulled away from Conall, patting at her hair self-consciously. "Thank you kindly, Floote. Very well done as always. I'm sorry to have drawn you away from your regular duties."

The elderly butler merely nodded, expressionless. "Of course, madam."

"Especially as there seem to be no drones about. Where are they all?"

The butler thought for a moment and then said, "I believe that it is bath night, madam."

Lady Maccon paled in horror. "Oh, goodness. We had best escape quickly, then, Conall, or I'll never be able to get away in time for—"

Clearly summoned by her fear of just such a delay, a knock sounded at Lord Akeldama's third closet door.

How Lord and Lady Maccon had come to be residing in Lord Akeldama's third closet in the first place was a matter of some debate among those privy to this information. A few speculated that there had been a negotiated exchange of spats and possibly promises of daily treacle tart. Nevertheless, the arrangement seemed to be working remarkably well for all parties, much to everyone's bemusement, and so long as the vampire hives did not find out, it was likely to remain so. Lord Akeldama now had a preternatural in his closet and a werewolf pack next door, but he and his drones had certainly weathered much worse in the way of neighbors, and he had certainly housed far more shocking things in his closet, if the rumors were to be believed.

For nigh on two years, Lord and Lady Maccon had maintained the appearance of actually living next door, Lord Akeldama maintained the appearance of still utilizing all his closets, and his drones maintained the appearance of not having full creative control over everyone's wardrobe. Most importantly, as it turned out, Alexia was still close enough to her child to come to everyone's rescue. Unforeseen as it may have been when they originally concocted the arrangement, it had become increasingly clear that the home of a metanatural required the presence of a preternatural or no one was safe—particularly on bath night.

Lady Maccon opened the closet door wide and took in the sorry sight of the gentleman before her. Lord Akeldama's drones were men of fashion and social standing. They set the mode for all of London with regards to collar points and spats. The handsome young man who stood before her represented the best London society had to offer—an exquisite plum tailcoat, a high-tied waterfall of white about his neck, his hair curled just so about the ears—except that he was dripping with soap suds, his neck cloth was coming untied, and one collar point drooped sadly.

"Oh, dear, what has she done now?"

"Far too much to explain, my lady. I think you had better come at once."

Alexia looked down at her beautiful new dress. "But I do so like this gown."

"Lord Akeldama accidentally touched her."

"Oh, good gracious!" Lady Maccon seized her parasol and her beaded reticule—now containing a fan; her opera glassicals; and Ethel, her .28-caliber Colt Paterson revolver—and charged down the stairs after the drone. The poor boy actually squelched in his beautifully shined shoes.

Her husband, with a grumbled, "Didn't we warn him against that?" came crashing unhelpfully after.

Downstairs, Lord Akeldama had converted a side parlor into a bathing chamber for his adopted daughter. It had become clear rather early on that bathing was going to be an event of epic proportions, requiring a room large enough to accommodate several of his best and most capable drones. Still, this being Lord Akeldama, even a room dedicated to the cleanliness of an infant was not allowed to be sacrificed upon the unadorned altar of practicality.

A thick Georgian rug lay on the floor covered with cavorting shepherdesses, the walls were painted in pale blue and white, and he'd had the ceiling frescoed with sea life in deference to the troublesome child's evident unwillingness to associate with such. The cheerful otters, fish, and cephalopods above were meant as encouragement, but it was clear his daughter saw them as nothing more than squishy threats.

In the exact center of the room stood a gold, clawfooted bathtub. It was far too large for a toddler, but Lord Akeldama never did anything by halves, especially if he might double it at three times the expense. There was also a fireplace, before which stood multiple gold racks supporting fluffy and highly absorbent drying cloths and one very small Chinese silk robe.

There were no less than eight drones in attendance, as well as Lord Akeldama, a footman, and the nursemaid. Nevertheless, nothing could take on Prudence Alessandra Maccon Akeldama when bathing was at stake.

The tub was overturned, saturating the beautiful rug with soapy water. Several of the drones were drenched. One was nursing a bruised knee and another a split lip. Lord Akeldama had tiny soapy handprints all over him.

One of the drying racks had fallen on its side, singeing a cloth in the fire. The footman was standing with his mouth open, holding a bar of soap in one hand and a wedge of cheese in the other. The nanny had collapsed on a settee in tears.

In fact, the only person who seemed neither injured nor wet in any way was Prudence herself. The toddler was perched precariously on top of the mantelpiece over the fire, completely naked, with a very militant expression on her tiny face, yelling, "Noth, Dama. Noth wet. Noth, Dama!" She was lisping around her fangs.

Alexia stood in the doorway, transfixed.

Lord Akeldama straightened where he stood. "My *darlings*," he said, "tactic number eight, I think—circle and enclose. Now brace yourselves, my pets. I'm going in."

All the drones straightened and took up wide boxer's stances, forming a loose circle about the contested mantelpiece. All attention was focused on the toddler, who held the high ground, unflinching.

The ancient vampire launched himself at his adopted daughter. He could move fast, possibly faster than any other creature Alexia had ever observed, and she had been the unfortunate victim of more than one vampire attack. However, in this particular instance, Lord Akeldama moved no quicker than any ordinary mortal man. Which was, of course, the current difficulty—he *was* an ordinary mortal. His face was no longer deathless perfection but slightly effete and perhaps a little sulky. His movements were still graceful, but they were mortally graceful and, unfortunately, mortally slow.

Prudence leaped away in the manner of some kind of high-speed frog, her tiny, stubbly legs supernaturally strong but still toddler unstable. She crashed to the floor, screamed in very brief pain, and then zipped about looking for a break in the circle of drones closing in upon her.

"Noth, Dama. Noth wet," she cried, charging one of the drones, her tiny fangs bared. Unaware of her own supernatural strength, the baby managed to bash her way between the poor man's legs, making for the open doorway.

Except that the doorway was not, in fact, open. Therein stood the only creature who little Prudence had learned to fear and, of course, the one she loved best in all the world.

"Mama!" came her delighted cry, and then, "Dada!" as Conall's shaggy head loomed up from behind his wife.

Alexia held out her arms and Prudence barreled into them with all the supernatural speed that a toddler vampire could manage. Alexia let out a harrumph of impact and stumbled backward into Conall's broad, supportive embrace.

The moment the naked baby came into contact with Alexia's bare arms, Prudence became no more dangerous than any squirming child.

"Now, Prudence, what is this fuss?" remonstrated her mother.

"No, Dama. No wet!" explained the toddler very clearly, now that she did not have the fangs to speak around.

"It's bath night. You don't have a choice. Real ladies are clean ladies," explained her mother, rather sensibly, she thought.

Prudence was having none of it. "Nuh-uh."

Lord Akeldama came over. He was once more pale, his movements quick and sharp. "Apologies, my little dumpling. She got away from Boots there and hurled herself at me before I could dodge." He moved one fine white hand to stroke his adopted daughter's hair back from her face. It was safe to do so now that Alexia held her close.

Prudence narrowed her eyes suspiciously. "No wet, Dama," she insisted.

"Well, accidents will happen and we all know how she gets." Alexia gave her daughter a stern look. Prudence, undaunted, glared back. Lady Maccon shook her head in exasperation. "Conall and I are off to the theater. Do you think you can handle bath night without me? Or should we cancel?"

Lord Akeldama was aghast at the mere suggestion. "Oh, dear me no, *buttercup*, never that! *Not* go to the theater? Heaven forfend. No, we shall shift perfectly well here without you, now that we've weathered this one teeny-tiny upset, won't we, Prudence?"

"No," replied Prudence.

Lord Akeldama backed away from her. "I'll stay well out of range from here on, I assure you," continued the vampire. "One brush with mortality a night is more than enough for me. It's quite the *discombobulating* sensation, your daughter's touch. Not at all like your own."

Lord Maccon, who had been placed in a similar position on more than one occasion with regard to his daughter's odd abilities, was uncharacteristically sympathetic to the vampire. He replied with a fervent, "I'll say." He also took the opportunity of Prudence being in her mother's arms to ruffle his daughter's hair affectionately.

"Dada! No wet?"

"Perhaps we could move bath night to tomorrow," suggested Lord Maccon, succumbing to the plea in his daughter's eyes.

Lord Akeldama brightened.

"Absolutely not," replied Lady Maccon to both of them. "Backbone, gentlemen. We must stick to a routine. All the physicians say routine is vital to the well-being of the infant and her proper ethical indoctrination."

The two immortals exchanged the looks of men who knew when they were beaten.

In order to forestall any further shilly-shallying, Alexia carried her struggling daughter over to the tub, which had been righted and refilled with warm water. Under ordinary circumstances, she would have plopped the child in herself, but worried over the dress, she passed Prudence off to Boots and stepped well out of harm's way.

Under the watchful eye of her mother, the toddler acquiesced to full immersion, with only a nose wrinkle of disgust.

Alexia nodded. "Good girl. Now do behave for poor Dama. He puts up with an awful lot from you."

"Dama!" replied the child, pointing at Lord Akeldama.

"Yes, very good." Alexia turned back to her husband and the vampire in the doorway. "Do have a care, my lord."

Lord Akeldama nodded. "Indeed. I must say I had not *anticipated* such a challenge when Professor Lyall first suggested the adoption."

"Yes, it was foolish of all of us to think that Alexia here would produce a biddable child," agreed the sire of said child, implying that any flaw was Alexia's fault and that he would have produced nothing but the most mild-mannered and pliant of offspring.

"Or even one that a vampire could control."

"Or a vampire and a pack of werewolves, for that matter."

Alexia gave them both a *look*. "I hardly feel I can be entirely at fault. Are you claiming Sidheag is an aberration in the Maccon line?"

Lord Maccon tilted his head, thinking about his great-great-great-granddaughter, now Alpha werewolf of the Kingair Pack, a woman prone to wielding rifles and smoking small cigars. "Point taken."

Their conversation was interrupted by a tremendous splash as Prudence managed to pull, even without supernatural strength, one of the drones partly into the bath with her. Several of the others rushed to his aid, cooing in equal distress over his predicament and the state of his cuffs.

Prudence Alessandra Maccon Akeldama would have been difficult enough without her metanatural abilities. But having a precocious child who could take on immortality was overwhelming, even for two supernatural households. Prudence actually seemed to steal supernatural abilities, turning her victim mortal for the space of a night. If Alexia had not interfered, Lord Akeldama would have remained mortal, and Prudence a fanged toddler, until sunrise. Her mother, or presumably some other preternatural, was the only apparent antidote.

Lord Maccon had accustomed himself, with much grumbling, to touching his daughter only when she was already in contact with her mother or when it was daylight. He was a man who appreciated a good cuddle, so this was disappointing. But poor Lord Akeldama found the whole situation distasteful. He had officially adopted the chit, and as a result had taken on the lion's share of her care, but he was never actually able to show her physical affection. When she was a small child, he'd managed with leather gloves and thick swaddling blankets, but even then accidents occurred. Now that Prudence was more mobile, the risk was simply too great. Naked touch guaranteed activation of her powers, but sometimes she could steal through clothing, too. When Prudence got older and more reasonable, Alexia intended to subject her daughter to some controlled analytical tests, but right now everyone in the household was simply trying to survive. The toddler couldn't be less interested in the importance of scientific discoveries, for all her mother tried to explain them. It was, Alexia felt, a troubling character flaw.

With one last glare to ensure Prudence remained at least mostly submerged, Alexia made good her escape, dragging her husband behind her. Conall held his amusement in check until they were inside the carriage and on their way toward the West End. Then he let out the most tremendous guffaw.

Alexia couldn't help it—she also started to chuckle. "Poor Lord Akeldama."

Conall wiped his streaming eyes. "Oh, he loves it. Hasn't had this much excitement in a hundred years or more."

"Are you certain they will manage without me?"

"We will be back in only a few hours. How bad can it get?"

"Don't tempt fate, my love."

"Better worry about our own survival."

"Why, what could you possibly mean?" Alexia straightened and looked out the carriage window suspiciously. True, it had been several years since someone tried to kill her in a conveyance, but it had happened with startling regularity for a period of time, and she had never gotten over her suspicion of carriages as a result.

"No, no, my dear. I meant to imply the play to which I am being dragged."

"Oh, I like that. As if I could drag you anywhere. You're twice my size."

Conall gave her the look of a man who knows when to hold his tongue.

"Ivy has assured me that this is a brilliant rendition of a truly moving story and that the troupe is in top form after their continental tour. *The Death Rains of Swansea*, I believe it is called. It's one of Tunstell's own pieces, very artistic and performed in the new sentimental interpretive style."

"Wife, you are taking me unto certain doom." He put his hand to his head and fell back against the cushioned wall of the cab in a fair imitation of theatricality.

"Oh, hush your nonsense. It will be perfectly fine."

Her husband's expression hinted strongly at a preference for, perhaps, death or at least battle, rather than endure the next few hours.

The Maccons arrived, displaying the type of elegance expected from members of the ton. Lady Alexia Maccon was resplendent, some might even have said handsome, in her new French gown. Lord Maccon looked like an earl for once, his hair *almost* under control and his evening dress *almost* impeccable. It was generally thought that the move to London had resulted in quite an improvement in the appearance and manners of the former Woolsey Pack. Some blamed living so close to Lord Akeldama, others the taming effect of an urban environment, and several stalwart holdouts thought it might be Lady Maccon's fault. In truth, it was probably all three, but it was the iron fist of Lord Akeldama's drones that truly enacted the change—or should one say, iron curling tongs? One of Lord Maccon's pack merely had to enter their purview with hair askew and handfuls of clucking pinks descended upon him like so many mallard ducks upon a hapless piece of untidy bread.

Alexia led her husband firmly to their private box. The whites of his eyes were showing in fear.

The Death Rains of Swansea featured a lovelorn werewolf enamored of a vampire queen and a dastardly villain with evil intent trying to tear them apart. The stage vampires were depicted with particularly striking fake fangs and a messy sort of red paint smeared about their chins. The werewolves sported proper dress except for large shaggy ears tied about their heads with pink tulle bows— Ivy's influence, no doubt.

Ivy Tunstell, Alexia's dear friend, played the vampire queen. She did so with much sweeping about the stage and fainting, her own fangs larger than anyone else's, which made it so difficult for her to articulate that many of her speeches were reduced to mere spitting hisses. She wore a hat that was part bonnet, part crown, driving home the queen theme, in colors of yellow, red, and gold. Her husband, playing the enamored werewolf, pranced about in a comic interpretation of lupine leaps, barked a lot, and got into several splendid stage fights.

The oddest moment, Alexia felt, was a dreamlike sequence just prior to the break, wherein Tunstell wore bumblebee-striped drawers with attached vest and performed a small ballet before his vampire queen. The queen was dressed in a voluminous black chiffon gown with a high Shakespearian collar and an exterior corset of green with matching fan. Her hair was done up on either side of her head in round puffs, looking like bear ears, and her arms were bare. *Bare!*

Conall, at this juncture, began to shake uncontrollably.

"I believe this is meant to symbolize the absurdity of their improbable affection," explained Alexia to her husband in severe tones. "Deeply philosophical. The bee represents the circularity of life and the unending buzz of immortality. Ivy's dress, so like that of an opera girl, suggests at the frivolousness of dancing through existence without love."

Conall continued to vibrate silently, as though trembling in pain.

"I'm not certain about the fan or the ears." Alexia tapped her cheek thoughtfully with her own fan.

The curtain dropped on the first act with the bumblebee-clad hero left prostrate at the feet of his vampire love. The audience erupted into wild cheers. Lord Conall Maccon began to guffaw in loud rumbling tones that carried beautifully throughout the theater. Many people turned to look up at him in disapproval.

Well, thought his wife, *at least he managed to hold it in until the break.*

Eventually, her husband controlled his mirth. "Brilliant! I apologize, wife, for objecting to this jaunt. It is immeasurably entertaining."

"Well, do be certain to say nothing of the kind to poor Tunstell. You are meant to be profoundly moved, not amused."

A timid knock came at their box.

"Enter," yodeled his lordship, still chuckling.

The curtain was pushed aside, and in came one of the

people Alexia would have said was least likely to visit the theater, Madame Genevieve Lefoux.

"Good evening, Lord Maccon, Alexia."

"Genevieve, how unexpected."

Madame Lefoux was dressed impeccably. Fraternization with the Woolsey Hive had neither a deleterious nor improving effect on her attire. If Countess Nadasdy had tried to get her newest drone to dress appropriately, she had failed. Madame Lefoux dressed to the height of style, for a man. Her taste was still subtle and elegant with no vampiric flamboyances in the manner of cravat ties or cuff links. True she sported cravat pins and pocket watches, but Alexia would lay good money that not a one solely functioned as a cravat pin or a pocket watch.

"Are you enjoying the show?" inquired the Frenchwoman.

"I am finding it diverting. Conall is not taking it seriously."

Lord Maccon puffed out his cheeks.

"And you?" Alexia directed the question back at her erstwhile friend. Since Genevieve's wildly spectacular charge through London and resulting transition to vampire drone, no small measure of awkwardness had existed between them. Two years on and still they had not regained the closeness they had both so enjoyed at the beginning of their association. Madame Lefoux had polluted it through the application of a rampaging octomaton, and Alexia had finished it off by sentencing Genevieve to a decade of indentured servitude.

"It is interesting," replied the Frenchwoman cautiously. "And how is little Prudence?"

"Difficult, as ever. And Quesnel?"

"The same."

The two women exchanged careful smiles. Lady Maccon, despite herself, liked Madame Lefoux. There was just something about her that appealed. And she did owe the Frenchwoman a debt, for it was the inventor who had acted the part of midwife to Prudence's grossly mistimed entrance into the world. Nevertheless, Alexia did not trust her. Madame Lefoux always promoted her own agenda first, even as a drone, with the Order of the Brass Octopus second. What little loyalty and affection for Alexia she still had must, perforce, be a low priority now.

Lady Maccon moved them on from the platitudes with a direct reminder. "And how is the countess?"

Madame Lefoux gave one of her little French shrugs. "She is herself, unchanging, as ever. It is on her behest that I am here. I have been directed to bring you a message."

"Oh, yes, how did you know where to find me?"

"The Tunstells have a new play, and you are their patroness. I admit I had not anticipated *your* presence, my lord."

Lord Maccon grinned wolfishly. "I was persuaded."

"The message?" Alexia put out her hand.

"Ah, no, we have all learned never to do *that* again. The message is a verbal one. Countess Nadasdy has received instructions and would like to see you, Lady Maccon."

"Instructions? Instructions from who?"

"I am not privy to that information," replied the inventor.

Alexia turned to her husband. "Who on earth would dare order around the Woolsey Hive queen?"

"Oh, no, Alexia, you misunderstand me. The instructions came *to* her, but they are *for* you."

"Me? Me! Why . . . ," Alexia sputtered in outrage.

"I'm afraid I know nothing more. Are you available to call upon her this evening, after the performance?"

Alexia, whose curiosity was quite piqued, nodded her acquiescence. "It is bath night, but Lord Akeldama and his boys must really learn to muddle through."

"Bath night?" The Frenchwoman was intrigued.

"Prudence is particularly difficult on bath nights."

"Ah, yes. Some of them don't want to get clean. Quesnel was like that. As you may have noticed, circumstances never did improve." Genevieve's son was known for being grubby.

"And how is he muddling along, living with vampires?"

"Thriving, the little monster."

"Much like Prudence, then."

"As you say." The Frenchwoman tilted her head. "And my hat shop?"

"Biffy has it marvelously well in hand. You should drop by and visit. He's there tonight. I'm certain he would love to see you."

"Perhaps I shall. It's not often I get into London these days." Madame Lefoux began edging toward the curtain, donning her gray top hat and making her good-byes.

She left Lord and Lady Maccon in puzzled silence, with a mystery that, it must be said, somewhat mitigated their enjoyment of the second act, as did the lack of any additional bumblebee courtship rituals.

CHAPTER TWO

Wherein Mrs. Colindrikal-Bumbcruncher Does Not Buy a Hat

"Don't you believe this would suit the young miss better?" Biffy was a man of principle. He refused, on principle, to sell a huge tricolored pifferaro bonnet decorated with a cascade of clove pinks, black currants, and cut jet beads to Mrs. Colindrikal-Bumbcruncher for her daughter. Miss Colindrikal-Bumbcruncher was plain, dreadfully plain, and the bonnet was rather more of an insult than a decoration by contrast. The hat was the height of fashion, but Biffy was convinced a little gold straw bonnet was the superior choice. Biffy was *never wrong about hats*. The difficulty lay in convincing Mrs. Colindrikal-Bumbcruncher of this fact.

"You see, madam, the refined elegance complements the delicacy of Miss Colindrikal-Bumbcruncher's complexion."

Mrs. Colindrikal-Bumbcruncher did not see and would have none of it. "No, young man. The pifferaro, if you please."

"I'm afraid that is not possible, madam. That hat is promised elsewhere."

"Then why is it out on the floor?"

"A mistake, Mrs. Colindrikal-Bumbcruncher. My apologies."

"I see. Well, clearly we have made a *mistake* in patronizing your establishment! I shall take my custom *elsewhere*. Come, Arabella." With which the matron marched out, dragging her daughter in her wake. The young lady mouthed an apology behind her mother's back and gave the little gold straw bonnet a wistful look. *Poor creature*, thought Biffy, before returning both hats to their displays.

The silver bells attached to the front of the shop tinkled as a new customer entered. Some evenings those bells never seemed to stop. The store was increasingly popular, despite Biffy's occasional refusal to actually sell hats. He was getting a reputation for being an eccentric. Perhaps not quite so much as the previous owner, but there were ladies who would travel miles in order to have a handsome young werewolf refuse to sell them a hat.

He looked up to see Madame Lefoux. She carried in with her the slightly putrid scent of London and her own special blend of vanilla and machine oil. She was looking exceptionally well, Biffy thought. Life in the country clearly agreed with her. She was not, perhaps, so dandified in dress and manner as Biffy and his set, but she certainly knew how to make the most of somber blues and grays. He wondered, not for the first time, what she might look like in a proper gown. Biffy couldn't help it, he was excessively fond of female fashions and could not quite understand why a woman, with so many delicious options, might choose to dress and live as a man.

"Another satisfied customer, Mr. Biffy?"

"Mrs. Colindrikal-Bumbcruncher has the taste level of an ill-educated parboiled potato."

"Revolting female," agreed the Frenchwoman amiably, "and her gowns are always so well made. Makes her that much more vexing. Did you know her daughter is engaged to Captain Featherstonehaugh?"

Biffy raised one eyebrow. "And he's not the first, I hear."

"Why, Mr. Biffy, you talk such scandal."

"You wrong me, Madame Lefoux. I never gossip. I observe. And then relay my observations to practically everyone."

The inventor smiled, showing her dimples.

"How may I help you this evening?" Biffy put on his shopboy persona. "A new chapeau, or were you thinking about some other fripperies?"

"Oh, well, perhaps." Madame Lefoux's reply was vague as she looked about her old establishment.

Biffy tried to imagine it through her eyes. It was much the same. The hats still dangled from long chains so that patrons had to push their way through swaying tendrils, but the secret door was now even more well hidden behind a curtained-off back area, and he had expanded recently, opening up a men's hats and accessories section.

The Frenchwoman was drawn into examination of a lovely top hat in midnight blue velvet.

"That would suit your complexion very well," commented Biffy when she fingered the turn of the brim.

"I am sure you are right, but not tonight. I simply came to visit the old place. You have tended it well."

Biffy gave a little bow. "I am but a steward to your vision."

Madame Lefoux huffed in amusement. "Flatterer."

Biffy never knew where he stood with Madame Lefoux. She was so very much outside his experience: an inventor, a scientist, and middle class, with a marked preference for the company of young ladies and an eccentricity of dress that was too restrained to be unstudied. Biffy didn't like enigmas—they were out of fashion.

"I have recently come from seeing Lord and Lady Maccon at the theater."

Biffy was willing to play along. "Oh, indeed? I thought it was bath night."

"Apparently, Lord Akeldama was left to muddle through alone."

"Oh, dear."

"It occurred to me that we have switched places, you and I."

The French, thought Biffy, *could be very philosophical*. "Come again?"

"I have become a reluctant drone to vampires and you nest in the bosom of the Maccon home and hearth."

"Ah, were you once in that bosom? I had thought you never quite got all the way inside. Not for lack of trying, of course."

The Frenchwoman laughed. "Touché."

The front door tinkled again. *Busy night for new moon.* Biffy looked up, smile in place, knowing he made a fetching picture. He wore his very best brown suit. True, his cravat was tied more simply than he liked—his new claviger needed training—and his hair was slightly mussed. His hair was *always* slightly mussed these days despite liberal application of Bond Street's best pomade. One, apparently, had to bear up under such tribulations when one was a werewolf.

Felicity Loontwill entered the shop and wafted over to him in a flutter of raspberry taffeta and a great show of cordiality. She smelled of too much rose water and too little sleep. Her dress was very French, her hair was very German, and her shoes were quite definitely Italian. He could detect the odor of fish oil.

"Mr. Rabiffano, I was so hoping you would be here. And Madame Lefoux, how unexpectedly delightful!"

"Why, Miss Loontwill, back from your European tour already?" Biffy didn't like Lady Maccon's sister. She was the type of girl who would show her neck to a vampire one moment and her ankle to a chimney sweep the next.

"Yes. And what a bother it was. Two years abroad with absolutely nothing to show for it."

"No delusional Italian count or French marquis fell in love with you? Shocking." Madame Lefoux's green eyes twinkled.

The door jingled again and Mrs. Loontwill and Lady Evelyn Mongtwee entered the shop. Lady Evelyn headed immediately toward a spectacular hat of chartreuse and crimson, while Mrs. Loontwill followed her other daughter up to the counter.

"Oh, Mama, do you remember Mr. Rabiffano? He belongs to our dear Alexia's household."

Mrs. Loontwill looked at the dandy suspiciously. "Oh, does he, indeed? A pleasure to meet you, I'm sure. Come away, Felicity."

Mrs. Loontwill didn't even glance in Madame Lefoux's direction.

The three ladies then gave their undivided attention to the hats while Biffy tried to comprehend what they were about.

Madame Lefoux voiced his thoughts. "Do you think they are actually here to shop?"

"I believe Lady Maccon is not receiving them at present, so they may be after information." He looked suspiciously at the Frenchwoman. "Now that Felicity has returned, will she be rejoining the Woolsey Hive?"

Madame Lefoux shrugged. "I don't know, but I shouldn't think so. I can't imagine it holds much appeal, now that the hive is located outside London. You know these society chits—only interested in the glamorous side of immortality. She may find herself another hive. Or a husband, of course."

At which juncture Felicity returned to them, in clear defiance of her mother's wishes. "Mr. Rabiffano, how is my *dear* sister? I can hardly believe how long it has been since I saw her last."

"She is well," replied Biffy, utterly passive.

"And that child of hers? My darling little niece?"

Her face sharpened when she was being nosy, noted Biffy, rather like that of an inquisitive trout. "She, too, is well."

"And how is Lord Maccon? Still doting upon them both?"

"Still, as you say, doting."

"Why, Mr. Rabiffano, you have grown so dreary and terse since your accident."

With a twinkle to his eye, the dandy gestured at the little gold straw bonnet. "What do you think of this one, Miss Loontwill? It is very subtle and sophisticated."

Felicity backed away hurriedly. "Oh, no, mine is too bold a beauty for anything so insipid." She turned away. "Mama, Evy, have you seen anything to your taste?"

"Not tonight, my dear."

"No, sister, although that green and red toque makes quite the statement."

Felicity looked back at Madame Lefoux, on point. "How unfortunate that you are no longer in charge here, madame. I do believe that the quality may have fallen."

Madame Lefoux said nothing and Biffy took the hit without flinching.

"Do, please, give my sister and her husband my best regards. I do hope they remain blissfully enamored of one another, although it is terribly embarrassing." Felicity whirled to the French inventor. "And give the countess my compliments as well, of course."

With that, the rose-scented blonde led her mother and her sister out into the night with nary a backward glance.

Biffy and Madame Lefoux exchanged looks.

"What was *that* about?" wondered the inventor.

"A warning of some kind."

"Or an offer? I think I should return to Woolsey."

"You are turning into a very good drone, aren't you, Madame Lefoux?"

As she made her way out, the Frenchwoman gave him a look that suggested she preferred it if everyone thought that. Biffy hoarded away that bit of information. He had much to tell Lady Maccon when he saw her next.

Alexia and Conall arrived home from the theater prepared to go out immediately to call on the Woolsey Hive. One did not ignore an invitation from Countess Nadasdy, even if one was a peer of the realm. Alexia alighted from her gilded carriage in a flutter of taffeta and intrigue, marching into her town residence with strides of such vigor as to make the bustle of her dress sway alarmingly back and forth. Lord Maccon eyed this appreciatively. The tuck-in at his wife's waist was particularly appealing, emphasizing an area ideally suited to a man's hand, particularly if one had hands as large as his. Alexia turned in the doorway and gave him a look.

"Oh, do hurry." They were still making a show of living in their own house and so had to move swiftly up the stairs and across the secret gangplank into Lord Akeldama's residence in order to effect a change of attire.

Floote's dapper head emerged from the back parlor as they did so. "Madam?"

"Not stopping, Floote. We have been *summoned*."

"Queen Victoria?"

"No, worse—a queen."

"Will you go by rail or shall I have the groom switch to fresh horses?"

Alexia paused halfway up the grand staircase.

"Train, I think, please."

"At once, madam."

Prudence, much to everyone's delight, was down for her nap, nested with her head atop Lord Akeldama's cat and her feet tucked under the Viscount Trizdale's lemon-satin-covered leg. The viscount was looking strained, obviously under orders not to move for fear of waking the child. Prudence was wearing an excessively frilly dress of cream and lavender plaid. Lord Akeldama had changed into an outfit of royal purple and champagne to complement it and was sitting nearby, a fond eye to his drone and adopted daughter. He appeared to be reading a suspiciously embossed novel, but Alexia could not quite countenance such an activity in Lord Akeldama. To her certain knowledge, he never read anything, except perhaps the society gossip columns. She was unsurprised when, upon catching sight of them lurking in the hallway, the vampire put his book down with alacrity and sprang to meet them.

Together they looked at the lemony drone, calico feline, and plaid pile of infant.

"Isn't that just a *picture*?" Lord Akeldama was adrift on a sea of candy-colored domestic bliss.

"All is well?" Alexia spoke in hushed tones.

The vampire tucked a lock of silvery blond hair behind his ear in an oddly soft gesture. "*Excessively.* The puggle behaved herself after you departed, and as you can see, we had no further incidents of note."

"I do hope she grows out of this dislike for soap suds."

Lord Akeldama gave Lord Maccon a significant sort of once-over where he lurked behind his wife in the hallway. "My *darling* chamomile bud, we can but hope."

Lord Maccon took mild offense and sniffed at himself subtly.

"Conall and I have been summoned to visit Woolsey. You will manage without us for the remainder of the night?"

"I believe we may, *just possibly*, survive, my little periwinkle."

Lady Maccon smiled and was about to head upstairs to change her gown when someone pulled the bell rope. Being already in the hallway and hoping to keep Prudence from waking, Lord Maccon dashed to answer the door despite the fact that this was most unbecoming for a werewolf of his station, and it was someone else's house.

"Oh, really, Conall. Do try *not* to behave like a footman," remonstrated his wife.

Ignoring her, Lord Maccon opened the door with a flourish and a tiny bow—as behooved a footman.

Lady Maccon cast her hands up in exasperation.

Fortunately it was only Professor Lyall on the stoop. If any man was used to Lord Maccon's disregard for all laws of propriety and precedence, it was his Beta. "Oh, good, my lord. I was hoping to catch you here."

"Randolph."

"Dolly *darling*!" said Lord Akeldama.

Professor Lyall didn't even twitch an eyelid at the appalling moniker.

"You had a visitor, my lord," said the Beta to his Alpha, looking refined.

Alexia was confident enough in her assessment of Lyall's character to spot a certain tension. He displayed quick efficiency under most circumstances. Such forced calm as this indicated a need for caution.

Her husband knew this, too. Or perhaps he smelled something. He loosened his stance, prepared to fight. "BUR or pack business?"

"Pack."

"Oh, must I? Is it terribly important? We are required out of town."

Alexia interrupted. "I alone am required. You, as I understand it, my love, were simply coming along out of curiosity."

Conall frowned. His wife knew perfectly well that the real reason he wished to accompany her was for security. He hated sending her into a hive alone. Alexia waggled her reticule at him. As yet, there was no new parasol in her life, but she still carried Ethel, and the sundowner gun was good enough when pointed at a vampire queen.

"I'm afraid this is important," said a new voice from behind Professor Lyall, in the street.

Professor Lyall's lip curled slightly. "I thought I told you to wait."

"Dinna forget, I'm Alpha. You canna order me around like you do everyone else."

Alexia thought that a tad unfair. Professor Lyall was many things, but he was not at all tyrannical. That was more Conall's style. It might be better said that Professor Lyall *arranged* everyone and everything around him just so. Alexia didn't mind in the least; she was rather fond of a nice arrangement.

A woman moved out of the gloom of the front garden and into the light cast by the bright gas chandeliers of Lord Akeldama's hallway. Professor Lyall, polite man that he was, shifted to one side to allow their unexpected visitor to take center stage.

Sidheag Maccon, the Lady of Kingair, looked much the same as she had almost three years earlier, when Alexia had seen her last. Immortality had given her skin a certain pallor, but her face was still grim and lined about the eyes and mouth, and she still wore her graying hair back in one heavy plait, like a schoolgirl. She wore a threadbare velvet cloak that would do nothing to ward off the evening's chill. Alexia noted the woman's bare feet. Clearly, the cloak was not for cold but for modesty.

"Evening, Gramps," said Lady Kingair to Lord Maccon, and then, "Grams," to Alexia. Considering she looked older than both, it was an odd kind of greeting to anyone unfamiliar with the Maccon's familial relationships.

"Great-Great-Great-Granddaughter," responded Lord Maccon tersely. "To what do we owe this honor?"

"We have a problem."

"Oh, do *we*?"

"Yes. May I come in?"

Lord Maccon shifted, making an open-hand gesture back at Lord Akeldama, this being the vampire's house. Vampires were odd about inviting people in. Lord Akeldama had once muttered something about imbalance in the tether ratio after Lady Maccon entertained Mrs. Ivy Tunstell overly long in his drawing room. He seemed to have adjusted tolerably well to Prudence and her parents living under his roof, but after the Ivy tea incident, Alexia always made certain to entertain her guests next door, in her own parlor.

Lord Akeldama peeked over Lady Maccon's shoulder, standing on tiptoe. "I don't believe we have been introduced, young lady." His tone of voice said much on the subject of any woman darkening his doorstep with plaited hair, a Scottish accent, and an old velvet cloak.

Alexia pivoted slightly and, after a quick consideration, decided Lady Kingair was just lady enough to warrant the precedence, and said, "Lady Kingair, may I introduce our host, Lord Akeldama? Lord Akeldama, this is Sidheag Maccon, Alpha of the Kingair Pack."

Everyone waited a breath.

"I thought as much." Lord Akeldama gave a little bow. "Enchanted."

The female werewolf nodded.

The two immortals evaluated each other. Alexia wondered if either saw beyond the outrageousness of the other's appearance. Lord Akeldama's eyes gleamed and Lady Kingair sniffed at the air.

Finally Lord Akeldama said, "Perhaps you had best come in."

Alexia felt a surge of triumph at the achievement of such civilized discourse under such trying social circumstances. Introductions had been made!

However, her pleasure was interrupted by a high-treble query from behind them. "Dama?"

"Ah, I see *somebody* is awake. Good evening, my puggle darling." Lord Akeldama turned away from his new acquaintance to look fondly down the corridor.

Prudence's little head poked out from the drawing room. Tizzy stood behind her, looking apologetic. "I *am* sorry, my lord. She heard your voices."

"Not to worry, my ducky *darling*. I know how she gets."

Prudence seemed to take that as an invitation and padded down the hallway on her little stubby legs. "Mama! Dada!"

Lady Kingair, momentarily forgotten, was intrigued. "This must be my new great-great-great-aunt?"

Alexia's forehead creased. "Is that correct? Shouldn't it be great-great-great-great-half sister?" She looked at her husband for support. "Immortality makes for some pretty peculiar genealogy, I must say." *No wonder the vampires refuse to metamorphose those with children. Very tidy of them.* Vampires preferred to have everything in the universe neat. In that, Alexia sympathized with their struggles.

Lord Maccon frowned. "No, I believe it must be something more along the lines of—"

He never finished his sentence. Prudence, seeing that there was a stranger among her favorite people, and assuming that all who came into her presence would instantly adore her, charged Lady Kingair.

"Oh, no, *wait*!" said Tizzy.

Too late, Alexia dove to pick up her daughter.

Prudence dodged through the legs of the adults and latched on to Lady Kingair's leg, which was quite naked under the velvet cloak. In the space of a heartbeat, the infant changed into a small wolf cub, muslin dress ripped to tatters in the process. The cub, far faster than a toddler, went barreling off down the street, tail waving madly.

"So that's what *flayer* means," said Sidheag, pursing her lips and arching her eyebrows. Her unnatural pallor was gone and the lines in her face were more pronounced—mortality had returned.

Without even a pause, Lord Maccon stripped smoothly out of his full evening dress in a manner that suggested he had been practicing of late. Alexia blushed.

"Well, welcome to London Town, indeed!" exclaimed Lord Akeldama, whipping out a large feather fan and fluttering it vigorously in front of his face.

"Oh, Conall, really, in full view!" was Alexia's response, but her husband was already changing midstride from human to wolf. It was done with a good deal of finesse. Even if it was done right there for all the world to see. Sometimes being married to a werewolf was almost too much for a lady of breeding. Alexia contemplated divesting Lord Akeldama of his fan—her face was quite hot, and *he* no longer possessed the ability to blush. As if reading her mind, he angled about so that he could fan them both.

"That is a lovely fan," said Alexia under her breath.

"Isn't it marvelous? From a little shop I discovered off Bond Street. Shall I order one for you as well?"

"In teal?"

"Of course, my blushing pumpkin."

"I do apologize for my husband's behavior."

"Werewolves will happen, my pickled gherkin. One has to merely keep a stiff upper lip."

"My dear Lord A, you keep stiff whatever you wish—you always do."

"Doesn't it hurt her?" Lady Kingair asked rather wistfully as Alexia exited the vampire's house down the front stoop to stand next to her, watching as the massive wolf chased the tiny cub.

"Not that we can tell."

"And how long will this last?" Sidheag made a gesture up and down her own body, indicating her altered state.

"Until sunrise. Unless I intervene."

Sidheag held a naked arm out at Lady Maccon hopefully.

"Oh, no, not you. The preternatural touch has no effect on you anymore. You're mortal. No, I have to touch my daughter. Then immortality, sort of, well, reverberates back to you. Difficult to explain. I wish we understood more."

Professor Lyall stood off to one side, a tiny smile on his face, watching the chaos in the street.

Prudence tried to hide behind a pile of delivery crates stacked on one side of the road. Lord Maccon went after her, knocking the crates to the ground with a tremendous clatter. The wolf cub went for the steam-powered monowheel propped against the stone wall of the Colindrikal-Bumbcruncher's front yard. Mr. Colindrikal-

Bumbcruncher was particularly fond of his monowheel. He had it specially commissioned from Germany at prodigious expense.

Prudence took refuge behind the spokes of the center area. Lord Maccon was having none of it. He wiggled one mighty paw through to get at her. The spokes bent slightly, Lord Maccon got stuck, and Prudence dodged out, pelting once more down the street. Her tail wagged even more enthusiastically at the delightful game.

Lord Maccon extracted himself from the monowheel, shaking loose and causing the beautiful contraption to crash over with an ominous crunch. Lady Maccon made a mental note to send a card of apology around to their neighbors as soon as possible. The unfortunate Colindrikal-Bumbcrunchers had suffered great travails over the past two years. The town house had been in Mr. Colindrikal-Bumbcruncher's family for generations. Its proximity to a rove vampire was well known and tolerated, if not exactly accepted. Just as all the best castles had poltergeists, so all the best neighborhoods had vampires. But the addition of werewolves to their quiet corner of London was *outside of enough*. Mrs. Colindrikal-Bumbcruncher had recently snubbed Lady Maccon in the park, and frankly, Alexia couldn't fault her for it.

She squinted at the Colindrikal-Bumbcruncher house, trying to see if an inquisitive face at a window might have observed Conall's transformation in Lord Akeldama's hallway. That would require an even more profound apology, and a gift. *Fruitcake, perhaps.* Then again, perhaps the sight of Lord Maccon's backside might warrant less of an apology, depending on Mrs. Colindrikal-Bumbcruncher's preferences. Lady Maccon was distracted from this line of thinking by Professor Lyall's shout of amazement.

"Great ghosts, would you look at that?"

Alexia could not recall Professor Lyall ever raising his voice. She whirled about and looked.

Prudence had reached a good distance away, near to the end of the street, where an orange-tinted lamp cast a weak glow on the corner. There she had turned abruptly back into a squalling, naked infant. It was very embarrassing for all concerned. Particularly, if her screams of outrage were to be believed, Prudence.

"Well, my goodness," said Alexia. "That's never happened before."

Professor Lyall became quite professorial. "Has she ever gotten that far away from one of her victims before?"

Lady Maccon was slightly offended. "Must we use that word? *Victim*?"

Professor Lyall gave her an expressive look.

She acquiesced. "Quite right, it *is* unfortunately apt. Not that I know of." She turned to look at Lord Akeldama. "My lord?"

"My darling *sweet pea*, had I known that if we simply let her run a little distance she would work herself out, I would have let her *gallivant* about at will."

Lord Maccon, still in wolf form, trotted over to pick up his human daughter. Possibly by the scruff of her neck.

"Oh, Conall, wait!" said Lady Maccon.

The moment he touched her, Prudence turned once more into a wolf cub, this time stealing her father's skin, and he was left to stand in the middle of the street, starkers. Prudence tore off back toward the house. Lord

Maccon made to follow, this time in his lumbering mortal form.

Alexia, forgetting the delicacy of the Colindrikal-Bumbcrunchers' finer feelings, was seized with the spirit of scientific inquiry. "No, Conall, wait, stay there."

Lord Maccon might have disregarded his wife, particularly if he had any thought of his own shame or the dignity of the neighborhood, but he was not that kind of husband. He had learned all of Alexia's cadences and tones, and that one meant she was *on to something interesting.* Best to do as she asked. So he stood, watching with interest, as his little daughter dashed back the way they had come and then past the house in the opposite direction.

Just as before, at a distance from her victim, she turned back into a toddler. This time Lady Maccon went to retrieve her. *What must the surrounding households think of us? Screaming baby, wolf cub, werewolves.* Really, she would never put up with it herself were she not married into the madness. As she hoisted Prudence, she looked up to see Mr. and Mrs. Colindrikal-Bumbcruncher and their butler glaring daggers at her from their open front door.

Conall, with a little start, turned back into a wolf before heads turned in his direction and someone would be forced to faint. Knowing the Colindrikal-Bumbcrunchers, that someone would probably be the butler.

Sidheag Maccon began to laugh. Lord Akeldama hustled her swiftly inside, fanning himself with the feather fan.

Lord Maccon, once more a wolf, was in the door next. Alexia and her troublesome offspring followed, but not before she heard the Colindrikal-Bumbcrunchers' door close with a definite click of censure.

"Oh, dear," said Lady Maccon upon attaining the relative safety of Lord Akeldama's drawing room. "I do believe we have become *those* neighbors."

CHAPTER THREE

―――――

In Which Lord Maccon Wears a Pink Brocade Shawl

I don't have much time," said Alexia, sitting down with Prudence cuddled in her lap. After her exhausting shape-changing laps up and down the street, the infant had done the most practical thing and fallen asleep, leaving her parents to handle the consequences.

"That was a remarkable display of whatnot," remarked Lady Kingair, settling herself gingerly into one of Lord Akeldama's highest and stiffest-looking wingback chairs. She drew her shabby velvet cloak closely about her and tossed her long plait behind her shoulder.

"And an interesting newfound aspect of your daughter's abilities." Professor Lyall looked as though he might like a notepad and a stylus of some kind to make a note for BUR's records.

"Or failing." Lady Maccon was not so certain she liked the idea of her invincible little daughter having this weakness. Given Alexia's own experience, it was more likely than not that someone, more probably several someones, would try to kill Prudence over the course of her lifetime. It was far less comfortable knowing that all they would have to do was determine the limits of her abilities.

"That's what it is, isn't it?" Alexia looked to Professor Lyall, the only one who might qualify as an expert so far as these things went. "It's a tether, much like a ghost's to her corpse."

"Or a queen's to her hive," added Lord Akeldama.

"Or a werewolf's to his pack," added Lord Maccon.

Lady Maccon pursed her lips and looked down at her daughter. The poor thing had inherited her mother's complexion and curly hair. Alexia hoped the nose would not follow. She brushed back some of that dark hair. "Why should she be any different, I suppose?"

Lord Maccon came over to his wife and placed his hand on the back of her neck, caressing the nape with his calloused fingers. "Even you have limits, my dear wife? Who would have thought?"

That wrested Alexia out of her maudlin humors. "Yes, thank you, darling. We must press on. Woolsey is calling. So, if Lady Kingair would like to inform us as to the nature of her visit?"

Lady Kingair, it seemed, was a tad reluctant to do so in Lord Akeldama's well-appointed drawing room surrounded by the expectant faces of not only her great-great-great-grandfather, but also his wife, his Beta, a very eccentric sort of vampire, that vampire's lemon-colored drone, a sleeping child, and a fat calico cat. It was more audience than any lady of quality should have to endure when paying a social call on family.

"Gramps, could we nae go somewhere more private?"

Lord Maccon rolled his eyes around, as if only now

noticing the crowd. He was a werewolf, after all; he naturally acclimatized to the pack around him, even if that pack had gotten a little bizarrely dressed of late.

"Well, what I know, my wife and Randolph know. And, unfortunately, what Alexia knows, Lord Akeldama knows. However, if you insist, we could put out the drone." He paused while Tizzy tried to look as if butter wouldn't melt in his mouth, or on his trousers for that matter. "And the cat, I suppose."

Lady Kingair emitted an exhalation of exasperation. "Oh, verra well. To cut to the crux of it: Dubh has disappeared."

Lord Maccon narrowed his eyes. "That's not like a Beta."

Professor Lyall looked concerned by this news. "What happened?"

Alexia wondered if he and the Kingair Beta had ever met.

Sidheag Maccon was clearly searching for a way of putting it that would not make her seem in the wrong. "I sent him away to investigate some small matter of interest to the pack, and we havena heard back from him."

"Begin at the beginning," instructed Lord Maccon, looking resigned.

"I sent him to Egypt."

"Egypt!"

"To track down the source of the mummy."

Lady Maccon looked to her husband in exasperation. "Isn't that just like one of *your* progeny? Couldn't just let sleeping mummies lie, could she? Oh, no, had to go off, nosing about." She rounded on her several-times-removed stepdaughter. "Did it occur to you that I exhausted my parasol's supply of acid to destroy that blasted creature for a *very good reason*? The last thing we need is more of them entering the country! Just look at the havoc the last one caused. There was mortality simply everywhere."

"Oh, really, no. I dinna want to collect another one. I wanted to find out the particulars of the condition. We need to know where it came from. If there are more, they need to be controlled."

"And you couldn't have simply suggested that to BUR instead of trying to manage the situation yourself?"

"BUR's jurisdiction is homeland only. This is a matter for the empire, and I had the feeling that *we* wolves needed tae see tae it. So I sent Dubh."

"And?" Lord Maccon's expression was dark.

"An' he was supposed tae report in two weeks ago. He never made the aethographic transmission. Then again last week. Still naught. Then, two days past, this came through. I dinna think it's from him. I think it's a warning."

She threw a piece of paper down on the tea table before them. It was plain parchment of the kind employed by transmission specialists the empire over for recording incoming aetherograms. Only, instead of the usual abrupt sentence, one single symbol was drawn upon it: a circle atop a cross, split in two.

Alexia had seen that symbol before, on the papyrus wrappings about a dangerous little mummy in Scotland and later hanging from a chain around the neck of a Templar. "Wonderful. The broken ankh."

Lord Maccon bent to examine the document more closely.

Prudence stirred, giggling in her sleep. Alexia tucked

the blanket, one of Lord Akeldama's pink brocade shawls, more securely about her daughter.

Lord Maccon and Lady Kingair both looked at Alexia. Lord Maccon, it ought to be noted, was wearing another pink brocade shawl wrapped securely about his waist. It looked like a skirt from the East Indies. Alexia supposed her husband, being Scottish, was accustomed to wearing skirts. And he did have very nice knees. Scotsmen, she had occasion to observe, often did have nice knees. Perhaps that was why they insisted upon kilts.

"Oh, don't tell me I never told you about it?"

"You never told *me*, my little robin's egg." Lord Akeldama waved his closed feathered fan about in the air, inscribing the symbol he saw before him.

"Well, the ankh translates to 'eternal life' or so Champollion says. And there we see eternal life destroyed. What do you think it might mean? Preternaturals, of course. Me."

Lord Akeldama pursed his lips. "Perhaps. But sometimes the ancients inscribed a hieroglyphic broken to keep the symbol from leaking off the stone and into reality. When inscribed for that reason, the meaning of the hieroglyphic does not alter."

"But who would nae want immortality?" asked Sidheag Maccon. She had pestered her great-great-great-grandfather for years to be made into a werewolf.

"Not everyone wants to live forever," Alexia said. "Take Madame Lefoux, for example."

Lord Maccon brought them back around to the point. "So Dubh has gone missing, in Egypt? What do you want me to do about it? Isn't this a matter for the dewan?"

Lady Kingair cocked her head. "You are family. I

thought you might make some inquiries without having tae involve official channels."

Lord Maccon exchanged looks with his wife. Alexia glanced significantly at Lord Akeldama's massive gilded cuckoo clock that dominated one corner of the room.

"We should be getting on," he said.

"I shall be fine without you, my love. I will take the train. Nothing unpleasant ever happens on the train," assured his wife.

Lord Maccon did not look reassured. Nevertheless, it was clear he was more concerned by troubles among werewolves than summons from vampires.

"Very well, my dear." He turned to Lady Kingair. "We had better adjourn to BUR headquarters. We will need the assets only the Bureau can provide."

Lady Kingair nodded.

"Randolph."

"I'm with you, my lord. But I prefer to travel a little more formally."

"Very well. We shall meet you there." At which Lord Maccon swooped down upon his wife, one hand firmly occupied in keeping the shawl secure about his midriff. "Please, be cautious, my love, train or no train."

Alexia leaned into his embrace. Uncaring for the watching eyes about them—everyone there was family, after all—she touched his chin with one hand and arched up into his kiss. Prudence, accustomed to such activity, did not move in her mother's lap. Conall disappeared out into the hallway to remove the pink brocade and change form.

Mere moments later, a shaggy wolf head peeked back into the room and barked insistently. With a start, Lady Kingair excused herself to follow him.

"My hallway," remarked Lord Akeldama, "has never before seen such *lively* action. And *that*, my sugarplums, is *saying* something!"

Lady Maccon left her daughter asleep in her adopted father's drawing room. She changed out of her evening gown and into a visiting dress of ecru over a bronze skirt with brown velvet detailing. It was perhaps too unadorned for a vampire queen, but it was eminently appropriate for public transport. She commandeered one of the drones to assist her with the buttons, seeing as Biffy—her *lady's valet*, as she liked to call him—was busy with his hats. She tucked Ethel into a brown velvet reticule, checking to ensure the gun was fully loaded with sundowner bullets. Alexia detested the very idea that she might have to actually *use* her gun. Like any well-bred woman, she vastly preferred merely to wave it about and make wild, menacing gestures. This was partly because her marksmanship was limited to sometimes hitting the side of the barn—if it was a very large barn and she was very close to it—and partly because guns seemed so decidedly *final*. Still, even if all she intended to do was threaten, she might as well be able to fulfill that threat adequately. Alexia abhorred hypocrisy, especially when munitions were involved.

She took a moment to lament her lack of parasol. Every time she left the house, she felt keenly the absence of her heretofore ubiquitous accessory. She had asked Conall for a replacement, and he had muttered mysterious husband-with-gifts-afoot mutters, but nothing had resulted. She might have to take matters into her own hands soon. But with Madame Lefoux indentured to the Woolsey Hive, Alexia was at a loss as to how to locate an inventor capable of producing work of such complexity and delicacy, not to mention fashion.

Floote materialized with two first-class tickets from London to Woolsey on the Tilbury Line's Barking Express.

"Lord Maccon will not be joining me, Floote. Are any of the men available to act as escort?"

Floote took a long moment to consider his mistress's options. Alexia knew she had tasked her butler with quite a conundrum. With drones, werewolves, and clavigers to choose from, distributed among two households and currently bumbling about most of London, there was quite the crowd for even a butler of Floote's cranial capacity to keep account of. All Alexia knew was that Biffy was working and that Boots was visiting relations in Steeple Bumpshod.

Floote took a small breath. "I'm afraid there is only Major Channing immediately available, madam."

Alexia winced. "Really? How unfortunate. Well, he will have to do. I can't very well travel by train alone, can I? Would you tell him I request his attendance as escort, please?"

This time it was Floote's turn to wince, which for him was a mere twitch of one eyelid. "Of course, madam."

He glided off, reappearing moments later with her wrap and Major Channing, the London Pack's toffee-nosed Gamma werewolf.

"Lady Maccon, you require my services?" Major Channing Channing of the Chesterfield Channings was a man who spoke the Queen's English with that unctuous precision instilled only by generations of the best schools, the best society, and an overabundance of teeth.

"Yes, Major, I must visit Woolsey."

Major Channing looked as though he would quite like to object to the very idea of accompanying his Alpha female into the countryside, but he knew perfectly well that Lady Maccon would ask for him only if she had no other alternatives. He also knew who was most likely to bear the brunt of Lord Maccon's wrath if she were allowed to travel alone. So he said the only thing he could say under such circumstances.

"I am, of course, at your disposal, my lady. Ready, willing, and able."

"Don't overdo it, Channing."

"Yes, my lady."

Lady Maccon eyed the Gamma's outfit with a critical eye. He was in his military garb, and Alexia wasn't entirely certain that was appropriate for calling on vampires. *But do we have time for him to change?* To give insult by being very late indeed or by bringing a soldier into the house of a vampire queen? Quite the conundrum.

"Floote, what time does our train depart?"

"In one half hour, madam, from Fenchurch Street Station."

"Ah, no time for you to change, then, Major. Very well, collect your greatcoat and let's be away."

They rode the train in an uncomfortable silence, Alexia pondering the night out the window and Major Channing pondering an exceedingly dull-looking financial paper. Major Channing, Alexia had discovered much to her shock, was interested in figures, and as such was bursar to the pack. It seemed odd for a man of breeding and snobbery to dally with *mathematics*, but immortality did strange things to people's hobbies.

Some three-quarters of an hour into their journey, they consumed some very nice tea and little crustless sandwiches provided by an obsequious train steward who seemed very well aware of the dignity of Major Channing and rather less of that of Lady Maccon. As she nibbled her cucumber and cress, Alexia wondered if this were not one of the reasons she disliked the major so very much. He was awfully good at being aristocratic. Alexia, on the other hand, was only good at being autocratic. Not quite the same thing.

Alexia became increasingly aware of a prickling sensation at the back of her neck, as though she were being scrutinized carefully. It was a most disagreeable sensation, like stepping one's bare foot into a vat of pudding.

Pretending travel fatigue, she arose to engage in a short constitutional.

There were few other occupants in first class, but Alexia was startled to find that behind them and across sat a man in a sort of floppy turban. That is to say, she was not startled that there was someone else in the carriage but that a man was in a *turban*—most irregular. Turbans were well out of fashion, even for women. He seemed unduly interested in his daily paper, suggesting he had, until very recently, been unduly interested in something else. Lady Maccon, never one to take anything as coincidence, suspected him of observing her, or Major Channing, or both.

She pretended a little stumble as the train rattled along and fell in against the turbaned gentleman, upsetting his tea onto his paper.

"Oh, dear me, I *do* apologize," she declaimed loudly.

The man shook his damp paper in disgust but said nothing.

"Please allow me to fetch you another cup? Steward!"

The man only shook his head and mumbled something low in a language Alexia did not recognize.

"Well, if you're quite sure you won't?"

The man shook his head again.

Alexia continued her walk to the end of the car, then turned about and returned to her seat.

"Major Channing, I do believe we have company," she stated upon reseating herself.

The werewolf looked up from his own paper and over. "The man in the turban?"

"You noticed?"

"Hasn't taken his eyes off you most of the ride. Bloody foreigners."

"You didn't think to tell me?"

"Thought it was your figure. Orientals never like to see a lady's assets."

"Oh, really, Major, must you be so crass? Such language." Alexia paused, considering. "What nationality would you say?"

The major, who was very well traveled, answered without needing to look up again. "Egyptian."

"Interesting."

"Is it?"

"Oh, Major, you do so love to annoy, don't you?"

"It is the stuff of living, my lady."

"Don't be pert."

"Me? I wouldn't dream of it."

No further incidents occurred, and when they alighted at their stop, the foreign gentleman did not follow them.

"Interesting," said Alexia again.

The Woolsey Station, a new stopover, was built at

considerable expense by the newly relocated Woolsey Hive with an eye toward encouraging Londoners to engage in country jaunts. The greatest disappointment in Countess Nadasdy's very long life was this exile to the outer reaches of Barking. The Woolsey Hive queen had commissioned the station to be built and even allocated a portion of Woolsey's extensive grounds. From the station, visitors could catch a tiny private train, conducted by a complicated tram apparatus without an engineer. The location of the hive was no longer a not-very-well-kept secret. The vampires seemed to feel some sense of security in the country, but they were still vampires. There was no longer a road leading directly to Woolsey; there was only this special train, the operation of which was tightly controlled by drones at the castle terminus.

Lady Maccon approached the contraption warily. It looked like a chubby flat-bottomed rowboat on tracks, with a fabric-covered interior and two massive parasols for protection from the elements. Major Channing helped her to step inside and then followed, settling himself opposite. At which juncture they sat, staring at the scenery so as not to look at each other, waiting for something to happen.

"I suppose they must be alerted to the fact that we have arrived." Alexia looked about for some kind of signaling device. She noticed that off to one side of the bench sat a fat little gun. After subjecting it to close examination, she shot it up into the air.

It made a tremendous clap. Major Channing started violently, much to Alexia's satisfaction, and the gun emitted a ball of bright white fire that floated high up and then faded out.

Alexia looked at the weapon with approval. "Ingenious. Must be one of Madame Lefoux's. I didn't know she dabbled in ballistics."

Channing rolled his ice-blue eyes. "That woman is an inveterate dabbler."

They had no further time to consider the gun, for the rowboat jolted once, causing Alexia to fall back hard against one of the parasol supports. It was Major Channing's turn to look amused at her predicament. They rolled forward, first at quite a sedate pace and then at increasing speed, the tracks running up the long, low hill to where Woolsey Castle crouched, a confused and confusing hodgepodge of architecture.

Countess Nadasdy had done what she could to improve the Maccons' former place of residence, but it did little good. The resulting building merely looked grumpy over the indignity of change. She'd had it painted, and planted, and primped, and festooned, and draped to within an inch of its very long life. But it was asking too much of the poor thing. The result was something akin to dressing a bulldog up like an opera dancer. Underneath the tulle, it was still a bowlegged bulldog.

Major Channing helped Alexia out of the tram, and they made their way up the wide steps to the front door. Alexia felt a little odd, pulling the bell rope at what once had been her home. She could only imagine what Major Channing felt, having lived there for goodness knew how many decades.

His face was stoic. Or she thought it was stoic; it was difficult to tell under all that handsome haughtiness.

"She certainly has made"—he paused—"adjustments."

Lady Maccon nodded. "The door is painted with silver swirls. Silver!"

Major Channing had no opportunity to answer, for said door was opened by a beautiful young maid with glossy ebony hair, decked out in a frilled black dress with crisp white shirt and black pin-tucked apron front. Perfect in every way, as was to be expected in the countess's household.

"Lady Maccon and Major Channing, to see Countess Nadasdy."

"Oh, yes, you are expected, my lady. I'll inform my mistress you are here. If you wouldn't mind waiting one moment in the hall?"

Lady Maccon and Major Channing did not mind, for they were busy absorbing the transformation the countess had enacted upon their former abode. The carpets were now all thick and plush and blood red in color. The walls had been repapered in pale cream and gold, with a collection of fine art rescued from the wreckage of the hive's previous abode on prominent display. These were luxurious changes that neither appealed to a werewolf's taste nor suited his lifestyle. One simply did not live with Titian paintings and Persian rugs when one grew claws on a regular basis.

Major Channing, who hadn't seen the place since the pack left it, arched one blond eyebrow. "Would hardly have thought it the same house."

Lady Maccon made no answer. A vampire was oiling his way down the staircase toward them.

"Dr. Caedes, how do you do?"

"Lady Maccon." Dr. Caedes was a thin, reedy man, with a hairline paused in the act of withdrawal and an interest in engineering, not medicinal matters, despite his title.

"You know Major Channing, of course?"

"We may have met." The doctor inclined his head. He did not smile nor show fang.

Ah, thought Alexia, *we are to be treated with respect. How droll.* "My husband would have attended your summons, but he was called away on urgent business."

"Oh?"

"A family matter."

"I do hope it is nothing serious?"

Alexia tilted her head, playing the game of reveal with aplomb. She had been some time now a member of the Shadow Council and was a quick study in the fine art of conversing upon matters of great importance yet saying nothing significant. "More bedraggled, I suspect. Shall we proceed?"

Dr. Caedes backed down, having to follow the niceties of conversation that he and his kind had insinuated into society. "Of course, my lady. If you'd care to follow me? The countess is awaiting you in the Blue Room."

The Blue Room, as it turned out, was the room formerly occupied by the Woolsey Pack's extensive library. Alexia tried to hide her distress at the destruction of her favorite retreat. The vampires had stripped it of its mahogany shelving and leather seats and had papered it in cream and sky-blue stripes. The furniture was all cream in color with a decidedly Oriental influence and, unless Alexia was very much mistaken, Thomas Chippendale originals.

Countess Nadasdy sat in an arranged manner, draped to one side over the corner of a window seat. She wore an extremely fashionable and extraordinarily elaborate moss-green receiving dress trimmed with pale blue, the skirt tied back so narrowly that Lady Maccon wondered at the queen's ability to walk about, and the sleeves were so tight Alexia very much doubted the vampire could lift her arms at all. Biffy had tried to foist such absurdities upon Alexia, but only once, at which juncture she insisted that mobility was not to be sacrificed for taste, especially not with a child like Prudence dashing about. Biffy hunted down daringly cut fluid styles influenced by the Far East for his mistress to wear instead and said no more about it.

The countess had the ample figure of a milkmaid who had partaken too freely of the creamy results of her labors, which did not suit the style of the dress at all. Alexia would never have said a word, but she shuddered to think of Lord Akeldama's opinion on such a figure in such attire. She planned, of course, to describe it in detail to her dear friend as soon as possible.

"Ah, Lady Maccon, do come in."

"Countess Nadasdy, how do you do? You are adjusting to rural life, I see."

"For a girl with as unsullied a nature as I, the countryside is unobjectionable."

Lady Maccon paused, verbally stymied by the countess using the words *unsullied* and *girl* to describe herself.

The vampire queen glanced away from Lady Maccon's ill-disguised discomposure. "Thank you, Dr. Caedes. You may leave us."

"But, My Queen!"

"This is a matter for Lady Maccon and I, alone."

Alexia said quickly, "Countess, may I present Major Channing?"

"You may. Major Channing and I are already acquainted. I'm sure he won't mind allowing us a few moments of privacy?"

Major Channing looked like he would mind, but realizing that Dr. Caedes was about to leave his queen with a preternatural decided it was all in good faith.

"I shall be just outside the door, my lady, should you need anything."

Alexia nodded. "Thank you, Channing. I'm convinced all will be well."

So Alexia found herself alone in a blue room with a vampire queen.

After Felicity and Madame Lefoux departed, the shop turned into a frenzy of fashionable ladies in pursuit of hats, but Biffy's staff of assorted shopgirls had it well under control. He did a quick lap to ensure no lady was purchasing anything that did not suit her coloring, complexion, demeanor, station, or creed. He then left his accessories to the tender mercies of Britain's shopping public and retired down to the contrivance chamber to catch up on necessary paperwork. He was engaged at first, it must be admitted, in beautifying said paperwork by trimming the corners and adding necessary swirls and flowers to the text.

It had all happened rather organically. Because he was there most nights, and the contrivance chamber was the new dungeon for Lord Maccon's wolves, Biffy had assumed responsibility for a good deal of pack organization. Professor Lyall didn't seem to mind. In fact, he rather approved, so far as Biffy could tell. He wondered if the professor, after decades of sole stewardship, was relieved to have someone else take on part of the burden.

Since Madame Lefoux had removed all her machines, instruments, and gadgets, the contrivance chamber was a good deal more cavernous. Biffy thought it could use some nice rose-patterned wallpaper and a brocade cushion or two. But, given that its new purpose was as a full-moon prison, there was no point in wasting wallpaper on werewolves.

The dandy circled the huge room slowly, imagining himself swanking about a massive ballroom in one of Paris's fancy hotels—except he was checking the security of the pulley system, not waltzing with worldly Parisian ladies in obscenely large headdresses. Everything seemed to be secure. Gustave Trouvé had done an excellent job. The massive cages, iron coated in a silver wash, were strong enough to hold even Lord Maccon, yet they rose to the ceiling via a cranking mechanism that even the weakest claviger could operate. Biffy looked up contemplatively at the bottoms of the cages and wondered if he might not turn them into some kind of chandelier. Or at least ornament them with some ribbons and a tassel or two.

He settled behind his small desk in one corner of the room. There was pack business to attend to: a puzzle over one of the new recruits and a petition from a loner for one of his clavigers to be put up for metamorphosis. Several hours later, he stood, stretched, and packed away his work. He considered the fact that all around town, plays were ending, clubs were filling with smoke and chatter, and the gentlemen follies were at large. Perhaps he might change and catch the last of the evening's entertainment before sunrise. He had been required, by dint of association, to give over some of his dandified ways after becoming a werewolf, but not all of them. He fingered delicately the unruly curls of his hair. Some young men about town had recently assumed a certain level of scruff and simulated messiness. Biffy liked to think it was his influence.

The pack town house was dark. Everyone was taking advantage of the lures that London had to offer with little risk of accidental change for the youngsters or chronic boredom for the elders. He was making his way upstairs when he caught a smell, an unusual one not ordinarily associated with his abode. Something spicy and exotic and—he paused, trying to think—*sandy*. He turned, tracking with small short sniffs, following the alien scent toward the back of the house and the servants' domain.

Biffy heard the murmur of voices, his fine wolf hearing alerting him even through the shut kitchen door. Men's voices, one of them deep and authoritative, the other higher and more lilting. The first sounded familiar, but it was difficult to tell who it was, as they both were speaking in a foreign tongue Biffy couldn't quite place.

The conversation ended and the outer door to the kitchen opened and shut, letting in the sound of the back alley and a brief whiff of rubbish. Lightning fast, Biffy nipped into the shadows under the staircase at the far side of the hall, watching for the other party of the conversation.

Floote emerged from the room. The butler did not notice Biffy, merely gliding about his duties.

Biffy stood a long time in the dark, thinking. Then he realized what language it had been. Interesting that Lady Maccon's pet butler spoke fluent Arabic.

"Well." Alexia stood before the queen of the Woolsey Hive and narrowed her eyes at the woman. "Here I am, Countess, at your disposal. How can I help?"

"Now, Lady Maccon, is that any way to address your betters?" Countess Nadasdy didn't move from her stiff pose.

Alexia privately suspected, due to the tightness of the dress, that she couldn't.

"You have taken me away from an evening with my family, Countess."

"Yes, on the subject of which, we understood Lord Akeldama would have primary care for the abomination and yet..." The vampire let her words trail off.

Alexia understood perfectly. "Yes, and he does. Prudence lives with him. And please refer to my daughter by her name."

"But you live next door and visit quite frequently, I understand."

"It is necessary."

"A mother's love or a child's affliction?" The countess widened her cornflower-blue eyes significantly.

"Someone has to cancel her out."

The countess grinned suddenly. "Difficult is she, the soul-stealer?"

"Only when she isn't herself."

"Fascinating way of putting it."

"You simply must learn to relax your standards, Countess, or Prudence could run ragged all over London, even getting so far as Barking." Alexia, nettled that she had been offered neither seat nor tea, allowed some of her annoyance to creep into her voice. "Is this the nature of your summons or did you have something particular you wished to discuss with me?"

The vampire queen reached out to a small side table. Alexia was certain she heard the dress creak. The queen

gestured Alexia to come closer, using a small scroll of
parchment she had resting there.

"Someone wishes to meet the abomination."

"What was that? I'm afraid I didn't quite catch it.
Wishes to meet *who*, did you say?" Alexia looked pointedly out a nearby window.

Countess Nadasdy showed fang. "Matakara wishes to
meet your child."

"Mata-who? Well, many people wish to meet *Prudence*. Why should this particular person signify to
any—"

The countess interrupted her with a sharp gesture.
"No. You misunderstand. Matakara, queen of the Alexandria Hive."

"Who?"

"Oh, how can you be intimate with so many immortals, yet be so ignorant of our world?" The countess's
beautiful round face became pinched in annoyance.
"Queen Matakara is the oldest living vampire, possibly
the oldest living creature. Some claim over three thousand years. Of course, no one knows the actual number
with any certainty."

Alexia tried to fathom such a vast age. "Oh."

"She has shown a particular interest in your progeny.
Generally speaking, Queen Matakara hasn't shown an
interest in anything *at all* for five hundred years. It is a
great honor. When one is summoned to visit her, one does
not delay."

"Let me get this perfectly clear. She requires *me* to
travel, to *Egypt*, with *my* daughter, on *her* whim?" Lady
Maccon was, perhaps, less impressed than she ought to be
by the interest of such an august body.

"Yes, but she would prefer if the reason for your journey were not publicly known."

"She wants me to travel to Egypt with my daughter under subterfuge? You have heard of my daughter's antics, have you not?"

"Yes."

Alexia huffed out a breath in exasperation. "Not asking very much, is she?"

"Here." The countess passed her the missive.

The sum of the request, or more properly the order, written in a slightly stilted manner that suggested the writer's first language was not English, was indeed as had been discussed.

Alexia looked up from it, annoyed. "Why?"

"Because she desires it, of course." Clearly Queen Matakara had the same kind of superior social power over the countess as the Queen of England did the Duchess of Devonshire.

"No, I mean to ask, why should I inconvenience myself with a trip?"

"Ah, yes, preternaturals, so very practical. I understand Egypt is lovely this time of year, and I believe there is something more that you have overlooked."

Alexia read the letter again and then flipped it over. There was a postscript on the reverse side. "I believe your husband is missing a werewolf. And you are missing a father. I can help you with both."

Alexia folded the parchment carefully and tucked it into her reticule, next to Ethel. "I'll prepare to leave at once."

"My *dear* Lady Maccon, I surmised that might be the case." The countess looked sublimely pleased with herself.

Alexia sneered. Nothing was more annoying than a self-satisfied vampire, which, given that seemed to be their natural state, was saying something about vampires.

A great hullabaloo out in the corridor heralded some kind of emergency. There was a good deal of yelling and then a banging at the door to the Blue Room.

"I left orders not to be disturbed!" yelled the queen, moved to irritated vocalization, if not actually moved to, well, move.

Said orders, however, were clearly to be disregarded, for the door burst open and in stumbled Dr. Caedes, Major Channing, and Madame Lefoux. They were carrying between them an exquisite young woman with dark hair, whose eyes were closed and body ominously floppy. Her perfection was marred by a great gash at the back of her head that bled copiously.

"Oh, really! I just had this room made over," said Countess Nadasdy.

CHAPTER FOUR

Several Unexpected Occurrences and Tea

It's Asphodel, My Queen. Riding accident."

The vampire queen made a beckoning motion with two fingers. "Bring her to me."

The three carried the drone over to her mistress. The girl's breathing was shallow, and she did not move.

"Dead drones are so inconvenient. Not to mention the hassle in finding an adequately fit, able, and attractive replacement."

"I think you should try for the bite, My Queen."

Countess Nadasdy looked at her vampire companion skeptically. "You do, do you, Doctor? I suppose it has been a while since I took the gamble."

The door crashed open once more and Mabel Dair appeared in the aperture, resplendent in a bronze riding gown with red trim. The actress swept into the room. "How is she?"

Miss Dair sashayed across the thick carpet and cast

herself forward to kneel on the floor next to Countess
Nadasdy and the injured drone. "Oh, poor Asphodel!"

Alexia had to give the actress credit for a moving
performance.

Madame Lefoux stepped forward and bent to press
Miss Dair's shoulders soothingly. "Come away, *chérie*.
There's nothing we can do for her now."

Mabel allowed herself to be gentled into a standing
position and away from the hive queen. "Oh, you will try,
please, won't you, mistress? Asphodel is such a sweet
girl."

The queen wrinkled her nose and looked back down.
"I suppose she is quite pretty. Very well, bring me my
sippy goblet."

Dr. Caedes sprang into action. "At once, My Queen!"
He vanished from the room.

While they waited for him to return, Alexia turned to
the new arrivals. "Good evening, Madame Lefoux. Miss
Dair."

"Lady Maccon, how do you do?" replied the actress.
Hands were clasped to her trembling bosom, and the bulk
of her attention was still centered on the dying girl.

Madame Lefoux merely tipped her head in Alexia's
direction and gave her a small, tight smile. Then she
returned her attention to the actress, placing a solicitous
arm about the woman's waist.

Dr. Caedes returned, bearing a small silver goblet with
some kind of lid attached to the top. It looked like those
cup attachments designed for gentlemen with mustaches.
He passed it to the queen, who took it in one hand.

"Prepare the girl."

Dr. Caedes grabbed the comatose woman by the

shoulders and shifted her into his mistress's lap. His supernatural strength made the task an easy one, even had the girl not been relatively slight. He turned her head so that she rested with the side of her neck exposed.

The queen took a drink from the goblet, swished the contents around in her mouth, and paused, an intense look of contemplation on her face. Then Countess Nadasdy bared her teeth, both the longer regular fangs, the feeders, and the smaller fangs to either side, the makers. Alexia wasn't quite certain on the logistics of vampire metamorphosis. They were secretive about the details, and rarely were scientists, save their own, permitted to observe. But she knew the current theory held that feeders sucked the blood out while makers pumped blood in, so metamorphosis occurred by process of the queen literally giving her own blood over to the new vampire.

The countess opened her mouth wide. The makers were dripping perfect drops of dark blood, almost black. Alexia wondered if the contents of the sippy goblet acted as a catalyst.

Dr. Caedes bent and looked into his queen's mouth. "I believe we may proceed, My Queen."

Lady Maccon could only hope that the vampire metamorphosis process was less brutal than the werewolves. Her husband had practically eaten Lady Kingair whole in order to change her. It was most indelicate. The last thing Alexia wanted was to witness the vampire version of a three-course meal.

"Should we be watching this? Isn't unbirth a matter for family intimates only?" Alexia asked Major Channing on a hiss.

"I think we are remaining as witnesses apurpose, my

lady. She wants to prove her strength." The major seemed not at all perturbed by the prospect.

"Does she? Why? Did I look as though I doubted it?"

"No. But our Alpha has managed two successful metamorphoses in the past three years. That has got to smart something awful for the vampires."

"You mean, I have stumbled into some kind of eternal tiddlywinks match? Who can make the most immortals? What are you people, schoolroom children?"

Major Channing tilted his hands, palms up, in supplication.

"Oh, for goodness' sake," said Alexia, and then hushed, for the countess was biting down at last.

It was a good deal more elegant than with the werewolves at first. Countess Nadasdy sank her feeder fangs deep into the flesh of the girl's neck and then kept going until she was far enough in for the maker fangs to sink in as well. She cradled both arms about the woman and leaned back so that she was held up to her mouth like a tea sandwich. The girl's slack white face tilted toward the small audience. Countess Nadasdy closed her eyes, assuming an expression of ecstatic bliss. She moved not one muscle, except that Alexia could see a strange up and down fluttering in her neck, like a cow regurgitating its cud, only faster, smaller, and in both directions.

Asphodel remained limp in her mistress's arms for a long while, until her whole body jerked—once. Alexia jumped in reaction, as did Major Channing. Madame Lefoux gave them both a quelling look.

Asphodel's eyes popped open, wide, startled, looking directly at the observers. Then she began to scream. It was a deep, drawn-out cry of agony. Her pupils dilated, darkening and changing color, extending outward until her entire eyeball was a solid deep red.

The girl's eyes began to bleed. Drops of blood leaked out, running down the sides of her face and dripping off her nose. Her screams became gargles as blood began to pour out of her mouth, muffling the cries.

Dr. Caedes said, "Enough, My Queen. It isn't taking. There will be no making this one over."

The hive queen only continued to suck, her expression beatific. Her arms were beginning to lose their hold, however, and she was sagging over the girl.

Dr. Caedes stepped forward and ripped Asphodel off of his queen's fangs. Under normal circumstances, Alexia suspected he would not have been able to do so. All vampires were strong, but queens were reputed to be the strongest of them all. However, the countess's beautiful eyes, when they finally opened, were sunken with exhaustion.

Dr. Caedes yanked the maid from the countess's grasp and threw her to the floor like a used dishrag. The girl convulsed one final time and stilled.

Alexia went to bend over her solicitously, careful not to touch her in case, somehow, this was all as it was meant to be, and preternatural contact might interfere with the process of metamorphosis. The girl, however, was motionless. Lady Maccon looked up from her crouch at Major Channing. The werewolf shook his blond head.

Dr. Caedes spoke into the shocked quiet of the Blue Room. "My Queen, it did not take. You need to feed and restore your strength. Please, put the makers away. I will call in the drones."

Countess Nadasdy turned an unfocused gaze onto her

vampire companion. "Didn't it work? Another one gone. How unfortunate. I shall have to buy a new dress, then." She looked around, catching sight of the fallen girl and Lady Maccon bent over her. She laughed. "There's nothing you can do, soul-sucker."

Alexia stood, feeling queasy.

There was blood everywhere. Soaked into the countess's green gown, splattered across the cream and blue carpet, and pooling under the body of the unfortunate girl. It was really more than any lady should have to tolerate when making a social call.

Dr. Caedes gestured Mabel Dair forward. "See to your mistress, Miss Dair."

"Certainly, Doctor. At once." Mabel ran to the countess, her golden curls bouncing, and offered up her wrist.

Dr. Caedes followed, reaching around to support his queen's head. "Now remember, only feeders. You are weak, My Queen."

Countess Nadasdy drank for a long time from the actress's wrist, everyone watching in silence. Mabel Dair stood still and quiet in her beautiful bronze dress, but soon the rose bloom on her perfect round cheeks began to fade.

Dr. Caedes said gently, "Enough, My Queen."

Countess Nadasdy did not stop.

Madame Lefoux strode forward. Her movements were angular and sharp under the impeccable cut of her evening jacket. She grabbed Miss Dair's arm above the wrist and jerked it off the vampire queen's teeth, causing both women to gasp in surprise.

"He said enough."

The countess glared at the Frenchwoman. "Don't you dare dictate to me, *drone*."

"Haven't you had sufficient blood for one evening?" The inventor gestured with her hand at the body and the mess that resulted.

Countess Nadasdy licked her lips. "And yet, I am still hungry."

The Frenchwoman lurched away. Dr. Caedes stopped her by placing his hands on her shoulders. "You don't want the queen to take from Miss Dair anymore, do you, Madame Lefoux? Offering yourself in her place, are you? That's very generous. Especially considering how cautious you have been with your blood since you came to us."

Madame Lefoux pushed her hair back behind her ears, defiantly. She'd let it grow longer since becoming a drone, but it was still too short for a woman. She offered up her wrist without protest. The countess sank in her fangs. Madame Lefoux looked away.

"Perhaps the major and I should make our farewells," suggested Alexia, uncomfortable witnessing Genevieve's pretend disinterest. At which juncture they did, leaving Madame Lefoux dismissive, Mabel Dair drained, Dr. Cedes distracted, and the countess still at tea.

Fenchurch Street wasn't Alexia's favorite station. It was too close to the London Docks and, of course, the Tower of London. There was something about the Tower, with all its ghosts that would not be exorcized, that gave her the squirms. It was as if they were dinner guests who had overstayed their welcome.

Lady Maccon and Major Channing alighted. It was the

quietest time of the night, so there were no porters to be found. Lady Maccon sat in the first-class waiting room alone, impatient, while Major Channing went to see about a hackney.

A man unlike any Alexia had ever encountered burst in through the door just after Channing vanished out of sight. Alexia knew there were such people about London, but not in her part of the city! His hair was long and shaggy. His face was sunburned like that of a sailor. His beard was ferocious and untended. However, Alexia did not fear him, for the man appeared to be in a state of extreme distress, and he knew her name.

"Lady Maccon! Lady Maccon."

He spoke with a Scottish accent. His voice was vaguely familiar, for all that it was faint and cracked. For the life of her, Alexia couldn't place that gaunt, cooked-lobster face, not under all that unkempt.

She looked down her nose at the man. "Do I *know* you, sir?"

"Yes, my lady. Dubh." He cracked a weak smile. "I'm a mite different from when you saw me last."

The werewolf could not be but understating the case. Dubh had not been a particularly handsome or agreeable man, but now he was positively unsightly. A Scotsman, to be sure, and Alexia acknowledged her preferences seemed to lean in that direction. In the past, the man had not behaved much to Alexia's taste, having engaged in a bout of fisticuffs with Conall that destroyed most of a dining room and an entire plate of meringues. "Why, Mr. Dubh, what has brought about such a need for the barber? Are you unwell? Have you been the victim of an anarchist outrage?"

Alexia made to move over to him, for he had propped himself against the jamb of the door and seemed likely to slide right down it and fold up upon the floor.

"No, my lady, I beg you. I could not stand your touch."

"But, my dear sir, let me summon help. You have been much missed. Your Alpha is here in London looking for you. I could send Major Channing to fetch—"

"No, please, my lady, only listen. I have waited to catch you alone. 'Tis a matter for you alone. Your household... your household is nae safe. It is nae contained."

"Do go on."

"Your da... what he did... in Egypt. You need tae stop it."

"What? What did he do?"

"The mummies, my lady, they—"

A gunshot fired clear and sharp in the silence of the station. Lady Maccon cried out as a bloom of red blood appeared on Dubh's chest. The Beta looked utterly surprised, raising both hands to cup over the wound.

He pitched forward, facedown, showing that he had been shot in the back.

Alexia clasped her hands together and willed herself to stay away, although all her instincts urged her to help the injured man. She yelled out at the very top of her lungs, "Major Channing, Major Channing, come quickly! Something *untoward* has occurred."

The Gamma came dashing in using speed only supernaturals could achieve. He immediately crouched over the fallen werewolf.

He sniffed. "Kingair Pack? The missing Beta? But what is he doing *here*? I thought he went missing in Egypt."

"It appears he recently returned. Look—beard, tan, loss of flesh. He's been mortal for some length of time. Only one thing does that to a werewolf."

"The God-Breaker Plague."

"Can you think of a better explanation? Except, of course, that he is back here, in the country. He should be a werewolf once more."

"Oh, he is, or I wouldn't be able to smell the pack in him," answered Major Channing with confidence. "He's not mortal, only very, very weak."

"Then he's not dead?"

"Not yet. We'd better get him home and the bullet out or he might well be. Take care, my lady. The assailant may still be out there. I should go first."

"But," said Alexia, "I have Ethel." She withdrew the small gun from her reticule and cocked it.

Major Channing rolled his eyes.

"Onward!" Alexia trotted out of the waiting room, eyes alert for movement in the shadows, gun at the ready.

Nothing happened.

They made it to the waiting hackney easily. Major Channing offered the driver triple the fare for double the speed. They would have made it back home in record time had there not been a fire in Cheapside that caused them to double back and go around.

Once home, a single yell from Lady Maccon brought all the werewolves and clavigers running. It was getting near to dawn, so the house was full, clavigers waking up and werewolves preparing for bed. The injured Kingair Beta caused quite a hubbub. He was taken carefully inside and into the back parlor, while runners were sent to BUR to fetch Lord Maccon and Lady Kingair.

Dubh was looking worse, his breath rasped. Alexia was genuinely concerned for his survival. She sat down on the couch opposite, feeling utterly ineffectual, as she could not even pat his hand or wipe his brow.

Floote appeared at her elbow. "Trouble, madam?"

"Oh, Floote, yes. Where have you been? Do you know anything that could help?"

"Help, madam?"

"He's been shot."

"We should try to get the bullet out, madam, in case it is silver."

"Oh, yes, of course, do you—"

"I'm afraid not, madam, but I will send for a surgeon directly."

"Progressive?"

"Naturally, madam."

"Very good. Please do."

Floote nodded to a young claviger who jumped eagerly forward, and the butler gave him the address of a physician.

"Perhaps, madam, a little air for the invalid?"

"Of course! Clear the room, please, gentlemen."

All the worried-looking clavigers and werewolves filed out. Floote walked quietly off and returned moments later with tea.

They sat in silence, watching as Dubh's breathing became fainter. Their reverie was interrupted by a clatter at the door, indicating Lord Maccon had returned.

Alexia hurried to meet her husband.

"Alexia, are you unwell?"

"Of course not. Did the runner explain what has transpired?"

"Dubh appeared, found you at the train station, tried to tell you something, and was shot."

"Yes, that's about the whole of it."

"Dashed inconvenient."

Lady Kingair pushed up next to her great-great-great-grandfather. "How is he?"

"Not well, I'm afraid. We have done what we can, and a surgeon has been sent for. Follow me." Alexia led the way into the back parlor.

They entered to find Floote bent over the injured man. The butler's normally impassive face was creased with worry. He looked up as they burst in and shook his head.

"No!" cried Lady Kingair, her voice ringing in distress. She shoved the butler aside to bend over her Beta. "Oh, no, Dubh."

The werewolf was dead.

Lady Kingair began to weep. Full shaking sobs, the grief of an old friend and longtime companion.

Alexia turned away from such naked emotion to find her husband's face also suffused with sorrow. She forgot that Dubh had been a part of his pack as well. Not so close as a Beta back then, but still, werewolves lived a long time and pack members were always valued. There had been no love lost personality-wise, but a dead immortal was never to be taken lightly. It was a tragedy of lost information, like the burning of the Library of Alexandria.

Alexia went to Conall and held him close, wrapping her arms tightly about him, not caring that others could see. Taking charge of the situation—everyone needed a hobby and that was Alexia's—she guided her husband gently to a large armchair and saw him seated. She sent

Floote for a dram of formaldehyde and directed a claviger to fetch Professor Lyall. Then she made her way out into the hall to confirm what the waiting werewolves had already guessed from Lady Kingair's cry—that they had lost one of their own.

CHAPTER FIVE

———

Under Cover of Thespians

Needless to say, there was a good deal for Lady Maccon to take care of before she could broach the matter of Queen Matakara with her husband. No one got much sleep that day, except perhaps Biffy. The newest of the London Pack seemed to have come home, raised his eyebrows at the unholy hubbub, and, very sensibly, gone to bed with the latest copy of *Le Beaux Assemblée*.

Lady Maccon spent the morning finding a black dress for herself, black waistcoats for the pack, and mourning bands for the staff. Dubh hadn't exactly been family, but he had died in her house, and she felt that proper respects ought to be paid. BUR was in an uproar and the clavigers were all aflutter with the drama, so she had to keep an eye to them as well.

When evening finally did arrive, Lady Kingair insisted on departing immediately with Dubh's body for Scotland. However, she stated that she would be returning after the burial in all due haste to sort the matter of his murder out to her satisfaction. Her tone cast aspersions over the English's ability to properly tend to such matters. The abruptness of her departure left Lord and Lady Maccon standing dumbly in the hallway, staring at one another, exhausted by lack of sleep. When the knock came at their front door, they were entirely unprepared to meet Lord Akeldama's painted face, nor a chipper Prudence sitting happily on Tizzy's hip just behind him.

"Dada! Mama!" greeted their daughter.

"Oh, darling, good evening!" said her mother, trying to look pleased. "Lord Akeldama, Viscount Trizdale, do come in."

"Oh, no, thank you kindly, *pudding cheeks*. We thought we'd go for a little stroll in the park. I can't believe we will benefit from this delightful weather much longer. The puggle and I were wondering if you darlings would care to accompany us?"

"Oh, how kind. I do apologize, my lord, but we've had rather a trying day."

"So my little droney poos informed me. It was all go here last night *and* all day today, I understand. Someone had a *serious* accident. Not to mention the fact that *you* paid a visit to Woolsey Hive, my *dear* Alexia. But, my fabulous darling, *all black*? Surely that couldn't possibly be necessary?"

Lady Maccon faced this onslaught with composed grace until the very end. "Oh, good gracious me, Woolsey! Conall, my dear, I entirely forgot! I must talk with you about that directly. Yes, as you say, Lord Akeldama, very busy. I'm sorry to be so abrupt but I really am quite exhausted. Perhaps tomorrow night?" Alexia wasn't about to give the vampire the satisfaction of any further information.

Lord Akeldama knew when he was being dismissed. The vampire tilted his head graciously, and he and Tizzy returned to the street where an enormous pram awaited Prudence's pleasure. Lord Akeldama had had the contraption made shortly after the adoption was made official. It was a Plimsaul Brothers Perambulator Special Class. It had penny-farthing-style wheels, in brass, and a leather carriage gilded in gold and trimmed with an excessive number of swirls. The handle could be adjusted for height, and from it dangled a porcelain plate with the name *Proud Mary* in flowery scroll. There was a crank for raising and lowering the affixed protective parasol—also good for inclement weather. The pram—rather optimistically, felt Alexia—converted to take more than one child at a time. Lord Akeldama had ordered it designed with removable interior lining, lace trim, and ribbons. He had then commissioned a full set made in every possible color so as to match any outfit he might wear. In the light of the gas streetlamp, Alexia could just make out that they were all in teal and silver this evening. Prudence was in a darling cream lace dress and Tizzy in a complementary shade of pale gold. The nursemaid trailed behind looking put-upon. Somehow the vampire had even gotten her to don a teal ribbon in solidarity.

They paraded off. No doubt the vampire was prepared, nay delighted, to stop and be admired by many a curious bystander. It was likely to be a very slow amble about the park. Lord Akeldama did so enjoy making a spectacle of himself. Luckily, signs were beginning to indicate that Prudence felt similarly on the subject. Two peas in a very sparkly pod.

Lady Maccon grabbed her husband by the arm,

practically dragging him into their back parlor and closing the door firmly behind her.

"Oh, Conall, something else has happened, and in the horror of Dubh's unfortunate demise, I entirely forgot to tell you. I witnessed Countess Nadasdy try to metamorphose a new queen yesterday eve."

"You never!" Lord Maccon was shaken slightly out of his melancholy. He patted the seat next to him, and Alexia came willingly over to settle beside him.

"It was all a rather rushed affair. One of her drones had an accident. The countess failed the attempt, but it was fascinating, from a scientific standpoint. Did you know the feeder fangs go in first? Oh, and there was blood everywhere! But I get ahead of myself. That's not the important part. Now, where did I put my reticule? Oh, bother. I must have dropped it when I pulled out Ethel at the station." She tsked at herself. "Never mind, I think I can remember the sum of the note."

"Note? What are you on about, my dearest?" Lord Maccon was watching his wife in fascination. Alexia so rarely got flustered; it was charming. It made him want to grab and pull her close, stroke her into stopping all her verbal fluttering.

"Countess Nadasdy summoned me to visit Woolsey because Prudence and I have been summoned, commanded even, to visit the queen of the Alexandria Hive herself."

Lord Maccon stopped thinking about the fineness of his wife's figure. "Matakara? Indeed?" He looked impressed.

Alexia was surprised. Her husband was rarely impressed by anything to do with vampires. In fact, Lord Maccon was rarely impressed by anything period, except perhaps Lady Maccon on occasion.

"She commands us to attend her in Egypt as soon as possible. *In Egypt*, mind you."

Lord Maccon didn't flinch at the outrageousness of such a demand, only saying, "Well, I shall have to accompany you, if that is the case."

Alexia paused. She had her story all prepared. Her explanation as to why she should go. She was even formulating a plan to disguise her reason for traveling. Yet, here her husband went just knuckling under and wanting to go with her. "Wait, what? You aren't going to object?"

"Would it signify if I did?"

"Well, yes, but I would still go."

"My love, one does not deny Queen Matakara. Not even if one is Alpha of the London Pack."

Alexia was so surprised she handed her husband his own argument—the one she had been prepared to battle. "You don't want to stay and see to the murder investigation?"

"Of course I do. But I would never allow you to go to Egypt alone. It's a dangerous land and not simply because of the God-Breaker Plague. Lyall, Channing, and Biffy are rather more capable than I like to admit. I'm certain they can handle everything here, including Lady Kingair and a dead werewolf investigation."

Alexia's jaw dropped. "Really, this is too easy. What—" She paused. "Oh, I see! You want to investigate what Dubh was up to in Egypt—what he found out there—don't you?"

Lord Maccon shrugged. "Don't *you*?"

"Do you think Lady Kingair was lying to us about why she sent him?"

"No, but I do think he must have uncovered something significant. And why you in particular? Why not his pack?"

"This all has to do with my father. Dubh started to say something to that effect right before he was shot, and Queen Matakara's note intimated she knew secrets about my father. He spent some time in Egypt, I understand from his journals. Unfortunately, he seems never to have written anything down during those times. Although, he met my mother when he was over there."

Lord Maccon blinked. "Mrs. Loontwill traveled to Egypt?"

"I know, astonishing to think on, isn't it?" Alexia grinned at her husband's obvious confusion.

"Very."

"So, I should plan the trip? The vampires can't possibly object to us taking full charge of Prudence for a month or two. After all, it is at *their* behest."

"Vampires object to everything. They will probably want to send a drone as monitor."

"Mmm. Also, it'll be slower with you along, my love. I was hoping to travel by Dirigible Postal Express, but with a werewolf we'll have to go by sea." She patted her husband's thigh to modulate any insult inherent in the words.

He covered her hand with his large one. "The Peninsular and Oriental Steam Navigation Company has a new high-speed ship direct to Alexandria out of Southampton that takes ten days. It also crosses various dirigible flight paths, so we can get regular mail drops. Lyall can keep me informed on the Dubh investigation while we journey there."

"How very well informed you are, husband, on travel

to Egypt. One would almost think you anticipated the jaunt."

Lord Maccon avoided explaining by asking, "How do you propose to disguise the purpose of our journey?"

Alexia grinned. "Let me rest for a bit. I'll make a midnight call, determine if the other party is amenable, and let you know later."

"My dearest love, I hate it when you come over mysterious. It indicates that I will be made uncomfortable by the results."

"Pish-tosh, you love it. It keeps you on your very estimable toes."

"Come here, you impossible woman." Conall grabbed his wife and held her close, kissing her neck and then her lips.

Alexia perfectly understood the nature of the caress. "We should go to bed directly, my love, have a sleep."

"Sleep?"

Alexia was extremely susceptible to that particular tone in her husband's voice.

They made their way up the stairs in their own home and then out and across the little drawbridge into Lord Akeldama's town house, where they kept their secret bedchamber in his third best closet. Alexia did not summon Biffy, instead allowing Conall to fumble with her buttons and stays, far more patient with his fiddling than she ordinarily was. He managed her dress, corset, and underthings in record time, and she made short work of his clothing. Alexia had learned her way around a man's toilette after only a week or so of marriage. She had also learned to appreciate the warmth of Conall's bare flesh against her own. Terribly hedonistic of her, such unconditional surrender, and she should never admit such a thing to anyone. There was something about connubial relations that appealed, sticky as they might be. She found her husband's touch as necessary to her daily routine as tea. Possibly more difficult to give up.

Alexia let Conall swoop her up and deposit her onto the big feather mattress, following her down into the puffy warmth. Once there, however, she gently but firmly took the control from him. Most of the time, because her husband was a dear bossy brute in the best possible way, she let him take charge in the matter of bed sport. But sometimes he must be reminded that she, too, was an Alpha, and her forthright nature would not permit her to always follow his lead in any part of their life together. She knew, given Dubh's death, that Conall needed to be cared for, and she needed to look after him. The evening called for gentleness, long smooth caresses, and slow kisses, reminding them both that they were alive and that they were together. She wanted to make him believe through her touch that she wasn't going anywhere. Their customary rough, joyful, nibbling passion could wait until she had made her point as firmly as she could, in a language Conall understood perfectly.

Ivy Tunstell received Alexia Maccon in her sitting room. The advent of twins into Mrs. Tunstell's life had affected neither the decoration of her house, which was pastel and frilly, nor of herself, who was more so. How she and her husband afforded a nursemaid Alexia would never be so gauche as to ask. With such an addendum to their household staff, Ivy's domestic bliss and stage appearances were little affected by the unexpected double blessing. As a matter of fact, she looked, behaved, and spoke much as she had before she married.

Ivy's children, unlike Alexia's daughter, seemed unpardonably well behaved. On those few occasions when they had had occasion to meet, Lady Maccon had said the customary "goo," and the babies had cooed and batted their overly long eyelashes back until someone came and took them away, which was all that one could really ask of babies. Alexia found them charming and consequently was perversely glad they were abed when she arrived.

"My dearest Alexia, how do you do?" Mrs. Tunstell greeted her friend with genuine pleasure, hands outstretched to clasp both of Alexia's. She drew Lady Maccon in to blow air kisses at either cheek, an affectation Alexia found overly French but was learning to accept as a consequence of time spent in the company of thespians.

"Ivy, my dear, how do you do? And how are you enjoying this fine evening?"

"I am quite reveling in the commonplace refinement of family life."

"Oh, ah, yes, and how is Tunstell?"

"Perfectly darling as ever. You know, he married me when I was but a poor and pretty young thing. All that has changed since then, of course."

"And the twins?" Born some half a year after Prudence, they were named Percival and Primrose, but more commonly called Percy and Tidwinkle by their mother. Percy was, of course, understandable, but Alexia had yet to understand how Tidwinkle evolved from Primrose.

Ivy smiled her sweet mother's-little-angels smile—accompanying the expression with a sigh of devotion. "Oh, the *darlings*. I could just eat them up with a spoon.

They are asleep, sweet, precious things. And your little Prudence, how is she?"

"A tremendous bother and holy terror, of course."

Mrs. Tunstell tittered at that. "Oh, Alexia, you are too wicked. Imagine talking about one's own child in such a manner!"

"My dearest Ivy, I speak only the barest of truths."

"Well, I suppose young Prudence *is* a bit of a mixed infant."

"Thank goodness I have help or I'd be practically run off of my feet, I tell you!"

"Yes," Ivy said suspiciously. "I'm sure Lord Akeldama is invaluable?"

"He is taking Prudence for a stroll in the park as we speak."

Ivy gestured Alexia to sit and sent the maid for tea.

Alexia did as she was bid.

Ivy settled herself happily opposite her friend, delighted as always that dear Lady Maccon still afforded her any time at all. There was such a large disparity in their consequence as a result of marriage, no matter how much Alexia tried to convince Ivy otherwise, that Ivy always felt she was being honored by the continued acquaintance. Even a position as intimate as fellow member of a secret society and spy was not enough to reconcile Mrs. Tunstell to the fact that Lady Maccon, wife of an earl, came to take tea with her…in Soho! In *rented* apartments!

Still, it did not stop Mrs. Tunstell from reprimanding said Lady Maccon gently on the subject of Lord Akeldama. The man was, after all, too outrageous for fatherhood. The vampire side of his character being, in Ivy's universe, far less a thing than his scandalous comportment and flamboyant dress. Even her fellow actors were not so bad. "Couldn't you have gotten yourself a nice nursemaid, Alexia dear? For stabilization of the vital emotional humors? I can recommend them highly."

"Oh, Lord Akeldama has one of those as well. His humors are quite stable, I assure you. It makes no flour for the biscuit in the end with my daughter. Prudence requires all hands to man the forward deck, if you take my meaning. Twice as difficult as her father, even on his best days."

Ivy shook her head. "Alexia, really, you do say the most shocking things imaginable."

Lady Maccon, knowing such pleasantries might continue in this vein for three-quarters of an hour or more, moved on to a topic more in alignment with her visit. "I managed to catch the opening of your new play the night before last."

"Did you, indeed? How kind. Very patronly of you. Did you enjoy it?" Ivy clasped her hands together and regarded her friend with wide, shining eyes.

The maid came in with the tea, giving Alexia a moment to properly phrase her reply. She waited while Ivy poured and then took a measured sip before replying. "As your patroness, I approve most heartily. You and Tunstell have done me proud. A unique story and a most original portrayal of love and tragedy. I can safely say, I am convinced London has never seen its like before. Nor will it again. I thought the bumblebee opera dancer sequence was... riveting."

"Oh, thank you! It warms the cudgels of my heart to hear you say such a thing." Ivy positively beamed, her copious dark ringlets quivering in delight.

"I was wondering how long you're scheduled to run

this performance at this particular venue, and whether you had considered taking it on tour?"

Ivy sipped her tea and considered the question with all seriousness. "We have only a week in our contract. We had intended merely to test the waters with this new style, with an eye toward expanding to a larger venue if it went over well. Why? Have you something in mind?"

Lady Maccon put down her teacup. "Actually, I wondered if you might consider"—she paused for dramatic effect—"Egypt?"

Mrs. Tunstell gasped and put one small white hand to her throat. "Egypt?"

"I believe the Egyptian theatergoing public might find *The Death Rains of Swansea* truly moving. The subject matter is so very exotic, and I understand there is a lady of means in residence there who is particularly interested in performances of this kind. Had you thought to take the production outside of London?"

"Well, yes, Europe of course. But all the way to Egypt? Do they have tea there?" Ivy wasn't looking wholly opposed to the jaunt. Ever since her trip with Alexia to Scotland, Mrs. Tunstell had rather a taste for foreign travel. Alexia blamed the kilts.

She pressed her advantage. "I would, of course, fund the expedition and make the necessary arrangements."

"Oh, now, Alexia, please, you embarrass me." Ivy blushed but did not refuse the offer.

"As your patroness, I feel it my duty to spread the deeply moving message inherent in your play. The bumblebee dance alone was a masterpiece of modern storytelling. I do not think we should deny it to others merely because of distance and questionable beverage options."

Mrs. Tunstell nodded, her pert little face solemn at this profound statement.

"Besides"—Alexia lowered her voice significantly—"there is also a matter for the Parasol Protectorate to handle in Egypt."

"Oh!" Ivy was overcome with excitement.

"I may call upon you in your capacity as Agent Puff Bonnet."

"If that is the case, I shall speak to Tunny and we shall take measures and make preparations immediately! I shall need more hatboxes."

Alexia blanched slightly at this ready enthusiasm. The Tunstells' acting troupe numbered nearly a dozen, plus assorted sycophants. "Perhaps we could narrow the scope of your production down slightly? This is a delicate matter."

"Such a thing *might* be possible."

"Down to, perhaps, only you and Tunstell?"

"I don't know. There is the wardrobe to consider. Who will look after that? And one or two of the supporting roles are perfectly vital to the story. And what about the twins? I couldn't possibly leave my beloved poppets. We will need our nursemaid along, as I couldn't manage without her. Then there is..."

Mrs. Tunstell continued to prattle on and Alexia let her. After a good long negotiation, Ivy concluded she could narrow her entourage down to ten, Tunstell and the twins not included, and she would collect the names and paperwork and send them on to Floote as soon as possible.

It was decided that they could leave by the end of the next week, all details being finalized. Lady Maccon departed feeling that the hard part was over and that all she need do now was persuade her husband as to the sensibleness of hiding themselves in plain sight among a bunch of actors.

She sent a note round to Countess Nadasdy instructing her to tell Queen Matakara that if the Alexandria Hive were to express particular interest in seeing a performance of *The Death Rains of Swansea*, it might also get a visit from Lord and Lady Maccon and their unusual child. Queen Matakara was to demand the play be performed before her in person, in her own home, and to that end was asking the Tunstells' Acting Troupe a la Mode to travel to Egypt specially. Alexia and Conall would be invited along as patrons.

By the time Lady Maccon had completed this task, the pack was home and a general ruckus of large men had resulted. Conall stuck his head round the doorjamb to say there was nothing new concerning Dubh and did she know where Biffy had gotten to?

Alexia replied that, no, she didn't and would he please come in and let her explain her plan before he gallivanted off again. He did, and she did, and after a good deal of grumbling, he accepted the necessity of traveling under cover of thespians.

"And now," announced Alexia, "I am going to have a chat with Lord Akeldama. I want his perspective on this summons from Queen Matakara, and I should inform him of my imminent protracted absence from the Shadow Council. He will have to handle the dewan on his own."

"If you think it necessary."

"My dear, you really must come around to the fact that Lord Akeldama knows useful things. Things even you and BUR don't know. Plus, he is Prudence's legal guardian. If we wish to take her out of the country, even at a vampire's request, we must ask his permission. It is the way of things."

Lord Maccon gestured her on magnanimously, and Alexia took herself next door without further ado.

Upon waking that evening Biffy was understandably bothered to hear of Dubh's death. However, it was a middling bother. He had never met the man, and, if the rumors were to be believed, he hadn't missed out on much. Besides, it was difficult to mourn the loss of anyone who had spent a good deal of his life in Scotland. Biffy was tolerably more disturbed by the fact that he had developed a cowlick while asleep that would not lie flat no matter what he did.

Biffy wondered if this attitude might be considered crass. He wouldn't want to be thought crass. It was simply that he still felt disconnected from his werewolf brethren. They had little conversation that did not revolve around sports or ballistics. Major Channing had a well-tied cravat, but really, even Biffy could not forge a relationship based solely upon attractive neck gear.

Biffy skirted off early to see to the hat shop and returned for a midnight snack to find Lord and Lady Maccon out and those few others still in residence dressed in black waistcoats. With a sigh, he went to change, disliking Dubh more for the alteration in his wardrobe than the poor man probably deserved.

He was picking idly at a plate of kippers when Professor Lyall wandered in, spotted him, and said, "Oh, good, Biffy, just the man I was looking for."

Biffy was startled. Professor Lyall had always been scrupulously kind to him, but other than doling out responsibility for the contrivance chamber and associated paperwork, the Beta had had very little to do with Biffy. Taking care of Lord Maccon was a full-time job, a fact Biffy understood all too well. He was such a very large and fearsome man, and so very scruffy. Biffy was part afraid of the Alpha, part in awe, and part driven by a pressing need to get him to a tailor.

He swallowed his bit of kipper and rose slightly out of his seat in deference to rank. "Professor Lyall, how can I be of service?" Biffy was hoping someday to learn the secret of the Beta's tame coiffure. It showed such admirable restraint.

"We're hitting a spot of bother getting anything substantial in the way of onlookers from Fenchurch Street. I was wondering if perhaps you might have some contacts in that area, from your before days?"

"Lord Akeldama did have me visit a pub near there upon occasion. One of the barmaids might remember me."

"Bar*maids*? Very well, if you say so."

"Would you like me to inquire now?"

"Please, and if you wouldn't mind some company?"

Biffy looked the Beta over—quiet, unassuming, with excellent if understated taste in waistcoats and a generally put-upon expression. Not the type of company Biffy would have chosen in his past, but that was the past. "Certainly, Professor, delighted." Perhaps they might discuss the matter of controlling cowlicks.

"Now, Biffy, don't tell fibs. I know I'm not up to your standards."

If he still had the capacity, Biffy would have colored at that bold statement. "Oh, sir, I should never even hint that you were anything but ideally suited to—"

Professor Lyall cut him short. "I was only teasing. Shall we?"

Biffy finished his last mouthful of kipper, wondering if the Beta generally teased at table. Then he stood, grabbed his hat and cane, and followed the professor out into the night.

They walked in silence for a long moment. Finally Biffy said, "I was wondering, sir."

"Yes?" Professor Lyall had a very gentle voice.

"I was wondering if perhaps your appearance were not as calculated to be unobtrusive as that of Lord Akeldama's drones, only in a far more subtle way." Biffy saw white teeth flash in a quick smile.

"Well, it is a Beta's job to take to the background."

"Did Dubh do that?"

"Not as I understood it. But he was a far fly from a true Beta. Lord Maccon killed his Kingair Beta for treason before he left the pack. Dubh stepped in because there was no one better."

"What an awful mess that must have been."

Next to him, Professor Lyall's footsteps paused one infinitesimal minute. Without his supernatural hearing, Biffy never would have caught the hesitation. "For the Kingair Pack? Yes, I suppose it was. You know, at the time, I never even gave them a thought. The Woolsey Pack had its own problems."

Biffy had heard the rumors. He had also done his best to learn the history of his pack. "The Alpha prior to Lord Maccon had gone sour, I understand."

"That's a rather elegant way of putting it—as though he were curdled milk."

"You didn't like him, sir?"

"Oh, Biffy, don't you think you could call me Randolph by now?"

"Goodness, must I?"

"Everyone else in the pack does."

"Doesn't make it palatable. Can I rename you?"

"How very Lord Akeldama of you. Not Dolly, though, please."

"Randy?"

Sour silence greeted that.

"Lyall, then. Are you going to answer my question, sir, or avoid it?"

Lyall cast him a sharp look. "You're right. I didn't like him."

Biffy felt a small frisson of horror. "Do *all* Alphas go sour?"

"All of the old ones, I'm afraid. Fortunately, most of them die fighting off challengers. But the really strong ones, the ones who live past three or four hundred, they all go—as you say—sour."

"And how old is Lord Maccon?"

"Oh, don't you worry about him."

"But he'll get there?"

"I suspect he might be one of the ones who does."

"And you have a plan?"

Professor Lyall gave a small huff of amusement. "I believe *he* does. You believe ours is a far more ugly world than that of the vampires, don't you, young pup?"

Biffy said nothing at that.

"Perhaps they simply hide it better. Had you considered that?"

Biffy thought of his dear Lord Akeldama, all light heart, pale skin, and sweet fanged smiles. Again, he said nothing.

Professor Lyall sighed. "You're one of us now. You made it through the first few years. You're controlling the change. You're taking on pack responsibility."

"Barely. Have you seen the way my hair is behaving of late? Practically scruffy."

They hailed a hansom cab and slung themselves inside. "Fenchurch Street, please, my good man, the Trout and Pinion Pub."

The fly got them there in good time, and they alighted before a questionable-looking establishment. For this part of town, near the docks, being more of a mind to cater to the daylight folk, it was quiet late at night. Nevertheless, the pub looked unfortunately popular.

The locals quieted at the advent of strangers, especially one dressed as flawlessly as Biffy. A murmur of suspicious talk circulated as they made their way to the bar.

The barmaid remembered Biffy. Most women of her class did. Biffy was a good tipper and he never groped or expected anything. Plus he dressed so well he tended to make a favorable impression on females of the species.

"Well there's my fine young gentleman, and ain't it been an age since I clapped eyes on you last?"

"Nettie, my dove"—Biffy put on his most extravagant mannerisms—"how are you this *delightful* evening?"

"Couldn't be better, ducky. Couldn't be better. What can I get you boys?"

"Two whiskeys, please, my darling, and a little of your company if you have a mind."

"Make that three and I'll sit on your knee while we drink 'em."

"Done!" Biffy slapped down the requisite coin, plus a

generous gratuity, and he and Lyall made their way over to a small side table near the fire.

Nettie hollered back for a replacement barmaid, then joined them, carrying the three whiskeys, sloshed into tumblers. She settled herself, as threatened, on Biffy's knee, sipping her drink and twinkling hopefully at both men. She was a buxom thing, perhaps more round than Lyall favored, if Biffy was any judge of the man's taste, but of very pleasant disposition and inclined to chatter once steered in the correct direction. Her hair was so blond and fine as to be almost white, as were her eyebrows, giving her an expression of uninterrupted wonder that some might have taken for stupidity. Biffy had yet to determine whether this was actually the case.

"So, how's the pub fared since I visited last, Nettie my dove?"

"Oh, well, let me just tell you, love. Old Mr. Yonlenker—you remember, the bootblack down the block?—tried to clean his own chimney just last week, got himself wedged right proper for two days. They had to use lard to get him out. And then..." Nettie chattered on about all the various regulars round the neighborhood for a good twenty minutes. Biffy let the wave of gossip wash over him. Professor Lyall paid dutiful attention and Biffy asked enough questions to keep her going.

Finally he prodded gently, "I hear there was a bit of a flutter at the station the other night."

Nettie fell obligingly into the trap. "Oh, wasn't there ever? Gunshots! Young Johnny Gawkins round Mincing Lane said he's sure he saw a man taking off by private dirigible! Round these parts, can you imagine? And then of course there was the fire, same night. Can't say as how the two are linked, but I ain't saying they're not, neither."

Biffy blinked, confounded for a moment. "Young Johnny say anything about the man's looks?"

"Gentlemanly, think he said. Though nothing up to your standards, of course, me young buck. You sure ain't half curious about it, aren't ya?"

"Oh, you know me, Nettie, terrible one for scandalmongering. Tell me, has Angie Pennyworth had her baby yet?"

"Not as how! Twins I tell you! And her without two pennies to rub together, and no da never did come forward. Crying shame, that's what I say. Though of a certainty an' we're all thinking it's *you know who*." The barmaid gestured with her pale head at a skinny lad lurking in the far corner, nursing a pint.

"Not Alec Weebs? Never!" Biffy was appreciatively shocked.

"Oh, believe it." Nettie settled herself in for another round.

Biffy gestured at the replacement barmaid for more whiskey.

Professor Lyall nodded at Biffy imperceptibly in approval. A gentleman in a private dirigible wasn't much to go on since the recent upsurge in dirigible popularity, but it was better than nothing. And at least there were records of dirigible sales. That narrowed their suspect list.

CHAPTER SIX

In Which the Parasol Protectorate Acquires a New Member

Lord Akeldama was back from his walk, Prudence was down for her nap, and Tizzy and the nursemaid were relieved of their duties for the moment. The vampire was holding court in his drawing room with a small collection of drones arrayed around him, a bottle of champagne on the end table, and the fat calico cat on his lap. Truth be told, Lord Akeldama had transformed into rather a homebody since becoming a father, much to London's surprise. This was because home had become, under Prudence's influence, even more exciting than the social whirl of the ton. Besides, Lord Akeldama had nothing but time; he could afford a few decades to play at parenting. He had, after all, never indulged in such an experience before. When one was a vampire as long-lived as he, new experiences were hard-won, difficult to find, and treasured—like good-quality face powder.

"Alexia, my *dearest* custard cup, how *are* you? Was it a perfectly *horrid* night?"

"Pretty much horrid, yes. And how was your stroll in the park?"

"We were the statement of the hour!"

"Of course you were."

The drones amicably made room for Alexia to sit, standing prettily while she did so. They then returned to their own chattering, leaving their master and his visitor to carry on together. However, Alexia was very well aware that ears were perked. Lord Akeldama's drones were trained in such a way as to suit their own intrinsic natures, and in the end, one could never take the love of gossip out of a soul once embedded there. They were as much interested in Lord Akeldama's secrets as they were in everyone else's.

"Lord Akeldama, do you think we might have a little word, in confidence? I have had a rather interesting summons and I could use the benefit of your advice."

"Of course, my *dearest girl*! Clear the room, please, *my darlings*. You may take the champagne."

The drones rose and trooped obligingly out, closing the door behind them.

"Ah, the dears, they are probably all pressed in a huddle with their collective ear to the jamb."

"Prudence and I have been summoned to visit Queen Matakara, in Egypt. What do you make of *that*?"

Lord Akeldama was not as awed as Lady Maccon might have hoped. "Ah, my dearest *sugar drop*, I am only surprised it has taken her so long. You aren't *actually* considering going, are you?"

"Not to put too fine a point on it, but yes. I've always wanted to see Egypt. There is also a pack matter Conall wishes to investigate there. I have even devised a cover story."

"Oh, Alexia, my rose hip, I *really* wish you wouldn't. Not Egypt. It's not a nice place, so hot and smelly. Full of tourists in muted colors. The puggle might be endangered. And I, of course, could not accompany you."

"Endangered by bad smells and muted colors?"

"Not to mention local dress. Have you seen what they wear in that country? All loose and flowy, *abominable* concessions to comfort and practicality." Lord Akeldama's hand floated up and out in the air in a simulation of the flutter of robes worn by exotic tribesmen. He lowered his voice. "There are too many secrets and too few immortals to keep them."

Alexia pressed further. "And Queen Matakara, have you ever met her?"

"In a manner of speaking."

Lady Maccon looked at her friend sharply. "What manner?"

"A very long time ago, my dearest pudding drop, you might say she was *responsible for everything.*"

Alexia gasped. "Oh my giddy aunt! She *made* you!"

"Well, darling, there is no need to put it so crassly as all that!"

So many questions cluttered Alexia's mind at this revelation that her head very nearly did take to spinning. "But how did you get *here*?"

"Oh, silly child. We can move long distances, for a short period of time, right after metamorphosis. How else do you think vampires managed to migrate all over the world?"

Alexia shrugged. "I suppose I thought you simply expanded outward in ever-increasing circles."

Lord Akeldama laughed. "There would have to be considerably more of us for that, my darling sugar lump."

Lady Maccon sighed, then asked the best question she could, given Lord Akeldama's evasiveness. "What *can* you tell me about Queen Matakara?"

The vampire raised his gem-studded monocle and looked at her through the clear glass. "Not quite the right question, sweetling."

"Oh, very well. What *will* you tell me about Queen Matakara? Given that I will be taking your adopted daughter into her hive whether you like it or not."

"Hard line, my little *marmalade pot*, but better. I will tell you that she is very old, and her concerns are not that of the shorter lived."

"No advice at all, not even for Prudence's sake?"

The vampire looked at her, a slight smile on his face. "You are not above playing all the cards you have been dealt, are you, my darling girl? Very well. You want my advice? Don't go. More than that? Be careful. What Queen Matakara *says* is never the whole truth, and what Queen Matakara *is* has been hidden by the sands of time. It is not that she no longer cares to win; it is that she does not play the game at all. For you and I, my dear, who live for such petty diversions, this is practically impossible to comprehend."

"Then why ask to see Prudence? Why involve herself?"

"There you have the *real* danger, my clementine, and the *real* question, and, of course, there is no way for us to understand the answer."

"Because she is outside of our understanding?"

"Precisely."

"Unusual woman."

"You haven't yet seen the way she dresses."

While Lyall tracked down dirigible possession records, and Lord Maccon dashed about looking for clues, Lady Maccon planned her trip. Or, to be precise, she told Floote what she wanted and he made the necessary arrangements and procurements. The Tunstells were accounted for, and much to Alexia's disgust, Countess Nadasdy insisted on sending one of her drones along as ambassador for the English hives.

"She only wants to keep an eye on *me*," she objected to Floote while they contemplated which traveling gowns were best suited to an Egyptian climate. "Do you know who she's sending? Of course you do."

Floote said nothing.

Lady Maccon cast her hands up into the air in exasperation and began pacing about the room, gesticulating wildly in accordance with her Italian heritage.

"Exactly! Madame Lefoux. That woman simply cannot be depended upon. I'm surprised the countess trusts her so far as she can throw her. Although, I suppose being a vampire, she could throw her quite far. Then again, perhaps she is sending her along because she doesn't trust her. I mean, who is Genevieve favoring these days? Me, the vampire, the OBO, or herself?"

"A woman of conflicted loyalties, madam."

"To say the least! She must live a very complicated life. I'm certain I could never be so duplicitous."

"No, madam, not in your nature. I shouldn't let it concern you."

"No?"

"You can be guaranteed of at least one thing, madam. This time she doesn't want you dead."

"Oh, yes? How can I know this?" Alexia huffed, and sat on her bed, her lace robe floating out around her in a waterfall of opulence. "You know, Floote, I really enjoyed her company. That's the difficulty."

"You still do, madam."

"Don't be familiar, Floote."

Floote ignored this, in the manner of long-time family retainers everywhere. "It will be good for you to have someone like her along, madam."

"Like what? What do you mean, Floote?"

"Sensible. Scientific."

Alexia paused. "Are you speaking as my butler or as my father's valet?"

"Both, madam."

Floote's face was, as always, practically impossible to read. But after days of packing and organizing, Lady Maccon was beginning to get the distinct impression that he did not approve of Egypt.

"You don't want me to go, do you, Floote?"

Floote paused, looking down at his hands, perfectly gloved in white cotton, as was appropriate to upstairs staff.

"I made Mr. Tarabotti two promises. The first was to keep you safe. Egypt is not safe."

"And the second?"

Floote shook his head ever so slightly. "I can't stop you, madam. But *he* wouldn't want you to go."

Alexia had read her father's journals. "I have done a great deal in my life he would not have approved of. My marriage, for one."

Floote went back to packing. "He would want you to live as you wished, but not in Egypt."

"I am sorry, Floote, but it's time. If you won't tell me the missing parts of my father's life, perhaps someone there will." Alexia had always thought Floote's loyalty was absolute. Floote had stayed with her pregnant mother when Alessandro abandoned them. He had changed her nappies when she was a babe. He had left the Loontwill household to attend Alexia after her marriage to a were-wolf. Now, she thought for the first time, perhaps it was his loyalty to her dead father that was unshakable and she was merely a proxy player.

Later that night, when her husband came home, Alexia curled against him rather more fiercely than she ordinarily might. Conall knew his wife well enough to sense the confusion and offer physical comfort of the kind she had given him only a few evenings earlier. In his touch, Alexia found reassurance. She also realized that with both Conall and Ivy along, she was leaving her home interests unsupervised. Lyall owed his loyalty to Lord Maccon, and she considered him an unreliable source ever since she found out he was behind the Kingair assassination attempt. Lord Akeldama's motives were always his own. Who did that leave her?

Things remained excitedly on the go all that week. Biffy carved out what time he could for his precious hats but nevertheless found himself drawn into the excitement of Dubh's murder investigation and Egyptian travel. He simply couldn't abstain. He was overly intrigued by the affairs of others.

He did manage to return to his duties as lady's valet.

He rather adored Lady Maccon, and had from the moment she first appeared in Lord Akeldama's life. She had such an endearingly practical way of looking at the world. He had once described her to a colleague as the type of female who was born a grande dame. Everyone and everything had a proper place or she would see they were put into one of her own devising. Although she did require his guidance in the manner of her toilette. So far as Biffy was concerned, that, too, was an admirable quality in a lady. He enjoyed being needed, and Lady Maccon would be lost without him.

Which was precisely what she said as he fussed about with her hair. "Oh, Biffy, how do you do it? So lovely, you know I should be utterly lost without you."

"Thank you very much, my lady." Biffy finished cleaning the curling tongs and placed them into a drawer, standing back to take a critical look at his masterwork.

"That will do, my lady. Now, what would you like to wear this evening?"

"Oh, something sensible I think, Biffy. I won't be doing anything more exciting than packing."

Biffy went to look at her row of dresses. "How are preparations coming along for the trip?" He selected a day gown of cream striped in red with a cuirasse bodice of black velvet and a matched black underskirt. He paired this with a forward-tilting wide-brimmed hat with masculine overtones counteracted by a great array of feathers. Alexia thought the hat a little much but bowed to Biffy's judgment and allowed herself to be trussed up.

"Admirably, I believe. All of us should be prepared to leave the day after tomorrow. I am rather looking forward to it."

"I do hope you enjoy yourself."

"Thank you, Biffy. There was one more thing. I was wondering if I might prevail upon you. That is..." Lady Maccon paused, as though embarrassed or unable to find the words.

Biffy immediately left off fastening all the copious small buttons at the back of her gown and circled around to stand next to her, meeting her eyes via the looking glass. "My lady, you know you have only to ask."

"Oh, yes, of course. But this is a matter of some delicacy. I want it to be your own choice. Not one driven by pack or status."

She turned so they could look at each other face-to-face and took one of his hands in hers. He felt the effect of her touch instantly, an awareness of mortality, a dimming of his supernatural senses. It was a little like dropping out of the aether into the lower atmosphere, a sinking sensation in the stomach. He had learned to ignore the feeling. What with dressing and arranging Lady Maccon's hair, he experienced it frequently.

"I have a little private consortium. I was wondering if, perhaps, you might be persuaded to join."

Biffy was fascinated. "What kind of consortium?"

"A sort of secret society. I will, of course, require a vow of silence."

"Naturally. What do you call yourselves?"

"The Parasol Protectorate."

Biffy smiled. "I am enthralled by the concept of a society named after an accessory. Do go on, my lady."

"I am afraid you would be only our third member. Currently, the society consists of myself and Ivy Tunstell."

"Mrs. Tunstell?"

"She was rather invaluable in a matter of some considerable delicacy just before Prudence was born."

"What is the purpose of this society?"

"I suppose the root of the Protectorate is to seek truth and protect the innocent. In as polite and well accessorized a way as possible, of course."

"That seems quite glamorous enough to me." Biffy was rather taken with the idea of being in a club with the estimable Lady Maccon. It sounded most diverting. "Do I make a pledge?"

"Oh, dear. I did invent one for Ivy, but it is a tad ridiculous."

"Splendid."

Lady Maccon giggled. "Very well. Fetch me one of those parasols, please. I'm afraid the original pledge required my special parasol, but one of those will do as a replacement."

"Your *special parasol*, my lady?"

"Oh, just you wait. I'll have something made for you. Perhaps a particular top hat?"

"Particular?"

"Lots of hidden gadgets, concealed compartments, covert weaponry, and the like."

"What a horrid thing to do to a perfectly nice top hat!"

"Cane, then?"

Biffy tilted his head in consideration. Then he remembered Lord Akeldama's gold pipe that was actually a glaive. "Perhaps a cane. Now, about that pledge?" He was not about to allow Lady Maccon to deny him ready amusement.

His mistress sighed. "If you insist, Biffy. Spin the parasol three times and repeat after me: I shield in the name of fashion. I accessorize for one and all. Pursuit of truth is my passion. This I vow by the great parasol."

Biffy couldn't help it; he started to laugh, but he did as he was bid.

"Do try to keep a straight face," said his mistress, although she said it around her own grin. "Now pick the parasol up and raise it open to the ceiling."

Biffy did as instructed.

"Ivy insisted we seal the vow in blood, but I hardly think that necessary, do you?"

Biffy raised his eyebrows. It was fun watching Lady Maccon squirm.

"Oh, I had no idea *you* would be so difficult. Very well." She retrieved a small knife from her armoire. It was not silver, so in order to make the cut, she had to hold on to Biffy's wrist with her bare hand, keeping him mortal.

"May the blood of the soulless keep your own soul safe," she intoned, cutting a tiny slice in the pad of her thumb and then in his and pressing the two together.

Biffy had a moment of panic. What might her preternatural blood do to his werewolf blood? But the second she let go, his cut healed instantly, leaving no remnant mark behind.

"Now, Mrs. Tunstell goes by the sobriquet Puff Bonnet."

Biffy let out an uncontrolled bark of laughter.

"Yes, yes. Well, I go by Ruffled Parasol. What would you like your moniker to be?"

"I suppose it ought to be another accessory of some kind?"

Lady Maccon nodded.

"How about Wingtip Spectator?"

"Perfect. I will inform Ivy of your indoctrination."

"And now, my lady, I assume there is a reason for your recruiting me at this particular time?"

Lady Maccon looked at him. "You see, Biffy? That's what I mean. You are an adorably smart thing, aren't you?"

Biffy raised an eyebrow.

"I require someone to monitor London while Ivy and I are abroad. Keep me informed as to the nature of the murder investigation. Keep an eye on Channing's behavior—and Lyall's for that matter. And the vampires, of course."

"Tall order, my lady. Professor Lyall?"

"Everyone has secrets Biffy, even Lyall."

"Especially Professor Lyall, my lady. I'd say he is keeping a goodly number of everyone else's secrets as well as his own."

"You see, what did I say? Perceptive. Now, there will be irregular dirigible mail during our steamer crossing. I'll provide you with a schedule of the ones you'll need to utilize, depending on where we are. After that, I intend to set up an aethographic connection to the public access transmitter in Alexandria. I have the valve frequensor codes here, and I will give them mine. Thereafter, you will have to send all messages in code. I'll send you the first one just after sunset the day after we arrive—London sunset. Please coordinate the timing and be ready to receive. Lord Akeldama trained you in the use of an aethographic transmitter?"

"Of course." Biffy had known the workings of every single transmitter since the technology first came to London those many years ago. "This is going to be delightful fun, isn't it, my lady?"

At that, Lady Maccon put an arm about his waist and leaned her head on his shoulder. "That's the spirit!"

"Oh, dear heavens, Ivy, must you bring so many hats?"

They had let the entire first-class coach for the short haul from London to Southampton, where their steamer awaited the tides. Lady Maccon stood next to her husband on the platform waiting to board.

Mrs. Tunstell was wearing a traveling gown of pale pink and apple-green stripes, trimmed with multiple blue trailing ribbons. Her hat was a great tower of feather puffs, pink and green, through which peeked the heads of stuffed bluebirds and more ribbons. In addition to her hat-boxes, of which she took the greatest care and supervision, Mrs. Tunstell was accompanied by her husband, her children, their nursemaid, the wardrobe mistress, the prop master, a set designer, and six supporting cast members. Being actors, the whole lot of them performed the simple act of loading and boarding a train with all the pomp and circumstance of a three-ring circus.

Everyone was a flutter of broad gestures, eye-searing attire, and loudly projected voices. Tunstell was his usual cheery redheaded self, the excitement of travel merely causing him to grin more broadly at the world. Alexia wouldn't exactly accuse Tunstell of being the kind of man who wrote sonnets, but his britches were overly tight and in a vocal plaid, his top hat was purple, and his traveling coat was scarlet. In fact, his entire outfit seemed an impressionistic take on riding out for the hunt. Biffy, who had come to the station to see them off, looked as though he might faint at the very sight of it and took his leave quite hurriedly.

Alexia carried Prudence in her naked arms, waiting until the sun was properly up, at which juncture she could hand the squirming toddler off to her husband without fear of any furry recriminations. It was a great embarrassment to be seen in public without her gloves, but she was taking absolutely no chances. They had a train to catch. Prudence simply couldn't be allowed to delay matters by turning wolf and running off.

There had been a very tearful good-bye before they left their house. Lady Maccon held Prudence close while Lord Akeldama peppered his puggle with kisses. Tizzy, Boots, and all the other drones made their farewells as well, doling out an excessive number of coos and coddles to Prudence, as well as small gifts for the journey. Lady Maccon was beginning to suspect her child of being rather spoiled. All this excitement caused Prudence to come over tetchy for the duration of the ride to Waterloo Station. Alexia had only just gotten her settled when they were summarily immersed in the chaos of the Tunstells' acting troupe.

Of course, Prudence was beaming in delight at all the drama and color. She was very much Lord Akeldama's daughter in this and clapped her chubby little hands when Mrs. Tunstell ordered the porter to fit all her hatboxes inside the train car at once and the poor man went tumbling backward, hats flying everywhere.

"Stay!" Mrs. Tunstell ordered her hats.

"Oh, really, Ivy. Let the porter handle things. The man knows what he is doing. Get your party settled." Alexia was as annoyed as her daughter was delighted.

"But, Alexia, my hats, they simply can't be left to just anyone. It's the collection of a lifetime."

Lady Maccon told a calculated fib in order to expedite matters. "Oh, but, Ivy, I do believe I see the nursemaid trying to attract your attention from within. Perhaps the twins—"

Mrs. Tunstell immediately forgot all about her precious hats and climbed hurriedly up into the train to see if her little angels were indeed suffering any possible distress.

Unlike Prudence, the Tunstell twins were apparently bored by the prospect of foreign travel. Perhaps their ennui was brought on by near constant exposure to the theatrical lifestyle. Primrose was quietly entranced by all the trim and sparkle about her, clearly her mother's daughter. Periodically tiny arms would wave out from her bassinet, reaching for a feather or a particularly gaudy bow. Percy, on the other hand, had spit up obligingly all over the lead villain's velvet cape and then gone to sleep.

"Alexia, Lord Maccon. Good morning." A warm, faintly accented voice came wafting from behind them.

Alexia turned. "*Madame Lefoux*, you made it in good time, I see."

"As if I would miss this for the world, *Lady Maccon*."

"As you can see, it is quite the kerfuffle," Alexia said. They watched as the last of Ivy's entourage made their way on board, leaving a mound of luggage behind on the platform.

"Conall, tip the porters well, would you, please?" Lady Maccon prodded her husband into coping with the mountain.

"Of course, my dear." Lord Maccon wandered over to see to the logistics.

Alexia shifted Prudence to her other hip. "Prudence, this is Madame Lefoux. I don't believe you have met since your arrival into this world. Madame Lefoux, may I introduce Prudence Alessandra Maccon Akeldama?"

"Dama?" queried Prudence at that.

"No, dear, Lefoux. Can you say Lefoux?"

"Foo!" pronounced Prudence with great acumen.

The Frenchwoman shook Prudence's pudgy little hand solemnly. "A pleasure to make your acquaintance, young miss."

"Foo Foo," replied Prudence with equal gravitas. Then, after giving the lady dressed as a gentleman a very assessing look, she added, "Btttpttbtpt."

The inventor brought along only a small portmanteau for the journey and a hatbox Alexia remembered as being a hatbox only on the surface. Underneath it was a cleverly devised toolkit.

"Expecting trouble, are you, Genevieve?" Alexia forgot to be formal, falling all too quickly into the familiarity bred by a previous journey made together across Europe—a time when she and the inventor had been friends rather than cautious acquaintances.

"Of course. Aren't you? No parasol, I see. Or not a *real* one."

Alexia narrowed her eyes. "No. Mine happened to get destroyed when a certain person brought a certain hive house down around everyone's ears."

"I *am* sorry about that. Things got a touch out of hand." Madame Lefoux dimpled hopefully.

Alexia was having none of it. "Sorry isn't good enough. I *lost* my *parasol*." She practically hissed it. The absence still rankled.

"You might have said something. I could easily have made you a replacement. The countess has me very well set up."

Alexia arched her eyebrows.

"Ah. You don't trust me now that I belong to the Woolsey Hive. May I remind you that you put me there?"

Alexia sputtered.

"Dada," said Prudence, warning them both.

Lord Maccon had seen to the luggage. "Well, ladies, Madame Lefoux, shall we? The train is about to depart, and I believe everyone is aboard, save us." It took him a moment to sense the tension between his wife and her erstwhile friend.

"Now, now, what's all this about?"

"Foo!" pointed out Prudence.

"Yes, poppet, so I see."

"Your wife is still missing her parasol."

"Ah. My dear, I did order you a new one, but it is taking far longer than I expected. You know how scientists can be."

"Oh, thank you, Conall! I did think it might have slipped your mind."

"Never, my dear." He bent and kissed her on the temple. "Now, if that settles matters?"

The sun peeked up, outside the station but definitely rising. The train sounded its horn, loud and long, and the engine began to ramp up, belting bouts of smoke and steam out onto the platform like a sudden, smelly fog.

Lord Maccon grabbed Madame Lefoux's portmanteau and tossed it up into the coach to the waiting steward. His strength was taxed by the rising sun, but not so much as to make even a large piece of luggage much of a burden. He took Prudence from his wife. His daughter wrapped chubby arms about him in delight. Prudence was growing to love daylight, since she associated it with hugging her father. In addition, her aunt Biffy and her uncle Lyall were more likely to scoop her up and twirl her around when the sun was up.

"Dada," she said approvingly. Then she leaned forward toward his ear, as if to tell him a secret, and spouted a whole stream of incomprehensible babbling. Alexia figured this was Prudence's version of gossip. It was probably quite interesting and informative, had it actually been composed of words.

"Prudence, darling," said her mother as she climbed up into the train. "You must learn to use proper English. Otherwise, you can't possibly hope to be understood."

"No," said Prudence, most decidedly.

Madame Lefoux seemed to find this terribly amusing, for Alexia heard her chuckle behind her as she, too, climbed inside the coach.

The Tunstells' troupe had already struck up a rousing chorus of "Shine Your Buttons with Brasso," an extremely bawdy tune entirely ill-suited to the first-class compartment of the Morning Express to Southampton.

Lady Maccon looked at her husband as if he might be one to justify such behavior.

He shrugged. "Actors."

Prudence, lacking in all sense of dignity and decorum, squeaked in delight and clapped along with the song.

Madame Lefoux immersed herself in some papers from the Royal Society, humming along.

Tunstell demanded ale, despite it being early morning. One of the young ladies from the supporting cast began to dance a little jig in the aisle.

"What will the steward think of us?" said Alexia to no one in particular. "This is going to be a very long trip."

CHAPTER SEVEN

Biffy Encounters a Most Unsatisfactory Parasol

In the years that followed, when Lady Maccon had occasion to recall that nightmare morning, she would shudder at the horror of it all. She who has not traveled in the company of ten actors, three toddlers, a werewolf, and a French inventor cannot possibly sympathize with such torture. The chaos of the train station was a mere appetizer to the main course of utter insanity that was the Maccon party's attempt at boarding the steamer at Southampton. Miraculously, they managed to do so with few actual casualties. Ivy lost one of her hatboxes to the briny deep and had a fit of hysterics. The man playing the villain, a fellow named Tumtrinkle, barked his shin on the side of the entrance ramp, an occurrence that, for some strange reason, caused him to sing Wagnerian arias at the top of his lungs to withstand the pain for the next three-quarters of an hour. The wardrobe mistress was in a panic over the proper treatment of the costumes, and the set designer insisted on handling all of the backdrops personally, despite the fact that he had a dodgy back and a limp. One of the understudies was not pleased with the size and location of her room and began to cry, claiming that in her country, ghosts were tethered near water, so she could not possibly be in a room that overlooked the ocean...on a boat. Percy spit up on the captain's lapel. Primrose ripped a very long feather out of a lady passenger's hat. Prudence squirmed out of her father's grasp at one point, toddled over to the railing, and nearly fell over the edge.

Lady Maccon felt, if she were the type of woman to succumb to such things, a severe bout of nerves might have been called for. She could quite easily have taken to her apartments with a cool cloth to her head and the worries of the world far behind her.

Instead, she oversaw the loading of the mountain of luggage with an iron fist, distributed cleaning cloths to the captain and Percy, rescued and returned the feather to its rightful owner, sent a steward to Ivy's room with restorative tea, insisted Tunstell comfort the hysterical understudy, distracted the wardrobe mistress and set designer with questions, corralled her daughter with one arm and her frantic husband with the other, and all before the steamer tooted its departure horn and lurched ponderously out into a dark and choppy sea.

Finally, once everything was settled, Alexia turned to Conall, her eyes shining with curiosity. "Who did you order it from?"

Lord Maccon, exhausted, as only a man can be when put in sole charge of an infant, said, "To what could you possibly be referring, my dear?"

"The parasol, of course! Who did you order my new parasol from?"

"I took a good hard look at the available options, since Madame Lefoux was off the market, and thought we needed someone who at least knew something of your character and requirements. So, I approached Gustave Trouvé with the commission."

"My goodness, that's rather outside his preferred practice, is it not?"

"Most assuredly, but out of fond regard, he took the order anyway. He has, I am afraid to say, encountered some difficulty in execution. Hasn't Madame Lefoux's touch with accessories."

"I should think not, with a beard like that. Are you quite certain he is up to the task?"

"Too late now—the finished product was supposed to arrive just before we departed. I left instructions with Lyall to send the article on as soon as it appeared. It was meant to be a surprise."

"Knowing Monsieur Trouvé's taste, I'm certain it still will be. But thank you, my love, very thoughtful. I have felt quite bereft these past few years. Although, thank goodness, I have had very little need of it."

"Comparative peace has been nice." Conall moved Prudence, who had dozed off, to drape more artistically over one massive shoulder and shifted closer to his wife. They stood at the rear of the ship, watching the cliffs of England retreat into the mist.

"But?"

"But you have been getting restless, my harridan. Don't think I haven't noticed. You wanted to come to Egypt for a bit of excitement, if nothing else."

Alexia smiled and leaned her chin on his vacant shoulder. "You'd think Prudence would be excitement enough."

"Mmm."

"And don't place this all on me—you're harking after some adventure yourself, aren't you, husband? Or have you Egyptian interests?"

"Ah, Alexia, how do you know me so well?"

"Are you going to tell me?"

"Not yet."

"I loathe it when you do that."

"It's only fair. You practice the same policies, wife. Case in point: were you going to tell me about Biffy?"

"What about him?"

"You said something to him before we left. Didn't you?"

"Good gracious me, how could you possibly know that? Biffy has far too much circumspection to reveal anything to you."

"I know, my dear, because he changed. There was a lightness about him. He fit correctly into the pack, a role he has been reluctant to fill heretofore. What did you do?"

"I gave him a purpose and a family. I told you all along that was what he needed."

"But I tried that with the hat shop."

"I guess it had to be the right purpose."

"And you aren't going to tell me any more until I tell you about my reason for visiting Egypt."

"My love, now it is *you* who knows *me* too well."

Lord Maccon laughed, jiggling Prudence quite violently. Fortunately, much like her father, she was difficult to awaken.

It was a gray, wintry day, and there was little to see now that they had taken to the open ocean.

Alexia was beginning to feel the chill. "So long as we

understand each other. And now let's get our daughter
inside. It's a mite cold out here on deck, don't you think?"

"Indubitably."

Biffy felt the absence of his Alphas as a kind of odd ache.
It was difficult to describe, but the world was rather like a
tailored waistcoat without buttonholes—missing something important. It wasn't as though he could not function
without buttonholes; it was simply that everything felt a
little *unfastened* without them.

He returned from the station in good time only to find
a stranger at the door to his hat shop. A well-rounded
stranger with a narrow wooden box tucked under one
arm, an indifferent mode of dress, and an abnormally
proactive beard. From the quantity of dust about his person, Biffy surmised the man had been traveling. Without
spats, he noticed in alarm. There was a certain cut to the
stranger's greatcoat that suggested France, and from the
weathered appearance of the garment, Biffy deduced
he must have come by train directly from the Dover landing green, on the Channel Dirigible Express out of Calais.

"Good evening, sir," said Biffy. "May I help you
at all?"

"Ah, good evening." The man had a jovial way of
speaking and a French accent.

"Are you looking for Madame Lefoux, perhaps?"

"Cousin Genevieve, no. Why would you think...? Ah,
yes, this used to be her shop. No, I am in search of Lady
Maccon. I have a delivery for her. This was the address
given with the commission."

"Indeed? Is it something for the London Pack
perchance?"

"No, no. For her specifically, at Lord Maccon's request."

Biffy unlocked the shop door. "In that case, you had best come in, Mr. . . . ?"

"Monsieur Trouvé, at your service." The Frenchman doffed his hat, his button eyes twinkling, apparently at the mere pleasure of being asked to introduce himself.

Biffy felt the bushiness of his beard became less offensive in a man who seemed so very good-natured.

"Pardon me for a moment. I must see to the lights." Biffy left the Frenchman at the entrance and flitted quickly about in his practiced nightly ritual of turning up the gas in all the lamps and straightening gloves and hairmuffs from the day's activities. His head girl was good, but when she closed the shop for supper, she never left things quite up to his exacting standards. He remembered talking with Lady Maccon about her journey through Europe after Lord Maccon's unfortunate distrust of her moral fiber. At the time, he had been locked in a massive egg beneath the Thames. Later, however, Lady Maccon had related her side of the story, and it had included this French clockmaker, one Monsieur Trouvé. He was also the man who had designed the cages in the contrivance chamber below.

He completed his circuit of the shop and returned to his visitor.

"You are said by experts to be the last word on the subject of clocks. And I have heard of your exploits as relates to a certain ornithopter, the *Muddy Duck*. It is a pleasure to make your acquaintance."

The Frenchman threw his head back and let loose an infectious peal of laughter. "Yes, of course. It has been so long since I saw either Lady Maccon or Cousin Genevieve that I thought I might make the trip to London myself with the goods. An excuse for socializing, yes?"

"I am afraid you've missed them both. They left only a few hours ago for Southampton."

"Oh, how unfortunate. Will they be back soon?"

"Regrettably, no. They have taken a large party on an Egyptian tour. But if that box contains what I think it contains, Lady Maccon will want it as soon as possible. I am charged to send important items on to her. They are traveling by steamer in deference to Lord Maccon's, er, health."

"Ah, mail by dirigible has ample opportunity to bisect their journey? A most acceptable proposal, Mr. . . . ?"

"Oh, dear me, my sincerest apologies, sir. Sandalio de Rabiffano. But everyone calls me Biffy."

"Ah, the newest member of the London Pack. Genevieve wrote of your metamorphosis. A matter of some scientific interest not to mention political unrest. Not my field, of course." Knowing he was conversing with a member of Lord Maccon's pack seemed to relax the Frenchman. Yet France was not progressive in its approach to the supernatural.

"You are not afraid of me, Monsieur Trouvé?"

"My dear young man, why should I be? Oh, ah, your unfortunate monthly condition. I admit before meeting Lady Maccon I might indeed have been taken aback, but a werewolf came to our rescue on several occasions, and of wonderful use he was, too. Now vampires, I will say, I have little use for. But werewolves are good to have on one's side in a fight."

"How kind of you to say."

"Here is the box for her ladyship. The contents are quite durable, but I should not like to see it lost."

"Certainly not. I will ensure it is transported safely."

The twinkle reappeared from the depths of all the facial hair. Biffy dearly wanted to recommend the man the services of a good barber but thought this might be taken as an insult. So he bent his head to examine the package—a plain thing of untreated wood, cut thin like a cigar box.

"There is one other matter."

Biffy looked up from his inspection expectantly. "Yes?"

"Major Channing, is he also out of town?"

Biffy's good breeding took over, hiding his surprise. "No, sir, I believe he is at the pack's town residence." He tried to hide the curiosity in his voice, but the Frenchman seemed to sense it.

"Ah, that werewolf I spoke of, the one who came to our rescue. We ended up traveling through Europe together. Decent fellow."

At a complete loss, Biffy told him the pack address. He and the Gamma had very little to do with one another. Biffy showed the major his neck on a regular basis, and the major took control as needed and ignored him the rest of the time. But never before had anyone described Major Channing Channing of the Chesterfield Channings as a *decent fellow*.

The French clockmaker continued this surprising line of conversation. "I believe I will pay him a call, seeing as the ladies are away. Thank you for your time, Mr. Biffy. Good evening to you."

"I hope the rest of your London visit is more productive, Monsieur Trouvé. Good night."

As soon as the man left, Biffy popped open the long, skinny wooden box to look inside. It was terribly out of form, of course, to inspect someone else's mail. But he argued himself into believing it was to check on the safety of the contents, and he *was* now a member of Lady Maccon's Parasol Protectorate. It granted him, he felt, certain rights of familiarity.

He gasped in horror at the contents. Lady Maccon had carried with her many rather ill-advised parasols over the course of their association, one of which had been a good deal *more*. There was something to be said for such a weapon. But the parasol in the box before him was a travesty. Apart from everything else, it was utterly plain and undecorated except for the stitching of the supposedly *hidden* pockets. It was made of drab olive canvas! It was probably quite deadly, and there was no doubt the bobbles on the handle housed hidden dials and debilitating poisons. It was certainly heavy enough to do any number of things. But if such a thing could be said of a parasol, it looked like the kind of object a sportsman would carry, all function and no beauty. The brass handle positively clashed with the olive color. It looked— Biffy shuddered in utter horror—like an…umbrella!

He checked the delivery schedule. He'd have to place it on the early morning Casablanca-bound post in order for it to cross Lady Maccon's path as soon as possible. With a determined gait, he returned to the front of the shop and flipped the CLOSED sign. He had only six hours to rectify the situation. Taking the hideous thing in hand, he made room upon the counter. He pulled out all the laces, silk flowers, feathers, and other trims, dumped them all around him, found a needle and thread, and went to work.

The P & O's Express Steamer was constructed with luxury in mind. Built to take advantage of the new craze in antiquities collecting and Egyptian tours, the line was an attempt by the shipping industry to compete with dirigible carriers. Dirigibles had the advantage of being faster and more frequent, but a steamer had more space and carrying capacity. Lord and Lady Maccon's first class cabin was quite as large as Lord Akeldama's closet, perhaps even bigger, and outfitted with two portholes—an improvement on the closet, which had no windows at all. Of course, the portholes could be covered over with thick curtains, as the one clientele liners could guarantee was werewolves.

Lord and Lady Maccon knocked on the adjoining cabin, which they had rented for Ivy's nursemaid and the children, and deposited the sleeping Prudence into a small cot there. They could hear Ivy, still chattering to her husband in a distressed tone over the loss of her hat, in the cabin on the far side.

In the interest of limiting numbers, they had not included a butler, valet, or lady's maid among their personnel. This was an embarrassing breach in propriety, should the information get out. Alexia was nervous because it meant Conall had to help her with her toilette, but she supposed she might call upon the theatrical troupe's wardrobe mistress in dire emergencies. Her hair would simply have to be stuffed under a cap as much as possible. She had a few of Ivy's hairmuffs on hand as well, suspecting that the deck of a steamer got just as cold as that of a dirigible, possibly more so.

Being of the supernatural set, and rather confirmed in their habits and ways, the Maccons defied the breakfast bell and all tenets of fellow traveler obligation by undressing and taking to bed. Alexia figured the acting troupe was also likely to keep to nighttime hours, and as their visit in Egypt was to pay court on a vampire, she saw no reason to alter the entire pattern of her married life merely because of a sea voyage. No doubt the crew was accustomed to such idiosyncratic behavior. She left very clear orders with regard to meal times and postal deliveries. It was daylight, so even if Prudence did awaken, the infant couldn't cause more harm than any ordinary precocious toddler. Thus Alexia felt comfortable falling gratefully into Conall's welcome embrace. The world outside could await her pleasure.

Lady Maccon awakened late that afternoon. She dressed herself as much as she was able and left the cabin without disturbing her husband. Poor Conall, he looked as though he'd been hit by a train.

The designated nursery was quiet and still, but a certain waving of arms and burbling indicated that Prudence was awake, although not inclined to cry and unsettle her companions. Lord Akeldama had noted, on more than one occasion, that while Prudence's peculiar abilities made her somewhat of a handful, she was a very good-natured child. He then flattered Alexia by saying this rather reminded him of her.

Alexia made her way over to the cot and looked in.

"Mama!" announced Prudence, delighted.

"Shush," admonished her mother. "You will awaken the others."

The nursemaid came up behind Alexia. "Lady Maccon, is everything all right?"

"Yes, thank you, Mrs. Dawaud-Plonk. I think I'll take Prudence down with me, if you don't mind seeing to the necessities?"

"Of course, madam." The nursemaid whisked Prudence off behind an Oriental screen in one corner of the cabin. The infant emerged moments later wearing a fresh nappy and a pretty dress of cerulean muslin with a fur cape for warmth and a French-style hat. She looked quite smart and a little mystified by the rapidity with which she had been dressed. So, indeed, was Alexia. Such efficiency in relation to her daughter was a miracle of the highest order.

"I see why Ivy values your services so highly, Mrs. Dawaud-Plonk."

"Thank you, Lady Maccon."

"You aren't, by any chance, related to my butler, Mr. Floote, are you?"

"I am afraid not, madam."

"I had no idea there could be more than one."

"Madam?"

"Oh, nothing. I should warn you, as you are likely to have care of my child as well as the twins over the next few weeks, that Prudence has some very unusual habits."

"Madam?"

"Special."

"Every child is special in his or her own way, madam."

"Ah, yes, well, Prudence can be *quite* special indeed. Please try to keep her from touching her father after sunset, would you? She gets overly excitable."

The nursemaid didn't even flinch at such an odd request. "Very good, madam."

Alexia propped Prudence on one hip and together they went to explore the ship.

Up top, the day proved still dreary. The wind was running fierce and cold and there was nothing to see but whitecaps atop a darkened ocean. Alexia merely wished to ascertain that they were still going in the correct direction.

"Brrr," was Prudence's eloquent comment.

"Indeed, most inclement weather."

"Pttttt."

"Exactly, let us adjourn elsewhere."

She switched Prudence to her other hip and made her way to the forward section of the steamer, in front of the first smokestack, where the dining room and the library were situated.

Unsure as to the wakefulness of her party, Lady Maccon visited the library first for some light reading so that if she did have to dine alone, she might have some kind of intellectual discourse. Prudence was not quite yet up to her mother's standard of debate. The library was of questionable curation, but she found a scientific manual on human anatomy that she thought might prove absorbing, if not entirely appropriate to dining. The cover was innocuous enough, and there were some rather graphic pictures within that intrigued Prudence. Alexia was enough her father's daughter to relax some standards of propriety so long as scientific inquiry was the result. If Prudence was interested in anatomy, who was Alexia to gainsay her?

Despite it being very nearly teatime, the eatery was empty save for one gentleman in the far corner. Lady Maccon was about to settle on the opposite side of the room, feeling it a standard of common decency not to inflict a child on anyone, least of all a lone gentleman, when the gentleman in question rose and nodded at her, revealing that he was Madame Lefoux.

Reluctantly, but not wishing to appear rude, Alexia wended through the chairs and tables to join her.

Lady Maccon settled Prudence on her lap. The infant stared at Madame Lefoux with interest. "Foo?"

"Good afternoon, Miss Prudence, Alexia."

"No," objected Prudence.

"It's her latest word," explained Alexia, distracting her child with the book. "I'm not entirely certain she knows what it means. How have you settled in, Genevieve?"

A steward appeared at Lady Maccon's elbow with a small scrap of paper on which was printed the comestibles on offer.

"Interesting approach to food service," she said, fluttering the pamphlet about. Prudence grabbed at it.

"Saves the bother of having to hold everything in stock for the entirety of a journey and at the whims of passengers," replied the Frenchwoman.

Alexia was not interested in commerce, only tea. "A pot of Assam, if you would be so kind. One of the apple tarts and a cup of warm milk for the infant," she said to the hovering man. "Do you have any cinnamon sticks by chance?" The steward nodded. "Infant, do you want cinnamon?"

Prudence looked at her mother, her tiny rosy lips pursed. Then she nodded curtly.

"Shave some cinnamon on top for her, would you, please? Thank you."

The steward moved smoothly off to see to her needs.

Alexia snapped open a monogrammed serviette and tucked it into the neck of her daughter's dress. Then she sat back and took in her surroundings.

If not exactly decorated with Lord Akeldama's flair, the dining hall at least bowed to Biffy's taste. There was gilt and brocade aplenty, if judiciously applied. The room seemed to have been made by enclosing a deck, rather like a greenhouse, for there were large windows all around showing the gloomy outside.

"So what do you make of the SS *Custard*?" Madame Lefoux asked, pushing aside her papers and favoring Alexia with a dimpled smile just like the old days.

"It's rather posh, isn't it? Although I shall reserve judgment until I have sampled the comestibles."

"As you should." Madame Lefoux nodded, sipping her own beverage from a tiny demitasse teacup.

Lady Maccon sniffed the air. "Hot chocolate?"

"Yes, and a very good showing, by my standards."

Alexia rather preferred to drink tea and eat chocolate, but Genevieve was French and had to be allowed some measure of European behavior.

The steward arrived with her tea and tart, both of which proved to be well above average. Alexia began to think she might actually enjoy the crossing. Prudence was quite taken with her warm milk, spending a good deal of time dabbing at the cinnamon sprinkles on the top with her finger and then sucking them off. Terribly undignified, of course, but as yet the infant-inconvenience had shown very little interest in the proper use of utensils, her attitude seeming to be that fingers had come first in her life, so why mess with a good thing? Alexia kept an eye on her but didn't otherwise interfere. It was amazing what having a toddler had done to her much-vaunted principles.

"So, how are you, Genevieve?" Alexia asked finally, determined not to be made to feel embarrassed. After all, Madame Lefoux was in the wrong, not she.

"Better than could be expected. It is not so bad as I had feared, working for the hive."

"Ah."

"And Quesnel is enjoying himself, getting plenty of attention and an excellent education. Say what you will about vampires, they value knowledge. And an entire hive of vampires and drones actually keeps my boy in check. Although, that said, they have not managed to impress upon him any interest in fashion."

"Dama?" Prudence wanted to know.

"Exactly, Prudence," answered her mother.

"No," said Prudence.

Alexia remembered Quesnel as a scamp with a predilection for grubby workman's clothing that rendered him, in appearance, much like a newspaper boy. "So you both may survive until he has reached his maturity?"

Prudence finished her warm milk and shoved the cup away petulantly. Alexia caught it before it fell off the table. The child switched her attention to the printed menu that the steward had unwisely left behind. She flapped it about happily and then spent some time folding the corners.

Madame Lefoux's dimples reappeared. "We may. It is strangely restful, having the responsibility for his well-being partly removed, although there have been"—she paused delicately—"discussions with the countess. I can but temper their influence. I suppose it must be similar for you and Lord Akeldama."

"Thus far, Prudence seems perfectly capable of making up her own mind on most things. He does favor frilly dresses but I could hardly expect practicality from a vampire. Prudence doesn't seem to mind. Conall and I are happy to have the help. The werewolves have a saying. Do you know it? 'It takes a pack to raise a child.' In this case, a pack, Lord Akeldama, and all his drones may just possibly be sufficient to handle my daughter."

Madame Lefoux gave a doubtful look. The child looked about as innocent as a werewolf with a pork chop. She was content with the pamphlet, quietly humming to herself.

The Frenchwoman finished the last of the chocolate in her cup and poured herself another helping from the pot. "You have an easier time letting go than I."

"Well, I am less motherly than you, I suspect, and Lord Akeldama is my friend. We share sympathies and interests. Fortunately, he is *very* motherly."

"Not so the countess and myself."

Lady Maccon smiled into the last of her tart before probing gently. "Although I understand you do share *some* tastes."

"Why, Alexia, what could you possibly be implying?"

"Mabel Dair, perhaps?"

"Why, Alexia." Madame Lefoux brightened. "Are you jealous?"

Alexia had only meant to needle, now she found herself drawn into flirting and became embarrassed as a result. She should never have even broached such a scandalous topic.

"You would bring things back around to that."

Madame Lefoux took Lady Maccon's hand, becoming serious in a way that made Alexia quite nervous. Her green eyes were troubled. "You never even gave me a chance. To determine if you liked it."

Alexia was surprised. "What? Oh." She felt her body flush under the constriction of stays. "But I was married when we met."

"I suppose that is something. At least you saw me as competition."

Alexia sputtered, "I...I am very *happily* married."

"Such a pity. Ah well, that's one of us sorted. I guess you could do worse than Conall Maccon."

"Thank you, I suppose. And things cannot be so off with the hive and Miss Dair, or you would not be so forthcoming about it."

"Touché, Alexia."

"Did you think that while you were studying my character, I was not studying yours? We have not been much in each other's company these last few years, but I doubt you have changed that much." Alexia leaned forward. "Formerly Lefoux said to me, before she died, that you loved too freely. I find it interesting that you can be so loyal to the individual and to your much-vaunted technology yet be so unreliable where groups and governments are concerned."

"Are you accusing me of having my own agenda?"

"Are you denying it?"

Madame Lefoux sat back and let out a silvery tinkle of laughter. "Why should I wish to?"

"I don't suppose you are going to tell me to whom you are reporting on this particular trip. Order of the Brass Octopus? Woolsey Hive? Royal Society? French government?"

"Why, Alexia, didn't you just say I work only for myself?"

This time it was Alexia's turn to be amused. "Very nicely turned, Genevieve."

"And now, if you will excuse me, I have some business to attend to in my quarters." Madame Lefoux stood, made a little bow to both ladies. "Alexia. Miss Prudence."

Prudence looked up from her careful mutilation of the menu. "No."

The inventor retrieved her jacket and top hat from a stand by the door and made her way out into the blustery corridor.

"Fooie," said Prudence.

"I couldn't agree with you more, infant," said Lady Maccon to her daughter.

Alexia remained in the dining hall a goodly while. She enjoyed the ambiance, the constant supply of tea and nibbles, the efficiency of the staff, and the fact that it afforded her a general inspection of the other passengers. Everyone, after all, had to eat. Their fellow pilgrims were the expected assortment. She spotted several sets of pale ladies—invalids in search of health. The two emaciated fellows who were all floppy hair and elbows with ill-cut jackets could only be artists. The tweed-clad jovial chaps intent on drinking the steamer's entire stock of port before they reached port were obviously sportsmen keen upon crocodiles. There was a wastrel in black Alexia first thought might be a statesman, until he whipped out a notebook, which made her think he was that lowest of the low: a travel journalist. There were various unfashionable gentlemen with battered headgear and too much facial hair, either antiquities collectors or men of science.

Of course, her main reason for staying was that Prudence seemed equally content to sit, mutilating the menu pamphlet, and there was no point in messing with a good thing. Which was how it was that her husband found her still at tea even after sunset.

He arrived trailing Mr. and Mrs. Tunstell, the nursemaid,

the twins, and two members of the troupe, all looking bleary-eyed but dressed for dinner.

"Dada!" said Prudence, looking very much like she would appreciate some affection from her father. Alexia set her bare hand carefully on the back of her daughter's neck and then nodded at her husband.

"Poppet." Conall buzzed his daughter exuberantly on the cheek, making her giggle, and then did the same to his wife. "Wife." This elicited an austere look, which they both knew was one of affection.

Alexia supposed she ought to retire and dress for dinner herself, but she was terribly afraid of missing something interesting, so she remained, only transferring to a larger table so that the others could join her and Prudence.

"I do believe I might enjoy ocean transport even more than floating," pronounced Ivy, sitting next to Alexia without regard for proper table arrangement or precedence. Alexia supposed such standards had to be relaxed when traveling. Lord Maccon sat on Ivy's other side, keeping a good deal of room between him and his daughter.

"Is it the space or the fashion that appeals?"

"Both. Now, Percy, love, the furniture is not for eating." Baby Percival was busy gumming the back of the dining chair, arching over his father's arm in order to do so.

"Ahhouaough," said Primrose from her position on the nursemaid's lap. She had not yet developed the capacity for consonants.

This behavior, peaceable though it was, appeared to be too much for Mrs. Tunstell. "Oh, take them away, Mrs. Dawaud-Plonk, do. We will have a nice supper sent down to you. This simply isn't the place for children, I'm afraid."

Mrs. Dawaud-Plonk looked worried, faced with the logistical prospect of having to carry three toddlers. But Prudence, seeming to agree with Ivy that it was high time to leave, jumped down from her chair, removed the serviette from about her neck, handed it carefully to her mother, and stood waiting patiently while the nursemaid loaded herself up with twins. The little girl then preceded the nursemaid from the room, as though she knew exactly where she was going.

Ivy looked after, impressed. "I do look forward with pleasure to the time when mine are walking with greater stability."

"I wouldn't, if I were you. She gets into everything." It was a matter of some discussion in the Maccon–Akeldama household that Prudence seemed to walk sooner and with greater efficiency than was expected in an infant. It was generally thought that this might be because of her alternate forms—her vampire one being far faster and her werewolf one stronger. Together they probably bettered her burgeoning understanding of bipedal motion.

Ivy commenced to chatter about her experiences aboard the ship, for all they had been at sea only half a day, as though steamers were her life's work and main passion. "The windows in my cabin are actually *round*. Can you believe it?" The meal proceeded without incident, if the phrase *without incident* might be used to describe such an ordeal as objections to the type of sauce, the quality of the meat, and the color of the jellies. Lady Maccon began to suspect actors of being far more choosy in their preferences than even Lord Akeldama. She felt that the meal, comprised of giblet soup, fried turbot, beef shoulder, minced veal and poached eggs, corned pork, pigeon pies, croquettes of mutton, jugged hare, ham and tongue, and boiled potatoes was all that one might hope for aboard ship. And the seconds, always her favorite, far excelled such expectations, as they included both blackcap and rice puddings, jam tartlets, and a platter of excellent cheeses.

Lord Maccon declined after-dinner drinks and cards. Lady Maccon declined a stroll about the decks. Together they made their way back to their private quarters instead. Alexia, thinking of her filched book on anatomy, suggested they take advantage of the comparative peace of travel with no muhjah or BUR duties to distract them. Conall wholeheartedly agreed but seemed to believe books had no part in this activity.

They compromised. Alexia took out the book on anatomy and used Conall as a study specimen. She was taken with trying to determine where different organs were situated from the outside, which involved prods and pokes with her fingers. Since Conall was ticklish, this led to a small tussle. Eventually, Alexia lost possession of the book, her clothing, and her heart rate, but the study session was declared, by Conall at least, to be a resounding success.

CHAPTER EIGHT

Alexia Makes an Unexpectedly
Damp Discovery

The sea voyage was an oddly peaceful affair. This made Lady Maccon nervous. Because they kept to supernatural hours, the Maccons, the Tunstells, the collective progeny, and the acting troupe had nothing to do with the other travelers except at suppertime. During those convocations, when Alexia and her compatriots were commencing their waking hours, and the others their evening's amusement before bed, all travelers were required to socialize. The steamer was outfitted with only first-class compartments, unlike some of the less dignified Atlantic lines, and Alexia was delighted to find passengers behaving as first-class frequenters ought. Everyone was civil and politics never came up at table. The actors provided much needed entertainment, either through the acceptable avenues of conversation and the occasional musical interlude or through more dramatic means, like engaging in mad, passionate affairs with some dish on the menu and then having the vapors when the cook ran out or stealing the skipper's hat for a scandalous dance routine. They behaved themselves as much as could be expected and did not stray so far away from the upper crust as to commit any prank not already enacted by the young men of Oxford or Cambridge. Although one memorable evening of bread roll cricket certainly stretched the boundaries of propriety.

Trouble, when it inevitably came, originated in the most likely quarter—her husband and her daughter and her daughter's favorite toy, a large mechanical ladybug.

Early on in Prudence's life, Lady Maccon had written to her friend the clockmaker Gustave Trouvé, with an order for one of his mechanical ladybugs, only larger, slower, and less deadly. She'd had this outfitted with a small leather saddle and had, inadvertently, started a new craze in children's toys that kept that good gentleman busy for the next year. Lucrative, as it turned out, the market for rideable ladybugs.

Prudence showed this particular toy such favor as to make it entirely necessary to pack the thing for any trip— let alone one of several weeks—despite its bulky size. Alexia and Prudence had taken to occupying the first-class lounge and music room every evening after supper, Alexia with a book and a weather eye to her daughter, and Prudence with her ladybug and a gratifying willingness to wear herself out by running after it, or on top of it, or, on several occasions, under it. Sometimes one or two of the actors would join them to play the piano. Either Prudence or her mother might pause in their respective activities to listen, Lady Maccon sometimes driven to glare in disapproval when songs strayed too far toward the "Old Tattooed Lady" and the like.

It was when Lord Maccon joined them on the third night and Prudence, in a fit of excitement, ran her ladybug into his foot and fell against him that things went askew. They had been very careful, but it was so unexpected that even Lord Maccon's supernatural reflexes were not fast enough. This was compounded by the fact that, being a father, his instinct was to reach out and catch his daughter before she hit the floor, not, as it ought to have been, to leap away.

Prudence fell. Lord Maccon caught. And a werewolf cub dashed about the lounge causing chaos and panic. Prudence had been wearing a pretty pink dress with multiple frills, a nappy, and lace pantalettes. The nappy and the pantalettes did not survive the transition. The dress did. Prudence remained wearing it in wolf form, to Alexia's unparalleled amusement.

Prudence's werewolf nature seemed less driven by the need to hunt and feed than it was to run and play. Alexia and Conall had discussed whether this was a product of her youth or her metanatural nature. She also made for a very cute wolf cub, if Alexia did say so herself, so no one in the music lounge was *afraid* of her, but the unexpectedness of the cub's appearance did cause surprise.

"Gracious me, where did you come from, you adorable little fuzzball?" exclaimed Mr. Tumtrinkle, the gentleman playing the villain in *The Death Rains of Swansea*. He made a grab for said fuzzball, missed, and flew forward, crashing into the well-endowed lady soprano sitting at the piano. She shrieked in surprise. He grappled for purchase and ripped the bodice of her raspberry and green striped dress. She pretended a faint from embarrassment, although Alexia noted she kept an eye on a nearby steward to ensure her corseted assets were fully appreciated, which, from the young man's crimson blush, Alexia assumed they were.

Prudence the wolf cub made a circuit of the room, jumping up on people, trying to squirm under furniture and overturning it, and generally causing the kind of mayhem expected of an extremely energetic puppy wearing a pink frilly dress and confined to a small area. She completed her tour at her father's feet, at which point, operating on some infant memory, she attempted to try to ride the ladybug that had caused the accident in the first place, all the while avoiding her parents' grasp.

They probably would have caught her at some point. It was a large lounge, but it wasn't *that* large. Unfortunately, a deck steward opened the door, carrying a long package under his arm.

"Lady Maccon? This package just arrived for you by dirigible. And this letter. And here is a missive for you, Lord Maccon, and—Oh my goodness!"

Which was when Prudence made a break for freedom between the unfortunate man's legs.

"Catch her!" ordered Alexia, but it was too late. Prudence was off down the corridor. Alexia ran to the door, just in time to catch sight of the tip of her daughter's fluffy tail as it disappeared around a corner.

"Oh, dear."

"Lady Maccon," said the lounge steward sternly from behind her, "unregistered animals are not allowed on board this vessel! Even well-dressed ones."

"Oh, er, yes, of course. I will naturally pay any fine for the inconvenience or damages, and I assure you everything will be rectified the moment I get my hands on her. Now, if you will excuse me. Are you coming, Conall?"

With which Lord and Lady Maccon went dashing after their errant child.

Everyone left behind was very confused, especially when they found a torn child's nappy next to the forgotten ladybug and no evidence of little Lady Prudence anywhere in the lounge.

"You look tired, Professor. No insult intended, of course. And you make it intentionally difficult to tell, but I am beginning to believe that that little wrinkle about the pocket of your waistcoat indicates exhaustion."

"How very wise of you, young Biffy, to note my mood from the state of my waistcoat. Have you noticed anything else significant occurring around town of late?"

Biffy wondered if this was some kind of werewolf test to assess his skills of observation. Or perhaps Professor Lyall wanted to know what information Biffy might impart to a fellow pack member, or whether he would keep his own council, or whether he would tell Lord Akeldama, or whether he would tell Lady Maccon. He would, of course, tell all parties. He wouldn't tell them all everything, or even all the same thing, but he would tell them all *something*. What other point could there be in gathering the information in the first place? In this, he and his former master disagreed. Lord Akeldama liked to know things for their own sake. Biffy liked to know things for the sake of others.

He answered Professor Lyall in a roundabout way. "London's rove vampires are acting up. I had one in the shop this very evening, throwing his weight around like he was a queen. It's a good thing the contrivance chamber is hidden. His drones were nosing about after something, and it wasn't hats."

Lyall looked Biffy up and down, assessing. "You're coming along nicely, young Biffy. You'll make an excellent replacement."

"Replacement for what?"

"Ah, as to that, patience is a virtue, my dear boy. Now, this thing with the roves, how long has it been going on would you say?"

"They've been getting worse over the last few years, but it's gone quite tannic indeed since our Alphas left. Why, one rove accused me of purposefully not stocking gaiters. Made quite a fuss over it. I never stock gaiters! And just this evening I saw one of them feeding in the street. Assuredly, it *was* down near the embankment. But still, in the open air? I mean to say, that's almost as bad as picnicking in the park. Eating in *public*! It's simply not done."

Lyall nodded. "And the rove parties are getting rather wild as well. Do you know BUR had a missive from Queen Victoria on the subject? Bertie was seen at one of the Wandsworth events. She is a progressive, our dear Regina, but she is not all *that* progressive. Her son fraternizing with a hive on a regular basis—not at all acceptable. I understand the potentate got an earful on the subject."

"Oh, dear. Poor Lord Akeldama." Biffy brought all his new werewolf culture and his old vampire training to bear on the situation. "Is all this vampire ruckus because we werewolves are living inside their urban territory?"

"That is one theory. Any others?"

"Is it because Countess Nadasdy is no longer in May-fair? There is no queen for London central. Could that be causing dissonance?" Biffy watched Professor Lyall's face closely. He would never have called the Beta handsome, but there was something very appealing in the mildness of his expression.

"That is a thought. Lord and Lady Maccon and their Alpha nature might have held them back somewhat, but London is missing a queen, and the Grande Dame of Kentish Town is simply too far away to oversee matters in Westminster and the south side of the Thames."

Biffy knew a little of London's northern queen. "She also cares very little for the affairs of society. Not even fashion."

"There are some vampires," Lyall said, "very few, but *some*, gone off like *that*." He sniffed in a way that suggested the odor of rotten meat that undercut the scent of all vampires.

If Biffy understood nothing else, he understood significant emphasis in speech. "What can we do about it?"

"I shall have BUR keep a close eye on the roves, call in the rest of our pack if I have to, but full-moon revels are likely to be overly fervent this month. And there is little I can do then. We can but hope that Lord and Lady Maccon complete their business quickly and return home before a second full moon, as one alone may tax us to our limits."

Biffy said, off the cuff, "Or we could find a replacement queen."

"Volunteering for the position?"

"Why, Professor, is that wittiness I detect?"

"Only for you."

"Charmer." Biffy tapped him on the arm playfully.

Professor Lyall started slightly and then actually looked embarrassed by the casual contact.

Prudence led them on a merry dance about the ship, ending her jaunt hidden in a lifeboat on the port side of the promenade deck. Conall managed to catch her. Despite her supernatural strength, he also managed to hold on to her long enough to transfer her to his wife.

"Mama!" said the wriggling girl who resulted from this transaction. And then, as they were on the outer deck and she was wearing only a pink party dress, "Brrrr!"

"Yes, well, dear, you have only yourself to blame for that. You know you have to avoid your father at night."

"Dada?"

"Yes, precisely."

Lord Maccon waved shyly at his daughter, standing a good distance away to forestall any additional accidents.

"Oh, now, Prudence, look at that," said her mother, pointing up.

"No," said Prudence, but she looked up.

Above them was the postal dirigible, lashed to the moving steamer and being dragged along as deliveries were transferred between the two. Mail was dropped down a taut silk chute. Alexia thought it looked like fun and wondered if people ever came aboard in such a manner.

"Any mail for Casablanca?" the assistant deck steward yelled, marching to-and-fro. "Mail for Casablanca? Departure in ten minutes! Any mail?" He continued his call and went down to the lower decks.

The floating post was a good deal different-looking from the passenger dirigibles Alexia was accustomed to utilizing. Prudence was duly fascinated. Lord Maccon took it as an opportunity to skulk off in pursuit of port in the smoke room, and possibly a nice game of backgammon.

"Bibble!" was Prudence's opinion. The infant was excessively fond of air flight, although she had yet to try it personally. There was some fear that, like her father and other werewolves, she would fall victim to airsickness. Her fondness was merely exhibited in pointing at dirigibles and squeaking whenever she happened to spot one above the town or when she was taken on a walk to Hyde Park. Occasionally, she was even allowed to sit in Lord Akeldama's private air transport, *Dandelion Fluff Upon a Spoon*, when it was at rest upon the roof of the vampire's town house. And, of course, she had multiple toy dirigibles, including one that was an exact replica of *Dandelion Fluff Upon a Spoon*.

The postal dirigible was very sleek and stealthy in appearance. Alexia and her daughter were riveted. Its balloon section was narrowed for speed. It had six aether current propellers, and its barge section was mainly one massive steam engine. Any other available space was utilized by the post itself and a small number of passengers, mostly businessmen, who were willing to trade luxury and comfort for speed.

Prudence was enthralled and might have stayed a good deal longer, but her teeth started to chatter. Lady Maccon noticed and took her daughter to the nursemaid for a new nappy and some warmer clothing. It was some time before Alexia remembered that the deck steward had attempted to deliver mail to her.

Lady Maccon went in pursuit of her deliveries, finding them in good time and then, suspicious of the contents, went to find her husband. She guessed well what it was from the shape of the box and supposed Conall might want to witness the opening of her new parasol.

She found him at the backgammon tables, delivered to him his missives—one in Lyall's tidy block lettering and the other in Channing's untidy scrawl—and then turned her attention to her own mail. In addition to the box, there was a letter from Biffy. The front of this was addressed as required for float mail, but on the back, below the seal, the young werewolf had written, *To be opened before the box!* in block lettering.

Conall, dear man, got all bouncy when he saw the package. "Capital! It has arrived at last!"

Alexia had enough sensitivity not to blurt out her certain knowledge as to the contents. "I have a communication from Biffy. Silly boy seems to believe it important that I read his letter first."

"By all means," said her husband magnanimously, although his eyes were caramel colored with excitement.

Alexia duly seated herself, despite glares from various gentlemen at the presence of a *female* in the *smoke room*, and cracked open the seal. Inside, Biffy detailed not only the current state of the murder investigation (no appreciable change), Lord Akeldama's latest waistcoat purchase (navy and cream striped with gold braid), and Floote's odd behavior on the subject of roasted pheasant (dismissed from the larder forthwith), but also a visit from Gustave Trouvé (beard of substantial magnitude). He went into a colorful and very detailed description of her new parasol upon its initial arrival. And then into even more specificity over the improvements to its appearance that he had felt compelled to make. He apologized profusely for opening her mail without permission but articulated that he felt his actions were duly excused, as they spared her the horror of ever having to encounter the parasol in its original state. He signed the missive with his real name, but Alexia knew this was because this particular letter contained nothing delicate nor Parasol Protectorate related, aside, of course, from the parasol itself.

Thus forewarned, Lady Maccon *opened the box*.

What lay before her was as dissimilar a creature to Biffy's description of the original as could be imagined. The talented boy had taken the monstrosity in hand and subdued it with as much finesse as might be brought to bear upon drab olive canvas.

He had covered the exterior with black silk. There were delicate white chiffon ruffles along the ribs and three layers of fine embroidered lace ruffles at the edge of the shade, completely disguising the multiple pockets hidden there. He had managed to drape the fabric overlay in such a way that when the parasol was closed, it puffed out, disguising any suspicious bulges. At the top, near the spike, was another bit of white lace and then a great puff of black feathers, cleverly hiding the springs and arming mechanism that allowed the tip to open and shoot various deadly objects and substances. Unfortunately, he'd had very little to work with on the handle. It was brass, very simple, with three nodules, the twisting of which, according to Gustave Trouvé's notes, would cause different results. He hadn't Madame Lefoux's predilection for fancy hidden buttons or carved handles. Biffy, however, had fought back against the simplicity by wrapping pretty ribbon at various points about the handle, hopefully not interfering with its primary function. He had completed his decoration by lining the interior with white chiffon ruffles and looping two black pom-poms about the handle, which acted decoratively and, Alexia realized with delight, would allow her to fasten the accessory to her person so she might not misplace it.

It was a bit loud for her taste, but the clean black-and-white color scheme added an air of refinement, and all the additional froofs would better disguise the secrets within.

"Oh, Conall, isn't it perfectly lovely? Didn't Biffy do a splendid job?"

"Oh, yes, if you say so, my dear. But what of Mr. Trouvé?"

"What, indeed? To praise his side of the work, I must put it through its paces, must I not?"

Lord Maccon looked around at the still-glaring gentlemen whose peaceful card games and cigar puffs had been inexcusably disturbed by the brash Lady Maccon and her frivolous mail.

"Perhaps elsewhere, wife?"

"What? Oh. Of course, somewhere private, and in the open air. There's no knowing what might come flying out of this little beauty." Alexia stood eagerly.

They exited the smoking room, only to run into Mrs. Tunstell in the hallway.

"Alexia! Lord Maccon! How fortuitous! I was looking for you. Mrs. Dawaud-Plonk has put the children down, and Tunny and I were wondering if you would like to join us for a game of whist?"

"I don't play whist," said Conall, rather shortly.

"Oh, don't mind him," dismissed his wife at Ivy's offended expression. "He's difficult about cards. I might be able to, in a quarter of an hour or so, but I just this moment took delivery of a new parasol, and Conall and I are off to the promenade deck to test it."

"Oh, how topping. But, Alexia, it isn't sunny."

"Not that kind of testing." Lady Maccon gave Mrs. Tunstell a wink.

Ivy was taken aback for only a moment. "Oh! Ruffled Parasol?"

"Exactly, Puff Bonnet."

Ivy was enthralled. "Oh, *I say*." She raised her hand to her face and made a little finger wiggle toward the tip of her pert little nose. This was her not-so-subtle gesture for secrets afoot. Alexia counted her blessings. Ivy's first suggestion had been that they each hop about in a small circle when they had clandestine information to impart, and then stop, face one another, and point both fingers at the mouth in a most ridiculous fashion.

Still, Lord Maccon was fascinated by Ivy's absurdly wiggling fingers.

Lady Maccon poked him in the ribs to get him to stop staring.

Ivy stopped her odd gesture. "Can I see *it*?"

Lady Maccon proffered up the accessory.

Mrs. Tunstell was appropriately enthusiastic. "Black and white, very modish! And is that chiffon? Now, that is something *like*. Nicely done. Of course, you know scarlet and yellow are far more *the thing* for spring."

Alexia gave her a look that said she was on very dangerous ground.

Ivy backpedaled hurriedly. "But black and white is more versatile, of course, and you want this one to last."

"Exactly so."

"May I join you on deck?"

"To view its anthroscopy?"

"Its anthro-what? No, my dear Alexia, to witness its"—Ivy paused and blushed, looking around to see if they were being overheard—"*emissions*."

"That's what I said."

"Oh, did you? Well?"

Alexia figured Ivy was officially part of her inner circle, and this parasol was that circle's defining feature. "Of course you may, my dear Ivy."

Ivy clapped her blue-gloved hands in excitement. "I'll go fetch a wrap and my hairmuffs."

"We shall see you up top." Lady Maccon took her husband's arm and led him away.

"My dear, what is the meaning of that…" Conall waved his fingers at his nose in a fair imitation of Ivy's wiggle.

"Oh, let her have her fun, Conall."

"If you say so, my dear. Odd behavior, though. Like she had a fly about her snoot."

Accordingly, a good fifteen minutes later, Ivy, complete with wardrobe change, joined a shivering Alexia and an annoyed Lord Maccon on the promenade deck.

Ivy now sported an outrageous set of hairmuffs that Alexia had no doubt had been specially designed. They exactly matched Ivy's hair and consisted of multiple corkscrew curls in the Greek style falling about her ears and a coronet of plaits. Gold braid was woven throughout, with a gilt dagger over the left ear with a spray of leaves and gold fruit falling at the back. It looked more like a headdress for a ball than anything else. It was all of a piece and worn like a helmet over Ivy's own hair.

Because the hairmuffs entirely covered her ears as

well as her head, Mrs. Tunstell was warm but also rather deaf.

"Ivy, finally, what could possibly have taken you so long?" Lady Maccon wanted to know.

"You want a song? I couldn't possibly serenade you on an open deck. Perhaps later, in the lounge. You are meant to be anthropomorphizing the workings of that parasol, remember?"

"Yes, Ivy, I know. We have been waiting for you."

"What are you to do? Well, I assume the accessory came with instructions. It can't possibly be all that different from your original emissionous parasol."

Alexia gave up and turned to proceed with her experiments. She stripped off her gloves and passed them to Ivy, who took them gravely and tucked them into her reticule. Alexia consulted the instruction sheet.

Of the three nodules on the handle, the first, when twisted, appeared to do nothing whatsoever. As she was pointing the parasol out to sea, and this was the magnetic disruption emitter, this was the best that could be hoped for. Even Alexia was not so bold as to trot aft and try the parasol on the steamboat's engine.

"Nothing happened," objected Ivy in disappointment.

"Shouldn't with the emitter."

"Mittens? I suppose that is sensible in case of snow," replied Ivy.

The middle nodule, turned to the left, caused a silver spike to jut out, and to the right, a wooden one. Unlike Lady Maccon's previous parasol, both could not pop out at once.

Alexia wasn't certain about that change. "What if I need to fight off both vampires and werewolves together?"

Lord Maccon gave her a very dour look.

"Ooh, ooh, ooh!" Ivy was practically bouncing in excitement over some kind of revelation. "I had a thought," she said, examining the edge of the wooden stake with interest.

"Oh, yes?" encouraged Alexia loudly.

Ivy stopped and frowned, her pert little face creased in worry. "I said I *had* one. It appears to have vanished."

Alexia returned to her examinations. The bottom nodule, closest to the shade and nested in the puff of black feathers, was slightly more detailed. Alexia consulted her sheet and then opened and carefully flipped the parasol around. A twist to one direction and a fine mist spouted forth from the ends of the parasol's ribs. From the smell and sizzle of the liquid as it hit the deck, that was lapis solaris diluted in sulfuric acid. A twist in the other direction and lapis lunearis and water came out, causing a brown discoloration to the already pockmarked deck.

"Oops," said Lady Maccon, not very apologetically.

"There, you see, emissions! Really, Alexia, is there no more dignified approach?" Ivy stepped back from her friend and wrinkled her nose.

Finally, Alexia reached the very last point on Monsieur Trouvé's list of instructions.

Gustave Trouvé had written: "*My esteemed colleague included the two spikes in her original model, but I thought we might make additional use of them. Please ensure that you are well braced for this feature, my dear Lady Maccon, and that you have pointed the parasol at something substantial. Twist the nodule closest to the shade sharply clockwise while holding the parasol pointed steadily at your target.*"

Alexia backed up, leaning against the railing of the ship, and pointed the parasol at the wall on the other side of the promenade deck. She handed Conall the instruction sheet, braced herself, gestured Mrs. Tunstell well out of the way, and fired.

Later, Conall was to describe to her how the parasol's tip shot completely off, twisting slightly as it flew and pulling behind it a long, strong rope. The spike sank into the wall of the cabin and held. Alexia was to comment that this might have been quite useful the time she nearly fell off of the dirigible or out of the hive house. However, Gustave Trouvé had not exaggerated when he instructed her to be well braced, for the parasol jerked back against her violently, quite destroying her stability. Alexia let go of it in surprise.

Unfortunately, the railing was just low enough not to accommodate a woman of Lady Maccon's stature, girth, and corsetry. She overbalanced entirely, flipped in grace-less splendor backward over the railing, and plummeted down into the ocean below.

Alexia screamed in surprise and then in shock at the coldness of the water. She came up sputtering.

Without hesitating, her husband dove in after. He could swim better and catch up to her faster in wolf form, so he changed as he fell, hitting the water a massive brindled beast instead of man.

As the steamer churned swiftly away, Alexia heard Ivy screaming, "Woman overboard! Wait, no, man *and* woman overboard. Wait, no woman and *wolf* overboard. Oh, dash it, help! Help us please! Stop the ship! Man the lifeboats. Help! Summon the fire brigade!"

Conall arrowed through the icy black sea toward

Alexia, his fur slicked back, seal-like. After only a few moments, he reached her.

"Really, husband, I can swim perfectly well. There's no need for both of us to get all salty," instructed Alexia tersely, although she was already shivering and she well knew the real danger in being cast adrift came not from drowning but from cold.

Conall barked at her and swam closer.

"No, *don't touch me*! Then you'll be human, too. Then we'll both shiver to death. Don't be silly."

Ignoring her, the wolf came up next to her and wormed his way under one arm, clearly intending to help her stay afloat.

He did not change.

Not even slightly.

Alexia had removed her gloves for parasol examination and was gripping him reflexively with one bare hand. Nothing. He remained a werewolf.

"Well, would you look at that!"

Conall's wolf face looked shocked. But then again, the markings about his eyes and muzzle often caused that expression, so there was no way to tell if he was truly registering the peculiarity or still acting on instinct to protect her. Whatever the case, at least he did not give in to his werewolf nature and try to eat her, which for the first time in their long association he might have been able to do.

Alexia's teeth started to chatter. Conall was doing most of the work to keep them afloat. She figured she might as well let him, as he still had all his supernatural strength.

She cogitated upon this amazing occurrence, thinking back over her life and every preternatural touch: those times when she had been forced to use her naked flesh, and those times when it had functioned even through fabric.

"Wat-t-t-t-ter!" she chattered. "It's all wat-t-t-t-ter. Just like ghosts and t-t-tethers."

Conall appeared to be ignoring her, but Alexia was having a scientific breakthrough and being stranded somewhere near the Strait of Gibraltar in the Atlantic Ocean wasn't going to stop her epiphany. "It all makes per-r-r-fect sense!" She wanted to explain but she was chattering so hard she could no longer understand herself. Also her extremities were going numb. Science would have to wait.

I'm going to freeze to death, she thought. *I have figured out one of the greatest preternatural mysteries and no one will know the truth. It's so very simple. It was there all along. In the weather. How annoying.*

"Oh! There she blows!" she heard Ivy sing out in the dark night. A wave of displaced water crashed over her, and a second later a wooden box with handles splashed down next to her for her to latch on to. The box was followed by a knitted hammock she could use to pull herself inside.

Conall changed into his human form and pulled himself in next to her.

"Cover yourself with my skirts," hissed his wife through still-chattering teeth, pushing the ruination of her evening gown at him.

Her husband only looked at her, mouth agape. "What just happened?"

"We have made a g-g-g-reat discovery! We may have to p-p-p-publish," announced his wife, waving her goose-pimpled arms about. "Scientif-f-f-ic-c-c break-k-k-through!"

Conall threw his arm around her, hugging her close, and they were lifted to safety. By the time they reached the deck, he was mortal.

CHAPTER NINE

Biffy Experiments with Flirting
and Felicity

Everything ought to have proceeded smoothly with the investigation—or as smoothly as possible with Lady Kingair's brand of Alpha obnoxious interference. Biffy genuinely believed they were doing well, even after calling in at the eighth ball in an attempt to track down various private dirigible owners. Lucky for him, in the manner of all wealthy enthusiasts, the owners were quite willing to talk about their floating conveyances to the exclusion of all else, even with a slight young man to whom they had only recently been introduced. Biffy learned how the *Great Mitten Slayer* earned its name, where it was berthed, how often it was used, and what security measures were in place that prevented lone assassins from floating it to Fenchurch Street and killing werewolves. He ascertained similar details about *Her Majesty's Truss*, the *Lady Boopsalong*, and several others with names less easily recalled. He also learned that those gentlemen equipped with the means and inclination to purchase personal flotation devices were not so interested in tying their cravats with finesse. Dirigibles brought out the worst in people.

It was Professor Lyall's plan of inquiry. Biffy was to handle the high-society elements, while the professor looked in at registration offices and sequestered paperwork on pilots' credentials and private dirigible sales from Giffard's. Lady Kingair was of very little use, so they left her to stew at the house, pacing about the library and pouncing upon whoever stumbled in. Floote kept her in line as well as he was able with a constant supply of chewing tobacco, Scotch, and treacle tart. Just like Lady Maccon, she seemed to have an unholy passion for the dratted stuff. Biffy had never liked treacle tart, even as a human; he simply couldn't respect any kind of food that left a residue.

He came home from the eighth party, and yet another failed lead, to find Floote waiting for him in the hallway looking rather more concerned than he had previously thought Floote capable of looking, even after an entire evening spent with sticky, treacle-eating werewolf she-Alphas. The hallway smelled of roses.

"Is something wrong, Floote?"

"It's Miss Felicity, sir."

"Lady Maccon's sister? What could she possibly want with me?"

"Not you, sir. She called here to see Lady Kingair. They've been sequestered in the back parlor for over an hour."

"Good gracious me! They know each other from when the ladies visited Scotland, but I did not think they were on terms of any intimacy."

"No, sir, I don't believe they are."

"You think Miss Loontwill is *up to something*?"

Floote inclined his head. As much as to say, *Isn't she always?*

Biffy took off his hat and gloves, placing them both on the hall table and checking the state of his rebellious hair in the looking glass above it. Tonight it was frizzy. He sighed. "But what could Miss Loontwill possibly want with Lady Kingair?"

"Is that Professor Lyall?" came a roar from the back parlor. The door crashed open, revealing Lady Kingair in a towering fury.

Biffy, noting the rage, inclined his head, tugging down on his cravat to expose his neck.

This submissive stance only seemed to aggravate her further. "Oh, it's *you*. Where is Lyall, the little weasel? I'll see him flayed alive. You see if I don't."

Biffy glanced up through his lashes, trying to keep as unthreatening a demeanor as possible.

Felicity followed Lady Kingair out into the hall. She was wearing a dress of pale blue satin with royal blue velvet trim and a smug expression. Biffy had no idea why, but that expression terrified him more than Lady Kingair's rage. He wasn't particularly taken with the dress, either. Blue on blue always looked damp.

Lady Kingair came close enough for his hackles to rise, even in human form. "Did you ken, pup?"

"Know what, my lady?" Biffy kept his voice mellow.

"Did you ken it was him? Did you ken what he did?"

"I'm sorry, my lady, but I have no idea to what you are referring."

"Did you ken what he did to *my pack*? Stole Gramps

away from us! Lyall, that jackass. Stole him! Organized everything. Played us all like we were bally puppets. Got my pack to attempt treason and Gramps to feel betrayed so he would up and run to Woolsey. Do you ken what that did to my life? A *child* left to clean up dross? Have you any inkling what it was like? Did he give us a single thought? Destroy one pack to save another, will he? Bollocks to that! I'll skin him alive!"

Biffy could only shake his head, trying to understand, trying to put everything together. "This is all before my time, my lady."

She lashed out at him, backhanding him hard across the face, all werewolf strength and Alpha rage at anyone who would threaten her pack, past or present, real or imagined. The force of the blow thrust Biffy back against the wall and down to one knee, blood spattering the perfect points of his white starched collar.

Felicity gave a little squeak of alarm.

The pain was intense but fleeting. Biffy could feel the cut on his lip healing even as he regained his feet. It had taken him a long while to become accustomed to the sensation of flesh knitting back together again, like skin darning. He pulled out his handkerchief, lilac scented, and dabbed the spatter off of his cheek. He could feel the hunger starting, the need to consume bloody flesh to compensate for the blood he had lost. Felicity, standing so still behind the vibrating Lady Kingair, smelled delicious, even through the lilac of his handkerchief and the rose of her perfume—werewolf urges were so embarrassing.

"Now, Lady Kingair, there's no call for that kind of behavior. We are all civilized here, if you would just—"

But the Alpha was already away, ripping the dress

from her own body and changing to wolf form there in the hallway. She went charging out into the night. Floote had enough presence of mind to open the front door wide or she might have crashed through it.

Biffy was frightened for Lyall and momentarily at a loss given the suddenness and violence of the preceding few minutes. He knew he should warn the Beta somehow, but first he had to ascertain the particulars. He turned to face Felicity.

Out of the corner of his eye, he saw Floote subtly replacing a tiny pearl-handled gun into his inner coat pocket with his free hand. The butler must have armed himself when Lady Kingair turned violent. Biffy wasn't certain how he felt about this. Should butlers be hiding small firearms about their personage? Didn't seem very domestic.

Felicity tried to make her way to the now-open door.

Biffy moved supernaturally fast. He would never be as quick as Lord Akeldama, but he was certainly faster than Felicity Loontwill. He signaled Floote with a sharp gesture, and the butler, understanding perfectly, closed the door firmly in the young lady's face. In the same instant, Biffy took Felicity by one arm.

His hands—slender and fine and once so well suited to his preferred mortal pastime, playing the piano—were now more than equipped with the strength to waylay one frivolous female.

"I didn't know you knew Lady Kingair."

"I didn't until I met her."

Biffy glared.

Felicity started to prattle. "Why, Mr. Rabiffano, I've hardly seen you out in society at all since I returned from abroad. I'm finding private balls about town so very undiscriminating these days. They'll let practically *anyone* attend. Then again, you were at the Blingchesters last night, weren't you? Talking to Lord Hoffingstrobe about his new dirigible?"

Biffy decided, under the circumstances, it was not too rude to interrupt her. "Miss Loontwill, stop gargling, please. I think you had better tell me what, *exactly*, you just told Lady Kingair."

After being warmed by multiple hot water bottles and then cleaned of brine in the plushest of the SS *Custard*'s bathhouses, Lady Maccon was once more able to carry on a conversation without chattering.

"Alexia," Ivy reprimanded most severely once she was back in her friend's presence, "you had my heart in my chest! You really did."

Alexia disposed of Ivy's panic and solicitude by sending her off in search of comforting and obscure foodstuffs and took to her bed merely because it seemed the safest way to keep the gossipmongers at bay. Ivy had proved resourceful under such extreme circumstances as her favorite friend and patroness falling overboard. After calling for help, she had extracted the two parts of the new parasol, coiling the grapple about the tip like yarn about a spindle. She even spent time scuttling and hopping about, managing to stomp on the instruction sheet before it flew overboard.

"You see," said Alexia to her husband as Ivy dashed off to see about custard éclairs, "I told you she had hidden depths."

"Do you think it's only saltwater immersion that has

this kind of effect?" Lord Maccon was far more interested in their recent revelation. Ivy's peculiarities of character were nothing on his wife's peculiarities of ability.

Alexia was most decided on this point. "No. I believe it is any water. Even moisture in the air narrows the scope. Did you never wonder why the Kingair mummy's effect was so wide in London and so small when we reached Scotland? It was raining in Scotland. Also, there must be some kind of proximity and air contact as well, for I was only affected by the preternatural mummy when I was in the same room with it, unlike you, who could not change into a werewolf within a larger-ranging area."

"We have always known preternaturals and supernaturals functioned differently. Why should we not react differently to an alien agent in our midst? Werewolves are affected by the sun and moon; preternaturals are not."

"And it's clear the water was not enforcing your form?"

"Absolutely. I can change in water. Have done so many times."

"So it definitely limits preternatural touch."

"We know your abilities are related to ambient aether. We should not be so very surprised."

Alexia looked at her husband. "I wonder how wet I have to be."

"Well, my darling, we will have to perform a series of scientific tests . . . by bathing together." Lord Maccon waggled his eyebrows at her and leered.

"Could soap be a factor?" Alexia was willing to play his game.

"And how about underwater kisses?"

"Now you're getting silly. Do you think that's why our Prudence hates bath night so much?"

Conall sat up and stopped flirting. "By George, that *is* an idea! Perhaps she feels a limiting of her abilities, or perhaps she has a way of sensing others out of the aether that she relies upon that is shut off by water."

"You mean she feels blinded? Goodness, bathing would be quite a torture, then. She does always seem to notice when someone new is in the room before anyone else."

"That could simply be excellent powers of observation."

"True. Oh, dear, I wish she would acquire complete sentences. It would be so much more efficient to ask her these questions and get a sensible answer."

"Our curiosity will have to wait a few years."

Alexia worried her lower lip. "It's all to do with the aether in the end."

"Very poetical, my dear."

"Was it? I didn't know I had it in me."

"Well, do be careful, my love. Poetry can cause irreparable harm when misapplied."

"Especially with reference to our daughter."

Very little made Biffy lose his poise or posture, but after Felicity's story, he was practically slouching. "Let me see if I have this quite clear: Professor Lyall was responsible for Kingair losing Lord Maccon as Alpha?"

Felicity nodded.

"But how could *you* possibly know a thing like that?"

Felicity flicked a curl of blond hair over one shoulder. "I overheard Alexia accusing him of it when I was staying here. He didn't deny it and they agreed to keep the whole thing from Lord Maccon. I don't think that's right. Do you? Keeping secrets from one's husband."

Biffy was sickened, not so much by the information, as he could readily believe such a thing of Professor Lyall, who would do anything for his pack, but by Felicity's duplicity. "You have been sitting on this information for several years, waiting to distribute it until it could do the most damage. Why, Felicity?"

Felicity huffed out a little breath of aggravation. "You know, I told Countess Nadasdy. I told her! And she did *nothing*! She said it was a matter of werewolf internal politics and domestic relations, and none of her concern."

"So you waited, and when you heard Lady Kingair was in town, you decided to tell her? Why?"

"Because she will react badly and tell Lord Maccon in the worst possible way."

"You may, quite possibly, be evil," said Biffy in a resigned tone.

"It's always been Alexia: better, smarter, special in that way of hers. Alexia who married an earl. Alexia who visits the queen. Alexia who lives in town. Alexia with a baby. Who am I to be left behind by my great lump of a sister? Why is she so wonderful? She's not pretty. She's not talented. She has none of my finer qualities."

Biffy could hardly believe such pettiness. "You did this to destroy your sister's marriage?"

"Alexia had me exiled to Europe for *two years*! Now I'm too old for the marriage mart. But what does she care for my problems? She's well set up. Wife of an earl! She doesn't deserve to have any of it! It should be *mine*!"

"Why, you horrible little creature."

"No wife should keep a confidence from her husband like that." Felicity struggled to find the moral high ground.

"And no thought of what this will do to Professor Lyall or this pack?"

"What do I care for a middle-class professor or a gaggle of werewolves?"

Biffy suddenly couldn't stand to even look at the girl. "Get out."

"What?"

"Get out of my house, Miss Loontwill. And I hope never to see you again."

"What do I care for your ill opinion, either, Mr. Rabiffano? A mere hat-shop owner and a low-ranked werewolf."

"You may not care for mine, Miss Loontwill, but I still enjoy the friendship of Lord Akeldama, and I will see he knows exactly what you have done. Lady Maccon is his *very dear friend* and he will see you ostracized from polite society because of this. Rest assured, Miss Loontwill, you will become a social pariah. I recommend you plan an emigration of some kind. Perhaps to the Americas. You will no longer be welcome in any parlor in London."

"But—"

"Good evening, Miss Loontwill."

Biffy didn't know what good he thought it might do, but it was quarter moon—enough for him to change without difficulty and not so full he might lose control. Not that he did *that* much anymore. He was getting better and better at the shift, almost like adjusting to a new haircut or cravat. It still hurt like nothing else on earth, which made it less cravatlike than one would prefer, but at least now when he was a wolf, he was still himself. There had been some doubt of that once.

He had only one advantage over Lady Kingair. He

already knew where Professor Lyall was supposed to be. He did not have to track him through the city. He ran straight there, a lean chocolate-colored wolf with an ox-blood stomach and a certain mottling about his neck that was almost, Lady Maccon had kindly noted, cravatlike. He used the back alleys and side streets so as not to disturb anyone. Most of London knew they now boasted a werewolf pack residing in the city center, but there was a difference between knowing and meeting a wolf face-to-face when engaging in an evening constitutional. That said, he did encounter a group of sporting blunts at their cups, who all politely raised their hats to him as he passed.

The Bureau of Unnatural Registry occupied the first few stories of an unassuming Georgian near the *London Times* offices and generally kept itself to itself in the manner of all semisecret government operations. Tonight, however, there was clearly something afoot even from outside the building. Had not the bright lights and rapidly shifting shadows given this indication, the yells loud enough for even a normal human to hear would have. Not to mention the fact that the front door was wide open and hanging askew on its hinges.

Biffy nosed his way inside.

The hallway was filled with running men, demands for numbing agents, calls for the constabulary, and arguments over whether they were authorized to interfere.

"Clearly a personal werewolf matter!"

"Oh, you think so, Phinkerlington? Then why bring it to BUR?"

"Who knows the ways of werewolves? Ours is not to question pack protocol."

"But... but... but Professor Lyall *never* fights!"

"This is a matter of enforcement. BUR must enforce!"

At that juncture, the collective in the hallway noticed Biffy slinking in among them.

"Oh, spiffing, here's another one!"

"Now, now, perhaps he can help."

"They're in the stockroom, Mr. Werewolf, sir, and we may not have a stockroom soon if they don't quiet down."

Biffy was not all that familiar with the layout of BUR, but he could follow his ultrasensitive hearing, which directed him up the stairs toward a large cavernous room. The door to this room was also open, although unbroken, and crowded round it stood a group of BUR officers and agents watching a battle within. Money was exchanged as wagers were taken on the outcome, and now and then a cry of distress went up as something particularly dramatic occurred.

Biffy forced his way through the onlookers' legs and entered the room, still not certain what good he might do but determined to try.

Professor Lyall and Lady Kingair were faced off against one another. Professor Lyall was not doing well.

If one were to pass the professor in wolf form in the countryside, one might mistake him for some kind of overgrown off-color fox. He was a slender, elegant creature and not one to inspire confidence in battle. Biffy had learned since joining the pack that Professor Lyall's skill lay in his ability to fight smart and in his quickness and dexterity. He was almost beautiful as he battled the Alpha of Kingair, his movements lithe and graceful, calculated, yet impossibly swift.

But he was only a Beta. He simply wasn't strong

enough. He was holding his own, but his body was ripped open in a thousand places and he was fighting pure defense. Every good general knows that defense will never win.

Biffy couldn't help himself. Instinct took over. He'd been learning his werewolf instincts for two years now, so he was cogent enough to analyze their meaning. One urged him not to face an Alpha, but it was balanced out by another that urged him to help his packmate, to protect his Beta. That second instinct was the one that won.

Biffy launched himself at Lady Kingair, going for her face. As a human, he would never contemplate such a thing—to hit the face was ungentlemanly and to hit a lady unpardonable—but werewolves measured victory in challenge by the destruction of the eyes. Eyes were one of the few things a wolf could bite that took time to heal, rendering continued roughhousing impossible. There was also death, of course. It wasn't common, but it did happen, usually when an Alpha faced a much weaker opponent, or two Alphas fought in daylight.

Lady Kingair dodged easily out of Biffy's way. Professor Lyall barked at him, an order to stay out of it, but Biffy wasn't going to let him take on an enraged Alpha all alone. He charged Lady Kingair again.

The Alpha swung her head around and sliced at the side of his cheek, tearing it open with her teeth. Biffy felt the burning sting of profound pain and then the equally agonizing knitting sensation as his body repaired itself. Everything, he had realized shortly after his metamorphosis, was pain for werewolves. Which was probably why they were so mean—general buildup of peevishness.

Lady Kingair was on him again. Biffy realized what

Professor Lyall was up against. The female Alpha was vicious in battle. She gave no quarter and had no mercy. Oh, she was smart about it, as smart as Lord Maccon in a fight, but she was a lot less nice. She was almost taunting them, never going in for a kill strike or the eye mark that would bring about victory. She wanted the torture, like a cat with mice. She wanted Professor Lyall to suffer, and now that Biffy was there, she wanted him to suffer, too.

Biffy and Professor Lyall exchanged yellow-eyed looks. They really had only one option. They had to either exhaust Lady Kingair, or they had to keep her occupied until sunrise. A tall order indeed, but there were two of them.

For the next three hours, Biffy and Lyall traded off fighting Lady Kingair. They never once let her rest, while managing to grab a few minutes to flop down and pant one at a time, catch a breath, and heal slightly. Even two of them acting together could not defeat her or injure her enough to make her yield. She was far too much of an Alpha for that. So they simply kept fighting her. Hoping her anger would run dry. Hoping she might collapse in exhaustion. Hoping the sun might rise. Her anger was inexhaustible, as was her speed and abilities. And the sun refused to rise.

Biffy was beginning to flag. The loss of blood was catching up with him in a quintessential werewolf way. He wanted to turn upon the humans crowding the doorway and feed almost as much as he wanted to fight. But some lingering sense of gentlemanly behavior would not allow him to abandon his Beta. He fought on until all his muscles were shaking, until he thought he could not lift another paw. He could only imagine what poor Professor Lyall felt, who must have been fighting Lady Kingair at least an hour longer than he.

Yet she kept right on going, her claws wicked and fast, her teeth impossibly sharp.

She got that great jaw of hers around Biffy's hind leg and began biting down. She was no doubt strong enough to snap the bone in half. Biffy hoped Professor Lyall was prepared to jump in while he took the time needed to knit that bone back together. He also hoped he was prepared for the pain. When the bone broke, it was liable to be excruciating, and he'd hate to howl with all those men watching.

Except it became suddenly clear that *all* the bones in his body were involuntarily breaking, fracturing, and re-forming. Fur was moving toward his head, the feel of stinging gnats crawling up his skin. He was left lying, limp and panting, naked in the utterly destroyed stockroom of BUR headquarters.

The sun had peeked its cheery head above the horizon.

"I'll thank you, Lady Kingair, to remove my ankle from your mouth," he said.

Sidheag Maccon did so, looking exhausted, and spat in disgust.

"I took a bath recently," said Biffy in mild rebuke.

Professor Lyall crawled over to them, his wounds far greater than either Biffy's or Lady Kingair's. They would be slow to heal, now that the sun was up. But at least the fighting was over. Or so Biffy thought.

"You nasty, manipulative little maggot," said Lady Kingair to Professor Lyall, her words more rancorous than her tone, which was fatigued.

The Beta looked over at the door full of curious BUR employees. "Haverbink, close the door, please. This is none of BUR's concern."

"Oh, but, sir!"

"Now, Haverbink."

"Well, here you go, sir. Figured you might need these." The aforementioned Haverbink, a strapping lad who looked like he ought to be milking pigs, or whatever it was they did in the Yorkshire dales, tossed some blankets and three large muttonchops into the room. Then he shut the door, no doubt leaning his ear to the outside.

Despite the gnawing, raging hunger, Biffy reached for a blanket first, dragging it to cover over his lower half, for modesty's sake.

"Good lad, Haverbink," commented Lyall as he bit into a chop. He handed one to Biffy, and in exchange Biffy tucked half the blanket around Lyall solicitously, noting that Professor Lyall had very nice thighs.

Biffy took the meat gratefully, wishing he had a knife and fork. And a plate, for that matter. But the meat smelled so good he turned aside so the others couldn't quite see and took as delicate bites as he could.

Lady Kingair gave the Beta a long look when he offered her the last chop and then took it with a muttered "thanks." She tore into the bloody meat without regard for anyone's finer feelings.

Lyall was looking at Biffy with an odd expression in his hazel eyes. "Biffy, my dear boy, when did you learn to fight with soul?"

"Um, what do you mean, Professor?"

"Just now, you knew who you were, who I was, and what we were doing the entire time."

Biffy swallowed his mouthful. "Isn't that part of controlling the shape-shift?"

"Goodness no. It's a rare thing for a wolf to fight smart. Alphas, of course, and a few lucky Betas, and some of the oldest of the pack regulars. But most everyone else goes on instinct. It's quite a gift to have learned so young. I'm proud of you."

Biffy could feel himself blushing. Never before had he received a compliment from Professor Lyall, not even a fashion-related one.

"Och, how sweet." Lady Kingair's lip curled. "But perhaps the compliments could wait until you have explained yourself, *Beta*."

Lyall finished his repast and collapsed against an overturned stack of metal slates. Biffy pressed his back slightly against his Beta's legs, taking comfort from the contact, and leaned up on one elbow to look at Lady Kingair. The Alpha propped herself into a full seated position, using a massive box of ammunition. She looked tired, but still angry. They all stared at one another.

Finally Professor Lyall said, "I'll admit I did not see it from your perspective, my lady. And for that I extend my sincerest apologizes. But you have no idea what he was like. No idea."

Sidheag Maccon looked much like her great-great-great-grandfather as she popped the last bite into her mouth and gave the Beta an austere look. When she finished chewing, she said magnanimously, "I ken he went mad. I ken he was violent. I dinna think that's an excuse."

"He killed Alessandro."

"Aye? Well, Templar training will only get a man so far. And after, what? You planned for years to get your revenge. At my expense. At poor old Gramps's expense. He was happy in Scotland. What werewolf wants to come to England when he has the rolling green of the Lowland to run? You stole him against his will. Against our will."

The Beta fished about for a scrap of paper and cleaned his hands of blood as though with a handkerchief. "I provided the temptation. Your pack need not have followed it."

"Na good enough, Randolph Lyall. Na good enough."

Professor Lyall took a deep breath as though to fortify himself. Biffy felt a soft touch on his shoulder, and he craned his neck about to find the Beta leaning toward him. "You needn't have come, pup, although I'm glad you did. But I do wish you didn't have to hear what comes next."

But Biffy did hear, every messy, degrading, disgusting detail as Professor Lyall told Lady Kingair exactly what life had been like under the Alpha Lord Woolsey. Servicing him as Beta near the end had been humiliating—for five and a half long years. Lyall's face was deadpan as he relayed the details, as those who are tortured or raped will become when they retell the pattern of abuse. Biffy began crying quietly and wishing, indeed, that he did not have to hear it.

Lady Kingair lost much of her anger in the telling, but her sympathies were not entirely swayed. She could understand that Lyall had found himself in a situation with no possible way out except the one he took. But she could still not forgive that her pack had suffered the consequences of his choice.

"Oh, aye, and is that to be my lot as well? Tae be going

all over abusive and deranged? Will poor old Gramps face the same fate?"

"Not all Alphas go bad the way Lord Woolsey went bad. He already had the tendencies. It's simply that when he was sane, he acted with the consent of his partners. Take comfort, my lady—most Alphas die before the opportunity arises."

"Oh, aye, much obliged I'm sure. Verra comforting, that is. What now, Professor?"

"Well, in an odd way, I am glad it is known. But Lord Maccon will never forgive me or trust me again. I take it you wrote him the details?"

"Oh, aye."

"Poor Lady Maccon. She didn't want to keep my secret. Now she will have to handle Conall finding out."

"You telling me you're prepared to make reparations?" Lady Kingair looked less angry and more contemplative, examining Professor Lyall through half-lidded eyes.

Biffy, wary of that look, leaned in against his Beta. Relishing the intimacy, feeling oddly proprietary.

Professor Lyall squeezed his shoulder reassuringly. "Of course."

"And you ken what I will want of you?"

The Beta nodded, looking resigned.

Lady Kingair took a deep breath and looked down her nose at the slight, sandy-haired gentleman. And Professor Lyall was still a gentleman, Biffy realized, even without a stitch of clothing, lying on the floor of a stockroom.

"I'm thinking Kingair's needing a Beta right about now."

"No!" Biffy couldn't help the exclamation. He reeled away from Lyall, turning so that he faced him fully.

Professor Lyall only nodded.

"And you, for all yon manipulations, are one of the best. Possibly because of them."

Professor Lyall nodded again.

"Oh, no," Biffy cried. "You can't abandon us! What will we do without you?"

Professor Lyall only looked at him with a little smile. "Oh, now, Biffy, I think you will do very well."

"Me!" squeaked Biffy.

"Of course. You have the makings of an excellent Beta."

"But I...I...," Biffy stuttered.

Lady Kingair nodded. "That'll do nicely. Now dinna worry, pup, we won't keep him for all time—only until we find someone better."

"There is no one better," said Biffy with absolute confidence.

They were interrupted by a knock on the door. Haverbink stuck his head in without being summoned.

"Didn't I order you to stay away?" asked Professor Lyall placidly.

"Yes, sir, but it was so quiet I wanted to make certain you were all still alive."

"As you see. And?"

"And a massive gilt carriage has just pulled up out front. Lord Akeldama sent it with his compliments." Haverbink produced a mauve-colored scrap of paper. Lilac scent wafted into the room. "Said you would need a nice dark ride back home to get some sleep, and what were you *fluffy darlings* all doing still out and about?"

"How could he have known to send such a thing? He himself should already be comatose." Lyall blinked in mild confusion and looked to Biffy for an explanation.

"He would have left orders with his drones."

"Nosy vampire neighbors," sniffed Lady Kingair.

Afterward, Biffy could only just recall that ride back home, stumbling into the house and up the stairs, he and Professor Lyall leaning against one another in exhaustion. But he remembered perfectly the Beta's face, a single sharp look when they reached the door to his chamber, almost frightened. It was a look Biffy recognized. He had neither the strength nor the interest in allowing loneliness to pillage anyone else's peace of mind.

So he made the offer. "Would you like company, Professor?"

Professor Lyall looked at him, hazel eyes desperate. "I wouldn't…that is…I couldn't…that is…I'm not all that…capable." He gave a weak little flap of a gesture indicating his still-wounded state, his fatigue, and his disheveled appearance all in one.

Biffy gave a little puff of a chuckle. He had never seen the urbane professor discombobulated before. Had he known, he might have flirted more in the past. "Just company, sir. I should never presume even if we were both in perfect health." *Besides, my hair must look atrocious. Imagine being able to attract anyone in such a state, let alone someone of Lyall's standing.*

The corner of his Beta's mouth twitched, and he withdrew behind a veil of dispassionate hazel eyes. "Pity, pup? After you heard what Lord Woolsey did to me? It was a long time ago."

Biffy had no doubt Professor Lyall was as proud, in his way, as any other man of good breeding and refined tastes. He tilted his head, showing his neck submissively.

"No, sir. Never that. Respect, I suppose. To survive such things and still be sane."

"Betas are made to maintain order. We are the butlers of the supernatural world." An analogy no doubt sparked by the advent of Floote, who glided down the hallway toward them, looking as concerned as it is possible for a man to look who, so far as Biffy could tell, never displayed any emotion at all.

"You are well, gentlemen?"

"Yes, thank you, Floote."

"There is nothing I can get for you?"

"No, thank you, Floote."

"Investigation?" The butler arched an eyebrow at their fatigued and roughened state.

"No, Floote, a matter of pack protocol."

"Ah."

"Carry on, Floote."

"Very good, sir." Floote drifted away.

Biffy turned to make his way to his own sleeping chamber, assured now that his overtures had been rejected. He was forestalled by a hand on his arm.

Lyall had lovely hands, fine and strong, the hands of an artist who practiced a craft, a carpenter, perhaps, or a baker. Biffy had a sudden fanciful image of Lyall with a smudge of flour on his face, going comfortably into old age with a fine wife and brood of mild-mannered children.

The sandy head tilted in silent invitation. Professor Lyall opened the door to his bedroom. Biffy hesitated only a moment before following him inside.

By the time the sun set that evening, they were both fully recovered from the ordeal, having slept the day away without incident. Fully recovered *and* curled together naked in Lyall's small bed.

Biffy learned, through careful kisses and soft caress, that Lyall was not at all disturbed by messy hair. In fact, his Beta's hands were almost reverent, stroking through his curls. Biffy hoped that with his own touch he could convey his disregard for Lyall's past actions and suffering, determined that none of what they did together should be about shame. Most of it, Biffy guessed, was about companionship. There might have been a tiny little seed of love. Just the beginnings, but a tender, equality of love, of a kind Biffy had never before experienced.

Professor Lyall was as different from Lord Akeldama as was possible. But there was something in that very difference that Biffy found restful. The contrast in characters made it feel like less of a betrayal. For two years, Biffy had held on to his hope and his infatuation with the vampire. It was time to let go. However, he didn't feel that Lyall was edging Lord Akeldama out. Lyall wasn't the type to compete. Instead he was carving himself a new place. Biffy might just be able to make the room. Lyall was, after all, not very big, for a werewolf. Of course, he worried about Felicity's story of Alessandro Tarabotti, about whether Lyall was capable of loving him back, but it was early yet and Biffy allowed himself to revel in the simple joy that can only be found in allaying another's loneliness.

When Lyall lay flush against him, nuzzling up into his neck, Biffy thought they fit well together. Not matched colors so much as coordinated, with Lyall a neutral cream satin, perhaps, and Biffy a royal blue. Biffy said nothing concerning any such romantic flights of fancy. Instead he asked a more practical question.

"You truly intend to become Kingair's Beta, even after all you sacrificed for this pack?"

"I must make amends." Lyall did not stop his nuzzling.

"So far away from London?" *So far from me?*

"It won't be forever. But I'll have to stay away, at least until Lord Maccon retires."

Biffy was floored. He stopped smoothing the hair at Lyall's temple. "Retires? Retires from being Alpha?" *As though it were a position in a tradesman's firm?* "You think that is something he's likely to do?"

Lyall smiled. Biffy could feel the movement of his cheek against his chest. "Ah, Biffy, you think Lord Maccon is any less aware of the fate of Alphas who get too old than we are?"

Biffy's hand went involuntarily to his throat in shock. For there could be only one possible implication from such a statement. Lord Maccon intended to kill himself before he went mad. "Poor Lady Maccon!" he whispered.

"Now, now, not to worry. I shouldn't think it'll be all that soon. Decades or more. You must really learn to think like an immortal, my sweet Biffy."

"Will you come back here after?"

"I will try."

"So we must wait until Lord Maccon dies? How macabre."

"Much of immortality, you will find, is in surviving the deaths of others. And the waiting has not started yet. We have some time before our Alphas return." He began kissing Biffy softly on the neck.

"By all means, let us not waste time."

Which was how Biffy missed his last window to send a message by dirigible post, warning Lady Maccon of Lady

Kingair's letter to Lord Maccon. Which was why he used rather more colorful language than he ought upon realizing that he had mucked the timing up quite royally and would not have an opportunity to contact his mistress again until *after* she landed in Alexandria.

Timing, he realized, could work hard against one, even when one had, theoretically, all the time in the world.

CHAPTER TEN

Wherein Our Intrepid Travelers
Ride Donkeys

It was Sunday tea aboard ship and the Tunstells had been persuaded to perform their rendition of *Macbeth* to rousing applause and much comedic effect in the dining hall when the port of Alexandria was sighted. Ten days of familiarity will make strangers traveling together more friendly with one another than an entire season of town socialization. Alexia was not certain how she felt about such familiarity—it led to homegrown theatricals while *at table*, but the other passengers were enjoying themselves.

Ivy was dressed in a corseted medieval gown and lamenting her blood-covered hands—beet juice from a most excellent stewed vegetable tureen—and wearing a blond wig of epic proportions and ratty state. She was giving the tragedy her all, in a rather misguided and decidedly impressionistic take on the famous knife scene. Tunstell lay prone over a potted plant stage right—also known as the kitchen entrance. Mr. Tumtrinkle, sporting a substantial fake mustache and a waistcoat so tight it was near to popping over his well-padded circumference, was tiptoeing across the stage wielding another potted plant, Macduff with Birnam Wood, and carrying a baguette sword.

The diners were riveted. Particularly by the antics of the waitstaff, who had to dodge through the climactic fight scene carrying scones and jam.

It was no wonder, then, that Alexandria snuck up on all of them. The first thing that signified the momentous event was a slowing in their speed and a loud tooting noise. The captain hurriedly excused himself, tea unfinished, and the Tunstells stopped their antics and stood about dumbly.

The proximity bells clanged out and everyone made busy finishing their conversation and foodstuffs without the appearance of excitement or hurry, although clearly under the influence of both.

"Have we arrived?" Alexia asked her husband. "I do believe we have."

Conall, for whom high tea was an exercise in futility, there being little protein on offer and too many small fiddly sandwiches expressly designed to thwart a man of his ilk, stood without prompting. "Well, come along, my dear, to the upper deck!"

Alexia took up Prudence, who was ostensibly the excuse for awakening early and attending the tea. The toddler had yet to experience such an occasion as Sunday tea in a public assembly on a steamer, and Alexia had thought she might enjoy the treat. Prudence had indeed, although her good behavior might be better attributed to the performance than the comestibles. Prudence found the Tunstells' rendition of *Macbeth* more fascinating than anyone else, possibly because the antics were right about her education level or possibly because life with Lord Akeldama had given her to expect a certain degree of extravagant theatricality.

Prudence was particularly taken with the idea that Mr. Tumtrinkle now answered to the name Macduff, possibly because she could say Macduff but not Tumtrinkle. She was also hypnotized by his mustache, a fact made clear as they climbed out onto the promenade and the actor stood behind them. Prudence somehow ended up leaning over her mother's shoulder, misappropriating the mustache and wearing it rather proudly on her own tiny, fat face.

"Oh, really!" was her mother's comment, but she did not try to remove it.

Madame Lefoux came up next to them and gave Prudence a green-eyed look of approval. "Child after my own heart."

"Don't you start," said Alexia, possibly to both of them. "Prudence, darling, look: Egypt!" She pointed before them as the rays of the slowly setting sun caught the beige buildings of the last great Mediterranean port. The first thing to appear was the famous lighthouse, rising above the level of a colorless line of coast. Although, to Alexia's mind, it seemed a little smaller than one would hope.

"No," said Prudence, but she looked.

The steamer chugged to a halt, disappointing everyone.

"We have to wait to take a pilot on board," explained, of all people, Ivy Tunstell.

"We do?" Alexia looked down at her friend, mystified. Ivy had come to stand next to them still garbed in her medieval dress and long blond wig.

Ivy nodded sagely. "The channel into the harbor is narrow, shallow, and rocky. Baedeker says so."

"Well, then, it must be true." They spotted a small tug chugging through the water toward them. A sprightly, dark-skinned fellow in very ill-fitting and baggy clothing was allowed aboard. He saluted the watching passengers in a casual manner and then disappeared toward the captain's lookout.

Moments later, the steamer puffed back up into rumbling action and began making its way sedately into the port of Alexandria.

Lady Maccon was pleased to say the city quite lived up to her expectations. While Ivy prattled on about Pompey's Pillar, the Cape of Figs, the Arsenal, and various other guidebook sights of note, Alexia simply absorbed the quality of the place: the subdued tranquility of exotic buildings, broken only occasionally by the white marble turrets of mosques or the sharp knitting-needle austerity of an obelisk. She thought she could make out ruins in the background. It was mostly sand colored, lit up orange by the sun—a city carved out of the desert indeed, utterly alien in every way. The thing it most resembled was a sculpture made of shortbread.

Ivy excused herself, remarking that they, too, ought to go below, or at least in out of the sea air. "Too much sea air can detrimentally affect the mental stability, or so I've read."

"Why, Mrs. Tunstell, you must have traveled by boat before," said Lord Maccon.

Lady Maccon stifled a chuckle and returned her attention to the shore. She felt the heat for the first time as well, rolling at them off the land. True, it had been getting hotter over the last few days, but this heat brought new smells with it.

"Sand, and sewage, and grilled meat," commented her husband, rather ignoring the romance of it all.

Alexia shifted against him and took his hand with her free one, bracing Prudence against the railing.

The baby frowned at the city, which loomed larger and larger as they moved in to dock. "Ick," she said, and then, "Dama."

Alexia wasn't certain if the toddler was simply missing her adopted father or if somehow the ancient city reminded Prudence of the ancient vampire. The little girl shivered despite the heat and buried her mustachioed face in her mother's neck. "Ick," she said again.

As complicated and difficult as it had been getting on board the steamer, it was twice as problematical getting off of it. Of course, it was intended that passengers spend that last night aboard, to awaken the next morning in a new land and begin their adventures well rested and fully packed. But Alexia and her party were on a night schedule and had no intention of wasting precious evening hours by staying on the ship. They hurried back to their respective rooms and threw a collective tizzy gathering up attendants to help them pack, tracking down multiple missing items, paying steward's fees, and eventually disembarking.

Even after they were safely ashore and getting their land legs back, Ivy Tunstell had to return to her quarters no less than three times. The first under the impression that she had misplaced her favorite gloves—they were in a hatbox with her green turban, as it turned out. The second because she was assured her Baedeker's was left on the bedside table, only to discover it in her reticule. The third because she panicked, convinced she had forgotten Percy, asleep in his bassinet.

The nursemaid, who had charge of the twins, safely ensconced in a rather impressive sling contraption, held Percy up for his frantic mother to see, at which juncture the baby spit up on the strikingly large turban of a native gentleman as he injudiciously cut through their assembled party.

The gentleman made a very rude gesture and said something rapid-fire in Arabic before dashing on.

Ivy tried desperately to apologize to the man's retreating back. "Oh, my dear sir, how terrible. He's only a very little boy, of course, not yet under his own power so far as the proper operation of the digestive centers. I am so very sorry. Perhaps I could—"

"He is long gone, Ivy dear," interrupted Alexia. "Best turn our attention to our hotel. Where are we headed?" She looked at Conall hopefully. It really was rather a bother to travel without Floote; nothing went smoothly, and no one seemed to know exactly what to do next.

Madame Lefoux stepped into the breach. "The custom house is over there, I believe." She gestured at an ugly square building to their right, from which a military-looking group of local gentlemen were charging in their direction. Alexia squinted, attempting to discern the details of the group. The sun was mostly set at this point, the exotic buildings around them blanketed in shadow.

The customs officials, for that is what they proved to be, practically crashed into them and began garbling unintelligibly in Arabic. Ivy Tunstell whipped out her travel guide and began trilling some, quite probably, equally unintelligible phrases in, for some strange reason known only to Ivy, a lilting falsetto and what appeared to be Spanish. Tunstell began prancing about trying to be helpful, his red hair attracting a good deal of unwarranted attention. When one of the men tried grabbing at Mr. Tumtrinkle's carpetbag, Lord Maccon began yelling and gesticulating in English, descending rapidly into Scottish as he became increasingly annoyed.

During the hubbub, Madame Lefoux sidled up to Lady Maccon.

"Alexia, my dear, might I recommend relocating your gun to an inaccessible part of your apparel and opening the parasol as though the sun were quite up?"

Lady Maccon looked at the inventor as though she were mad. It was now evening, no time for a parasol, and Ethel was tucked away in her reticule, where any good firearm should be.

Madame Lefoux nodded significantly at one of the customs men just as he upended Mr. Tumtrinkle's carpet bag onto the dock, much to that gentleman's annoyance, and produced a prop musket triumphantly from within. Mr. Tumtrinkle's efforts to demonstrate that the firearm was, in fact, a fake did not meet with any kind of approval. Quite the opposite, in fact.

Using Prudence's body to hide her actions, Lady Maccon took her own tiny gun out of her reticule and shoved it down the front of her bodice. Then she reached for her parasol, dangling from a chatelaine hook at her waist, and opened it above her head. Prudence clung on dutifully while she did this and then insisted on holding the parasol handle herself. This delighted Alexia, as now it appeared as though the parasol were up at her daughter's childish whim, rather than her own eccentricity.

Lord Maccon was becoming red in the face as he argued violently with the customs officials over the rudeness of actually opening and looking through their luggage right there in public. The men were not intimidated by Lord Maccon's size, rank, or supernatural state. The first being the only thing they had any direct contact with, the second being irrelevant in Egypt, and the last virtually unknown. It was quite dark, and Conall looked to be in imminent danger of losing his temper altogether when the most curious savior appeared.

A medium-sized, medium-girthed native fellow arrived in their midst. He wore voluminous dark bloomers tucked into suede boots, a high-neck dark shirt of muslin, a wide yellow sash about his waist, and a fez upon his head with a long tassel. He had a beard neatly trimmed into sharp pointed aggressiveness and a serious expression. Alexia wasn't sure about the beard, nor the bloomers, but she did think that with a different hat and a very long sword, he would look most appealingly piratical. Except that with his figure, that would be more along the lines of a banker at a masquerade.

The newcomer introduced himself politely as Chancellor Neshi in perfect English. He interposed himself between Lord Maccon's bluster and the customs official's efficaciousness. Alexia saw her husband's nose wrinkle in a telltale way and noticed that slight wince that he never could hide if he wasn't anticipating a bad smell. She sidled up next to him, careful not to touch him just in case they needed all of his supernatural abilities.

"Vampire?" she whispered into his ear.

He nodded, not taking his eyes off of the stranger.

Chancellor Neshi said something in rapid staccato fashion to the officials and they instantly backed away and stopped fussing.

"This must be Lady Maccon? And the miracle progeny?" Their savior leaned forward a little too close for Alexia's comfort, staring hard at Prudence, and then looked away as though he could not tolerate the sight of the child.

The toddler pursed her little lips in consideration. "Dama," she said with certainty.

Alexia would wager her right glove that her daughter was picking up on the man's vampire nature and utilizing the only word in her vocabulary capable of articulating it. So she said, "Yes, my dear, very like."

Prudence nodded. "Dama Dama duck!"

"Queen Matakara has sent me to be your guide to Alexandria. One might say, perhaps, your dragoman. This is acceptable? I will see you through this business of customs and then safely to your hotel. I have arranged for your audience, and performance, later tonight. If that's not too soon?" He looked at the actors around him. "This is the famous troupe, I take it?"

Ivy and Tunstell pushed forward.

Alexia said, "Yes, indeed, Chancellor. This is Mrs. Tunstell and Mr. Tunstell, owners, performers, and artists extraordinaire. Your queen is in for a treat."

Tunstell bowed and Ivy curtsied. "She commands the performance right away? It is a good thing we have been practicing on the journey."

The dumpy man took in Ivy's hat and Tunstell's trousers and could only nod. Ivy had selected a gray felt cha-

peau with steel braid around the crown, a long gray
feather, and a turned-up brim that showed off a turban of
striped surah silk wound underneath. That went around
her head to form a bow over the left ear, ending in a fringe
down the back. The hat, Ivy no doubt felt, went with the
Egyptian aesthetic, and it was her way of honoring their
host country. Although, Alexia thought, looking about at
the peasants and dockworkers engaging in various tasks
around them, it was a little off the mark. Tunstell's trousers were, naturally, of a very aggressive purple and teal
plaid and quite tight enough to be a second skin.

They were led into the custom house at that point and
permitted to take seats in comparative comfort. Despite
their objections, they then had to witness their bags, hatboxes, and trunks opened and examined in detail. The
dragoman explained that it was best not to protest and that
everything would be put back except for items of contra-
band. Apparently they were looking particularly for
cigars and chewing tobacco, which was subjected to a
high tariff. Prudence held on to the parasol firmly. No one
gave it a second glance. They also did not check the gentlemen's hats, which was where, Alexia had no doubt, her
husband had stashed his sundowner and Madame Lefoux
her more nefarious gadgets.

Madame Lefoux's hatbox, full of tools and mysterious
widgets, did cause some consternation. Until, with her
usual aplomb, the Frenchwoman produced papers claiming she had special dispensation from the Pasha to work
on water pumps in Asyut. The officials seemed either to
not know or not care that she was a woman dressed as a
man. The vampire dragoman referred to her as Mr.
Lefoux and spoke and addressed her as though she were

male. He also continually referred to her as a Hawal, whatever that meant.

Ivy's many hats and some of the props and costumes came under close scrutiny, until the dragoman explained at great length about Queen Matakara's request for a performance. Or Alexia assumed that was what he was doing. Queen Matakara's favor acted as some kind of oil to soothe the balm of quarantine, for it was only another hour more of questions before they were permitted to leave. One of the younger officials was particularly taken with one of Ivy's hats, a large straw affair, covered in silk fruit, grapes, strawberries, and a large knitted pineapple. He seemed to find it not so much suspicious as fascinating. Eventually, Alexia took off her own hat, a practical little brown bowler meets pith helmet, and put the fruity one on to demonstrate its proper use.

This gave the customs man in question a case of the giggles, and they were waved off with much good humor and goodwill. Alexia had a quick word with Ivy, promising reparations, and gifted the hat to the gentleman in question. Laughingly, he put it atop his own turbaned head. Then he bowed and kissed Lady Maccon's hand. Alexia was left with the distinct feeling that she had made an ally for life.

The street outside was an entirely different world from the dockyard. It was bustling with humanity. People walked, talked, dressed, and interacted like no people Alexia had ever seen before. She had traveled through Europe, but this…this was a different world! She was instantly and completely in love.

Ivy was equally enthralled. "Oh my goodness, look at all the men in gowns!"

There were old-fashioned oil streetlamps about, and even a few torches, but no gas, and it was now dark enough to make any estimation of color difficult. Nevertheless, Lady Maccon had a feeling that the clothing about them was quite as colorful as the buildings were monotonously drab.

Lord Maccon sniffed and then gave a little cough.

Alexia's own senses were so assaulted she could only imagine what her husband smelled. There was the intoxicating scent of honey, cinnamon, and roasted nuts. There was also a rather noxious gas emanating from various water-based smoking devices, hoarded by elderly men crouching on stone steps to either side of the narrow street. Underneath the other smells came the unmistakable odor of sewage, not unlike that of the Thames during a hot summer.

Conall turned to her with a wide grin on his handsome face. "That smells like you!" he said as though he had made some great discovery.

"Husband, I do hope you aren't referring to that noxious smoke nor the scent of bodily waste."

"Of course not, my love. Those pastries over there. They smell like you. Would you like to try one?" He knew his wife so well.

"Is Ivy fond of hats? Of course I would *love* to try one!"

The earl moved with alacrity over to the cleanest looking of the street vendors and in short order returned bearing a small sticky, flaky object. Alexia popped it into her mouth without hesitation, only to have her sense of taste assaulted by honey, nuts, exotic spices, and crisp flakes of some impossibly thin pastry.

She chewed in silence. It was far too sticky for anything else. "Amazing!" was her official pronouncement once she had finally swallowed. "Remember what it is called, would you, dear? Then I can order more when we arrive at the hotel. I'm delighted you think I smell like something so delicious."

"You are delicious, my dear."

"Flatterer."

The dragoman took charge of their highly distracted and distractible party and shepherded them toward a long string of donkeys with companion donkey boys who stood waiting under a nearby awning.

"Oh, aren't they perfectly sweet!" exclaimed Mrs. Tunstell.

"They *are* very fine donkeys, aren't they, Ivy? Such long velvet ears. Look, Prudence." Lady Maccon directed her daughter's attention to the string.

"No!" said Prudence.

Ivy shook her head. "No, Alexia, I mean the donkey boys. Look at those lovely almond-shaped eyes and such thick lashes. But, Alexia, is their skin meant to be so dark?"

Alexia didn't dignify this question with an answer.

At which point Mrs. Tunstell came upon a realization that proved even more startling. "Are we expected to *ride* those donkeys?"

"Yes, Ivy dear, I do believe we are."

"Oh, but, Alexia, *I don't ride*!"

Despite Ivy's protestations, which continued vociferously, there commenced a great round of strapping bags onto donkeys and climbing aboard donkeys, while Alexia and the other ladies of the party attempted to negotiate sidesaddle. The toddlers were popped into woven baskets, which the donkeys wore like panniers. The Tunstell twins were suspended together in one set, and Prudence in another, counterbalanced by her mechanical ladybug, which peeked its little antennae over the edge of the basket coyly. Mr. Tumtrinkle went on one side of his donkey and immediately off the other, so that he, like the luggage, had to be strapped into place. After seeing his wife safely up top, Tunstell threw his leg over easily enough, for he was quite nimble and athletic. Unfortunately, his trousers were not so flexible. They ripped loudly, exposing much of his scarlet drawers to the evening air and causing his wife to shriek in horror and faint forward onto the neck of her donkey. Lord Maccon guffawed loudly. Prudence clapped in appreciation. Madame Lefoux made her way genteelly to a nearby stand where she purchased one of the robes so favored by the locals. This Tunstell donned with all the enthusiasm and amiability of an actor accustomed to odd apparel in front of a large audience.

Ivy awoke from her swoon, noted her husband now wore what amounted to a dress, in public, and fainted again. The donkey beneath her was composed and unimpressed by her histrionics.

Conall refused donkey transport, as did their vampire dragoman. Even donkeys, placid creatures as they were, preferred not to carry werewolves or vampires. Lord Maccon perfectly understood this. After all, he was a good deal faster on four paws anyway, so the very idea was preposterous, and he would far rather snack upon the beast than ride it—particularly at this moment with ten days at sea and no live meat the entire time. Lastly, riding a donkey was pointless even when he had been mortal, for his long legs would touch the ground on either side of the wee thing. So he and the guide walked at the front, leading the way and chatting in a forced manner that had nothing to do with the fact that they were from different cultures and everything to do with the fact that one was a vampire and the other a werewolf.

As they trundled through the street, it became clear that they were as much a spectacle for Alexandria as Alexandria was for them. The great port city had been made much of over the last few decades, and the British army called there regularly, but high lords and ladies, small pale children, and troupes of English actors were practically unheard of and quite enthralling as a result.

Many Egyptians came to watch them. The natives pointed with interest at the ladies' hats, the gentlemen's top hats, Alexia's parasol, the odd shapes made by wardrobe and props, as though they were some kind of circus come to parade among them.

Alexia spent a good deal of her time trying to absorb every aspect of the city in the dim light of evening. They arrived at their abode, Hotel des Voyageurs, all too quickly for her, and she could not wait until the next day when she might see Egypt in all its glory. There was the expected chaos once more that saw them all, after much discussion and exchange of moneys, settled into a single floor of the hotel. The ladies took to their rooms for tea and rest, the children went down for naps, and the gentlemen retired to either the nearest bathhouses or the hotel's dubious smoke room, as suited their individual natures.

Lord Maccon helped his wife disrobe, merely raising one eyebrow when a gun dropped out of her corset and clattered to the floor. One became accustomed to such things when one was married to Alexia. Then he reacquainted himself with every aspect of her body, as if he had not just done so onboard the SS *Custard* that morning. Alexia threw herself wholeheartedly into the activity, having learned early on in their marriage that this was an exercise she found both enjoyable and entertaining. It also left her, generally speaking, relaxed and pleased with the world. Not so her husband. Not on this particular night, for even lying next to her on what had proved to be quite a resilient bed, he was what could only be described as *twitchy*.

"Conall, my love, what is the matter?"

"Foreign land," he said curtly.

"And you don't know the lay of it?"

"Exactly so."

"Well," she said with a supportive smile, "go on, then. We shall be fine without you for a few hours."

"Are you quite certain, my dear?"

"Yes, quite."

"You aren't trying to get rid of me?"

"Now, Conall, why would I want to do a thing like that?"

He grunted noncommittally.

"You will be careful, won't you?"

"Of what, precisely?"

"Oh, I don't know, random God-Breaker Plagues running amok? We only just arrived. I'd greatly prefer you not go missing or die quite yet."

"Aye-aye, Captain."

With which her husband gave her a passionate kiss, sprang naked from the bed, and exited their room rather spectacularly by way of the balcony in wolf form. Alexia wrapped the woven blanket about herself and made her way across the room rather less precipitously. She looked to see if she could spot him dashing through the streets off into the desert, but he was already out of sight. It was quarter moon, but he was restless from little exercise on board and he needed to hunt. She tried not to imagine what poor mangy desert creature he would end up eating. As the wife of a werewolf, one had to ignore certain unsavory aspects of cuisine and ingestion.

Lady Maccon felt only a slight twinge of concern. Conall Maccon could certainly take care of himself, and the one thing Alexandria boasted of in plenty was stray dogs. Her husband would simply look like a very large version thereof.

Alexia, thus consoled, drank her tea, which turned out not to be tea at all but that most ghastly of beverages, coffee. It was served with a great deal of honey, which rendered it drinkable if not entirely palatable. She then managed to dress herself. In honor of her trip, she had ordered up a nice mushroom-colored muslin blouse and matched tiny bowler hat, with a duster-style puff of brown feathers. The blouse was designed to be cool in hot weather, while still preserving her modesty. The fastenings at the back gave her some trouble, and the corset underneath could not be laced tight at all. But the draped brown overskirt and modest bustle went on easily enough. Her hair, in response to the desert heat, refused to obey any commands, coiling into great loglike curls. She fussed with it for a bit and then, figuring she was abroad where certain standards might be allowed to slip, pinned it half up and left the rest to flop about as it will.

Downstairs, supper had commenced and the front entrance to Hotel des Voyageurs was empty as all the residents descended upon the comestibles.

"Any messages for Lady Maccon?" she inquired of the desk clerk.

"No, my lady, but there is one for a Lord Maccon."

Alexia took it, noted that the handwriting was not one she recognized, and figured it was a BUR report. She tucked it into her reticule.

"Can you arrange an aetheric transponder connection appointment for me? I have my own valve frequensors, but I understand there is only one transmitter for public access in the city."

"Indeed, my lady. We are a little overtaxed as a result, but I am certain your rank will guarantee access. You'll want the Boulevard Ramleh's west end, opposite the street leading to the Exchange."

Alexia determined she would have to borrow Ivy Tunsell's guidebook in order to make sense of these directions, possibly attached to Ivy herself, but she made a mental note of the details.

"Thank you, my good man. I'll need to book to send a message for just after sunset London time, from here to England. Can you arrange such a thing?"

"Certainly, my lady. That should be something on the order of six o'clock in the evening. But I will ascertain the particulars and make the appointment for you."

"You are most efficient." Alexia, missing Floote quite dreadfully, gave the man a generous gratuity for his pains and wandered into the dining room to see if any of her party were about yet.

Ivy, Tunstell, the nursemaid, and the children were all there causing a ruckus at one of the larger tables. Prudence had her mechanical ladybug and was trundling about banging into people's chairs in a most indiscriminate

manner. Alexia was mortified by such behavior. What was
the nursemaid thinking, allowing the infant to bring the
ladybug to a public eatery? Tunstell was explaining, in
large expansive gestures, the thrilling plot of *The Death
Rains of Swansea* to some poor unfortunate tourists at the
adjoining table. Ivy was fretting over her Baedeker's
guidebook, and the nursemaid was busy with the twins.

Lady Maccon scooped up her errant child.

"Mama!"

"Have you eaten, poppet?"

"No!"

"Well, food, then. Have you tried one of those cinnamon pastry thingamabobs?"

"No!"

Still unsure if *no* was Prudence's new favorite word or
if she actually knew what it meant, Alexia guided the
ladybug with her foot and made her way, baby on hip, to
the Tunstells' table.

"Oh, Lady Maccon, how delightful!" extolled Tunstell
upon seeing her. "Lady Maccon, may I introduce our new
acquaintances the Pifflonts? Mrs. Pifflont, Mr. Pifflont,
this is Lady Maccon."

One is never sure, upon being introduced, whether one
should trust in the arranger of the association, particularly
when that arranger was Tunstell. Nevertheless, it was
Lady Maccon's business to be gracious, so gracious she
was. The Pifflonts turned out to be antiquities experts of
some amateurish Italian extraction, quiet and well man-
nered and exactly the type of people one would like to
meet in a hotel. Careful inquiry, and control over Tunstell's exuberance, turned the conversation to the couple's
journey through Egypt, which was nearing its close. They

were about to return home, abiding only one or two more days before catching a steamer to Naples.

The following unexpectedly intellectual discourse was interrupted by the advent of Lord Conall Maccon wearing a cloak and, so far as Alexia could tell, nothing else. She was horrified. First her daughter went around bumping into people with a ladybug and now her husband appeared without shoes. *Well, there goes that acquaintance!* She couldn't even bear to look at the faces of those nice Pifflonts.

She stood and scuttled swiftly to the earl where he loomed in the doorway.

"Conall, *really*!" she hissed. "At least pull on some boots so you have a facade of decency!"

"I require your presence, wife. And the bairn."

"But, darling, at least a top hat!"

"Now, Alexia. There is something I wish you to see."

"Oh, very well, but do go away. There's blood at the corner of your mouth. I can't take you anywhere."

Lord Maccon vanished around a corner of the hall and Alexia hurried back to the table. She made their excuses and scooped up Prudence, despite her daughter's protestations.

"No! Mama. Nummies."

"Sorry, darling, but your father has discovered something of interest he wishes us to see."

Mrs. Tunstell glanced up. "Oh, is it a textile shop? I hear they produce the most lovely cottons in this part of the world."

"Something more along the lines of ruffled parasols, I believe."

Ivy was thick but not so thick as all that. "Oh, of course," she said immediately, winking in a very overt manner. "*Ruffled parasols.* Naturally. Now, my dear friend, you won't forget we have a private show in only a few hours. And while I know you are not integrated into the performance, your presence is desirable."

"Of course, of course. This shouldn't take very long."

"Carry on, then," said Mrs. Tunstell, although her friend was already trotting hurriedly away. Alexia heard Ivy say, "Lady Maccon is our particular patroness, don't you know? Such a very gracious and grand lady."

She was met outside the hotel by a large wolf. In order to make more of a thing of it, Alexia purchased a donkey rope off an obliging, though confused, donkey boy. This she clasped about Conall's brindled neck, quite a feat of loops and twists, as she could not touch him and had to keep hold of Prudence. Eventually she was successful and it looked as though she were taking a very large dog for a walk.

Lord Maccon gave her a baleful look but submitted to the humiliation for the sake of propriety. They wended their way through the still-vibrant city; sunset seemed more an excuse to visit than an ending to daily activities. He led her a long way, due south down the Rue de la Colonne, past the bastions, through the outer slums of the city until they reached the canal. Alexia was beginning to worry about the time, concerned they might not make it back by the vampire visiting hour. Conall, in his wolf form, had little estimation of distance, and while Alexia was a great walker and never one to shirk exercise, traversing an entire city in the course of only an hour was really rather extreme, especially when carrying a disinterested toddler. Eventually, they developed a method by which Prudence rode astride her father, with Alexia gripping one hand firmly so as to keep everyone in their correct forms and fur.

The earl stopped imperiously at the bank of the canal, and it took Alexia only a moment to surmise they must cross it.

"Oh, really, Conall. Couldn't this wait until tomorrow?"

He barked at her.

She sighed and waved over a reluctant-looking lad in command of a kind of reed raft obviously utilized to cross the canal.

The raft boy refused, with many shakes of the head and wide eyes, to allow the massive wolf into his little craft but was charmed into unexpected delight when said wolf took to the water and simply dragged his raft across. He had no need of the pole normally employed for the crossing. Lady Maccon forbore to say anything on the subject of the cleanliness of the water.

Alexia gave the lad a few coins and gesticulated in such a way as she thought might convince him to wait for them, while Conall shook out his coat violently.

Prudence clapped and giggled at her father's antics, twirling about in the spray of dirty water. Alexia caught her daughter's hand before she touched him.

Alexia thought it a good thing the locals were accustomed to the eccentricities of the English, for such a thing as Lady Maccon alone in the baser end of a foreign city with her only daughter and a large wolf should never be tolerated in any other part of the empire.

Nevertheless, she followed her husband dutifully, reflecting that this was one of the reasons she had married him, with the certain knowledge that life would never be dull. She often suspected it was one of the reasons he had married her as well.

The sensation was barely recognizable at first, but then

she began to feel it—a tingling push, a little like the aether breezes against her skin when she floated. Only this sensation felt like the reverse. Aether tingling was like very mild champagne bubbles against the skin; this felt as though those bubbles were being generated by her own flesh. It was a faint sensation and it was almost pleasant, but it was odd. Had she not been alert for some new experience, she might not have even noticed.

Waving her arms about excitedly, Prudence said, "Mama!"

"Yes, dear, odd, isn't it?"

"No." Prudence was very decided on this. She patted Alexia on the cheek. "Mama *and*—" She waved her arms about. "Mama!"

Alexia frowned. "Are you saying that to you the air feels like me? How very odd."

"Yes," agreed Prudence, using a word Alexia hadn't until that moment realized she possessed.

"Conall, is that what I think it is?" Alexia asked the wolf, her attention still on her wiggling daughter.

"Yes, my love, I believe it is," said her husband.

Lady Maccon nearly dropped Prudence in startlement, looking up to confirm that her ears were not playing tricks on her and that her husband was standing a short distance away, fully naked and fully human.

Lady Maccon set down her daughter. The child toddled eagerly over to Conall, who scooped her right up, without fear. No need of it—Prudence remained her own precocious human self.

Lady Maccon went to stand next to him. "This is the God-Breaker Plague?"

"Indubitably."

"I thought I should feel more repelled by it."

"So did I."

"On the other hand, when the mummy was in London—do you recall?—and caused half the city to come over all mortal, I didn't register any sensations at all. This is almost as mild. It was only when I was in the same room as that awful mummy that I felt true repulsion."

The earl nodded. "*Sharing the same air.* I believe that was the Templar's phrasing for two preternaturals in the same place."

Alexia looked out over the low mud brick houses of Alexandria's poorest residents to the wide low black of nothingness beyond. "Is that the desert?"

"No. Desert has more sand. I believe that used to be a lake, all dried up now. It's wasteland."

"So there once was water and now there is none. Is it possible that the God-Breaker Plague has moved close to the city only since then? After all, we know preternatural touch is affected by water."

"That is a thought. Hard to know. Of course, it is also possible that the city has expanded toward it. But if it has moved closer, you can bet the local vampires would not be happy about it."

"Matakara's real reason for summoning us?"

"Anything is possible with vampires."

CHAPTER ELEVEN

In Which Prudence Discovers Sentences

The Maccons made it back to the hotel in time to change and make themselves presentable before being taken to Queen Matakara and the Alexandria Hive. Chancellor Neshi was waiting for them expectantly in the lobby.

The Tunstells and their troupe were soon to follow, trotting down the stairs lugging set pieces and already dressed in their costumes for the first act, although the gentlemen were all sporting top hats for the journey. If their arrival at the hotel had been remarked upon with interest by the natives, their departure was even more noteworthy. Mrs. Tunstell's dress was silver satin with an enormous quantity of fake pearl jewelry. Mr. Tunstell was attired as any fine gentleman about town except that his suit was of crimson satin and he had a short gold cape buttoned over one shoulder like a musketeer. Mr. Tumtrinkle, villainous from spats to cravat, wore black velvet with diamanté buttons, blue leather gloves, and a cloak of midnight blue satin that he swooped and swirled about like wings as he moved.

This time there was no need of donkeys. The hive queen had sent them a steam locomotive, a massive contraption worthy of even Madame Lefoux's interest. The inventor, however, was nowhere to be found, having disappeared about her own business more hastily than Alexia had ever expected. Alexia felt, it must be admitted, rather abandoned and unimportant. After all, she had surmised that Madame Lefoux was sent along to Egypt to spy on *her*, and here she found herself the least of the Frenchwoman's attentions.

The locomotive was a rangy, rumbling beast, a little like a stagecoach in shape but open topped. The flat back end was piled high with rushes, presumably for the comfort of the occupants, as there were no seats. As the thing rumbled down narrow roads and alleys designed with donkeys in mind, the straw did very little good. Never before had Alexia experienced such a bumpy ride. The locomotive belched bouts of steam high into a dark evening sky out of two tall smokestacks and was so loud that polite conversation was impossible.

Prudence, ghastly child, enjoyed the whole arrangement. She bounced up and down excitedly with each bump and rattle. Alexia was becoming horribly afraid that her bluestocking tendencies had transferred to her daughter, in spades. The infant was taken with anything remotely mechanical, and her fascination with dirigibles and other forms of transport was only increasing.

The Alexandria Hive house was situated off of the Rue Ibrahim within sight of Port Vieux on the eastern side of the city. The facade of the building was Greek in style. It was two levels high, the first level sporting widely spaced, large marble columns, and the upper level showcasing a colonnade of smaller supports open to the air in one long balcony. Inside, however, it was more as Alexia imagined one of the famous rock-cut tombs of the Valley of the Kings. There were doorways leading off of a vestibule, without doors, and woven reed mats spread on the floor. Basalt statues of ancient animal-headed gods stood all about like sentries at a masquerade. The walls were painted with more animal gods engaging in brightly colored and beautifully articulated myths. There was sinuously carved wood furniture here and there, but it was all quite primitive in shape and without adornment. The very starkness and lack of opulence was almost as awe-inspiring as the overabundance of riches that so characterized the vampires of Alexia's homeland. Here was a hive that knew its wealth was purely and simply in the world it had created, not in the objects it had managed to accumulate.

The Tunstells and troupe trailed in behind Lord and Lady Maccon and stood in reverent silence, the atmosphere subduing even them for a short time.

Chancellor Neshi clapped loudly—Ivy started and emitted a little "Oh, my!" of surprise—and near on twenty servants appeared from one of the darkened doorways, all handsome, dark-eyed young men wearing white loincloths for the sake of modesty and nothing else. Each crouched expectantly at the foot of a visitor. Alexia glanced at Chancellor Neshi and realized, with a good deal of shock, that these young men were expecting to remove her shoes. Not only hers, but everyone's! The gentlemen, each caught in the act of removing his outside topper, replaced the hat hurriedly and looked wide-eyed at one another. Realizing they would take their cue from her, Alexia lifted her foot to the young man's knee and permitted him to unlace and pull off her sensible brown walking boots. Following Lady Maccon's lead, the party allowed themselves to be divested of footwear. Alexia shuddered to see that her husband wore no socks and that Tunstell's were mismatched. Only Prudence was delighted to have her shoes removed, not being a very great fan of shoes to begin with.

Chancellor Neshi bustled off, presumably to herald their arrival, at which juncture Mrs. Tunstell broke the hush with a startled, "My goodness gracious, would you look at that god creature there? Its head is nothing but a single feather."

"Ma'at," explained Alexia, who had a particular interest in ancient mythology, "goddess of justice."

"One would perhaps call her feather-head?" suggested Tunstell to much general hilarity. The spell of the ancient world around them was broken.

Chancellor Neshi returned. "*She* is ready to see you now."

He led them up a set of cold stone stairs to the second level of the house, full of more cool, dark, windowless stone rooms, tomblike and torch-lit. From the upper vestibule, they were led down a long hallway that ended in a small open doorway that let onto an enormous room.

They entered. The room was certainly big enough to stage a play. Against the wall directly opposite the hallway door and halfway down on each side stood a series of low wooden divans with red cushions. The floor was spread with more intricately woven reed mats and the walls were again painted. These were done in a similar style to the ancient-looking images below but depicted a wide range of current events, from the Turkish invasion to the incorporation of Western technology, from the great Nutmeg Rebellion to the antiquities trade and tourism. It was a record of Egypt's modern history in bright pigment and perfect detail. It was odd to see the figures of bustled and trussed Europeans, British uniforms and army ships, all in the awkward childish style of papyrus paintings.

On the divans against either wall sat a string of striking and somber young persons who could only be the drones of the hive. They wore native dress but, Alexia noted with interest, both the men and women, in defiance of all she had observed so far, had their heads uncovered. She supposed this must be a kind of rejection of native religion in favor of worshipful loyalty to queen and hive.

Directly opposite the door in the position of greatest importance was what looked to be a large parasol. It was suspended from the ceiling, with great swaths of silken cloth hanging from around the edge. Richly colored and strikingly beautiful, the drapes formed a kind of tent, just large enough for one person to stand within. Alexia couldn't help feeling that whoever was inside could probably see out and was watching her every move.

To one side of this shrouded parasol sat four vampires. There was no doubt that they were, indeed, vampires. For, out of some custom alien to England, they were all showing their fangs to the guests. Vampires in London rarely showed fang without prestated, postintroduction intent. To the other side sat one more vampire, whom Chancellor Neshi went to join. Next to the dragoman were two empty spots.

After a moment of silently watching the odd crowd of mixed aristocracy and overdressed thespians, all six vampires rose to their feet.

"The entirety of the Alexandria Hive," whispered Lord Maccon to his wife.

"We are honored," said his wife back.

A stunningly lovely drone stepped forward, moving with liquid grace across the wide, empty floor until she stood before them. Her features were strong without being manly, her brows heavy, her mouth generous, her lips stained dark red by skilled artifice. She wore full, wide black trousers that ballooned well out and then came in at the ankles. Over this was a long black tunic, nipped in tight along arms and torso with a wide swath of fabric at the wrists and hem, floating away from the hips like a gentleman's frock coat. The wider parts of the tunic and the bloomers were patterned in gold leaves, and she wore a great quantity of gold jewelry about fingers, wrists, neck, ankles, and toes.

"Welcome," she said in perfect Queen's English, making a graceful gesture with her arms, like a dancer, "to the Alexandria Hive." Her large, dark eyes, lined heavily in black, swept over the crowd of actors before her.

"Lord and Lady Maccon?"

Alexia wanted desperately to take her husband's hand, but she thought he might need his supernatural abilities at any moment. So she shifted Prudence more firmly on her hip, taking strange comfort from the presence of her child, and stepped forward. Out of the corner of her eye, she watched Conall also segregate himself from the group.

The dark-eyed drone came closer. She looked to Conall

first. "Lord Maccon, you are welcome to Alexandria. It has been many centuries since a werewolf visited this hive. We hope it will not be so long before the next one graces us with his presence."

Lord Maccon bowed. "I suspect," he said, because he had no tact, "that will rather depend on the course of this evening's events."

The drone inclined her head and turned dark eyes to Alexia. "Lady Maccon, soul-sucker. You, too, are welcome. We do not judge the daughter by the father's actions."

"Well, thank you I'm sure. Especially as I never knew him."

"No, of course you didn't. And is this *the child*?"

Prudence was quite riveted by the beautiful lady. Perhaps it was all the gold sparkles and jewelry, or the liquid way the drone moved. Alexia hoped it wasn't all the face paint; the last thing she needed was a daughter with a keen interest in feminine wiles. She would have to cede all such training to Lord Akeldama.

"Welcome to the Alexandria Hive, stealer of souls. Your kind we have never had the pleasure of entertaining before."

"Remember your manners, dear," said Alexia to her daughter without much hope.

Prudence proved unexpectedly equal to the challenge. "How do you do?" she said, enunciating very clearly and looking quite directly at the lady drone.

Alexia and Conall exchanged raised eyebrow looks. *Very good*, thought Alexia, *we got ourselves a peppery one*.

The drone stepped aside and waved one graceful hand,

offering the two empty spots on the divan next to Chancellor Neshi. "Please, be seated. The queen desires the performance to begin directly."

"Oh," protested Ivy, "but she is not here! She will miss the opening act!"

Tunstell put an arm about his wife's waist and hustled her to one corner of the room to prepare.

The drone clapped her hands and once more dozens of servants appeared. With their assistance, the actors managed to set up one half of the room as a stage, screening off the doorway in the middle. They had the servants move all of the many torches and lamps to that side of the room, throwing the other, where drones and vampires sat in perfect silence, into eerie darkness.

The Death Rains of Swansea was not a performance that improved markedly upon a second viewing. Still there was something appealing if not entertaining about Ivy and Tunstell's antics. Mr. Tumtrinkle pranced his evil prance, and twirled his dastardly fake mustache, and swirled his massive cloak most voraciously. Werewolf hero Tunstell strode back and forth, trousers ever in great danger of ripping over his muscled thighs, coming to the rescue as needed and barking a lot. Ivy fainted whenever there was cause to faint, and swanned about in hats of such proportions it was a wonder her head didn't collapse like a griddle cake under the weight. The supporting cast was, of course, much diminished in size, playing both vampires and werewolves as script demanded. In order to save time, but causing no little confusion as to the plot—no matter what their character at the moment—they wore both the fake fangs and the large shaggy ears tied about their heads with pink tulle bows.

The bumblebee dance went off a treat, the watching vampires and drones almost hypnotized by the spectacle. Alexia wondered if the allegory was wasted on them, or if they, like her, had an appreciation for the ridiculous. Of course, Alexia had only heard Chancellor Neshi and the beautiful drone speak, so it was also possible none of the others understood a word of English.

At the end, vampire queen Ivy returned to werewolf Tunstell's arms after much separation and anxiety, and all was sweetness and light. The torches were dimmed and then raised, and the servants brought in extras to fill the room with an orange glow.

Alexia and the actors waited with bated breath. And then, oh, and then, the assembled vampires and drones rose to their feet crying out in adoration, trilling their tongues in a great cacophony of vibratory sound that could only be utter appreciation. Alexia even observed one or two of the vampires wipe away sentiment, and the beautiful drone with the amazing dark eyes was weeping openly.

The lady drone stood and rushed forward to congratulate Ivy and Tunstell with open arms. "That was wonderful! Wonderful! We have never seen such a performance. So complex, so brilliant. That dance with the yellow and black stripes, so perfectly articulating the emotion of immortality. How can words even begin to describe ... so moving. We have been honored. Truly honored."

Tunstell and Ivy and the entire troupe looked quite overwhelmed by such an enthusiastic reception. Both Tunstells blushed deeply and Mr. Tumtrinkle began to blubber in an excess of emotion.

The drone wafted over to Ivy and embraced her

warmly. Then she linked one arm with Ivy's and the other with Tunstell's and guided them gently from the room. "You simply must tell me the meaning of that interpretive piece in the middle? Was that an illustration of the soul's perpetual struggle with infinity, or a social commentary on the supernatural state in continuing conflict with the natural world as both host and food supply?"

Tunstell replied jovially, "A bit of both, of course. And did you notice the series of tiny leaps I performed stage right? Each one a hop in the face of eternity."

"I did, I did, I did indeed."

Thus agreeably conversing, they wandered down the hallway. There was a brief rustle of activity, and Ivy came bustling back, having extracted herself from her escort. She hurried into the room and made for Lady Maccon.

"Alexia," she said in a significantly hushed tone. "Have you your *ruffled parasol*?"

Alexia, did, in fact, have her parasol with her. She had found over the years it was always better to be on the safe side when visiting a hive. She gestured to her hip where it dangled off of a chatelaine at her waist.

Ivy tilted her head and winked significantly.

"Oh," said Alexia, making the connection. "Pray do not concern yourself, Ivy. Do go enjoy a well-earned repast. The parasol is fine."

Ivy nodded in a slow, suggestive way. Feeling that her secret society duties had been satisfactorily discharged, she went bustling after her husband.

After a moment's hesitation, the rest of the drones moved forward and introduced themselves, those who spoke English at least, to the acting troupe. After an exchange of pleasantries, mention of coffee was made, and they, too, were guided expertly from the room. This left Lord and Lady Maccon behind with Prudence and the six vampires.

Chancellor Neshi stood. "Are you ready now, My Queen?" he asked of the curtained off area.

No verbal response emanated from within, but the draped cloth twitched slightly.

Chancellor Neshi said, "Of course, my queen." He gestured for Lord and Lady Maccon to stand and come to face the front of the draped parasol. Then he pulled aside the curtains, tying them back with gold cords to each side.

Had Alexia not spent a good deal of time in Madame Lefoux's contrivance chamber prior to it being repurposed as a werewolf dungeon, she might have been startled by the contraption revealed. But she had seen an octomaton rampage through London. She had been attacked and then rescued by mechanical ladybugs. She had flown in an ornithopter from Paris to Nice. This was nothing by comparison. And yet, it was probably the most grotesque invention of the modern age. Worse than the disembodied hand in a jar under that temple in Florence. Worse than a dead body in an afterlife extension tank. Worse even than the wax-face horror of the Hypocras automaton. Because those creatures had all been dead or manufactured. What sat in the raised dais behind that curtain was still alive or still undead—at least in part.

She, for Alexia assumed it must be a she, sat atop what could only be called a throne. It was mostly made of brass. Its base was some kind of tank housing two levels of liquid, the bottom a bubbling mess of yellow that heated the upper composed entirely of a viscous red fluid that could only be blood. The arms of the throne were fitted with levers, nozzles, and tubes, some under the emaciated hands of the occupant, others going into or coming out of her arms. It was as though the woman and the chair had become one and not been separated for generations. Some parts of the chair were bolted directly into her flesh, and there was a bronze half mask covering the lower part of her face from nose to throat, presumably providing a constant supply of blood.

Only Lady Maccon's good breeding kept her from committing the vile act of involuntary purging right then and there on the reed mat. There was something particularly horrific about knowing that, because the queen was immortal, all those places where the chair speared into her flesh must be constantly trying to heal themselves.

Chancellor Neshi did a most humiliating thing. He knelt upon the floor and bowed forward all the way to the ground, touching his forehead to the reed mat. Then he stood and waved Alexia and Conall farther forward. "My Queen, may I present Lady Maccon, Lord Maccon, and Lady Prudence. Maccons, may I present Queen Matakara Kenemetamen of Alexandria, Ruler of the Ptolemy Hive ad Infinitum, Lady Horus of Fine Gold in Perpetuity, Daughter of Nut, Oldest of the Vampires."

With the lower half of her head concealed, it was difficult to determine Matakara's exact appearance. Her eyes were large and very brown, too large in that emaciated face. She had the dark complexion of most native Egyptians, grown darker as it shrunk in against the bone, like that of a mummy. She had a blue wig atop her head and a snake coronet made of gold set with turquoise eyes on top of that. Over the parts of her body not attached to the throne, she wore simple white cotton draped and pleated stiffly and a quantity of gold and lapis jewelry.

Despite the grotesqueness of the contraption and the pathetic appearance of the woman confined within it, Alexia was hypnotized by those huge eyes. Rimmed in black kohl, they stared fixedly at her. Alexia was convinced the queen was trying to communicate with her a message of great import. And she, Alexia Maccon, was too thick to comprehend it. The expression in those eyes was one of immeasurable desperation and eternal misery.

Lord Maccon made his bow, removing his hat in a wide, sweeping gesture and doing a creditable job of it. He did not look as surprised by the queen's appearance as Alexia felt, which made her wonder if BUR had received some kind of prior warning. She believed that she made a decent effort at disguising her own shock as she curtsied. Prudence, standing quietly by her side, hand firmly gripped in Alexia's, glanced back and forth from monstrosity to mother before performing her own version of a half bow, half curtsy.

A sound of disgust emanated from the queen and her contraption.

"She wants you to bow," hissed the chancellor.

"We just did."

"No, Lady Maccon, all the way."

Alexia was quite shocked. "Like an *Oriental*?" Her gown would barely permit kneeling and her corset certainly would not permit her to bow forward.

The earl looked equally taken aback.

"You are in the presence of royalty!"

"Yes," Alexia agreed in principle, "but to kneel on the *ground*?"

"Do you know how many strangers the queen has allowed into her presence over the last few centuries?"

Lady Maccon could hazard a guess. After all, if *she* looked as bad as Matakara did... "Not a lot?"

"None at all. It is a great honor. And you should bow, properly. She is a great woman, an ancient lady, and she deserves your respect."

"She does?"

Conall sighed. "When in Rome."

"That's just it, dear, we aren't. We are in Alexandria."

But it was too late; her husband had already swept off his hat a second time, knelt, and bowed forward.

"Oh, Conall, the knees of your trousers! Don't put your head all the way down. We don't know where that floor has been! Oh, now, Prudence, you don't have to follow Daddy's example. Oop, there she goes."

Prudence had nothing like her mother's reticence. Frilly yellow frock notwithstanding, she pitched forward and put her head to the ground with alacrity.

Feeling she was the last holdout, Alexia glared at her husband. "You'll have to help me back up. I can't possibly manage on my own without ripping my dress." So saying, she knelt slowly down and tilted herself forward as much as her foundation garments would allow, which wasn't very much. She nearly overbalanced to her left. Her corset creaked under the strain. Conall hoisted her back up, turning human for that one moment.

Chancellor Neshi went to stand next to his queen, on a pedestal of just the right height to bring his ear to her mouth area but ensuring he was no higher than she. The vampire queen spoke to him in a whisper. Alexia looked at her husband inquiringly, wondering if his supernatural hearing picked up anything.

"No language I know," he said unhelpfully.

"The queen says that Europeans do everything wrong, writing from left to right, uncovering the head to enter a room yet leaving the feet confined." Chancellor Neshi stood stiff-backed to state this, like a town crier, acting the mouthpiece for his queen. Then, without waiting for an answer to these accusations of backward behavior, he turned to listen once more.

"My queen wishes to know why all foreign children look the same."

Alexia gestured with her free hand at her daughter, who was standing in unusual docility by her side. "Well, this particular child is Prudence Alessandra Maccon Akeldama."

"No," said Prudence. No one listened. Prudence was to find this all too common in her young life.

Chancellor Neshi continued to speak for his queen. "Daughter of a hellhound, named for a soul-sucker and a bloodsucker. The queen wishes to know if she works."

"Pardon?" Alexia was confused.

"Is she a Follower of Set? A Stealer of Souls?"

Lady Maccon considered. It was a fair question, of course, but Alexia was too much a scientist to answer in the affirmative. Instead she said carefully, "She manifests the abilities of a supernatural creature after having touched him, if that is what you are asking."

"A simple yes would have sufficed, soul-sucker," said the chancellor.

Lady Maccon looked hard into Queen Matakara's sad eyes. "Yes, but it would not be true. Your names for her are not my names for her. Have you called my daughter and me here, Venerable One, simply to insult us?"

Chancellor Neshi bent to listen and then seemed to

engage in a brief argument. Finally he said, "My queen wishes to be shown the truth."

"What truth, exactly?"

"Your daughter's gifts."

"Oh, now wait a moment there!" interjected Conall.

"It can be tricky," hedged Alexia.

Queen Matakara's finger twitched on the arm of the chair, lighting a small spark of flame for a brief moment. This seemed to be a signal, for one of her hive darted forward and, in a flash of smooth movement, scooped Prudence up. Prudence let go of her mother's hand and was otherwise untroubled. Alexia let out a cry of anger. The vampire in question, however, instantly dropped the toddler because he had unexpectedly lost the strength he had no doubt enjoyed for centuries. He probably possessed the ability to maintain his grip, but the surprise was overwhelming. His fangs vanished. Prudence hit the ground with a thud but, being now immortal, sustained no injury. She leaped up, little fangs bared, grubby hands reaching. She was intrigued by the bronze chair with all of its switches and levers. Prudence was one to manhandle first, ask questions later. Much *later*, perhaps when she was grown up and could formulate a complete study. Most of the time this was mere childish enthusiasm and no more disconcerting than Baby Primrose's constant groping for trim and feathers, but now Prudence was a vampire, and she had more than enough strength to do some serious damage to that chair.

Lady Maccon dove forward. Luckily, Prudence was so fascinated she did not bother to flee. Alexia got a hand around her arm in quick order, averting catastrophe.

The vampires, all frozen in startled horror for those

brief, awful minutes, jumped to their collective feet and
placed themselves between the Maccons and their queen.
They were all shouting accusations at Alexia and Prudence in rapid, high-volume Arabic.

One of them nipped forward, hand back to strike
Alexia full across the face.

Holding Prudence in both hands, Alexia could not
go for her parasol, even had she been fast enough. She
flinched away, curling protectively about her daughter,
shielding Prudence from the blow.

Suddenly, standing between Alexia and the vampire
was a very large, very angry brindled wolf. His hackles
were raised, his huge white teeth were bared, and saliva
dripped down from the pink of his gums.

It was a terrifying thing to confront for any creature,
let alone those who had not seen a werewolf in hundreds
of years.

Lord Maccon interposed himself between his wife and
the hive and backed up until he was flush against the fabric of Alexia's skirt.

Alexia took the opportunity, with the vampires' attention now focused on this new threat, to switch Prudence
firmly to one hip and release the parasol from the chatelaine with her free hand. She raised it up, arming the tip
with a numbing dart. At the same time, understanding the
meaning behind her husband's consistent furry pressure
against her legs, she began backing slowly toward the
door.

One of the vampires feinted in the earl's direction. At
the same time, another made a lunge for Alexia. Without
break for thought, the werewolf charged the first, grabbing him about the hamstring and hurling him hard into

the other vampire. Both vampires crumpled to the floor
for a short moment before bouncing back to their feet.
Alexia, without pause, shot one of them with a numbing
dart. He fell right back down again, and this time stayed
there for a while before reeling groggily to his feet.

Alexia began backing with greater intent toward the
doorway, not shifting her attention from the milling clot
of angry vampires. Conall stuck close, maintaining a
snarling, barking, growling ferocity that encouraged space
between the vampires and his wife and daughter.

Chancellor Neshi stepped forward, slowly and with
empty hands held up in supplication. "Please, Lord Maccon, we are unused to such antics."

Conall only growled, low and furious.

If Alexia had expected an apology at that juncture, she
was sorely disappointed. The man, showing not insignifi-
cant bravery, only inched closer and gestured the wolf
toward the door like a porter. "This way, my lord. We
thank you for your visit."

Taking that as a statement of permission, Alexia turned
and strode from the room with all haste. No sense in dawdling where one was unwanted. After a moment's hesitation, Conall followed.

Prudence struggled mightily in her mother's arm, but
Alexia had had enough of *that* for one night and gripped
her tightly.

The infant cried out, "No! Mama, no. Poor Dama!" in
her high treble and strained back to the room.

Feeling her daughter's attention shift and possessed by
the same compulsion, Alexia paused and turned to look
back. The hive vampires stood in a huddle before their
mistress, but the dais raised Queen Matakara high enough

for Alexia's eyes to meet those of the vampire queen above the crowd. Alexia was struck once again by the profound unhappiness there and by the belief that Matakara wanted something of her, wanted it enough to bring her all the way to Egypt. *How can I help you with anything?* Alexia felt a tug at her dress and saw Conall had his teeth firm about her hem and was tugging her into motion. She did as she was bid.

Chancellor Neshi had to jog to catch up. After a moment's thoughtful regard, the vampire directed his conversation at Alexia, rather than her now-hairy husband. As if nothing unbecoming had happened, he inquired politely, "May we offer you some coffee before you leave?" They walked down the cold stone stairs to the entrance.

"No thank you," responded Alexia politely. "I think we had better depart."

"Mama, Mama!"

"Yes, my dear?"

Prudence took a deep breath and then said slowly and carefully, "Mama, get her out."

Alexia looked to her daughter in startlement. "Are we speaking in complete sentences now, Prudence?"

Prudence narrowed her eyes at her mother suspiciously. "No."

"Ah, well, still, that is an interesting theory. Trapped, you think. Against her will? I suppose anything is possible."

Biffy and Lyall spent that night much as though nothing of significance had happened in the previous one. They met with Lady Kingair and proceeded with the investigation as if there had been no fight, no life-altering decision, and no beginnings of a romance.

Lady Kingair sniffed and then glared at the two men suspiciously when they entered the room, but apart from that, made no comment about any change in state. If she noticed they were more relaxed around one another or the little touches they sometimes exchanged without quite realizing, she made no comment.

Biffy was sure Floote knew, because Floote always seemed to know such things. The butler attended to their requirements with the same solicitous efficiency as always. Perhaps more so, as it seemed that without Lady Maccon's demands to occupy his time and attention, he was ever on hand to help them with anything they might need.

Lyall spent his time looking over all the evidence they had gathered on the owners of private dirigibles in London. He compared these to political and tradesmen's concerns in Egypt but was unable to come up with any connections. Lady Kingair delved into the manufacture and distribution of sundowner bullets, trying to determine who might have access and why, but this also seemed fruitless. Biffy concentrated his efforts on Egypt and what Dubh might have found there. The man had clearly been inside the God-Breaker Plague zone to have emerged so weakened. Biffy gathered together passenger manifests on trains and steamers out of Egypt, attempting to access baggage information on the theory that, due to his emaciated state, Dubh must have been traveling in the company of at least *part* of a preternatural mummy on the voyage home. He must have disposed of it, or it had been stolen, as no supernatural creature in London had experienced ill effects upon his return.

Biffy was not one to get easily distracted, but after several hours immersed in manifests of one kind or another, he found himself drawn into an obscure treatise on the nature of the God-Breaker Plague written some fifty years ago. That, in turn, referenced a different report from the very first antiquities expeditions some hundred and twenty or so years prior. Something in the two documents struck him as odd, though he could not pinpoint the particulars. This sent him into a flurry of activity, pulling books on Egypt down from the library and sending Floote off to collect reports from the foreign office on the subject. The God-Breaker Plague was of peculiarly little interest to daylight folk and of particular secrecy to vampires and werewolves, so there was very little substantial information.

"Biffy, I don't mean to disturb your readings, but you appear to be getting a tad distracted from our original objective."

Biffy looked up at his Beta, rubbing his eyes blearily. "Mmm?"

"You seem to be delving further and further back in time. Away from our murder investigation. Are you tracking something of relevance?"

"There is something *peculiar* going on with this plague."

"You mean aside from the fact that it exists at all, a pestilence of unmaking affecting only supernatural folk?"

"Yes."

"What, exactly, are you on to, my boy?" Lyall crouched down next to Biffy, where he sat on the floor, surrounded by books and manuscripts.

Lady Kingair looked up from her own papers.

Biffy pointed at a line in one of the older texts. "Look here, one hundred and twenty years ago, reports of the plague being situated as far as Cairo. See here, particular mention of the pyramids being *clean*."

Lyall tilted his head, a sign Biffy was to continue.

"And here, a similar mention. No one seems interested in charting the exact extent of the plague, possibly because it would take a werewolf interested in scientific investigation, and willing to turn mortal on a regular basis as he walked through the desert. But so far as I can tell, fifty years ago, the God-Breaker Plague stretched from Aswan to, still, Cairo."

"Well?"

Biffy shook out a map of the Nile River Valley. "Taking into account topography and allowing water features and territory markers, much as werewolves and vampires do themselves, the plague would have extended like so." He drew a loose circle on the map with a stick of graphite. "So far as I can tell, the initial extent, here, remained fixed for thousands of years, ever since werewolves were divested of their rule and the plague began."

Lyall bent over the map, intrigued. "So what has you worried? This all seems to be as the howlers sing it. Ramses, the last pharaoh, who lost the ability to change and became old and toothless because of the God-Breaker Plague."

"Yes, except sometime after this last report, the one dated 1824, it moved."

"What! What moved?"

"Well, perhaps not moved. Perhaps *expanded* is a better word. Look at the more recent reports on the plague BUR got hold of, dated a few decades ago. Admittedly they

come out of the Alexandria Hive and one loner wolf who
braved the desert out of some kind of religious fervor. But
I would say, at a conservative guess, that the God-Breaker
Plague has expanded some one hundred miles in the last
fifty years." Biffy drew a second larger circle on his map.
"Here. It now includes Siwah and Damanhúr and stretches
all the way to the outskirts of Alexandria."

"What!"

"Something happened five decades ago that caused the
plague to start up again."

"This is not good," stated Professor Lyall baldly.

"You think our Dubh might have been carrying this
information back to us?" wondered Lady Kingair.

"He was sent looking for preternatural mummies.
What if he found more than any of us had wagered on?"

"Why be so obsessed with contacting Lady Maccon on
the subject?" Lady Kingair seemed to find this point particularly aggravating.

"Well, she *is* a preternatural," said Biffy.

"We must send them an aetherogram immediately
with this information. Do you have an appointment scheduled with Lady Maccon, Biffy?" asked Lyall.

"Yes, I... How did you know?"

"Because it's what I would have done in your place.
When is it?"

"Tomorrow at sunset."

"You must relay this information to Lady Maccon."

"Of course."

"And you must warn her of... you know..." Lyall gestured with his head at Lady Kingair.

"Yes, that your secret is out, that our pack is about to
change. I know."

"You are still not resigned to the change?" Lyall cocked his head to the side and lowered his voice.

"You will leave me, and you will leave me with a great deal of responsibility." Biffy looked up at him out of the corner of his eye, pretending further interest in the map of Egypt so as to disguise any sentiment.

"I believe you might have just proven how well placed my faith is in you."

"Well, gentlemen," interrupted Lady Kingair, "how about you prove Lord Maccon's faith and figure out who shot my Beta?"

CHAPTER TWELVE

Wherein Alexia and Ivy Meet a Man with a Beard

Lady Alexia Maccon awoke midafternoon. The light was rich and golden, peeking around the edges of the heavy curtains. She checked her husband's slumbering face, handsome and innocent in sleep. She trailed one fingertip down his fine profile and giggled when he snuffled a little snore at the familiarity. Sometimes she allowed herself to wallow in the sentimentality of knowing that this wonderful man, overbearing, impossible, and werewolf though he might be, was hers. Never in her old days as spinster and social outcast could she have imagined such a thing. She had thought that some kind, unassuming scientist might be persuaded to take her, or some midgrade clerk, but to have landed such a man...her sisters must envy her. Alexia would have envied herself, had that not proved logistically rather complicated. She kissed the tip of her husband's nose and climbed out of the bed, eager to investigate Egypt in the daylight.

She was not, however, to enjoy the pleasures of such an

exploration alone. The gentlemen were still abed, but
Mrs. Tunstell, the nursemaid, and the children were all
awake and enjoying coffee in the room dedicated as the
nursery.

"Mama!" came Prudence's excited cry upon seeing
Lady Maccon in the doorway. She slid down off the chair
and toddled over excitedly. Alexia bent to pick her up.
Prudence grabbed her mother's head, one chubby hand to
each cheek, and directed her attention at her own intent
little face. "Tunstellings! Silly," she explained. "Eeegypttt!"

Alexia nodded slightly. "I agree with you on all points,
my darling."

Prudence stared seriously into her mother's brown
eyes, as though trying to determine whether Alexia was
addressing the matter with due attention to the important
details. "Good," she said at last. "Go go go."

Mrs. Tunstell stood back politely while Lady Maccon
and her child conversed. At this she said, "Alexia, my
dear, are you perhaps pondering what I am pondering?"

Alexia replied, without hesitation, "My dear Ivy, I very
much doubt it."

Ivy took no offense, possibly because she did not per-
ceive the insult, only saying, "We were considering a little
stroll about the town. Would you be interested in joining us?"

"Oh, indeed. Do you have your Baedeker's? I need to
get to the local aethographor by six o'clock or thereabouts."

"Oh, Alexia, do you need to *transmit* something significant? How exciting!"

"Oh, nothing of any material consequence, simply a
matter of coordination. You have no objections to us making it one of the objectives of the excursion?"

"Certainly not. Taking the air is so much more enjoyable when one has purpose, don't you feel? I ordered up a donkey. Would you believe they don't have perambulators in this part of the world? How do they transport infants in style?"

"Apparently by donkey."

"That," stated Ivy most decidedly, "is *not* style!"

"I thought we could pop Primrose and Percival into those adorable little basket panniers, and Prudence here might like to try to ride."

"No!" said Prudence.

"Oh, come now, darling," remonstrated her mother. "You come from a long line of horsewomen, or so I like to believe. You should start while you are young enough to get away with riding astride."

"Pttttt," said Prudence.

A polite tap came at the open door and Madame Lefoux stuck her head in. "Ladies"—she tipped her elegant gray top hat—"and Percy," she added, remembering that one, at least, was a very minor gentleman.

Percy burped at her. Primrose waved her arms about. Prudence nodded politely, as did Alexia and Ivy.

"Madame Lefoux," said Mrs. Tunstell. "We were about to head out on an exploratory expedition around the metropolis. Would you care to join us?"

"Ah, ladies, I should ordinarily be quite eager, but I am afraid I have my own business to attend to."

"Ah, well, don't let us detain you," said Alexia, quite burning with curiosity as to the nature of Madame Lefoux's business. Was the Frenchwoman acting for the Order of the Brass Octopus, Countess Nadasdy, or herself? Lady Maccon wished, not for the first time, she had

her own team of BUR-style field agents she could set to
tail suspicious individuals at will. She looked with consideration at her tiny daughter, who was occupied playing
with a curl of Alexia's hair. *Perhaps I should train Prudence in covert operation procedures? With an adopted
father like Lord Akeldama, half my work will already be
completed.* Prudence blinked at her and then stuffed the
curl into her mouth. *Perhaps not just yet.*

Madame Lefoux made good her escape, and Alexia,
Ivy, and the nursemaid dressed and mobilized the three
infants. They made their way down and out the front of
the hotel where a docile, soft-eared donkey and companion boy stood awaiting them. The twins took up basket
position with little fuss, Percy being given a bit of dried
fig to gnaw upon and Primrose a length of silver lace to
play with. Both wore large straw hats, Primrose looking
quite the thing with her dark curls peeking out and her big
blue eyes. Percy, on the other hand, looked rather uncomfortable, like a fat, redheaded boatman unsure of the high
seas.

Prudence, set astride the donkey, drummed her chubby
legs and grabbed the creature's neck like a seasoned pro-
fessional. What little sun she had experienced aboard ship
had turned her skin a faint olive. Alexia was horribly
afraid her daughter had inherited her Italian complexion.
This spectacle, of three foreign children dressed in all the
frills and lace of England's finest, plus donkey, caused a
stir in the streets of Alexandria. It was just as well, since
they couldn't move very quickly without Prudence falling
off. The nursemaid walked alongside, keeping a watchful
eye to them all, neat as a new pin in her navy dress, white
apron, and cap. Mrs. Tunstell and Lady Maccon strode at

the front, leading the way, parasols raised against the sun.
Lady Maccon was dressed in a fabulous walking gown of
black and white stripes, courtesy of Biffy, and Mrs. Tunstell in a complementary day dress of periwinkle blue and
maroon plaid. Periodically they would pause to consult
Mrs. Tunstell's little guidebook, until this took too long,
at which juncture Lady Maccon would simply pick a
direction and stride on.

Alexia fell deeply in love with Egypt on that walk.
There really was no other way of putting it. As suggested
by Ivy's Baedeker, Egypt had no concept of bad weather
in the winter months, giving them instead a mild summer.
The sandstone and mud brick buildings basked under the
friendly orange glow, and the slatted rushes high above
their heads made crisscrosses of shade at their feet. The
flowing garb of the locals provided an endless shifting of
bright colors against a muted monotone background. The
native women carried baskets of food balanced upon their
heads. Ivy, at first, thought this a peculiar kind of hat and
was very interested in procuring one for herself, until she
saw a woman lift the basket down and dole out bread to an
eager donkey boy.

The gentlemen and ladies of Egypt seemed to possess
a self-respect and innate gracefulness of manner, regardless of societal rank, that could only be thought engaging.
That said, they also seemed inclined to sing while they
worked, or sat upon their heels, or stretched out upon a
mat. Alexia was not a particularly musical person, and her
husband, a noted opera singer in his human days, had
once described her bath time warblings as those of a
deranged badger. But even she could recognize complete
tunelessness, coupled to a certain rhythmic vocalization.

The resulting renditions seemed a means of lightening labor or sweetening repose, but Alexia thought them monotonous and displeasing to the ear. However, she learned, as she had done with the harmonic auditory resonance disruptor, to disregard it as mere background hum.

As they tottered happily along, Alexia felt compelled to stop at many a small shop and one or two bazaar stands to investigate the goods on offer, mainly drawn, as was her wont, by delicious and exotic foodstuffs. Ivy and the child-burdened donkey trailed in her wake. The nursemaid paid due attention to her charges and was properly shocked by the foreignness of the city about them the rest of the time. "Oh, Mrs. Tunstell, would you look at that? Stray dogs!" or "Oh, Mrs. Tunstell, would you believe? That man is sitting cross-legged, on his front step, and his legs are bare!"

Mrs. Tunstell, meanwhile, became increasingly addle-pated over their getting lost in a foreign land.

Prudence held on with all her might, and after taking in her surroundings with the jaundiced eye of a seasoned traveler, tilted her little head back, nearly losing her hat, and cooed in delight over the amazing sight of the many massive colorful balloons that hovered above the city. Egyptians were not yet proficient in dirigible travel but had for many hundreds of years played host to the balloon nomads of the desert skies, bronzed cousins to the Bedouin. The first of the English settlers named them Drifters, and the moniker stuck. A vast number hovered above Alexandria during the day, having come in for the markets and the tourist trade. They were every color of every hat Ivy had ever possessed, many of them patchwork or striped. As fascinating as the daily life of the natives might be, Prudence was lured by the promise of flight high above. She warbled her glee.

Thus pleasantly entertained, the group made its way through the city, pausing overlong only once, in one of the bazaars when Alexia was particularly taken by a fine display of leatherwork. Looking up, she noticed that the man seated behind the goods attractively arrayed on a colorful striped rug was not the same in looks as all the others they had encountered thus far. He had a different garb and bearing. His sharp, bearded features and steady gaze betokened firmness, resolution, and an autocratic nature. He was also *not singing*. This was no Alexandrian local but one of the Bedouin nomads of the desert, or so Alexia believed at first. Until she noted that a long rope ladder was tied to the building behind him, a ladder that stretched all the way up into the sky above, attached to the basket of one of Prudence's beloved balloons. The man was uncommonly handsome, his dark eyes intent, and he stared hard at Alexia for a moment.

"Leather for the pretty lady?" he asked.

"Oh, no thank you. Simply looking."

"You should look farther south. The answers to your questions lie in Upper Egypt, Miss Tarabotti," said the Drifter, his accent thick but his meaning unmistakable.

"Pardon me. What did you just say?" Alexia was startled into asking. She looked for Mrs. Tunstell. "Ivy, did you hear that?" By the time she had turned back, the man was gone, shimmying up his rope ladder into the sky with remarkable dexterity and speed, almost supernaturally quick—impossible, of course, as it was still daylight.

Alexia watched him go with her mouth slightly open until a new voice said, "Leather for the pretty lady?" and a small boy, in typical Alexandrian garb, looked hopefully up at her from the exact place the man had just been.

"What! Who was that bearded man? How did he know my name?"

The boy only blinked his fringe of lashes at her, uncomprehending. "Leather for the pretty lady?"

"Alexia, are we finished here? I hardly see what you would want with such goods."

"Ivy, did you see that man?"

"What man?"

"The balloon nomad who was just here."

"Oh, really, Alexia, it says right here in my little book—Drifters don't fraternize with Europeans. You must have imagined it."

"Ivy, my dearest boon companion, have I ever *imagined* anything?"

"Fair point, Alexia. In which case, I am very sorry to say that I did not observe the interaction."

"A disappointment for you, I'm sure, for he was a remarkably fine specimen."

"Oh, my, Alexia, you shouldn't say such things! You're a married woman."

"True, but not a dead one."

Ivy fanned herself vigorously. "La, Alexia, such talk!"

Lady Maccon only smiled and twirled her parasol. "Ah, well, I suppose time is of the essence. We should press on." She tried to memorize the stall's location and the color of the man's balloon, a patchwork of varying shades of deep purples.

With no further disruptions, they made their way to the west end of Boulevard Ramleh, arriving by six o'clock exactly. Alexia left her party in ecstasies over Port Neuf, glittering rich and blue under the low light of the late afternoon sun. She strode swiftly inside and, finding it was English run and quite up to snuff, had her own valve in place exactly on time to transmit a message to Biffy. At least she hoped it was the right time; so many things could go wrong with aethographors.

"Ruffled Parasol in place," her message ran. "Booking this time this location until departure." She then added the Alexandria codes and waited with bated breath. Within moments, as ordered, there came a reply. Unfortunately, it was not the reply Lady Alexia Maccon would have wished.

Biffy's sleep was troubled and not only by the fact that Professor Lyall boasted rather a small bed for two occupants. While neither of them was very large, Biffy was a good deal taller than his companion, which caused his feet to dangle off the end. Still neither would even think to suggest that they sleep apart, not now that they had discovered each other. Besides, once the sun rose fully, they both slept solidly enough to be thought dead, limbs wound together, breathing soft and deep. Nevertheless, Biffy's dreams were colored by missed appointments, canceled events, and forgotten messages.

Channing Channing of the Chesterfield Channings had caught Biffy following Lyall into his room that morning. He raised one blond eyebrow in silent criticism but said nothing. However, they both knew they were due to come under a good deal of teasing that evening, for all the pack would be informed. Werewolves were terrible gossips, especially about their own. Vampires preferred to talk about other people's business; werewolves were a tad more incestuous in their interests. Knowing that their new arrangement, as yet unformed in the particulars, was public fodder for the rumor mill allowed Biffy to give his claviger instructions to see him awakened a few minutes before sunset *in Lyall's chamber.*

"Sir, sir, wake up." As ordered, Catogan Burbleson, a nice boy with considerable musical talent, shook Biffy hard some fifteen minutes before sunset. It took a good deal of force to rouse a werewolf before sundown, especially one of Biffy's youth.

"Everything all right, Mr. Burbleson?" Biffy heard the Beta whisper.

"Yes, sir. Mr. Biffy asked me to see him up before sunset, something about not missing an important appointment."

"Ah, yes, of course."

Biffy felt a nuzzle at the back of his neck and then sharp teeth as Lyall bit him hard on the meat of his shoulder.

He stopped pretending to be asleep and said, "Now, now, Professor, save that for later. Naughty man."

Lyall laughed, actually laughed, and poor Catogan looked horribly embarrassed.

Biffy rolled out of bed and his claviger helped him into a smoking jacket, silk trousers, dressing gown, and slippers. Under ordinary circumstances, he would not leave his room, nor Lyall's for that matter, in anything less than shoes, spats, trousers, shirt, waistcoat, cravat, and jacket. But there was no time to waste, and he would have to complete his toilette at leisure later. He only hoped he should not encounter anyone with fixed opinions on his foray to the aethographor—a faint hope in a den of werewolves.

Thus informally attired, he hurried up to the attic of the house, where Lady Maccon had had her aethographic transmitter installed. The device looked on the outside to be nothing more than an enormous box, large enough to house two horses, raised up off the floor via a complex system of springs. The exterior was quilted in thick blue velvet to prevent ambient noise from reaching its interior. The box was divided into two small rooms, each filled with a precise arrangement of machinery. As he was supposed to be waiting for the Alexandria codes from Lady Maccon, Biffy took up vigil in the receiving chamber.

With everything switched to the on position, he sat as still as possible. Utter silence was necessary or the receivers might be disrupted in their response to aetheric vibrations. He watched intently and just as the sun set—he could feel the sensation in his werewolf bones—a message came through. Before him were two pieces of glass with black particulate sandwiched between, and a magnet mounted to a small hydraulic arm hovering above began to move. One by one, letters formed in the particulate. "Ruffled Parasol in place. Booking this time this location until departure." And there came a short string of numbers. Biffy had an excellent memory, so he simply made a mental note of the codes and then dashed out and over to the transmitting chamber.

As quickly as supernaturally possible, he dialed the aetheromagnetic setting into the frequency transmitters. Lady Maccon had insisted on commissioning only the latest and most sophisticated in aethographors. Biffy needed no companion valve on his end. That done, he double-checked his numbers and then picked up an acid stylus and an etching roll. He composed his message, careful to print each letter neatly in a grid square. This first communication was simple and had to be sent immediately. "Wait," it said, "more follows. Wingtip Spectator." He slotted the metal slate into the brackets and activated the transmitter. Two needles passed over the grid squares of the slate, one on the top side and the other underneath, sparking whenever they were exposed to one another through the etched letters.

Without waiting for a reply, he bent to compose his second message, the one carrying the bulk of his recent discoveries. It was a lot of vital information to transfer in code, but he did his very best. Once more he activated the aetheric convector. Barely breathing, he watched the sparks fly and hoped against hope that the message was away and that he was not too late.

"Wait," Biffy's message said, "more follows. Wingtip Spectator." Lady Maccon looked from the clerk to the scrap of papyrus paper he had passed to her and then back again.

"Is the receiving chamber booked just now?"

"Not for another few minutes, madam."

"Then allow me the privilege of renting it for one additional message." Alexia passed over a generous amount of money. The clerk's eyebrows rose.

"As you wish, madam." He hurried off, back to the Alexandria aethographor's receiving chamber, graphite pencil in one hand, a fresh scrap of papyrus in the other.

He returned a few moments later with another message. Alexia snatched it from him. The first part said, "50 years ago GBP start expand." Alexia puzzled over this for only a moment before she realized that Biffy must have figured out that the God-Breaker Plague was increasing and that this expansion had commenced some five decades ago. A fact that confirmed what she and Conall had surmised. She wished she knew how much and with what rapidity but guessed it must be quite significant for Biffy to think it important enough to mention. Also, Biffy had given her a time frame—fifty years. *What happened in Egypt fifty years ago? This must have something to do with Matakara's summons. But what good can I do? Or Prudence, for that matter. Neither of us can stop a plague.* Given that Biffy had determined the rate of expansion, Alexia wondered if he had also determined a possible epicenter. *If the plague moves far enough into Alexandria, I suppose Queen Matakara will have to swarm.* Could a vampire in her condition, grafted into a chair, afterlife supported by artificial means, still swarm? Then again, someone had once said that the older the queen, the shorter amount of time she had to swarm. Was Matakara simply too old to manage it at all? Had she lost the capacity?

Troubled by these thoughts, Lady Maccon almost didn't notice that there was a second scrap of paper with another message.

It read, "Lady K knows PL past. Wrote Lord M."

Alexia Maccon felt her heart sink down and lodge somewhere in the vicinity of her stomach where it caused no little upset. Her cheeks tingled as the blood drained out of her face, and she was certain, had she been the kind of woman to faint, she would have done so right then and there. But she was not, so she panicked instead.

The message was cryptic to be sure, but it could only mean one thing. Lady Kingair had somehow found out that Professor Lyall had rigged the Kingair assassination attempt and she had written to Conall informing him of Lyall's duplicity. This should not, ordinarily, upset Alexia all that much. Except, of course, that she, too, had known. And in knowing such an awful thing, she had also chosen for the last few years to keep it secret from her husband. A wifely betrayal she had hoped would not be revealed in her lifetime. For Conall would find it difficult to forgive such subterfuge.

At that moment, Lady Maccon remembered the innocent little letter, the one with the handwriting she had not recognized. The one she had picked up from the hotel clerk the other evening and placed upon Conall's bedside table, thinking it a missive from one of his BUR operatives.

"Oh, my giddy aunt!" she cried, crumpling the little scraps of paper in her hand and dashing out without further conversation. The surprised clerk had not the time to even wish her a good evening, merely bowing to her retreating back.

"Ivy! Mrs. Tunstell! Ivy! We must return to the hotel directly!" Alexia yelled upon exiting the offices.

But Ivy and the children, having grown tired of waiting in the street, were busy exploring the exotic world around them. Some species of little old lady in black robes, her face wrinkled into obscurity, was telling an animated story to a highly appreciative audience on the far side of the street. The crowd participated and responded to her words with cries of excitement. Ivy stood among the watchers, with Primrose on one hip and Percival on the other. Behind her was the nursemaid and the donkey with Ivy's parasol and the babies' hats. Prudence, however, was nowhere to be seen.

Seized by additional panic, Alexia dashed over, narrowly missing being hit by a cart full of oranges. The vendor hurled obscenities at her. Alexia shook her parasol at him.

"Ivy, Ivy, where is Prudence? We must return to the hotel directly."

"Oh, Alexia! This lady is an *Antari*, a singer of tales. Isn't she marvelous? Of course, I can't understand a word, but simply listen to the verbal intonations. And her projection is one of the finest I've ever experienced, even on the London stage. Such somnolence. Or do I mean resonance? Anyway, would you look at this crowd? They are riveted! Tunny would be so intrigued. Do you think we should go back to the hotel and wake him?"

"Ivy, *where is my daughter*?!"

"Oh. Oh, yes, of course. Just there." Ivy gestured with her chin. When Alexia still looked about frantically, she said, "Here, hold Tidwinkle," and passed Primrose off to her.

Alexia adjusted the little girl in her arms, and Primrose became fascinated by the white ruffles on the hem of her parasol. Alexia gave it to her obligingly to hold.

One arm now free, Ivy pointed into the crowd to the very front, where Alexia could just make out her daughter, sitting cross-legged and hatless in the dust of the road, exactly like the Antari, absorbing the story with great interest.

"Oh, really, has she no decorum at all?" wondered her mother, relieved beyond measure, but also back to frantic rushing, in the hopes that she might make it to the hotel in time to stop Conall from reading that letter.

Alexia was making her way back to the nursemaid to deposit Primrose so she could go scoop up her own daughter when something unpleasant happened. A group of white-clad, turbaned men descended upon her and surrounded her. Their faces were all veiled like those of Egyptian females, and their intent was clearly hostile. They were grabbing and pulling at her, trying to separate her from Primrose, or perhaps from her purse or parasol; it was difficult to tell.

Primrose set up a thin wail of discouragement and wrapped her chubby arms more firmly around Alexia's parasol like a good little assistant accessory guardian. Alexia used her free hand to beat off their attackers, exclaiming in anger and whirling about as much as possible, making it difficult for any to find purchase on her or the baby. It was not good odds, and she seemed to have no free moment at all to grab the parasol and bring the full capacity of its arsenal into the fray.

Help came from a most unlikely quarter. Perhaps it was motherly instinct, or perhaps being an actress had somehow expanded her gumption over the intervening years, or perhaps she felt it more appropriate as a member of the Parasol Protectorate, but Ivy Tunstell waded into the fray. Clutching Percy with one arm, she screamed her version of obscenities. "How dare you? You ruffians!" And, "Cads! Unhand my friend." And, "Can't you see there is a child involved? Behave!"

The nursemaid, donkey in tow, also joined the kerfuffle. She was wielding Ivy's parasol with a skill Alexia quite admired, bashing at the men and also yelling.

The storyteller paused in her recitation when it became clear that a pair of foreign ladies with children were under assault. No decent person, not even a native of this wild land, would condone such a thing in the middle of the street.

Their entertainment curtailed, the crowd pressed back against the men. The street was alive with flying limbs and staccato Arabic shouting. Alexia, fist flying, elbows prodding, did her best to keep herself and Primrose from being injured or separated, but there were many men all constantly grasping at her with brutal intent.

Suddenly she found herself seized by the shoulders and dragged out of the milling throng into the comparative safety of an alleyway. She looked up, panting slightly from the exertion, to thank her rescuer, only to find she was face-to-face with the balloon nomad from the bazaar. She would recognize that handsome face with its neatly trimmed beard anywhere. He nodded at her once, in a friendly manner.

Alexia took stock of her situation. She seemed to have only a few bruises to show for the battle. Primrose was still crying but was safe in her arms, parasol firmly clasped to her little breast.

Alexia felt a weight against her legs and looked down to see that Prudence had glommed on to her skirts and was looking up at her with wide, frightened eyes. "Whoa, Mama," she said.

"Indeed." *Well that is two accounted for.*

The Drifter dove back into the crowd, robe flapping behind him, while Alexia extracted her parasol from Primrose and armed the tip. One of the white-clad men broke away and made for her, murder in his eyes, and

Alexia shot him in the chest without compunction. The numbing dart was only partly effective on supernatural creatures, but it brought that daylight thug down before he took even one more step in their direction. He crumpled in a heap of white fabric to the dirty street. Then her mysterious savior reappeared, dragging behind him a screaming and thrashing Ivy Tunstell.

"He seems to be on our side, Ivy. Do stop fussing."

"Oh, oh, dear, Alexia. Can you believe? Why I never, in all life's flutterings!"

Ivy looked a little worse for wear. Her hat was gone, her hair loose, and her dress torn. Percival was red-faced and crying like his sister, but otherwise both seemed unbowed. The nursemaid, still with donkey—remarkably placid and undisturbed by the ruckus—came behind them.

Ivy plunked her squalling child into one of the panniers and Alexia did the same with Primrose. The twins continued their thin treble wails of distress but remained inside their respective baskets.

Alexia bent and lifted Prudence up. Her daughter was sobered by the experience, although much less overset by the excitement than the two younger infants. Not a tear tracked down the dust covering her face. In fact, her eyes glittered with hidden excitement.

"Oh-ah Eeegypt!" she said as a kind of commentary.

"Yes, dear," agreed her mother.

Ivy leaned back against the donkey, fanning herself with one gloved hand. "Alexia, I am quite overset. Do you realize we were attacked! Right here, in a public thoroughfare. Really, I feel quite faint."

"Well, can it wait? We must make for safety."

"Oh, my, yes, of course. And I could hardly faint with a bare head in a foreign country! I might catch something," Ivy exclaimed.

"Exactly."

Their bearded savior gestured. "This way, lady."

With no other options—Ivy having dropped her guidebook in the excitement—they followed.

The Drifter set a brisk pace through hidden streets and alleys, up small sets of stone steps in a direction Alexia could only hope was toward their hotel. She was beginning to worry that they might have gone from boiler to steam engine, trading one danger for another. She shifted so that her parasol pointed at the man's unprotected back, wary that she still did not recognize the city around them.

Then at long last, they burst out onto a familiar square and saw the front entrance to Hotel des Voyageurs sitting in peaceful serenity before them across a bustling bazaar. Alexia glanced over to thank their guide, but the man had melted off into the crowd, leaving the ladies to make their way this last little bit without escort.

"What a mysterious gentleman," commented Alexia.

"He probably had to make it back to his balloon."

"Oh?"

"Baedeker says that the balloons heat during the early part of the day and rise up. Most Drifters allow them to sink back down at night as they cool, wherever they are in the desert, until the morning heat again. He said that once the balloon is up, a Drifter will never allow it back down again until evening," Ivy explained as they pushed their way through the milling throng.

"How very ingenious."

"So, you see, his home is probably sinking. He has to go meet it or he wouldn't know where it landed."

"Oh, Ivy, I hardly think..." Alexia trailed off.

Lord Conall Maccon stood in the doorway to the hotel, holding a letter in one hand, and he did not look pleased.

CHAPTER THIRTEEN

In Which Idle Letters Waste Lives

Alexia Maccon adored her husband and she should never wish to cause him any pain. He was a sensitive werewolf type, unfortunately, for all her efforts, prone to extremes in emotion and with a particular, perhaps even obsessive, regard for such noble concepts as honor, loyalty, and trust.

"Wife."

"Good evening, husband. How was your repose?" Alexia paused at the threshold to the hotel, trying to angle herself to the side so they did not entirely block the entranceway. Given her husband's bulk, this was no mean feat.

"Never mind repose. I have received a most upsetting letter."

"Ah, yes, well. I can explain."

"Oh, ho?"

"Do you think we might repair to our room to discuss the matter?"

The earl ignored this entirely sensible suggestion. Alexia supposed she was in for a well-deserved bout of public humiliation. Behind Conall's looming form, in the foyer of Hotel des Voyageurs, she could see guests turn to look at the tableau in the doorway. Her husband had raised his voice rather more than was common, even for Alexandria.

Lord Maccon boasted a barrel chest and companion booming vocalization at the best of times. As this was the worst of times, he could have roused the undead—and probably did in some areas of the city. "Randolph Lyall, that squirrely snot-nosed plonker, rigged the whole darn thing: caused Kingair tae betray me, got me tae come tae Woolsey, saw me eliminate his old Alpha. All of it! He never saw fit tae tell me this little fact." The earl's tawny eyes were narrowed and yellow in fury, and it looked as though a bit of canine was showing out the corners of his mouth.

His voice went very cold and clipped. It was terrifying. "Apparently, *you* know all of this, wife. And you dinnae tell me. I canna quite ken tae such a thing. But my own great-great-great-granddaughter assures me of the truth of it, and why should she lie?"

Alexia raised her hands, placating. "Now, Conall, please look at this from my perspective. I didn't *want* to keep it secret. I really didn't. But I saw how upset you were about Kingair and that betrayal. I couldn't bear to see you hurt again if I told you about Lyall. He didn't know you intimately way back when. He had no thought to your loss. He was trying to save his pack."

"Oh, trust me, Alexia. I ken what old Lord Woolsey was like. And I ken verra well what Lyall was up against.

I can even ken what love and loss drove him tae do. But tae keep such a secret from me even after we became kin? After I had grown tae trust him? And worse, that you should do the same! You who have nothing like his excuse."

Alexia bit her lower lip, worried. "But, Conall, even knowing how awful it was for him, Lyall and I both knew you would never trust him again. And you need him—he is a good Beta."

Lord Maccon looked at her, even more coldly than before. "Make no bones about it, Alexia. I *need* no one! Least of all a wife like you and a Beta like *that*! If you owe me naught else in this marriage, you owe me truth about pack! I wouldna ask for truth in anything else. But *my pack*, Alexia? It was your duty tae tell me the moment you found out!"

"Well, to be fair, at the time I had other things on my mind. There was an octomaton, and Prudence to be born—you know, little trifles like that." Alexia tried to smile weakly, knowing there could be no real excuse.

"Are you making light of this, woman?"

"Oh, dear. Conall, I *wanted* to tell you! I really did. I simply knew you would react...well, you know."

"Do I?"

She sighed. "Badly. I knew you would react badly."

"Badly! You have no idea how bad this is going to get."

"See?"

"So you thought you might wait it out, that I shouldna find out?"

"Well, I thought perhaps, since I'm a mortal, I might at least die first."

"Don't go playing the sympathy card with me, woman.

I know verra well you'll be dying afore me." Then he sighed.

The earl was such a massive man, yet as Alexia watched in concern, he seemed to shrink in upon himself. He leaned back against the side of the door, old and tired. "I canna believe you would do this tae me. Alexia, I *trusted* you."

It was said in such a small, little boy voice that Alexia felt her own heart contract in response to his pain. "Oh, Conall. What can I say? I thought it was for the best. I thought you would be happier not knowing."

"You thought, you thought. Never did you *think* it might be better tae have been told by you than to have you ally against me? You have made a chump of me. To hell with the lot of you." With that, he crumpled the letter and tossed it to the street before striding off into the crowded city.

"Where are you going? Please, Conall!" Alexia called after him, but he only raised one hand into the air in disregard and strode away.

"And with no top hat," came a small addendum comment from behind her.

Alexia turned in a daze, having entirely forgotten until that moment that Mrs. Tunstell, the nursemaid, the children, and the donkey—all of them grubby, sunburned, and tear-stained—stood waiting patiently to enter the hotel, except the donkey, although he probably wouldn't have minded going inside.

Alexia could only blink down at Ivy, experiencing a kind of emotional distress heretofore alien to her makeup. Oh, Conall had been angry at her in the past, but to the best of *her* knowledge, he had never been in the right before. "Oh, Ivy. I am so very sorry. I forgot you were there."

"Goodness, that doesn't happen often," replied Ivy. Although she had heard much of the conversation, she was ignorant as to the significance of the tirade, for she asked at that juncture, looking with concern into her dear friend's ashen face, "Why, Alexia, my dear, are you quite well?"

"No, Ivy, I am not. I do believe my marriage may be in ruins."

"Well, it's a good thing we are in the land of such things, then, isn't it?"

"What things?"

"Ruins."

"Oh, Ivy, *really*."

"Not even a smile? You must truly be afflicted by sentimental upset. Do you feel faint? I've never known you to faint, but I suppose one is never too young to start trying."

Then, much to Ivy's shock and Alexia's horror, the bold-as-brass Lady Maccon—paragon of assertive behavior and wielder of stoicism, parasols, and the occasional cryptic remark—burst into tears, right there on the front step of a public hostelry in central Alexandria.

Mrs. Tunstell, horrified beyond measure, wrapped one consoling arm about her friend and hustled her quickly inside Hotel des Voyageurs and into a private side parlor where she called for tea and instructed the nursemaid to see that the children were cleaned and put down for a nap. Alexia had just enough presence of mind to babble out that under no circumstances was anyone to attempt to bathe Prudence.

Alexia continued to blubber incoherently and Ivy to pat her hand sympathetically. Mrs. Tunstell was clearly at a loss as to what else she might do to allay her friend's anguish.

Tunstell appeared in the doorway at one point, riding atop Prudence's mechanical ladybug—he had always been fond of ladybugs—his knees up by his ears and grinning like a maniac. Even that failed to cheer Alexia. Ivy sent her husband off with a quick shake of her head and a stern, "Tunny, this is a serious matter. Bug off. We are not to be disturbed."

"But, light of my life, what has happened to your hat?"

"Never mind that now. I have an emotional crisis on my hands."

Tunstell, shaken to the core by the fact that his wife was clearly not disturbed by the loss of one of her precious bonnets, elected to take Alexia's tears seriously and stopped smiling. "My goodness, what can I do?"

"Do? Do! Men are useless in such matters. Go see what is delaying the tea!"

Tunstell and the mechanical ladybug trundled away.

Finally a beverage did arrive, but it was once again honey-sweetened coffee, not tea. This only made Alexia cry harder. What she wouldn't give for a cup of strong Assam with a dollop of quality British milk and a piece of treacle tart. Her world was crumbling around her!

She sobbed. "Oh, Ivy, what am I to do? He will never trust me again." She must have been feeling quite undone to ask Mrs. Ivy Tunstell for advice.

Ivy clasped Alexia's hand in both of hers and made sympathetic shushing noises. "There, there, Alexia, it will all be all right."

"How will it be all right? I lied to him."

"Oh, but you've done that heaps of times."

"Yes, but this time it was about something that matters. Something he cares about. And it was wrong of me to do it. And I knew it was wrong but I did it anyway. Oh, blast Professor Lyall. How could he get me into this mess? And blast my father, too! If he hadn't gone off and gotten himself killed, none of this would have happened."

"Now, Alexia, language."

"Right when I have important information about this plague and I need Conall here to help me figure out the particulars. But, no, he has to go storming off. And it's all destroyed, all lost."

"Really, Alexia, I've never known you to be fatalistic before."

"Too many viewings of *The Death Rains of Swansea*, I suppose."

There came a bustle at the door and another familiar face peeked in. "What on earth has happened? Alexia, are you well? Is it Prudence?" Madame Lefoux came hurrying into the room. Tossing her hat and gloves carelessly aside, she dashed over to the divan and sat next to Alexia, on the other side from Ivy.

Lacking Mrs. Tunstell's natural British reticence, the Frenchwoman scooped Alexia into a full embrace, wrapping her bony arms around her friend and pressing her cheek to the top of Alexia's dark head. She stroked Alexia's back up and down in long, affectionate caresses, which reminded Alexia of Conall and made the tears, which were almost under control, start up once more.

Genevieve looked at Ivy curiously. "Why, Mrs. Tunstell, whatever could cause our Alexia to be so overset?"

"She has had a most trying argument with her husband. Something to do with a letter, and Professor Lyall, and a trifle, and some treacle, I believe."

"Oh, dear, it sounds gummy."

The absurdity of Ivy's interpretation was the boost Alexia needed to rein in her runaway sentimentality. *Really*, she thought, *there is no point in wallowing. I must get myself in order and come up with a way to fix this.* She took a deep, shaky breath and a long sip of the horrible coffee to calm her nerves. She then developed a bad case of the hiccoughs, because, as she could only surmise, the universe was against her retaining any dignity whatsoever.

"Old history," she said at last. "With werewolves, it is never so very well buried as one might hope. Suffice it to say that Conall has discovered something and I am to blame in part for his not knowing it to start with. He is not happy about this. Sticky, indeed."

Genevieve, sensing Alexia was beginning to recover, let her go and sat back, pouring herself a cup of coffee.

Mrs. Tunstell, wishing to provide some distraction while Alexia composed her emotions, began prattling on about their adventures at the bazaar in highly embellished terms. Madame Lefoux listened attentively and gasped in all the right places, and by the time the telling was complete, Alexia was feeling better, if not entirely up to snuff.

Alexia turned the full focus of her attention onto the French inventor. "And how about you, Genevieve? I trust your explorations about the metropolis have proved more enjoyable than ours?"

"Well, they were certainly less exciting. I had a matter of business to conduct. It seems, however, to have opened up more questions than it answered."

"Oh?"

"Yes."

Alexia took a gamble. "While I know that ostensibly the countess sent you along to keep an eye on me and figure out what Matakara wants with Prudence, I don't suppose your true purpose in visiting Egypt is to investigate the expansion of the God-Breaker Plague for the OBO. Is it?"

Genevieve dimpled at her. "Ah. I see. You've noticed it, too, have you?"

"Conall and I suspected as much the evening we arrived, and a missive from Biffy recently confirmed it. Some fifty years ago, or thereabouts, it began an accelerated push."

Madame Lefoux tilted her head in acknowledgment. "Actually, we are thinking that it was more like forty."

"You have an idea of what might have set it into motion?"

"Well…," Madame Lefoux hedged.

"Genevieve, we have been through this before. Don't you think it wiser simply to tell me what you are thinking? It saves burning half of London and having to build weapons of immense tentaclization."

The Frenchwoman pursed her lips and then nodded. She stared for a moment at Ivy out of suspicious green eyes and then finally said, "I suppose. It's not that we know exactly what caused it, more that there is a terrible coincidence. How to put this? You see, Alexia, your father happened to be in Egypt right about that time."

"Of course he was." Alexia wasn't surprised in the slightest by this information. "But, Genevieve, how would you know a thing like that? Even with all your contacts."

"Ah, yes, that. Well, that's the problem. Alessandro Tarabotti was working for the OBO at the time."

"It was after he broke with the Templars? Go on. There must be more."

"Well, yes, yes, there is. He came here and something happened, and he abandoned the OBO with no warning."

"That sounds like my father. He wasn't particularly loyal to any organization."

"Ah, but he took half the OBO underground information network with him."

Alexia had a sinking sensation. "Dead?"

"No, turned. They stayed alive, only working for him instead of us. And we never did get them back, even after he died."

Alexia felt a slight wiggle of butterflies in her stomach, which she was beginning to label her *sensation of significance*. Something was, quite defiantly, *up*.

"It's sealed under the Clandestine Scientific Information Act of 1855." Professor Lyall sat down with a thump next to Biffy on the small settee in the back parlor. He shoved him over gently to make room. Biffy bumped back against him affectionately but moved. Lyall had just returned from BUR and he smelled like a London night, etching acid, and the Thames.

"Have you been swimming?"

The Beta ignored this to continue his complaint. "It's all sealed."

"What is?"

"Records to do with Egypt, for a period of twelve years, starting right about the time the plague began to expand. Familiarity with clandestine-level scientific secrets is beyond my rank and authority. Especially mine, as no supernaturals, drones, clavigers, or persons with suspected excess soul are allowed access. I was working for BUR at the time, and I didn't know anything about the Clandestine Scientific Information Act until after it had passed into law." Professor Lyall seemed mildly annoyed by this. It wasn't that he was particularly troubled by not knowing, in the way of Lord Akeldama, it was more that he did not approve of anything that upset the efficient running of pack life or BUR duties.

Biffy thought back to some bits of information that Lord Akeldama had once let slip. "Wasn't the Clandestine Act linked to the last of the intelligencers before they were disbanded?"

"Under the previous potentate, yes. It also had something to do with the Great Picklemen Revolt and the disposal of patents of domestic servitude. What a mess things were in those days."

"Well, that's that, then." From what Biffy could recall, very serious action had been taken and there was nothing even the hives could do to countermand the restrictions that were put into place as a consequence.

"Not entirely. All this material about Egypt is locked under a cipher, and that cipher is linked to the code name of a known provocateur. A provocateur whose loyalties were unreliable and true allegiance unknown."

"Yes?"

"Fortunately, his is a cipher I know, without having to go up against the Clandestine Act."

"Oh?" Biffy sat up a little straighter, intrigued.

"He went by Panattone, but his real name was Alessandro Tarabotti."

Biffy started. "Again? My goodness, your former amour certainly had his fingers in many pies."

"Preternaturals are like that. You should know their ways by now."

"Of course—worse than Lord Akeldama. He has to know everyone's business. Lady Maccon has to know everyone's business *and* interfere in it."

Professor Lyall turned to face Biffy fully on the small couch, placing his hand on the young werewolf's knee. His calm demeanor might have been slightly shaken, although not a hair was out of place. Biffy wondered if he might persuade him to share this secret.

"The thing is, he was there. I *know* Sandy was there. It's in his journals—several trips to Egypt starting in 1835. But there is nothing about what he did while he was there nor the name of his actual employer. I knew he was involved in some pretty dark dealings, but to require an official seal?"

"You think it might have something to do with the God-Breaker Plague, don't you?"

"I think preternaturals, mummies, and the God-Breaker Plague go together better than custard and black-currant jelly. Alessandro Tarabotti was one powerful preternatural."

Biffy wasn't comfortable with Lyall talking about his former lover in such a reverent tone, but he kept his mind on the business in question, finding reassurance in the fact that Lyall's hand was still on his knee. "Well, I have only one suggestion. And Egypt is not exactly his forté. But you know..."

"We should see what Lord Akeldama has to say on the matter?"

"You suggested it, not me." Biffy tilted his head and examined Lyall's sharp vulpine face for signs of jealousy. Unable to discern any, he stood and offered the Beta a quite unnecessary hand up. *Any excuse for a touch.*

The two men clapped top hats to their heads and made their way next door to call upon the vampire in question.

Lord Akeldama's house was in an uproar. A very frazzled-looking drone opened the door a good five minutes after they had yanked on the bellpull for the third time.

"Werewolf on the loose?" asked Professor Lyall casually.

Biffy pretended to blush, remembering just such an incident a few years back when he had broken into his former master's abode. He had written a long letter of apology but had never quite recovered from the humiliation. Lord Akeldama had been decent about the whole incident, which somehow made it worse.

"No, not so bad as that, but something untoward certainly has happened." Biffy looked around, eyes bright with curiosity.

A gaggle of excited drones rushed through the hallway at that juncture, carrying various-sized empty jam jars. Two of the drones were wearing large brown leather gloves.

"What ho, Biffy," called out one excitedly.

"Boots, what's afoot?" Biffy asked.

Boots separated from the gaggle and slid to a stop before the two werewolves. "Oh, it's all go around here! Shabumpkin let loose a lizard in the front parlor."

"A lizard? Whatever for?"

"Just because, I suppose."

"I see."

"Can't seem to catch the darn thing."

"Big lizard is it?"

"Huge! Almost the size of my thumb. No idea where Shabumpkin got it. Cracking teal color."

Then came a crash from said front parlor and a deal of squealing. Boots hastily excused himself and went dashing after the sound.

Biffy turned to Professor Lyall, grinning. "A lizard."

"Massive one," agreed the Beta, pretending seriousness.

"It's all go at Lord Akeldama's place."

"As if I would have it any differently!" sang out the vampire himself, wafting in to greet them on a wave of lemon pomade and champagne cologne. "Did you hear what that *silly* boy let loose in my house? A reptile of all things. As if I should admit any creature *born out of an egg*. I don't even like poultry. *Never* trust a chicken— that's what I say. But enough about my little problems. How are you, my *fuzzy darlings*? To what do I owe the honor of this visit?"

Lord Akeldama was wearing a black-and-white-checked jacket with black satin trousers, the beginnings of what might have been subtle and elegant evening dress. Except that he had paired this with a burnt umber waistcoat and orange spats.

He received them with every sign of pleasure and led them into his drawing room with alacrity. Once seated, however, his bright blue eyes darted back and forth between the two werewolves with a hint of suspicion. Had the opportunity presented itself, and had it not been a delicate and highly personal matter, Biffy might have tried to tell his former lord of his new sleeping arrangements. But the opportunity did not arise, nor was it likely to. One did not, after all, gossip about oneself. It was simply *not done*.

Lord Akeldama's drones, however, would be pretty poor spies if they had not already informed their master as to the Beta's new chew toy, which meant that Lord Akeldama's odd expression was one of a man hunting for confirmation. It wounded Biffy deeply to know that he might be causing his former master emotional pain, but it had been two years, and he was tolerably assured that Lord Akeldama had moved on to better, younger, and more mortal morsels himself. Werewolves also liked to gossip about their neighbors.

As was often the case with Lord Akeldama, while he seemed to be doing a good deal of the talking, in the end Biffy and Lyall found themselves transferring to him the bulk of the information. Professor Lyall was not happy with this, but Biffy was comfortable knowing that the vampire enjoyed collecting information, but rarely did he put it to any concrete use. He was rather like a little old biddy who collected demitasse teacups that she then set upon a shelf to admire.

Biffy found himself telling Lord Akeldama all about Egypt and the expansion of the God-Breaker Plague. Lyall was convinced to tell him what he could about Alessandro Tarabotti and his trips to Egypt and how they all might be connected.

Once they had relayed all they could, the two werewolves stopped and sat, looking expectantly at the thin blond vampire as he twirled his monocle about in the air and frowned up at his cherub-covered ceiling.

Finally the vampire said, "My furry *darlings*, this is all very interesting indeed, but I fail to see how I could possibly be of any assistance. Or how this might connect to that tiny upset the Kingair Pack experienced. Losing a Beta. So sad. When was it? Last week or the week before?"

"Well, Dubh did say something to Lady Maccon about Alessandro," said Lyall.

Lord Akeldama stopped twirling the monocle and sat up straighter. "And there is Matakara to consider. The hive queen wanted to meet *my little puggle*. And the puggle is your Alessandro's granddaughter. You are correct to be suspicious, Dolly dear. But there are so many threads, and it is not so much that you are trying to untangle them, as weave them back into a pattern someone else already set."

The vampire stood and began to mince around the room. "You are missing something key, and while I should hate to mention it, given his *most excellent* service, there is only one person who knows what happened— *what really happened*—to your Sandy when he was in Egypt, my dear Dolly."

Biffy and Lyall looked at one another. They both knew to whom Lord Akeldama was referring.

Lyall said, "It's always difficult to get him to talk."

Biffy said, "I've often wondered if he could say anything more than the obligatory 'yes, sir.'"

Lord Akeldama smiled, showing his teeth. "So, lovely boys, in this instance it is not me you want for information. Who knew I should ever be outclassed by a butler?"

Professor Lyall and Biffy stood, bowing politely, knowing that what Lord Akeldama said was true and that they might be facing, for the first time in their collective careers in covert inquiry, a true challenge: convincing Floote to talk.

They tracked Lady Maccon's butler down to the kitchen where he was overseeing the menus for next week's repasts.

Biffy had never really looked at Floote before. One didn't, as a rule, examine one's domestic staff too closely. They might think it interfering. Floote was the perfect servant, always there when needed, always knowing what was desired, sometimes before the sensation registered in his employers.

Professor Lyall said softly, "Mr. Floote, might we have a moment of your time?"

The butler looked up at them. A nondescript man with a nondescript face, he could outdo Professor Lyall at his own game. Biffy noticed for the first time how weather-beaten Floote's skin was and that there were deep wrinkles about his nose and mouth and the corners of his eyes. He noticed that the butler's shoulders, once ramrod straight, were beginning to curve with age. Floote had acted as valet to Alessandro Tarabotti, so far as Biffy knew, since Alexia's father first appeared in the Bureau's official registry. Floote had worked for Alexia after that. *He must be*, thought Biffy, *well over seventy years of age!* He'd never even thought to ask.

"Of course, sirs," said Floote. There was some wariness in his tone.

They adjourned into the back parlor, leaving the cook and the housekeeper to finish the menu without Floote's input. Floote did not seem happy with this arrangement.

Professor Lyall gestured with one of his fine white

hands, his vulpine face pinched. "Please, take a seat, Mr. Floote."

Floote would do nothing of the kind. To sit in front of his betters? Never! Biffy knew the man's character well enough to know that. So did Lyall, of course, but the Beta was trying to make the man uncomfortable.

Lyall asked the questions while Biffy simply crossed his arms and observed the butler's behavior. He had been trained in just such a skill by Lord Akeldama. He watched the way Floote's eyebrows moved slightly, the dilation of his pupils, and the shifting of weight in his knees. But very little changed about the butler during the course of the questioning, and Floote's responses were always abbreviated. Either the man had nothing to hide, or Biffy was in the presence of a master whose skills far exceeded his own powers of observation.

"Sandy was in Egypt at least three times, according to his journals, but he makes few comments as to his business there. What happened the first time?"

"Nothing of consequence, sir."

"And the second?"

"He met Leticia Phinkerlington, sir."

"Alexia's mother?"

Floote nodded.

"Yes, but what else did he *do* in Egypt? He can't have gone merely to court a girl."

No response came from Floote.

"Can you tell us who he was working for, at the very least?"

"The Templars, sir. It was always the Templars, right up until he broke with them."

"And when was that?"

"After you and he . . . sir."

"But he went to Egypt after that. I remember his going. Why? Who was he working for then? It wasn't us, was it? I mean, England or BUR. I know Queen Victoria tried to recruit him. She offered him the position of muhjah. He turned it down."

Floote blinked at Professor Lyall.

The Beta began to get a little frustrated.

"Floote, you must give us something. Unless . . . Are you, too, sealed into silence under the Clandestine Act?"

Floote nodded the tiniest of nods.

"You *are*! Of course, that would make perfect sense. You couldn't talk to any of us, not even Lady Maccon, because we are all enemy agents under the terms of that act. It prevents supernaturals and their associates, including preternaturals, from access to certain scientific information. Or that's the rumor. I don't know the particulars, of course."

Floote only gave one of his little nods again.

"So Sandy discovered something in Egypt so severe it was included under the act even though it was outside the homeland. For the good of the Commonwealth."

Floote did not react.

Professor Lyall seemed to think they would get nothing more useful out of the butler. "Very well, Floote, you may return to your menu planning. I'm certain Cook has made a botch of it without your supervision."

"Thank you, sir," said Floote with a hint of relief before gliding quietly out.

"What do you think?" Lyall turned to Biffy.

Biffy shrugged. He thought that Floote still had more information. He also thought that Floote didn't want to tell them, even if he could. He thought there was something else going on—that it wasn't just acts of parliament and games of politics and science. He thought that Lyall would want to believe the best of Lady Maccon's father, no matter how unworthy the gentleman. If Alessandro Tarabotti had been doing good deeds during any one of his visits to Egypt, he, Sandalio de Rabiffano, would eat his own cravat. Under the Templars, the OBO, or his government, Mr. Tarabotti was a nasty piece of work.

Instead of any of these things, Biffy said, "Mr. Tarabotti broke with the Templars out of love, not principle. Or so I thought. But you would understand the man's character far better than I."

Professor Lyall hung his head and looked like he might be hiding a small smile. "I see your point. You think that something more than a major act of parliament would be required to influence Sandy."

"Don't you?"

"So while Floote may be obeying the law, something else was keeping Sandy silent about Egypt for those few years we had together before he died?"

Biffy only raised his eyebrows, allowing the Beta time to think through what he had known of his former lower.

Lyall nodded slowly. "You are probably right."

CHAPTER FOURTEEN

―――――

Wherein Alexia Loans Mr. Tumtrinkle Her Gun

The Tunstells had been encouraged by Chancellor Neshi to perform an encore of *The Death Rains of Swansea* at a local theater for the benefit of the public. The theater was open air, much in the manner of Ancient Rome. Alexia was persuaded to attend and endure a third viewing of the dratted spectacle in an effort to distract her from her worries. Lord Maccon was still off in his huff when they departed for the theater.

The play was as much admired by the masses as it had been by the vampire hive. Or at least Lady Maccon *believed* it was much admired. It was difficult to determine with any accuracy, when praise was heaped upon the theatricals in a tongue entirely alien to all. However, the approbation did seem genuine. Lady Maccon, patroness, waited for Mr. and Mrs. Tunstell afterward, but so, too, did a collection of excited Egyptians, eager to touch the hero and heroine of the play, press small gifts into their hands, and in one extreme case kiss the hem of Ivy's gown.

Ivy Tunstell took such accolades in stride as her due, nodding and smiling. "Very kind" and "Thank you very much" and "Oh, you really shouldn't have" were her pat responses, although no one understood her any more than she them. Alexia thought, if she was reading body language properly, that the locals were convinced that the Tunstells' Acting Troupe a la Mode represented some species of prophesiers of the American tent-preacher variety. Even the secondary actors, like Mr. Tumtrinkle, seemed to have gained unexpected notoriety and companion acclaim.

Alexia congratulated her friends on yet another fine performance. And, since it looked like otherwise they might never leave, the group wended their way back to the hotel on foot, followed by a collective band of sycophants and admirers. They made quite the raucous crowd through the otherwise quiet streets of Alexandria.

It was only a few hours before dawn, but Alexia was not surprised to find, when she inquired after her key at the hotel, that Lord Maccon had not yet returned. Still angry, she supposed.

They were making their farewells for the evening, Mrs. Tunstell solicitous in her care for Lady Maccon's low spirits, particularly in light of the buoyancy that admiration had given her own. The hotel was busy trying to eject the legion of Tunstell devotees, when a vision of horror came down the stairs and into the hotel reception area.

No one would have described poor Mrs. Dawaud-Plonk as attractive, even at the very best of times. The Tunstells' nursemaid had not been selected for her looks but for her ability to tolerate twins plus Mrs. Tunstell, while not crumbling under a strain that would have felled lesser females. She was old enough to be mostly gray, but not so old that her limbs had been sapped of the strength needed to carry two infants at once. She wasn't particularly tall, but she was sturdy, with the arms of a boxer and the general expression of a bulldog. Mrs. Dawaud-Plonk, Alexia supposed, had some species of hearty leather armchair somewhere in her ancestry. However, the Mrs. Dawaud-Plonk who came down those stairs that early morning was far from sturdy. In fact, she looked to have cracked at last. Her face was a picture of horror, her normally tidy pinafore was wrinkled, her cap was askew, and her graying hair fell loose about her shoulders. She clutched Percival to her breast. The baby boy was crying, his face as red as his hair.

Upon catching sight of Lady Maccon and the Tunstells' party, she cried out, raising her free hand to her throat, and said, on great gulping sobs of terror, "They're gone!"

Alexia broke free of the crowd and went up to her.

"The babies, the babies are gone."

"What!" Alexia brushed past the distraught nursemaid and charged up the stairs to the nursery room.

The chamber was in an uproar, furniture overturned, probably by the distraught nursemaid in her panic. The Tunstells' two bassinets were empty, as was Prudence's little cot.

Alexia felt her stomach wrench up into the most tremendous knot and a cold, icy fear trickled through her whole body. She whirled away from the room, already calling out instructions, although the hallway was empty behind her. Her voice was hard and authoritative. Then she heard, from behind her, a querulous little voice say, "Mama?"

Prudence came crawling out from under the bed, dusty, tear-stained, but present.

Alexia ran to her, crouching down to wrap her in a tight embrace. "Prudence, my baby! Did you hide? What a good, brave girl."

"Mama," said Prudence seriously, "no."

Alexia let her go slightly, grabbing on to her shoulders and speaking at her straight on. Grave brown eyes met grave brown eyes. "But where is Primrose? Did they take Primrose? Who took her, Prudence? Did you see?"

"No."

"Bad men took the baby. Who were they?"

Prudence only tossed her dark curls, pouted, and burst into unhelpful tears. Partially a response to her mother's frantic behavior, Alexia supposed, trying to calm herself.

"Dama!" the little girl wailed. She broke free of her mother's grasp and ran to the door, turning back to look at her mother. "Dama. Home. Home Dama," she insisted.

"No, dear, not yet."

"Now!"

Alexia marched over to her daughter and scooped up the child's struggling form. She strode back down the stairs into the hotel reception room, where all was still chaos.

Mrs. Dawaud-Plonk began to weep openly upon seeing Prudence clutched safely in Lady Maccon's arms and dashed over to coo over the toddler.

"Prudence hid under the bed, but it does look as though they took Primrose," announced Alexia baldly. "I am so very sorry, Ivy. Who knows why or what they want from a baby, but she is definitely gone."

Mrs. Tunstell let out a high keening wail and fainted back into her husband's arms. Tunstell looked as though he, too, might be in favor of fainting. His freckles stood out starkly against his white face and he stared at Alexia with desperate green eyes.

"I don't know where my husband is," replied Alexia, guessing at the nature of the plea in those eyes. "Of all the times for him to be off in a huff!"

The Tunstells were well loved by their troupe, so this misfortune threw all the other actors into sympathetic paroxysms of distress. The ladies fainted or had hysterics, whichever better suited their natures. Some of the gentlemen did the same. One ran out into the night with a fake sword, determined to track down the dastardly culprits. Mr. Tumtrinkle began stuffing his face with those little honey pastries and blubbering into his mustache. Percival was busy screaming his head off, only pausing to spit up all over anyone who came near.

Lady Maccon really could have used her husband's booming voice at that juncture. However, knowing the onus fell on her, and relieved her own daughter was accounted for, she took charge. Alexia was quite worried for Primrose's safety, but she was also clear on two fronts. Either the baby had been kidnapped in order to extract a ransom, in which case they could expect contact relatively soon, or they had the wrong baby, in which case they could expect her return momentarily. After all, why would anyone want the daughter of an actress? No matter how popular said actress was in Egypt.

Alexia cast a desperate look about for the only other person who might still have as level a head as she under such circumstances, but Madame Lefoux was nowhere to be found. She inquired of the hotel clerk, interposing herself in front of the poor man as he attempted to control the bedlam in his reception chamber.

"My good man"—Lady Maccon pulled him away from one of the hysterical actresses—"have you seen Madame Lefoux? One of our fellow travelers, the Frenchwoman inventor who dresses as a man. She might be useful at this juncture."

"No, madam." The man bowed hurriedly. "She's gone, madam."

"What do you mean *gone*?" Alexia did not like this turn of events. Now two ladies were missing! Well, Primrose was barely half a lady and Madame Lefoux dressed as a man, so Alexia supposed together they made up only one whole lady, but— Alexia shook herself out of spiraling thoughts and returned to the clerk.

"Left the hotel, madam, not one hour ago. Moving rather quickly, I must say."

Lady Maccon turned back to the pandemonium, a little floored. *Gone, Genevieve, but why?* Had she perhaps sent the kidnappers? Or was she on their trail? Or could it be that she was the kidnapper herself? *No, not Genevieve.* The Frenchwoman might build a massive octopus and terrorize a city, but that had been because someone kidnapped her own child. She would hardly put another mother through such an ordeal. *I suppose it could be coincidence?*

Still puzzling over the matter, Alexia stopped dead in the center of the room and took stock of her situation. "You—fetch smelling salts, and you—get cold compresses and wet towels. Everyone else—do be quiet!"

In very short order, she had the staff trotting to her

bidding. She ordered them not to touch the nursery, as the offenders could have left clues behind. She had them set up the still-hysterical nursemaid in a new room, one with very secure windows and better locks. She left her there with Prudence, Percy, Ivy, Mr. Tumtrinkle, and several other actors now restored to sense and ready to do battle. She gave Mr. Tumtrinkle her gun, as he assured her he had pointed many a prop firearm at many a hero in his day and shooting a real one could hardly be much different. Alexia assured him that she would be back as soon as possible and to please make certain he ascertained the truth of any enemy attack before shooting Ethel at *any-one*, particularly a hero.

She sent Tunstell to alert the local constabulary, the other actors and actresses back to their rooms, and the now-rather-worried-looking collective of Tunstell Troupe admirers off about their business. She had to use gesticulations, shushing sounds, and, eventually, a broom in order to accomplish this last.

The sky was beginning to pink and things were finally calm at Hotel des Voyageurs, when a dark shadow loomed in the doorway and Lord Maccon, wearing only a cloak and a sour expression, entered the room.

Alexia hurried up to him. "I know you are still angry with me, and you have a perfect right to be. It was beastly of me to keep the information from you, but we have a far more serious problem that needs your attention now."

The frown deepened. "Go on."

"Primrose appears to have been baby-napped. She was taken from her room several hours ago while the Tunstells were engaged in a performance. I was with them. Madame

Lefoux has also vanished. Apparently, the nursemaid was asleep and when she awoke, she found both Primrose and Prudence had disappeared."

"Prudence is gone, too?!" Lord Maccon roared.

The clerk, dozing fitfully behind his desk, snapped to attention with the expression of a man near to his breaking point.

Alexia put a hand on her husband's arm. "No, dear, do calm down. It turned out ours had taken refuge under a bed."

"That's my girl!"

"Yes, very sensible of her, although she seems to be having some difficulty describing the kidnappers to us."

"Well, she is only two."

"Yes, but as she really must learn coherent phrasing and syntax eventually, now would be an excellent time to complete the process. And she *has* let forth a complete sentence lately. I was hoping...never mind that now. The fact is, Primrose is gone and so is Genevieve."

"You believe Madame Lefoux took the baby?" The earl was frowning and chewing on his bottom lip in that darling way Alexia loved so much.

"No, I don't. But I think Madame Lefoux may be chasing the kidnappers. She was around the hotel at the time, and the clerk said she left in a great hurry. Perhaps she spotted something out her window. Her room is near the nursery."

"It's a possibility."

"I've sent Tunstell to the local authorities. I haven't let anyone into the room. I thought you might be able to smell something."

Lord Maccon nodded crisply, almost a salute. "I'm still

angry with you, wife. But I can't help but admire your efficiency in a crisis."

"Thank you. Shall we go check the scents?"

"Lead on."

Unfortunately, up the stairs and in the nursery, the earl smelled nothing of significance. He did say he thought he caught a whiff of Madame Lefoux and that it was possible she had grappled with the assailants or perhaps simply stuck her head in to see what had happened. It was also possible that it was a lingering remnant from the previous evening. He said he smelled a trace of the Egyptian streets about the place, but nothing more than that. Whoever had taken Primrose had hired ruffians to do it. He traipsed back out into the hallway, still sniffing.

"Ah," he said, "there is Madame Lefoux again— machine oil and vanilla. And here." He began walking back down the steps. "You know, wife, I do believe I have a fresh trail. I'm going after her." He dropped his cloak, revealing an impressive bare chest matted with hair, and shifted form. Luckily the lobby was deserted but for the extremely harried clerk who watched, openmouthed, as his esteemed guest, a real British earl, changed into a wolf right there in front of him.

The poor man's eyes rolled up into his head and he followed in the path of many a young lady that evening and fainted dead away behind the desk.

Alexia watched him fall, too dazed to make any effort to help him, and then turned back to her husband, now a wolf, carefully picking up his discarded cloak with his mouth.

"Conall, really, the sun is almost up. Do you think you'll have time...?"

But he was already gone, dashing out the door, nose lowered before him like a scent hound after a fox.

Lord Conall Maccon returned well after sunup. Alexia was coping with an utterly distraught Mrs. Tunstell. She had finally convinced Ivy to take a dram of poppy to quiet her nerves. At which point both Ivy and her nerves became rather floppy and confused.

Ivy managed to raise her head from where it bent low over Percy, asleep in her lap, when Lord Maccon tapped quietly at the door.

Mr. Tumtrinkle, seated facing the door with Alexia's gun in his lap, started violently and fired Ethel at the earl. Lord Maccon, slower than usual after a long evening's run and a good few hours dashing about as a human under the scorching heat of an Egyptian sun, ducked too late, but the bullet missed him.

Alexia tsked at the actor and put out her hand for the return of her pistol. The man handed it over, apologized profusely to Lord Maccon, and resumed his chair in embarrassed silence. Lady Maccon noted, however, that he did take one of the rapiers, tipped for use in stage fights and thus rather useless, and placed it to hand. Alexia supposed he could ferociously poke someone if he tried hard enough.

"Osh, Lord Maccon!" cried out Ivy, head lolling back and eyes rolling slightly. "Ish that you? Hash you any ... indigestion ... no ... information?"

The earl gave his wife a pained look.

"Laudanum," explained Alexia succinctly.

"Not as such, Mrs. Tunstell. I am very sorry. Wife, if you could spare me a moment?"

"Aleshia!"

"Yes, Ivy dear?"

"We should go dancing!"

"But, Ivy, we're in Egypt and your daughter is missing."

"But I can't see myself from here!"

Alexia stood up from where she was seated next to her nonsensical friend, experienced some difficulty in convincing Ivy to let go of her hand, and followed her husband out the door.

He spoke in a hushed voice. "I traced Madame Lefoux to the dahabiya docks. A peculiar sort of place. Lost the scent there. I'm afraid she may have boarded a ship. I'm going to go ascertain how Tunstell is getting on with the local authorities. Then I think we might need to notify the consular general. Bad publicity, very bad, a missing British baby on his watch."

Alexia nodded. "I'll go back to the docks, shall I? See if I can work my womanly charm and discover who accepted Madame Lefoux's fare and where she might be headed."

"You have womanly charm?" The earl was genuinely surprised. "I thought you simply harangued a blighter until he gave in."

Alexia gave him a look.

Lord Maccon snorted. "Only one direction to head if one is going by dahabiya."

"Up the Nile to Cairo?"

"Indeed."

"Well, they might at least tell a female if a passenger had a baby. They might even be convinced to say if she was chasing after someone."

"Very well, Alexia, but be careful, and take your parasol."

"Of course, Conall. I shall require a parasol, as the sun is up. Don't tell me you hadn't noticed."

"Yes, very amusing, wife."

Neither of them mentioned sleep, although Alexia was feeling the strain of having been awake since four the previous afternoon. Bed would have to wait; they had a baby to catch and a Frenchwoman to trace.

Biffy awoke before sunset and, after struggling with his hair for a quarter of an hour, returned to the maps he'd laid out of Egypt and the expansion of the God-Breaker Plague. He'd awakened with a certain feeling that he was missing something. He went back to the circles he'd drawn and reviewed notes on times indicating the plague's expansion and general location. He began to extrapolate inward, trying to determine its course. What if the plague had always been expanding, very slowly? What if there was a starting point?

He got so distracted he very nearly missed his appointment with Lady Maccon and the aethographor. He took the maps with him to the receiving chamber to await any missive, studying them carefully.

It was while he was waiting alone in that tiny attic room that he came upon the missing piece of the puzzle. All signs pointed to the fact that the epicenter for the God-Breaker Plague was near Luxor, at one prominent bend in the Nile River close to the Valley of the Kings. His books said very little on the archaeology of the area, but one report indicated that the bend housed the funerary temple of the expunged and vilified Pharaoh Hatshepsut. He had no idea how this might tie into the plague, but he resolved to send Lady Maccon the information, should she contact him that evening.

He was about to creep out and gather together some
acid and a metal slate when the receiving chamber activated, the metal particles between the receiver panes
shifted about, and a message appeared.

"Ruffled Parasol. Conall upset. Primrose kidnapped.
Uproar."

Biffy recoiled. What interest could Egyptian kidnappers possibly have in Mr. and Mrs. Tunstell's daughter?
The child of thespians. How odd. He awaited further
information but nothing more came through. He moved
next door, dialed in the appropriate frequensor codes, and
sent his message back.

"GBP center is Hatshepsut's temple, Nile River, Luxor.
Wingtip Spectator."

Silence met that and after a quarter of an hour, Biffy
supposed his message had been received and there was
nothing else to relate. He shut down the aethographor,
made certain his own missive was tucked securely away,
and ate the scrap of paper on which he'd scribbled Lady
Maccon's. He'd witnessed Lyall do so in the past with delicate information and figured it was a werewolf tradition
he'd better uphold. Then he went to find his Beta, not certain he was authorized to relay either bits of information.

It was in thinking about this, and wondering who
might kidnap Primrose and how Lady Maccon might be
coping with this new crisis—violently, he suspected—
that Biffy came upon another realization. Following that
realization to its inevitable, horrible conclusion, he detoured
toward the servants' quarters.

Floote was sitting alone at the massive table in the
kitchen, polishing the brass candlesticks, a sturdy apron
tied about his waist. His jacket was off and draped over

the back of a nearby chair. The moment he saw Biffy, he made a move toward it, but Biffy said hastily, "No, Floote, please don't trouble yourself. I simply had a question."

"Sir?"

"When Mr. Tarabotti traveled in Egypt, did he visit Luxor?" Biffy came casually over to Floote's shoulder, standing a little too close, pretending to inspect the polishing. He bent down as though particularly interested in one of the candlesticks and with one hand behind his back, quick as any vampire, snaked the tiny little gun out of the inside pocket of Floote's jacket.

Biffy tucked the gun up his own sleeve, wondering that there weren't more werewolf and vampire conjurers; sleight of hand was easy when one had supernatural abilities.

Floote answered him, "Yes, sir," without looking up from his polishing.

"Well, ahem, yes. Thank you, Floote, carry on."

"Very good, sir."

Biffy escaped to his own room where he locked the door and immediately took out the gun.

It was one of the smallest he had ever seen, beautifully made with a delicate pearl handle. It was of the single-shot variety popular some thirty years ago or more, outdated in this age of revolvers. It must be sentiment that urged Floote to keep it, for it wasn't the most useful of weapons. Difficult to hit anything at more than five paces and it probably shot crooked. Biffy swallowed, hoping against hope he wasn't about to find what he predicted. With a twist, he opened and checked the chamber. It was loaded. He tipped the bullet out into his hand. Such a small thing to damn a man so utterly. For that bullet was made of hardwood, capped in metal to take the heat and caged in silver. It was not quite the same as the modern ones, of course, but still undoubtedly a sundowner bullet.

At first Biffy didn't want to believe it, but Floote *had* been at liberty the night that Dubh was shot—with all his employers out of the house. Floote had access to Lord Akeldama's dirigible, for no drone would comment on Lady Maccon's butler coming and going from Lord Akeldama's house. Floote owned a gun that was loaded with sundowner bullets of exactly the kind with which Dubh was shot. Then later, when Lady Maccon rushed in with the injured man, Floote had been left alone with Dubh, and Dubh had died. Floote certainly had the opportunity. But why? Would the butler really kill to protect his dead master's secrets?

Biffy sat for a long time, rolling the bullet about in his hand and thinking.

A polite knock disturbed his reverie. He stood to open the door.

Floote walked quietly in, his jacket back on.

"Mr. Rabiffano."

"Floote." Biffy felt strangely guilty, standing there holding Floote's gun, which was obviously very precious to him, the damning bullet in his other hand.

Biffy looked at Floote.

Floote looked at Biffy.

Biffy knew, and he knew that Floote knew he knew—so to speak. He handed the butler his gun but kept the bullet as evidence, tucking it into his waistcoat pocket.

"Why, Floote?"

"Because he left his orders first, sir."

"But to kill a werewolf on a dead man's orders?"

Floote smiled the tiniest of half smiles. "You forget what Alessandro Tarabotti was, sir. What the Templars trained him for. What he trained me to help him do."

Biffy blanched, horrified. "You have killed werewolves before Dubh?"

"Not all werewolves, Mr. Rabiffano, are like you, or Professor Lyall, or Lord Maccon. Some of them are like Lord Woolsey—pests to be exterminated."

"And that's why you killed Dubh?"

Floote ignored the direct question. "Mr. Tarabotti gave his orders, sir," the butler repeated himself, "long before anyone else. I was to see it through to the end. That was my promise. And I've kept it."

"What else, Floote? What else have you been keeping in motion? Was Mr. Tarabotti responsible for the God-Breaker Plague expanding? Is that what he was doing over there?"

Floote only moved toward the door.

Biffy went after him, hand to his arm. He didn't want to use his werewolf strength and was horrified by the idea that he might have to, on a member of Lady Maccon's domestic staff! A longtime family retainer, no less—the very idea!

Floote paused and stared at the floor of the hallway, rather than at Biffy. "I really must see that carpet cleaned. It's disgraceful."

Biffy firmed up his grip.

"He left me with two instructions, sir—protect Alexia and protect the Mandate of the Broken Ankh."

Biffy knew from the way the butler's face closed over that he would get no more out of Floote that evening. But Biffy also could not afford to be wrong. Even knowing that it would disrupt the smooth running of the household, even knowing there was danger both at home and abroad, even knowing that Floote was elderly, even knowing that there would be werewolves traipsing around with badly tied cravats as a result, Biffy stuffed down his scruples. He drew back his fist and with supernatural speed and strength, tapped the butler on the temple hard enough to knock him senseless.

With a very sad sigh, the dandy flipped Floote's limp body easily over one well-dressed shoulder and carried him down to the wine cellar. There he removed the man's guns—there were two, as it transpired—from his pockets, searched for anything else of interest, and locked him in. It was ironic that the wine cellar had originally been fortified as a prison to hold Biffy only two years ago.

Biffy didn't feel victorious. He didn't feel as though he had solved some great mystery. He was simply sad. He was also grateful it would be up to Lyall to sort this mess out. His dear Beta would have to decide whether to tell Lady Kingair or not. Biffy did not envy him that conversation. With the heavy heart of a man burdened with unpleasant news, Biffy went looking for Lyall.

Alexia didn't want to awaken Conall—he was catching up on a few hours of sleep after a very hectic day—but she had news to relate and she was near to dropping from exhaustion herself.

She'd been awake over twenty-four hours with no trace of poor Primrose. No ransom note, no trail, nothing. The sun would set in less than an hour, and Alexia felt like she'd been at her inquiries for an age.

"Conall!"

He snuffled into the pillow.

She reached out to touch his bare shoulder with her bare hand, turning him human. Even that didn't awaken him. He was knackered. Lord knows what he had been up to, gallivanting around angry and then tracing the baby and dealing with politicians. He had probably expended a lot of energy. *And* the sun was very hot and bright in Egypt.

"Conall, really. Wake up."

The earl blinked tawny eyes open and glared at her. Before she could react, he gathered her in against him in a warm embrace. Always amorous, her husband. Then he seemed to remember that not only was there a crisis, he was still angry over her siding with Professor Lyall.

He pushed her away petulantly, like a small child. "Yes, Alexia?"

Alexia sighed, knowing he needed time to forgive her, if he ever would, but finding it hard not to be able to hold him under such nerve-wracking circumstances. "I've just had a message from Biffy. Or, better said, I remembered at the last minute my standing aethographor appointment. I managed to relay to him the current crisis, not that he could do anything, but I thought home ought to know. He sent a note back. Then I had to stop. The transmitter was booked and they booted me off. *Me!* Now, of all times! You know, I tried to extend the time, but the little old lady behind me in the queue had a terribly important message for her grandson and would not be reasoned with!"

"Someday, Alexia, *you* will be that little old lady."

"Oh, thank you very much, Conall."

"The message?" her husband prodded.

"Biffy says that he has traced the epicenter of the

God-Breaker Plague to one particular bend in the Nile River, near Luxor."

"And this relates to Primrose how?"

"It might. Because I managed to, well, um, bribe a few of the dahabiya captains down at the dock."

The earl raised an eyebrow.

"Madame Lefoux definitely hired a boat, one of the fastest and best on the line, to take her upriver. But not to Cairo, only *by way* of Cairo. No, her fare was for Luxor, or that's what one man said, based on the amount of money he observed changing hands. She had a mysterious bundle with her and she asked a lot of questions. So what do you think?"

"Very suspicious. I think we should go after her."

Alexia bounced slightly. "Me too!"

"How are Mr. and Mrs. Tunstell?" Lord Maccon switched topics.

"Coping tolerably well. Tunstell, at least, has been responding to direct questions. Ivy is difficult but then that is Ivy for you. I think we can leave them for a few days and follow Genevieve up the Nile."

"Right, then. The sooner we set out the better." Conall lurched out of bed.

Alexia tried to be practical. "But, my love, we both need rest."

"Still mad at you," he grumbled at her using an endearment.

"Oh, very well. But, *Conall*, we still need rest."

"Ever the pragmatist. We can rest on the train to Cairo. I think we can still catch one. It won't be as fast as Madame Lefoux, not if she hired one of the new steam-modified dahabiyas. But it will put us only a day behind her."

Alexia nodded. "Very well, I'll pack. You tell the others. And get Prudence, please. She's asleep in the nursery. I'm not leaving her behind with a baby snatcher on the loose."

The earl lumbered from the room, shirt hanging loose about his wide frame and his feet bare, before Alexia could stop him and make him dress. She supposed Ivy and Tunstell would be too distraught to take umbrage. She began a whirlwind of packing, throwing everything she could think of into two small cases. She had no idea how long they might be but figured they ought to travel as light as possible. Prudence would have to leave her mechanical ladybug behind.

Lord Maccon returned a quarter of an hour later with a sleeping Prudence tucked casually under one arm and Tunstell trailing behind.

"Are you certain I can't accompany you, my lord?" The redhead was looking frazzled. His trousers were not as tight as usual.

"No, Tunstell, it's best if you stay. Hold down the home front. It's possible we could be on the wrong track, that Madame Lefoux isn't the culprit or isn't following the culprits. Someone with a reasonable sense of responsibility must remain here to deal with the authorities, keep making a stink, keep them hunting."

Tunstell's face was serious, no smiles for once. "If you think it best."

Conall nodded his shaggy head. "I do. Now, don't hesitate to bandy my name about if you need the authority."

"Thank you, my lord."

Alexia added, "If Ivy feels up to it, there are messages coming in for me at the aethographor station every evening just after six. Here is a letter of permission granting Mrs. Tunstell the authority to receive them in my stead. Even so, they may not accept a substitute without my presence, but it's the best I can do at short notice. Only if she feels up to it, mind you."

"Very well, Lady Maccon, if you're certain I won't do?" Tunstell was clearly falling back on his claviger training in order to deal with this crisis.

"I'm afraid not, Tunstell my dear. The individual sending the messages from London will only respond to me or Ivy."

Tunstell looked puzzled but didn't question Lady Maccon further.

"Good luck, Tunstell. And I *am* sorry this has happened to you and Ivy."

"Thank you, Lady Maccon. Good luck to you. I hope you catch the bastards."

"As do I, Tunstell. As do I."

CHAPTER FIFTEEN

In Which We Learn Why Werewolves Don't Float

There were no more trains to Cairo that day, which meant Lady Maccon and her husband were forced to return to the dock and hire river transport. It was easier said than done. Despite the fact that they were now familiar with Lady Maccon and her autocratic demands, the captains did not want to set out until the following morning. Then there was the price to negotiate. Very few dahabiyas carried any kind of modern conveniences—augmented small-craft outboard steam propellers or tea kettles, for example—making them mere pleasure vessels designed to be pulled slowly up the river by mule or, worse, human power!

"It's all so very primitive!" huffed Alexia, who might ordinarily have enjoyed such a leisurely mode of transport.

Her excuse for such bad behavior must be that she was, at this juncture, exhausted, dusty, worried about Primrose, and tired of carrying Prudence. It was after sunset and the toddler was entirely in her charge. Under such circumstances, everyone's tempers were fraying, even Prudence, who was hungry. The quintessential Egyptian lack of urgency and insistence on haggling and negotiation was driving the efficient Lady Maccon slowly insane.

It was almost midnight and they were talking with the eighth captain in a row when a tap came on Alexia's shoulder. She turned around to find herself face-to-face with an extraordinarily handsome man, his features familiar, his beard cut neat and sharp—their Drifter rescuer from the bazaar.

"Lady? You are ready now, to right the wrong of the father?" His voice was deep and resonant, his words clipped by an Arabic accent and limited English.

Alexia looked him over. "If I say yes, will that get me any closer to Luxor?"

"Follow." The man turned and walked away, his dark blue robe a swirl of purpose behind him.

Alexia said to her husband, "Conall, I believe we may have to follow that gentleman."

"But, Alexia...what?"

"It has worked in my favor before."

"But who on God's green earth is the man?"

"He's a Drifter."

"Can't be—they don't fraternize with foreigners."

"Well, this one does. He rescued us at the bazaar when we were attacked."

"What? You were *what*? Why didn't you tell me?"

"You were busy yelling at me about Professor Lyall's manipulations."

"Oh. So tell me now."

"Never mind, we have to follow him. Do come on." Alexia firmed up her grip on Prudence and dashed after the rapidly disappearing balloon nomad.

"Oh, blast." Conall, bless his supernatural strength, hoisted all of their luggage easily and trundled after.

The man led them toward the Porte de Rosette. Eventually he veered off and, rounding a corner in the street, came upon a medium-sized obelisk carved of red rock that glittered in the moonlight. He was using it as a mooring, a heavy rope wrapped about the base, and his balloon hovered above like—Alexia tilted her head back—well, like a big balloon. The man stopped and made a move to take Prudence from Alexia. She jerked back but when he gestured at a rope ladder significantly, she nodded.

"Very well, but my husband goes first."

Conall was looking with white-faced horror at the swinging ladder. Werewolves do not float. "No, really. I'd prefer not, if you don't mind."

Alexia tried to be reasonable. "We must get to Luxor somehow."

"My dear wife, you have seen nothing in your life so pathetic as a werewolf with airsickness."

"Do we have a choice? Besides, with any luck we'll be flying into the God-Breaker Plague zone soon. At which point you should be fine and human once more."

"Oh, you think that, do you? What if the plague doesn't extend upward?"

"Where's your spirit of scientific inquiry, husband? This is our opportunity to find just such a thing out. I promise to take lots of notes."

"That's very reassuring." The earl did not look convinced. He eyed the ladder with even greater suspicion.

"Up you go, Conall. Stop dawdling. If it's that bad, I can simply touch you."

Her husband grumbled but began to climb.

"There's my brave boy," said his wife condescendingly.

Being supernatural, he heard her but pretended not to, eventually making it over the edge and into the balloon basket.

Alexia noticed that the balloon was much lower than the first time she had seen it, during the day. She was grateful for this—less ladder to climb.

The Drifter shimmied up, Prudence strapped to his back in a sling. The toddler squealed in delight. She, unlike her father, was very excited by the prospect of floating.

After a moment's hesitation, Alexia followed suit.

A little street urchin, all unobserved until that moment, darted forth and unwound the rope from the obelisk mooring. Alexia found herself unexpectedly climbing a free-floating ladder drifting down the street. This was not quite so easily done as one might think, particularly not in a full skirt and bustle, but no one had ever called Lady Maccon a spiritless weakling. She hung on for dear life and continued to make her way up by slow degrees, even as the ladder on which she clung headed for a very large building at a rate rather more alarming than reassuringly dignified.

She made it up into the basket just in time, somewhat hampered by the restrictions proper dress imposed upon the British female. She thought, not for the first time, that Madame Lefoux might have the right of it. But then she simply could not get around the idea of wearing trousers, not as a female of her proportions. The Drifter met her at the top with a strong hand of assistance, quickly hauling the rope ladder up after her.

So it was that the Maccons found themselves floating low above the city of Alexandria in one of the famous nomadic balloons completely at the mercy of a man to whom they had not been formally introduced.

The earl, with a muttered oath, lurched to the basket edge and was promptly sick over the side. He continued to be so for a good long while. Alexia stood next to him rubbing his back solicitously. Her touch turned him human, but it seemed that he was a man ill suited to travel by air, immortal or no. Eventually, she respected his dignity and his mutters of "do shove off" and left him to his misery.

The Drifter unstrapped Prudence from his back and set her down. She began to toddle around investigating everything—she had her mother's curiosity, bless her. The crew of the balloon, Alexia surmised after a short while, must be the man's family. There was a wife, upon whom the harsh features of the desert were not quite so attractive but who seemed more ready to smile than her dour husband. This lent her an aura of beauty, as is often the case with the good-natured. The woman's many scarves and colorful robes wafted in the slight breeze. There was also one strapping son of perhaps fourteen and a young daughter only slightly older than Prudence. The entire family was amazingly tolerant of Prudence's curiosity and evident interest in trying to "help." They pretended to let her steer with the many ropes that dangled in the center of the basket, and the boy held her up high so she could look out over the edge—an action that was met with peals of delighted laughter.

The balloon remained rather low, especially for a lady

accustomed to dirigible travel. Alexia remembered Ivy's comment about the Drifters ordinarily landing at night because of the cold and then rising up with the heat of the day. It made her wonder.

With the initial flurry of float-off past, Alexia left her self-imposed position of noninterference, checked once more on poor Conall, who was still expunging, and made her way slowly to their rescuer. It was difficult to walk for, while the sides of the basket were made of wicker, the floor was a grid of poles with animal skins stretched between—not the easiest thing for a woman of Alexia's girth and shoe choice. Add to that the fact that her moving about shook the entire basket most alarmingly.

"Pardon me, sir. It's not that I'm not grateful, but who are you?"

The man smiled, a flash of perfect white teeth from within that trimmed beard. "Ah, yes, of course, lady. I am Zayed."

"How do you do, Mr. Zayed."

The man bowed. Then he pointed in turn. "My son, Baddu; my wife, Noora; and my daughter, Anitra."

Alexia made polite murmurs and curtsied in their direction. The family all nodded but did not leave their respective posts.

"It is very kind of you to offer us, a, er, lift."

"A favor to a friend, lady."

"Really? Who?"

"Goldenrod."

"Who?"

"You do not know, lady?"

"Evidently not."

"Then we will wait."

"Oh, but..."

The man's face closed down.

Alexia sighed and switched topics. "If you don't think
it interfering, may I ask? We are very low—how can we
float at night?"

"Ah, lady. You know some of our ways. Let me show
you." He made his way over to the middle and threw several blankets off what looked to be a container of gas, of
the kind used for lamp lighting back home in London.
"For special, we have this."

Alexia was instantly intrigued. "Will you show me?"

The man flashed a brief grin of excitement and began
unhitching and hooking in various tubes and cords. He
hoisted the canister so its mouth pointed into the massive
balloon.

While he was busy fussing, Alexia took a moment to
take in her surroundings.

The balloon was utterly unlike the British-made dirigibles Alexia had utilized in the past. She had traveled in
both small pleasure-time floaters and the larger mail post
and passenger transports—the company-owned monsters.
This balloon was similar to neither. For one thing, the
balloon part itself hadn't the shape of a dirigible and was
entirely made of cloth. It was guided by means of opening
and closing flaps rather than by a propeller of any kind.
For another, the basket was bigger than a personal jaunt
dirigible but much smaller than one of the larger cross-
country behemoths. It was twice the length of a rowboat
but basically square. In the center was the mooring for the
balloon and all the associated straps and contraptions
required to see it float and directed properly. As the basket slowly spun with the balloon, there seemed to be no

particular front or back. There was an area clearly used for sleeping, another for cooking, and one tented corner that Alexia could only assume was meant for doing one's private business. She supposed that the family lived in the basket and that the various hanging sacks over the edge and from the base of the balloon—which she had assumed were ballasts—were probably goods and supplies.

Prudence went wobbling past, the Drifter girl on her tail, both of them giggling madly and having a grand old time. Alexia made her way to Conall, to defend him from possible contact with his daughter. The last thing they needed was an airsick werewolf pup dashing about the craft. Better to have a large airsick man instead.

A blast of flame and a whoop of delight from the boy, Baddu, and the balloon began a stately rise upward, fuel from the gas giving them a boost of speed high toward the aethersphere. There was no lurching sensation; in fact, the movement hardly registered except that the ground retreated below them and Alexia's ears popped.

Alexia knew in principle what the Drifters were aiming for. If they could get the balloon up and into an aether stream, they could hook into a current that would carry them south, up the Nile. It was a tricky maneuver, for should the balloon rise too much into the aether, there was a possibility of it getting torn apart, or caving with the sheer of crosscurrents, or the gas flame blowing out, causing them to drop out and down toward the desert.

Alexia tried not to think about it, instead looking down as Alexandria fell away under them.

Poor Conall, at this point reduced to dry heaving and little whimpers of distress, had his eyes tightly shut and his big hands white-knuckled about the side of the basket.

Alexia wondered if she shouldn't get Prudence to take on wolf form. Perhaps they could trap her as a pup in the corner? Prudence didn't seem to feel the pain of werewolf shift, so perhaps she didn't get airsick either? She certainly wasn't suffering from the affliction now. She was having a wonderful time. And, Alexia noted with pleasure, always stopping politely should any of their hosts wish to show her the correct anchoring of a cord or explain to her the thermodynamics of floating—in Arabic, mind you. If Lord Akeldama did nothing else, he was instilling in his adopted daughter the very best manners.

Soon they had risen high enough to turn Alexandria into a spot of faint torchlight. Below and ahead, Alexia could see only the dark of the desert, here and there a lonely fire, and, glinting under the moonlight, the hundreds of long silver snakes that made up the Nile Delta. A sudden flurry of activity in the basket, and Alexia looked over to see Zayed hauling hard on one of the ropes while Baddu offloaded some weight. Then there came a jerk and a woof noise, and the top of the balloon caught an aether stream. Zayed turned up the gas and angled the canister toward the cave-in and the balloon rose up fully into the aether stream. It immediately began to float, with much greater speed, due south. Despite this change in pace, Alexia felt almost nothing. Unlike a dirigible, there were no breezes; the balloon was moving with the currents.

Conall straightened, looking markedly better and less green.

Alexia patted him sympathetically. "Human?"

"Yes, but that doesn't do much good. I think I simply got everything, well, out. If you know what I mean?"

Alexia nodded. "Could it be our current proximity to the aether?"

"Could be. Well?"

"Well, what?"

"Are you going to make a note of it, wife? Seems that the God-Breaker Plague reaches all the way up to the aether."

"Either that, or the aethersphere itself counteracts your supernatural abilities."

"Well, if that were the case, scientists would have figured that out by now, wouldn't they?"

Lady Maccon took out a tiny notebook from one of the secret pockets of her parasol and a stylographic pen from another. "Oh, yes? And how would they have done that? Vampires can't float up that high, because they are tethered too short. And werewolves don't float at all, because they get sick."

"You can't tell me no one has transported a ghost and body via float before?"

Alexia frowned. "I don't know, but it's worth researching. I wonder if Genevieve and her deceased aunt came via float or ferry when they left Paris for London."

"You'll have to ask her when we catch up." They paused in their conversation, awkward for a moment; then Conall asked, "Can you feel the plague?"

"You mean that odd tingly sensation I felt at the edge of Alexandria?"

He nodded.

"Difficult to tell, since the feeling was already similar to that of aether breezes." Alexia closed her eyes and leaned her arms out of the balloon basket, embracing the air.

The earl immediately grabbed her shoulder and pulled her backward. "Don't *do* that, Alexia!" He was looking green again, this time with fear.

Alexia sighed. "Can't tell. Could be the plague, could be proximity to the aethersphere. We'll simply have to wait and see what happens as we move farther toward the epicenter."

"Did no one ever tell you, wife, that it's rather dangerous to do scientific experiments on oneself?"

"Now, dear, don't fuss. To be fair, I'm doing them on you as well."

"How verra reassuring."

Biffy knocked politely on Lyall's office door. He sniffed the air while he waited to be bidden entrance. He smelled the usual odors of BUR—sweat and cologne, leather and boot polish, gun oil and weaponry. In the end it was most similar to a soldier's barracks. He did not scent another pack. Wherever she was at the moment, Lady Kingair was not there.

"Enter," came Lyall's mild bidding.

Biffy was shocked by how warm simply the sound of that voice made him feel. Almost reassured. Whatever they were building together, Biffy decided at that moment that it was *good* and worth fighting for. Which, being a werewolf, he supposed might actually be more of a literal than figurative way of putting matters.

The young dandy took a breath and entered the room, his pleasure subdued under the weight of the information he had to impart. The burden of a spy, Lord Akeldama always said, was not in the knowing of things but in knowing when to tell such things to others. That and the

fact that creeping around could be dusty work, terrible on
the knees of one's trousers.

Biffy felt that there was no point in barking about the
dell. "I know who killed Dubh, and no one is going to like
it." He moved across the room, pausing only to remove his
hat and place it on the stand near the door. The poor hat
stand was already overloaded with coats and wraps and
chapeaus as well as a number of less savory items—
leather collars with gun compartments, Gatling straps, and
what looked to be a plucked goose made of straw.

Once he stood across the cluttered desk from Lyall,
Biffy removed the bullet from his waistcoat pocket and
slapped it down on the dark mahogany.

Professor Lyall put aside the papers he had been studying and picked up the bullet. After a moment of close
examination, he tipped a pair of glassicals down from
where they perched atop his head and studied the bullet
even more carefully through the magnification lens.

He looked up after a long moment, the glassicals dis-
torting one hazel eye out of all proportion.

Biffy winced at the asymmetry.

Lyall took the glassicals off, set them aside, and handed
the bullet back to Biffy. "Sundowner ammunition. Old-
fashioned. Of the kind that shot Dubh."

Biffy nodded, face grave. "You'll never guess who
from."

Professor Lyall sat back, vulpine face impassive, and
raised one dark blond eyebrow patiently.

"Floote." Biffy waited for a reaction, wanted one.

Nothing. Lyall was good.

"It was all Floote. He had opportunity. He was free at
the time of the initial attack at the train station. He had

access to Lord Akeldama's dirigible, which he could fly back, setting part of London on fire to delay Lady Maccon. Do you recall, Dubh mentioned something to her ladyship about not wanting to go with her home? He said it wasn't safe. I believe that was because he knew Floote would be there. Then when Lady Maccon brought the wounded Beta back, who did she leave him alone with in the sickroom for those few minutes?"

"Floote."

"And what happened?"

"Dubh died."

"Exactly."

"But opportunity is not motive, my dear boy." Professor Lyall, for all his passivity, was unwilling to believe.

"I confronted him, but you know Floote. He claimed it was something to do with Alessandro Tarabotti, orders left behind when he died. Something wasn't supposed to get out. Lady Maccon wasn't supposed to know. Of course, she left for Egypt anyway. You know what I think? I think Alessandro Tarabotti somehow set the God-Breaker Plague into motion, and Floote has been seeing that it continues to expand. Those were the orders Mr. Tarabotti left, and Floote's been secretly conducting a long-distance supernatural extermination mandate ever since. I think Dubh simply got in the way and Floote had no other choice."

"Ambitious, but what do you—" Lyall paused and sniffed the air. "Oh, dear," he said succinctly.

Biffy sniffed as well. He caught a whiff of open fields and country air, although not of the kind he might be familiar with from his own pack. This was a damp, lush, impossibly green field leagues to the north—Scotland.

Biffy whirled and ran to the door, throwing it open, only to see Lady Kingair's graying tail tip disappear out the front entrance of BUR and into the night, at speed.

He felt Lyall's presence next to him. "What did you do with Floote, my dandy?"

"Locked him in the wine cellar, of course."

"This is not good. Given half a chance, she'll kill him before we extract any additional information out of him."

"Not to mention that it's a bad idea to eat one's domestic staff."

The two men looked at one another and then, by mutual accord, began to strip out of their clothes. At least, Biffy consoled himself, BUR agents were accustomed to such eccentricities.

Professor Lyall gave up about halfway through and simply sacrificed his wardrobe to the cause. Biffy watched him run after the Alpha. He hoped fervently they weren't in for another fight with the she-wolf; he didn't think he had it in him. However, Biffy did spare a few moments to divest himself of his favorite waistcoat and cravat before shifting form. The trousers and shirt could be replaced, but not that waistcoat; it was a real pip.

Biffy took off after Lyall, pushing himself hard, so hard he caught up to the slighter wolf just before they reached the pack's town house. Professor Lyall was reputed to be one of the fastest fighters in England, but Biffy still had enough muscle mass on him to catch up in a straight race. He was inordinately proud of himself.

They pushed in the open door to the Maccon's town house to find Lady Kingair snuffling about, dashing frantically from room to room, evidently having started her hunt for the butler on the top floor in the servants' quarters. Luckily, she had not yet reached the wine cellar. Floote's scent was so prevalent throughout the house it must be throwing her off.

Biffy and Lyall looked at one another, yellow eyes to yellow eyes. Then they both leaped toward the angry Alpha and backed her into the front parlor by dint of surprise, rather than power.

Biffy lashed out with his tail, slamming the door closed behind them.

Professor Lyall changed form, standing before the furious she-wolf. "Lady Kingair, don't you think we might talk about this civilly, just this once?"

The rangy wolf sat back on her haunches, as though considering this proposition, and then, after a moment, the graying fur of her coat retreated, and she stood before Lyall.

Sidheag Kingair was a fine figure of a woman for all she had been converted later in life. She crossed her arms, utterly unself-conscious. "Professor, I dinna want tae be civil. If that man killed my Beta, 'tis my right tae take his blood."

"If."

She looked at Biffy, now sitting back on his haunches, tongue out and panting after such a run. "But I heard him say that—"

"You heard him speculate. Nothing has been proven."

"That dinna sound like speculation tae me."

Biffy wondered if he, too, should change his form, or if such a thing would be wasted on the Alpha's rage. He wanted to have some input, however, aside from wagging his tail and twitching his ears, so he sought out his reserves of courage, faced the pain, and shifted.

"We need to act within the confines of British law, Lady Kingair, as well as pack protocol. The first thing to do is confront the man and inquire further."

Lady Kingair's lip curled. "Inquire? If you insist."

Professor Lyall turned to Biffy. "If you would like to lead the way?"

Biffy would not like, but he did as he was told by his Beta, moving with a certain amount of embarrassed poise through the house in full view of half the servants.

Thus they trooped down to the wine cellar—to find the door slightly open with no sign of being forced and the cellar itself completely empty.

Floote was gone.

Lady Kingair erupted into immediate fury. "He's escaped!"

Professor Lyall shook his head. "Not possible. We secured this room to hold werewolves."

"Then *someone* must have let him out. Or not locked the room down properly." She snarled at Biffy.

Biffy was affronted. "I assure you, it was securely locked, and I searched his person for tools."

"You must have missed something, pup!"

"Perhaps I missed the utterly ridiculous idea that a butler could pick locks!"

"Perhaps you did, you little—"

Professor Lyall stepped in. "Now wait just a moment, Lady Kingair. Did you search Floote's room just now when you were looking for him?"

The Alpha shrugged, the long fall of her thick hair shifting against her naked breasts. She still glared at Biffy.

Unashamed, knowing he had done all that could be

asked of someone in his position, Biffy pretended to examine his manicure. For some reason, shifting forms played hell on the cuticles.

Lyall continued his questioning. "Had he taken his belongings?"

Lady Kingair wasn't interested in figuring out the minutiae of Floote's disappearance. She was interested in blaming someone for it—Biffy.

Biffy turned away to poke about the cellar, trying to find any clues that might represent Floote's ability to escape a heretofore impenetrable wine cellar.

He did not see her shifting forms. The only warning he got was Lyall's shout.

Afterward, Biffy was never quite certain what he did or why it happened. He reacted out of instinct, but there were two instincts in place—the werewolf one that wanted to shift forms out of self-preservation and the Biffy one that hated the pain of shifting more than any-thing, more than a badly cut jacket or a loose cravat. Those two instincts went to battle against each other as the great vicious she-wolf charged toward him.

He shifted.

He simply didn't quite manage to shift everything.

Only his head went over.

That action stopped Lady Kingair in a way that noth-ing else possibly could. She halted her charge, stood on four legs stiffed in surprise, and stared at him.

Biffy didn't understand what was going on. He still felt like himself, and there was very little pain, but his head felt swollen and heavy, as though he had caught a cold, and his senses were suddenly far more acute.

Professor Lyall moved forward, brushed past Lady

Kingair, and stood quietly in front of him. The Beta's mouth was open ever so slightly in shock, not an expression Biffy had ever thought to see on his lover's face.

He tried to ask, "What's going on?" But all he could manage was a bit of a whine and a small bark.

"Biffy," said Professor Lyall softly. "Did you know you had an Anubis form?"

Biffy barked at him again. He was beginning to shake slightly. It was from the fear and the stress, not from being naked in a cellar. Werewolves rarely felt cold even in human skin. Or half-human skin.

Lady Kingair shifted back into her *fully* human guise. She was still looking angry and impatient, but she also seemed far less inclined to fight him than she had mere moments before.

"He dinna *act* like an Alpha."

All Lyall's attention was on Biffy; he barely glanced at the Kingair Alpha. "He does in some areas," he replied.

Biffy argued he must look beyond ridiculous. The head of a wolf, all fuzzy and yellow-eyed, on the lean pale body of a dandy. *I don't want to be an Alpha*, he cried out internally. *I don't want to spend half my time fighting challengers. I don't want to have the responsibility of a pack. I don't want to die early or go mad. Make it go away!*

But again, all he could do was whine.

"It's all right, pup," soothed Lyall. "You simply shift it back. At least I think that's how it works." He frowned to himself. "I've served several Alphas and I never thought to ask if Anubis worked any differently than full wolf fur. Some professor I am."

Biffy only whined again. He was trying. He was reaching for that place deep inside that could force the shift, that tingling pressure of bones re-forming. It wasn't working. He couldn't go either direction, couldn't return to wolf or human. He was trapped in the in-between of Anubis state.

"Oh, dear. Are you stuck?" asked Lyall.

Smart man. Biffy nodded his shaggy head vigorously.

"Och, I've nae time for this! We must catch that blighter Floote." Lady Kingair was at her limit. Clearly Biffy's predicament was merely an added insult to her evening.

She went up the stairs. Preparing, no doubt, to chase after Floote into the night. "Where would he go?" she shouted back at the two werewolves.

With a shrug, Lyall and Biffy followed.

The Beta said, "If he was still working for Sandy, and if he was operating under that agenda all along, we must assume that it is an antisupernatural agenda. Sandy promised me…" The Beta winced slightly at this, an old lie only now uncovered. "Never mind what he promised. If the plan all along was to expand the plague, then it may be that even I couldn't change his mind."

Lady Kingair concurred. "I guess you weren't as alluring as you thought, Beta. So where would he go?"

Biffy came to stand close behind Lyall, placing a supportive hand on the man's shoulder. He wanted to reassure Lyall that he found him alluring, but he could only growl in annoyance.

Biffy knew what he would do were he in Floote's situation. Were he a mortal man with werewolves on his tail, there was only one truly safe place—the air. And Floote, loyal to the last, would try to get to Lady Maccon to explain his actions to her. To see that she was safe, as that, too, was part of Alessandro Tarabotti's mandate. Biffy might have said all these things, but he had no proper mouth and his neck was part wolf as well, including, apparently the voice box. *Good Lord*, he thought, *what if I'm permanently stuck like this? I'll never be able to carry off a pointed collar again!* Then he realized with relief that Anubis was wolf form, at least in part, and wolf form would not survive the sunrise. *Only a few more hours, then.*

Lyall had reached the same conclusion as Biffy regarding Floote's probable course of action. "He'll head to the nearest dirigible."

Lady Kingair dashed off.

Biffy whined and gestured with his wolf head at the stairs. The stairs that led to the second-story hallway that ended in a balcony that had a secret drawbridge to Lord Akeldama's house. If Floote wanted to take to the air quickly, he'd go for *Dandelion Fluff Upon a Spoon*. After all, he'd used Lord Akeldama's private dirigible before.

Lyall concurred, but he didn't try to stop Lady Kingair. He allowed her to rush off into the night, presumably toward the ticket stations of the larger public dirigibles at the green. She was not a woman accustomed to London and its extravagances. It had not even occurred to her that there might be a *private* dirigible nearby.

The Beta began making his way upstairs to cross over into the vampire's abode.

Biffy held back.

"Don't you want to see if you're correct? See if he did manage to steal Lord Akeldama's dirigible a second time?" Lyall goaded him gently.

Biffy gestured down at his naked body and furry head with one fine white hand.

Professor Lyall understood perfectly. "You're embarrassed?"

Biffy nodded.

"Don't be foolish. This is something to be proud of—very few werewolves boast Anubis form, not even all Alphas. And it's highly unusual in a pup so young as you. Generally, it takes a decade or more to manifest. This is brilliant."

Biffy whined in a sarcastic manner.

"Don't be silly. It really is."

Biffy gave a huffy bark that he hoped sounded like a snort of derision.

"Trust me, my dandy, this is a *good* thing. Now, do come along."

With a sigh, Biffy did as ordered and followed his Beta across the small drawbridge and into his former master's house.

Only three years earlier, all would have been chaos at the sight of two naked men, one of them with a wolf head, wandering the halls of Lord Akeldama's domicile. Several of the drones, possibly Biffy included, might even have had the vapors.

It was not that Lord Akeldama and his boys objected to nudity; in fact, all were coolly in favor of it—in the boxing ring, for example, or the bedroom. But wandering the hallways underdressed, let alone undressed, was frowned upon unless cursed by extreme inebriation or emotional instability. And a werewolf was not to be tolerated in the house of a vampire except when socially mandated. All that had shifted when Lady Maccon installed herself in

Lord Akeldama's closet. For where Lady Maccon went, Lord Maccon was soon to follow, and that good gentleman had somewhat improved the general outlook of Lord Akeldama's household on the subject of nudity and wolves, particularly in combination.

It was universally held among the drones that Lord Maccon had a particularly fine physique, and there had been quite the scuffle over who would be allowed to dress him in the evenings. After Floote assumed that role, it became a trickster's challenge to ascertain who among the boys could arrange such little incidences as would cause the London Alpha to bluster out into the hallway in the altogether of an afternoon.

As a result, the entire Akeldama household was markedly tolerant of Lyall's and Biffy's unexpected appearance and absent attire, although they did give Biffy some odd looks. Many of them had never seen Anubis form. Biffy took great solace in the fact that, as his head was that of a wolf, none of them knew it was him. Until, of course, they ran smack dab into Lord Akeldama, coming out of his aethographor chamber as they were making their way up onto the roof.

The vampire was dressed in an outfit that most closely resembled the waters of some tropical island, varying shades of turquoise, teal, and blue, accessorized with pearls and white gold. His effeminate features were screwed up in concentration over some small scrap of paper on which was scribbled, no doubt, an aetheric message of grave political, social, or fashionable import.

Lord Akeldama took a long look at Professor Lyall's physique and then gave him a little nod of academic approval. Then he directed an even longer look at Biffy.

Finally he said, "Biffy, my *darling* boy, what *have* you done to your hair? Something new for the evening?"

Biffy inclined his wolf head, dreadfully mortified. Of course, there was no chance of Lord Akeldama needing to see his face to recognize him; the vampire had a long, and somewhat inconvenient, memory for body parts.

Lord Akeldama smiled ever so slightly, the hint of a fang peeking out one corner of his mouth. "Now, my dear Dolly, did *you* know this would happen? You are a fortunate werewolf as well as a fortune man, now, are you not? Anubis form could be the solution to all your problems given some patience and a few well-placed suggestions."

Professor Lyall only inclined his head.

"But of course, you would have known *that* the moment he manifested."

The Beta's expression did not alter.

Lord Akeldama smiled fully, his fangs sharp and bright and fierce, as pearly as the cravat pin about his neck. "I don't trust serendipity, Professor Lyall. I don't trust it at all." No one missed the fact that the vampire was, for once, using someone's proper name.

Biffy's wolf head swayed back and forth between the combatants, wondering at all the unspoken undercurrents.

"I never underestimate the same man twice," said Lord Akeldama, fiddling with his cravat pin with one hand while he surreptitiously tucked the bit of paper with the aethographic message away with the other.

"You give me too much credit, my lord, if you thought I could anticipate this." Professor Lyall nodded at Biffy's altered state.

"Well, Biffy, what do you have to say on the subject?"

The vampire regarded his former drone, his expression friendly, if a little distant.

"He's stuck, my lord." Lyall came to Biffy's rescue.

"Goodness, how unnerving."

"Indeed. Imagine how Biffy must feel."

"That, my dear Dolly, is beyond even *my* capacities. And now, how may I help you gentlemen? Do you require *garments*, perhaps?"

Professor Lyall rolled his eyes slightly. "Shortly. We were hoping if first we might ascertain the condition and state of your lordship's dirigible."

"*Buffety*? I believe she's moored up top. Haven't sent her out in many a moon. No need with my dear Alexia right here, I suppose. Why?"

"We believe she might have been used for nefarious purposes."

"Really? How wonderfully *salacious*! I can't believe I wasn't invited."

Professor Lyall said nothing.

"Ah, are you perhaps here in your BUR capacity, Dolly, my pet?"

Professor Lyall knew better than to give Lord Akeldama any more information than strictly necessary.

"No? Pack business, then? Has my little *Buffety* something to do with that unfortunate incident concerning *the other Beta*?" The vampire tsked around his fangs. "So sad."

With still no response from Professor Lyall and none possible from Biffy, the vampire waved an aqua-gloved hand magnanimously at the ladderlike staircase that led up onto his roof. "By all means."

The three gentlemen climbed up to find that the *Dan-*

delion Fluff Upon a Spoon was, indeed, no longer in residence. They could see it, some distance away, floating high in the aether stream heading in a southwesterly direction. Lyall and Biffy were unsurprised. Lord Akeldama pretended outrage, although he was surely warned there might be something amiss.

"Why, I do declare! How unsporting, to purloin a man's dirigible without asking! I suppose you two have a very good idea who borrowed my beauty?"

The werewolves exchanged looks.

"Floote." Lyall no doubt figured Lord Akeldama would discover the truth soon enough.

"Ah, well, at least I know he'll take good care of it and return it in first-rate condition. Butlers are like that, you know? But where's he taken it? Not *too far* I trust—my little darling isn't made for long distances."

"Probably to try to make an in-air transfer to one of the postal dirigibles."

"Going after my darlingist of Alexias, is he? To Gyppie?"

"Most likely."

"Well, well, well."

"So you say."

"She'll be cast adrift, poor thing. I had better alert the authorities, let them know she's gone missing, so as I'm not held responsible if she drifts into anything *important*. Unless you, *my dear Dolly*, being BUR might count as..."

The Beta shook his head.

"Ah, well, so I shall send Boots to the local constabulary. Our beautiful boys with the silver pins."

Professor Lyall nodded. "That is probably a good plan. Although, I shouldn't think they need know who took it.

Not just yet. Right now all we have is coincidence and speculation."

The vampire regarded Lyall up and down in a very considering sort of way. "Look at you, Dolly, controlling information like an old intelligencer. One would almost think you vampiric. And, of course, *my darling Alexia* wouldn't like it, not her butler with a police record."

"Exactly. We must take into account Lady Maccon's feelings on the matter."

"I suppose...Lady Kingair?" Lord Akeldama twiddled his fingers casually in the air.

The Beta only lowered his eyes.

"Indeed, werewolf business. Just so. Well, Dolly my love, I *do* wish your werewolf business hadn't absconded with *my dirigible*."

"I do apologize about that, Lord Akeldama."

"Well, never you mind. Nice to have something for my boys to do. London has been awfully quiet without Lady Maccon. And now I see the sun will be rising soon, if you gentlemen will excuse me?" The vampire made a little bow at Professor Lyall. "Beta," and then to Biffy, pointedly, "*Alpha*."

Biffy and Lyall stayed, naked, on the roof of Lord Akeldama's town house watching the sunrise. As the sun eased itself up over the horizon, Biffy found himself inching closer and closer to Lyall's slight frame, until they stood, shoulders touching. When the first rays peeked over the horizon, he knew Lyall could feel the shudder of change that wrenched him back from Anubis to fully human.

The sunlight felt harsh, causing the sensation of dry and stretched skin. It was a condition, Biffy had learned, that was the price werewolves paid for being out during the day. But it was a relief to experience it once more, pulling at his nose and eyes. He reached up a tentative hand to feel, finding his own face instead of the wolf's.

"I do not want to be an Alpha," was the first thing he said, testing out his vocal cords for functionality.

Lyall bumped closer against his shoulder. "No, the best ones never do."

They continued to stand, not looking at one another, staring out over the awakening city, as though trying to see a small dirigible long since gone.

"Do you think he made it to the post?" Biffy asked at long last.

"It's Floote. Of course he made it."

"Poor Lady Maccon, a butler who murders, a father who betrays, and a husband who wants to die."

"Is that why you think Lord Maccon was so eager to visit Egypt?"

"Don't you? What man wants to go mad. It seems to me the God-Breaker Plague is an excellent solution to the problem of Alpha immortality." Biffy was, of course, thinking of his own future now.

"An interesting way of putting it."

"I cannot believe no werewolf has thought to use it so before."

"How do you know they have not? Who do you think gathered that data you were so interested in, on the extent of the plague?"

"Ah."

"Ah, indeed. Are you reassured by this?" The Beta turned to face him. Biffy could feel those concerned hazel eyes fixed on his profile. He kept resolutely facing the far horizon. *At least I have a good profile*, he consoled himself.

"You mean now that we know I am an Alpha?" Biffy considered the question. To be reassured that he had a safe place to die as a werewolf when once, an age ago now, he had thought to live forever as a vampire? He gave a tiny sigh. "Yes, I suppose I am." He paused. "How long do I have?"

Professor Lyall gave a little huff of amusement. "Oh, a few hundred years at least, possibly more, if you settle well. You still have to do military service, of course. That's always a risk."

"Learn to fight?"

"Learn to fight. I shouldn't worry, my dandy. Lord Maccon will make an excellent teacher."

"You think he's coming back?"

"Yes, I do. If only to yell at me over the sins of the past."

"Optimistic."

"I think, in this matter, young pup, I know our Alpha better than you."

"He will tolerate my presence, even with...?" Biffy gestured at his head.

"Of course. You are young yet and certainly no challenge to an Alpha of his standing."

"Funny, I was beginning to feel rather old."

Professor Lyall gave a tiny smile. "Come on, then, to bed with us, and I will remind you, in the best possible way, how young you really are."

"Very good, sir."

"Ah, Biffy, I rather think that *now* that is my line."

Biffy laughed and straightened his spine, grabbing the Beta by the hand. "Right'o, come along, then."

"*Very* good, sir." Professor Lyall managed, somehow, to make his reply sound like a change in rank, a promise of wickedness, and the approval of a favorite teacher, all in one simple phrase.

CHAPTER SIXTEEN

The Curative Properties of Nile Bathing

Alexia, Conall, and Prudence were five days with the balloon nomads of Egypt floating south. Five days drifting at speed above the long rope of the Nile River, a deep, dark blue-green during the day and a silvered strand at night. During those five days, the full moon came and went, with Conall, for the first time in hundreds of years, unaltered by its presence. The earl could freely play with and, much to Lady Maccon's delight, take care of his daughter any time of the day or night without repercussions. He also grew a very large and scruffy beard, with which she was far less delighted.

"A man's virility is in his beard," he insisted.

To which Alexia replied, "And a woman's is in her décolletage. Yet you don't see me allowing mine to get out of control, now, do you?"

"If wishes were balloons," was his only response.

Drifting was, thought Alexia, a most agreeable pas- time. True, the accommodations on board left something

to be desired and were rather cramped, but there were
some wonderful moments that could only be experienced
on a trip by way of balloon. For two days they linked up
with what appeared to be most of Zayed's extended family. They, too, sported bright balloons, mostly of a purple
color, which drifted up close to Zayed's, then floated a
short distance off and hitched in to the same aether current. Zayed cast out a massive circular net, and as each
new balloon arrived, they would pick up a section of net,
until there they were, all linked together, with a kind of
immense hammock dangling under and between them.
This became the walkway by which certain matters of
business were conducted and a playground for the children. Conall, still mostly uncomfortable with being up
high at all, refused point-blank to even test it, but Alexia
was never one to shirk a new experience when it presented
itself with such appeal. She set forth, even knowing that
should anyone on the ground have binoculars they might
very well see up her skirts. Soon enough, she found herself bouncing and tumbling across the wide net. It was not
so easy to traverse as it looked. She was entirely unable to
effect the smooth bobbing walk of the Drifter women,
who managed to go from basket to basket, in an odd
reflection of the British housewife paying a social call,
with great mounds of food balanced atop their heads.

Prudence, of course, took to the new sky-high transport like a newly minted vampire to blood, springing
about with little Anitra, who was her new favorite person
in the world. Alexia was tolerably assured that Anitra,
who had been raised on such folderol as nets in the aether,
knew more than the average child about falling. Alexia
also noticed that there always seemed to be older children

or mothers about with a watchful eye to the net's edge, and so she relaxed some of her own vigilance. Not so Conall, whose eyes stayed fixed in horrified terror on first his daughter and then his wife. Each of whom he would yell to in turn. "Now, Prudence, don't jump so high!" "Alexia, if you fall off, I shall kill you!" "Wife, look to our daughter!" Prudence, blissfully uncaring of her father's concern, continued to bounce. Alexia ignored his rantings as those of a man whose feet, two or four, ought to always be on the ground.

During their five days of travel, they landed only once, on the evening in which they were linked to the other balloons. Zayed insisted that they needed to rest and restock both fuel and water. They drifted down slowly after the sun had set, pulling the net in as they went and coming to ground by a little oasis. The tingly feeling of the God-Breaker Plague was much stronger in the desert. It was almost uncomfortable for Alexia, as it had not been while floating. She felt the beginnings of that odd little push, that physical repulsion she had first experienced in the presence of one very small mummy, decorated with a broken ankh. Prudence, too, wasn't happy grounded. "Up," she kept saying. "Mama, up!" Only Conall was pleased, rolling about in the sand like a puppy before stripping down to bathe in the oasis. Alexia supposed not even the God-Breaker Plague could really get the wolf out of Lord Conall Maccon.

Two days later, they arrived at the bend in the Nile.

Alexia was hypnotized by the spot as they floated over it. It was the early evening, so their descent was slow and measured. From the sky, the place looked oddly familiar, the wide curve of the river forming a shape in the desert that Alexia was certain she recognized. But it was like trying to see a figure in the clouds. Then, as they dropped down closer and closer, she realized what it was.

She beckoned autocratically at her massive husband. "Conall, do come over here. Do you see that?"

The earl gave his wife a very dour look. "Alexia, I am trying *not* to look down." But he made his way over to her.

"Yes, but, please? Just there. Zayed, if you could spare a moment? What *is* that?"

Their host came over to where the Maccons stood, Alexia leaning over the basket's edge, looking down intently.

He nodded. "Ah, yes, of course. The Creature in the Sands."

Alexia pointed it out for the benefit of her husband, even though Conall clearly wasn't interested. "See there, the curve of the river? That is its head, and there, stretching out in ribbons into the desert, those are its legs. Are those pathways, Zayed?" The earl, unwilling to study further the ground he would probably describe as *rushing* toward them, went over to lie down on a pile of colorful blankets, shutting his eyes.

Zayed confirmed Alexia's assessment. "Ghost trails into the desert."

"Really, made by actual ghosts? Before the plague, I assume?"

"So they say. Not just any ghosts, lady. Ghosts of kings and queens and the servants of kings and queens. Must be ghosts, lady. What living man would walk voluntarily into the desert sands?"

"Eight trails, eight legs," ruminated Alexia thoughtfully. *It is an octopus. But an upside-down octopus? Of course, because the Nile runs backward!* She continued interrogating her host. "And that spot there? The one that represents its eye?"

"Ah, lady, that is, how you might say, a temple."

"For which of the many Ancient Egyptian gods?"

"Ah, no, not for a god, lady. For a queen. A queen who would be king."

Alexia knew enough of Egyptian history to know that could mean only one person. "Hatshepsut? Indeed. How *very* interesting."

Zayed gave her a very funny look. "Yes, lady. What might she say to you visiting here?"

"Goodness, why should her opinion matter? Has it been properly excavated yet, that temple?"

Before Zayed could answer, several things happened at once. The balloon lost altitude, as the air began to cool with proximity to the river, dropping down toward the very point under discussion—the Eye of the Octopus. Alexia felt a sensation of total repulsion, one she had only experienced heretofore from a preternatural mummy. Only this time it was ten times worse. She felt as if she were being pushed, literally pushed, by hundreds of invisible hands. All of them were trying to press her skin inward so that it melted back into flesh and bone. It was a horrible sensation and she wanted more than anything to beg Zayed to take the balloon back up into the aether. But she also knew that the answers to all her many questions lay down below.

At the same time, Conall said, "Oh, I feel much better," and sat upright.

Prudence cried out, "Mama, Mama, Mama. No!"

Alexia, dizzy from the repulsion, sank forward, tilting

over the edge of the basket slightly, and spotted, moored near that fateful octopus eye, a large modern-style dahabiya.

Oblivious to the internal chaos of his lady passenger, Zayed answered Alexia's question. "One should never disregard the opinion of a queen. But *that* queen changed the pathways of the world."

Alexia felt as though she were missing something. As though the earth were spinning away from her, as fine and silvery fast as the Nile in full flood. The pushing came on harder and harder until it was as though she were being suffocated in a vat of molasses.

The balloon bumped down not ten paces from the Temple of Hatshepsut, but Alexia knew none of this. For only the second time in her adult life, she had fainted dead away.

Lady Maccon awoke to the sensation of cool water being splashed on her face and cool water surrounding her body.

Someone had thrown her into the Nile River—fully dressed.

She sputtered. "Oh my goodness, what?"

"It was my idea." Genevieve Lefoux's mellow, slightly accented voice came from behind Alexia's head. The Frenchwoman seemed to be supporting her by the shoulders so that she could float with the current.

Her husband's worried face appeared, blocking out the stars in the evening sky far above. "How do you feel?"

Alexia assessed the situation. The pressure was still there, the sense of repulsion, but mostly around her head and face now. Where her body was fully immersed in water, she felt nothing at all. "Better."

"Well, good. Don't scare me like that, woman!"

"Conall, it wasn't my fault!"

He was truculent. "Still, quite un-Alexia of you."

"Sometimes even I behave unexpectedly."

He was not to be mollycoddled. "Don't do it again."

Alexia gave up; there was no way he would be reasonable. She tilted her head back to look at Madame Lefoux, upside down. "It was a good idea, Genevieve. But I can't stay here in the Nile indefinitely. I have an octopus to investigate." Then she remembered something. "Primrose! Genevieve, did you steal Primrose and bring her with you?"

"No, Alexia. I did not even know she was missing until your husband asked me that same question not ten minutes ago."

"But we thought…"

"No, I am sorry. I was in a rush to leave the hotel because I had uncovered some very telling information and wanted to make my way here as quickly as possible. I had no idea there was a kidnapping. I do hope the little girl is all right."

"Don't we all? Blast it, we were hoping you saw something and were on the trail of the kidnappers. What was so interesting, then?" Alexia had no subtlety.

The Frenchwoman sighed. "Well, as you are here now, we might as well combine forces. Perhaps you are in possession of some missing pieces of my puzzle."

"How do you know it's not the other way around?" interjected the earl.

Genevieve continued as though he hadn't interrupted her. "I found myself in the company of Edouard Naville, a burgeoning archaeologist."

"An OBO member? I knew you had some other reason for visiting Egypt."

Madame Lefoux made no acknowledgment of any connection to the Order of the Brass Octopus. That, in and of itself, was an admission. "He has recently received the concession for Deir el-Bahri."

"Oh, indeed," encouraged Alexia, understanding none of this. She paddled frantically to right herself, touching her feet down into what she was certain was a filthy river bottom, but as she still had her walking boots on, it was impossible to tell. She stayed crouched down to keep as much of herself immersed as possible.

Conall offered his assistance with the maneuver. Alexia made note that while they had not bothered to remove *her* dress, Conall was quite naked, and Genevieve was wearing some kind of gentleman's undergarment as a bathing costume. Behind her, on the shore, Alexia could make out Zayed's balloon, mostly deflated, and a party of human shadows that must be made up of Zayed's family and the crew of Genevieve's dahabiya. They were engaging in some kind of trade, or meal, or both. Alexia could hear Prudence, with her usual lack of interest in water, shrieking with laughter. The infant was utterly unperturbed by her mother's ailment or resulting damp predicament.

Madame Lefoux gestured behind her at the shore. "*This* is Deir el-Bahri. You can make out some of the ruins of the temple behind our party. Beyond it is the Valley of the Kings. But this...this is the Eye of the Octopus."

Alexia nodded. "Yes, I had figured as much."

"Naville is young yet, but he hopes eventually to excavate here. I was sent to investigate, you know, *the source*."

Alexia was one step ahead of her. "The source of the God-Breaker Plague. You too?"

Lord Maccon interrupted, "Whose temple did you say it was?"

"I didn't, but Monsieur Naville believes it to be the mortuary temple of Queen Hatshepsut."

At which Conall, quite unexpectedly, busted out with a great crack of booming laughter. It echoed out over the river. "Well, well, well, I'm certain she won't like us visiting."

Alexia frowned. "Mr. Zayed said much the same thing."

Her husband continued. "And it could hardly be a mortuary temple. A metamorphosis temple, perhaps, but not mortuary."

Alexia began to comprehend what he was getting at, almost falling backward into the Nile in her surprise. "Are you telling me...?"

"Matakara is Hatshepsut's other name. Well, one of the many. You didn't know?"

"Of course I didn't know! Why should I? And why didn't you *tell* me? My goodness, she really is *very* old!"

Lord Maccon tilted his handsome head in that annoying way of his that was meant to be coy. "I dinna think it was of particular import."

"Oh, *dinna* you? Wonderful. And now, do you think it might be important *now*?" Alexia thought even harder, difficult to do with the sense of repulsion pressing in against her brain. She splashed her head back down into the river, immediately feeling better. She resurfaced, wondering at the no-doubt-horrible state of her hair, pleased that someone at least had thought to remove her hat and parasol before her dunking. "But, Conall, didn't you once tell me that Ancient Egypt was ruled by werewolves?"

"Only inasmuch as Ancient Rome was ruled by vampires. There were still vampires around Egypt, even then. Hatshepsut was quite an upset. Made some people very angry. Tuthmosis, of course, put everything to rights again. He was one of *ours*."

"It makes no sense. Why would Matakara's temple be the epicenter of the God-Breaker Plague? Why would a vampire be involved in such a thing? Her kind, too, would be exterminated."

Genevieve Lefoux said, "May I suggest we look to the scientific evidence, and the reality of the situation first, and speculate afterward?"

"I take it you haven't yet explored the temple?" Alexia was surprised.

"I only recently arrived here myself. We were mooring when your balloon touched down. How did you, by the way, manage to convince a Drifter to carry you?"

"I am supposed to right my father's wrong," replied Alexia cryptically, twisting up her face in disdain.

"Goodness, which of the many?" the inventor wanted to know. "Anyway, the temple is completely unexcavated, so it is still filled with sand. It would take years to dig it out. I wouldn't know where to start."

Alexia splashed at her. "My dear Genevieve, I don't see that our answers are going to lie inside the temple."

"No?"

"No. Remember what we have found out, that preternatural touch requires air—preferably dry air—to work? Don't you think dead preternaturals might function the same way?"

"Dead preternaturals? Is that our source?"

Alexia only pursed her lips.

"How long have you known that might be a possibility?"

"Since Scotland."

"The artifact of humanization was a mummy?"

"Of a preternatural, yes."

"But why didn't you *tell* me?"

Alexia gave her sometime friend a very funny look.

Madame Lefoux clearly understood. Alexia could not reveal such a dangerous scientific fact to a member of the OBO. "You think we should look for the epicenter outside the temple?"

"Indeed I do."

"Can you manage it?"

Alexia frowned. "I can manage anything if we get some answers at the end of it."

Thinking of the fact that she had recently fainted, Conall said, "We'll bring water along and keep your dress as damp as possible. That might help."

"Oh." Alexia felt guilty for maligning her husband's actions in her head. "Is that why you chucked me into the Nile fully clothed?"

Lord Maccon made a funny face. "Of course, dear."

They paddled to shore and climbed out onto the muddy bank. The moment she was free of the river, Alexia began to feel that awful sense of repulsion against her skin.

"I think I may have to sleep in the river tonight," she said to no one in particular.

"You've done stranger things, I suppose," was her husband's reply.

Early the next morning, before the heat of the sun, Lady Maccon, Lord Maccon, and Madame Lefoux climbed up the hill above Hatshepsut's temple—or squelched up in

Alexia's case. She was all pruned from a night spent in the river, a kind of hammock having been made to support her while she slept. It had not been very restful at all, and she was peevish and annoyed as a result. A trail of Egyptians followed in their wake, each carrying a large urn or canteen of river water. At Alexia's signal, one would step forward and splash her with it, rather too enthusiastically and much to Prudence's amusement.

"Mama, wet!"

"Yes, darling." Alexia could almost hear her daughter's adult commentary behind the baby phrases: *Sooner you than me, Mother.*

The sand-covered hill they scaled formed the back part of the roof of the temple, where it had been carved into the side of a cliff. Alexia took the lead, despite her damp dress hindering her stride, her parasol raised against the vicious sun. Then came Genevieve, and then Conall and Prudence. They left Zayed and family back at camp.

It was there, on the top of that hill, they began to see the bodies. Or to be more precise, the mummies. Or to be even more precise, it was where Lord Maccon accidentally stepped on a long-dead preternatural.

It made a sad, dry, cracking noise and let out a little puff of brown dust.

"Conall, do be careful! Inhale one of those and you could be mortal forever! Or something equally nasty."

"Yes, dear." The earl wrinkled his nose and shook off his boot.

Madame Lefoux held up a hand and they all stopped walking and simply looked. They could see down the sloping back side of the hill the eight long pathways out into the desert.

"Ghost trails," said Alexia, repeating Zayed.

"I hardly think so. Quite the opposite." Madame Lefoux was crouched down examining one of the bodies.

They were all mummies, or at least they looked to be mummies. As they followed along one of the trails down the hill, they eventually came across unwrapped bodies, baked and charred into a mummylike state by the dry desert sun. A thin coating of sand covered most of them, but once brushed aside, it became clear that it was these bodies that formed the octopus's tentacles. Hundreds of mummies, stretching out into the desert, spaced farther and farther apart. Maximizing the expansion, perhaps? Each one was marked by a headstone, some made of carved rock or wood. They bore no legend or the names of the dead. They were all carved with the same shape—or to be precise, two shapes, an ankh, broken.

Alexia looked out over the tendrils extending off into the sands, disappearing from sight. "My people."

Madame Lefoux stood up from where she had crouched down to examine yet another mummy. "Preternaturals, all of them?"

"That would do it."

"Do what, exactly?" The Frenchwoman goaded her into saying it out loud.

"Cause the plague. Dry desert air combined with hundreds of dead preternaturals, basically—oh, I don't know how to put it properly—*outgassing*."

"That's a lot of dead preternaturals," said her husband.

"Collected from all around the world for hundreds and hundreds of years, I suppose. There aren't that many of us to start with. Could also be that originally they were all piled up and that forty years ago *someone* decided to start spreading them out."

Lord Maccon glanced over at Genevieve. "That would take quite an operation."

Alexia added, "Two operations: one to get it started originally and another to start it up again forty years ago."

Madame Lefoux looked back at them, her dark head twisting between the two and her green eyes grave. "It isn't me! This is the first I've heard of it, I promise you!"

"Yes," agreed Alexia, "but it is the kind of thing that might require a secret society. A massive underground secret society, of scientists, perhaps, who might not get so squeamish as others about handling the dead and collecting them from all over the world."

"You think the OBO is doing this!" Madame Lefoux rocked back on her heels, genuinely surprised by the idea.

"It is an *octopus*." Alexia was having none of that kind of silliness.

"No, you mistake me. The Order did spawn the Hippocras Club. I read the reports. I know we are capable of monstrous things. I simply don't believe this is us. To have such knowledge, to know what the body of a dead preternatural could do and not tell any other members? It is all very well to have a secret society of geniuses, but to keep such information secret from the members defeats the purpose. It's ridiculous. Think of the weapons I could have devised against vampires and werewolves had I known this. No, not the Order. It must be some other operation. The Templars, perhaps. They certainly have the infrastructure and the inclination."

Alexia frowned. "Don't you think the Templars might

have done more with such knowledge? Might have developed weapons, as you say, from the technology. Or more likely, have collected the bodies in Italy to protect the homeland there. Move the God-Breaker Plague rather than expand it."

Conall Maccon joined the fray. "You know what I think?"

Both ladies turned to look at him, surprised that he was still there. Alexia's husband had their daughter propped on his hip. He was looking scruffy and hot. Prudence was inordinately quiet and somber, faced with all the bodies. She ought to have screamed and cried with fear, like any ordinary child, but instead she had merely looked at them, muttered, "Mama" in a very humble way, and buried her face in her father's neck.

"What do you think, oh, werewolf one?" asked Alexia.

It was hard to make out her husband's expression behind all that beard. "I think Matakara started it all those thousands of years ago. I think she started it to get rid of the werewolves and it got out of hand. She might even have done it at Alexander's behest. After all, when the Greeks came to Egypt and took over, they were very antisupernatural. She might have struck up a deal. A deal that left her the lone vampire in Alexandria and everyone else gone."

"It's as good a theory as any," agreed his wife.

"And then what?" Madame Lefoux wanted to know.

"Someone figured out what she did. Someone who wanted to expand it."

Alexia could guess that one. "My father."

Madame Lefoux picked up the story. "Of course. Alessandro Tarabotti had the contacts. The OBO tried to recruit him after he broke with the Templars. There were a number of people throughout Europe, including my father, who he might have turned to such a cause as this. Can you imagine? The promise of mass supernatural extermination? Start up a worldwide preternatural body-collecting scheme."

"How macabre." Alexia did not approve of this stain on the family name. "Why does my father always have to be so difficult? He's dead after all. Couldn't he have left it at that?"

"Well, you must have gotten the inclination for trouble from someone," ruminated her husband.

"Oh, thank you, darling. Very sweet." Alexia felt the repulsion building up, pressing against her skin. The sun had risen and it was already doing its best to see her dry and suffering. She turned to one of the Egyptians. "Splash, please."

He made a gesture down at the nearby mummy.

"Oh, yes, I suppose water would damage it." She moved away from the bodies, and the man doused her thoroughly.

"Lady," he said, "we are running out of water."

"Oh, dear. Well, I suppose that means I, at least, had better head back." She looked pointedly at her husband and the French inventor. "Are you coming? I don't think there is much more to learn here." Another thought occurred to her. "Should we stop it?"

Lord Maccon and the inventor looked at her, not quite understanding.

"End the plague, I mean to say. We could try. I'm not certain how. My parasol's acid worked on the mummy in Scotland, but I've nowhere near enough for all these.

Water might work, dissolve some of the mummies. It's the dry air that keeps them preserved. Just think, we might destroy the God-Breaker Plague right here and now."

Madame Lefoux looked conflicted. "But the loss of all the mummies. The science, I don't…" She trailed off.

Alexia said, with a tilt to her head, "Do I need to remind you that you are indentured to the Woolsey Hive? You must consider the best interests of your queen."

The Frenchwoman grimaced.

Lord Maccon interjected. "I think we should wait, Alexia. It is enough to know."

His wife was suspicious. "Why?"

"The plague has its uses."

"But to allow it to expand?"

"I didn't say *that* was a good idea. It might be a moot point anyway. Your father might not have known about the disruption of water. Will the plague even be able to cross the Mediterranean?"

"But if we can visit this location and discover the truth, so can others."

The earl was not about to give quarter. "It's important to have a part of the world that is free of supernaturals."

"Why is that?" Alexia was even more suspicious. It wasn't like her husband to argue against destructive behavior. She felt the repulsion building against her skin and decided it was an argument they might continue back at camp, preferably in the Nile. "We can discuss it later. Shall we?"

Madame Lefoux looked reluctant. "I should like to take a few samples, to see what…" She trailed off again, her eye caught by something behind them, up the hill above the temple.

A man was standing there, waving at them madly.

"Laydeeee," the man called out, "*they* are coming!"

"Is that Zayed? What is he...? Oh my goodness gracious!" Alexia turned to look in the direction Zayed pointed, and there across the desert, running low and fast, a *thing* was moving toward them. It was a thing straight out of one of Madame Lefoux's sketches. In principle it resembled an enormous snail, its eye stalks belching gouts of flame into the air. It couldn't possibly operate on steam power, for where would one get the water in the desert? It must have multiple wheels, like those on farming equipment, under its shell. It was made of brass and glinted in the sun.

The snail was fast in a way that, given its form, Alexia found rather insulting. Riding atop its head and neck and hanging down the sides of its back were a number of men. They were dressed in white robes and turbans.

Alexia, Conall, and Genevieve stood for a moment, transfixed by the snail sliding across the desert.

"High-pressure, air-compressed sand buggy operating on methane fumes, unless I miss my guess."

"What was that, Genevieve?"

"A gastropod transport. We've hypothesized about them, of course. I didn't think anyone had actually built one."

"Well, it looks like someone did." Alexia shielded her eyes against the glare.

As the contraption neared, spitting up a wake of sand to either side, it slurred between the tentacles of the octopus so as not to disturb the bodies laid out there.

"That's not good," said Alexia.

"They know what's going on here," said Genevieve.

"Run!" said Conall.

Alexia took off, as ordered, throwing her modesty to the wind. She snapped closed her parasol and clipped it to the chatelaine. Then she picked up her skirts high, showing ankle but not caring for once, and took off up the hill.

"Alexia, wait! Here, take Prudence," Conall called after her.

Alexia paused and held out her free arm.

"No!" yelled Prudence, but she clung like a limpet to her mother after the transfer, wrapping her chubby arms and legs tight about Alexia's corseted frame.

Alexia looked into her husband's face; it was set and determined. "Now, Conall, don't do anything rash. You're mortal, remember."

Lord Maccon looked hard at this wife. "Get our daughter to safety and protect yourself, Alexia. I don't think…" He paused, clearly searching for the right words. "I'm still mad, but I do love you and I couldna stand it if…" He let the sentence trail off, gave her a blistering kiss as hot and as fierce as the Egyptian sun, and turned, charging toward the oncoming snail.

The snail spat a blast of fire at him. He dodged it easily.

"Conall, you idiot!" Alexia yelled after him.

She ignored his instructions, of course, reaching for her parasol.

Madame Lefoux came up to her, pressing a firm hand to the small of her back, almost pushing her up the hill.

"No, here, take Prudence." Alexia passed the little girl off once more.

"No, Mama!" remonstrated Prudence.

"I have my pins and my wrist emitters," said Madame Lefoux, looking like she, too, might disobey orders.

"No, *you* get her to safety and get Zayed to inflate the balloon. Someone has to see to that dunce of a husband of mine." Alexia was white with fear. "I think he's forgotten he could *actually* die."

"If you're certain?"

"Go!"

Madame Lefoux went, Prudence shrieking and struggling under her arm. "No, Mama. No, Foo!" There was no way the toddler could break free. Madame Lefoux might be bony and tall, but she was wiry and strong from years of hoisting machinery.

Lady Maccon unhooked and flipped her parasol about and turned to face the gastropod.

CHAPTER SEVENTEEN

___

A Gastropod Among Us

Whoever they were, they were less interested in guns and hurling fire than in scrapping hand to hand with the big man who stood alone before them. They'd stopped their snail in front of Lord Maccon and were leaping off it to attack him. Alexia's husband stood, waiting for them, arms akimbo.

I married an idiot, thought his loving wife, and she rushed down the hillside.

The idiot glowered at the gastropod enemy. His hair was a shaggy mess, his face covered in a full beard, his expression ferocious. He looked like a mountain man come to raise hell among the desert folk.

The first of the white-clad men charged him.

Conall lashed out. He might be mortal but he still knew how to fight. What Alexia worried about was his remembering he wasn't nearly so strong nor so durable in his nonsupernatural state.

She came dashing up just as he engaged two more

robed men in combat. She drew back her parasol, took aim, and fired a numbing dart at one of the opponents.

At this action, the attackers paused and fell back to regroup behind the snail, nattering at each other excitedly in Arabic.

"Guess they weren't expecting projectiles," said Lady Maccon smugly.

"I told you to leave!" The earl was not pleased to see his lady wife.

"Be fair, my love. When have I ever done as ordered?"

He snorted. "Where's Prudence?"

"With Madame Lefoux, getting the balloon up, I hope." Alexia braced herself next to him, reaching into one of the secret pockets of her parasol. She pulled out Ethel and handed the small gun to him.

"Just in case." Even as she said it, they heard the sound of a gunshot, and sand near Conall's foot spat up sharp pellets at them.

Alexia and her husband both dove forward. They had the advantage of higher ground, but they also had no shelter.

Alexia opened her parasol defensively in front of them, trying to remember if this new one had armor.

Lord Maccon took careful aim and fired the gun.

A loud *ping* indicated the bullet had hit the metal of the gastropod's shell harmlessly.

"This is very decidedly not good," said Alexia.

Conall looked at her, his expression ferocious. "We are stuck on a hill, outmanned and outgunned."

Another barrage of shots came at them, this time narrowly missing Conall's head. Alexia and her husband began to squirm backward, up the hill. Alexia's bustle wiggled back and forth suggestively as she squirmed. Her skirts began to ride up scandalously high, but she had other things to worry about.

Lady Maccon was not happy about the situation. Not happy at all. She was also drying out, the sun beating relentlessly down, and all her water carriers had run off at the first sign of the gastropod. The pressure of the mummies around her was beginning to leak in and distract. Her entire being felt as though it were being pushed. All she could think was that she wasn't meant to be there. The dead didn't want her there. And neither did the living, if the white-clad snail men were anything to go by.

Another barrage of bullets came at them. Conall let out a sharp cry as one lucky shot hit the meat of his upper arm.

"See, what did I warn you of?" Alexia was concerned. In Alexia, concern, nine times out of ten, came out of her mouth as annoyance.

"Not now, wife!" Lord Maccon yanked off his cravat, and Alexia wrapped it quickly about his arm while he transferred Ethel to his other, working, hand.

"Should I?" she asked, offering to take the gun back.

"Even with the wrong hand I can still shoot better than you."

"Oh, thank you very much." Alexia glanced back up the hill and saw the purple rise of Zayed's balloon peek up behind it.

"He won't come get us," she said. "Not with bullets flying. The balloon would be at risk."

"Then I suppose we had better get to it."

Alexia was peeved enough to reply, "Well, yes. Couldn't you have done that in the first place?"

"I was trying to buy you ladies some time to escape. Precious little good it's done you."

"Oh, *very* gallant. As if I would let you take on a gastropod alone without any kind of weaponry."

"Must we argue right now?" Another round of gunfire spit the sand up around them.

They continued squirming up the hill and exchanging fire with the snail. Or Conall did; Alexia was out of the numbing darts.

Alexia closed the parasol so she could see where she was aiming. She reached for the first nodule on the handle and twisted it, activating the magnetic disruption emitter. Some of the gastropod must have been comprised of iron components, for the engine seized up, much to the bewilderment of the shouting driver.

Taking advantage of the confusion, Alexia and Conall jumped to their feet and dashed up the hill toward the balloon, the earl pushing his wife before him.

They almost reached the top. The balloon was higher now, and Alexia could make out the long rope ladder dangling down and trailing toward them in the sand. She ran to it, faster than she had ever thought possible. The repulsion pressure was bearing down on her hard, there being far more mummies at the top of the hill. She could feel the blackness closing in—too many dead preternaturals pressing against her skull.

I can't faint again. Now is not a good time, even if I were the fainting type, she remonstrated with herself.

Conall paused, turned, and fired. The snail was in motion again, the disruption worn off, but some of the men had given up waiting for it and had taken off after them on foot up the hill. When Conall paused to shoot, so did they.

Alexia heard her husband cry out and he jerked backward against her. The bottom fell out of her world as she turned frantically, half supporting his massive weight, desperately looking to this new injury. A bloom of red appeared over his ribs, staining the shirt. He wasn't wearing a waistcoat.

"Conall Maccon," she cried, shaking off the blackness, "I forbid you to die."

"Don't be ridiculous, woman. I'm perfectly fine," he replied, dropping Ethel to clutch at his side, gasping and terribly pale under the beard.

Alexia bent to scoop up her gun.

"Leave it. We're out of ammunition anyway."

"But!"

Conall began climbing up the hill, bent almost double against the pain.

Alexia turned to follow, only to find herself seized about the waist by one of the white-clad enemy. She screamed in rage and swung her parasol up and back hard, hitting the man squarely atop the head.

He let go of her.

She was out of numbing darts but there was more than that in her accessory's arsenal. She twisted the nodule closest to the shade, hoping she had the correct direction for the correct liquid. Either the acid for vampires or the silver nitrite for werewolves would work on humans, but the acid was nastier. She couldn't remember which was which, so she simply hoped.

Alexia met the man's eyes over the top of the parasol

and felt a brief flash of recognition. She had seen him before, on the train to Woolsey back in England.

"What?" she said, pausing in her action. Then remembering her husband's wounds, she let loose the spray.

The man, as shocked as she, leaped backward out of harm's way, tripped on his long robe, and tumbled down the hill before regaining his feet. Instead of continuing his pursuit, he whirled about, running back toward the gastropod waving his arms wildly in the air.

Alexia couldn't understand a word he said except one. He kept repeating something that sounded Italian, not Arabic: "Panattone."

The peace brought about by this startling reversal didn't last long for, despite his gesticulations, the other white-clad men continued to fire. One or two ran past their erstwhile companion and continued after her.

Conall, who had reached the ladder and was holding on to it, had turned back at Alexia's yell. He was looking even whiter, and there was a good deal more blood running down his side than Alexia had ever seen spilling out of anyone.

Her world was closing in. It was like being inside a black tunnel, the repulsion pressing against the corners of her eyes. Pushing herself, slogging that last short distance to her husband took herculean effort. But then she was there, and Conall was pressing the rope into her hands.

"Go on!" he yelled, pushing up on her bustle as though he might hoist her into the air. He was nowhere near strong enough for that in his current state.

Alexia stuffed the cloth of her parasol into her mouth, holding it with her teeth, and began to climb. She paused halfway up to glance back, making certain her husband was following her.

He was, but he did not look well. His grip must be very weak, particularly with that injured arm.

The moment they latched on to the ladder, Zayed, blessed man, gave the balloon some heat, and it floated up.

Below them they could hear more guns firing. Alexia felt one whiz past her ear and heard a thunk as it lodged itself in the wicker of the basket.

Madame Lefoux and Prudence's heads poked over the edge. They both looked terrified. There was nothing they could do to help.

"Genevieve, take Prudence to cover!" Conall yelled.

The heads disappeared for a moment and then only the inventor's reappeared.

Madame Lefoux had one of her deadly little wrist darts out and was aiming it down. Startled, Alexia thought she was pointing it at her or Conall. In that moment, she wondered, yet again, if she had misjudged the Frenchwoman's loyalty.

Genevieve fired. The dart hurtled past Alexia's ear. There came a cry, and it hit the man Alexia hadn't even realized was there. A man in white robes dangling off the very bottom of the ladder let go and fell, screaming.

The balloon lifted again, and Alexia felt a lightening of that horrible sensation of repulsion, the black tunnel receding from around her vision. She wished the balloon would go faster, but they were at the mercy of the sky now.

Finally, after what felt like an age, bullets whizzing by all the while, Alexia attained the basket lip and tumbled in. She spat out her parasol and instantly turned to see to her husband.

Conall was still some ways behind her, slowed by his wounds. Below him she could see the gastropod, tracking them across the sands, still close enough to be a danger. Alexia went for her parasol, prepared to use the grapple attachment.

The firing continued but the balloon was out of range.

Then, one of the enemy pulled out a different kind of gun, a huge fat rifle that looked like it was designed for large game. He fired. Whether he was aiming to bring down the balloon or not, he hit Lord Conall Maccon.

Alexia wasn't certain where he was hit exactly, but she could see her husband's face, already ashen under the beard, turned up toward her. A ghastly expression of profound surprise suffused his handsome visage and he let go and fell. Desperate, Alexia shot the parasol grapple at her husband and missed. Conall fell for what seemed leagues, silent, not screaming, not uttering a sound, to land in a broken heap in the desert far below.

Biffy was worried. He wasn't a man to let slide his training—the many years under Lord Akeldama, the few under Professor Lyall. His training taught him to be practical, to look to the evidence, to watch and observe, never to assume, and always to be stylish about it. But he was still worried, for something was wrong. He had received no message from Lady Maccon in three sunsets. He had faithfully, every evening, climbed to the attic aethographic chamber and waited, at first only for a quarter of an hour or so, but as the days passed, he waited longer and longer.

He mentioned his concerns to Professor Lyall and the

Beta made sympathetic murmurs, but what could they do? Their orders were to remain in London, keep things in check. That was difficult enough with Lady Kingair convinced they should send someone after Floote and Channing convinced they were lying about Biffy's new state.

"Prove it!" Major Channing said the moment Lyall made the announcement to the pack. "Go on. Show me Anubis form!"

"It's not like that. I can't control it yet." Biffy spoke calmly.

The Gamma was unconvinced. "There's no way you're an Alpha. You're a ruddy dandy!"

"Now, now, Channing. I saw it. So did Lady Kingair." Professor Lyall's voice was mellow and calm.

"I dinna ken what I saw," said that lady most unhelpfully.

"See? Do you see?" Channing turned back to Biffy, his shapely lip curled in disgust. His face, though handsome, was disagreeably set and his blue eyes icy. "Go on, then. Can't show me the head? Fight me for dominance." The Gamma really looked as though he might strip right there in the dining room and change to a wolf, simply to prove Biffy was lying.

"You think I desired this state?" Biffy was outraged at being accused of making such a thing up. "Do I look like the kind of man who *wants* to be Alpha?"

"You don't look like an Alpha at all!"

"Exactly. Look at Lady Kingair and Lord Maccon— clearly being Alpha plays hell with one's wardrobe!"

Professor Lyall stepped in again. "Stop it, both of you. Channing, you will have to take my word for it. You know how long it takes to control wolf form, let alone master a second one. Give the pup a chance."

"Why should I?" The white wolf was petulant.

"Because I said so. And because he might be your Alpha someday. Wouldn't want to get off on the wrong paw, now, would you?"

"As if Lord Maccon would allow any such thing."

"Lord Maccon is in Egypt. You take your orders from me."

Biffy had never heard Lyall sound so forceful before. He rather liked it. It worked, for Channing backed down. He was willing to fight Biffy, but not Lyall; that was clear.

"Such an unpleasant fellow, and so attractive; it makes it that much worse," commented Biffy to Lyall later that night.

"Now, don't you worry about Channing. You'll be able to handle him eventually. Attractive, is he?"

"Not so much as you, by any means."

"Right answer, my dandy. Right answer."

Someone was screaming.

It took Alexia a long time to realize it was her. Only then did she stop, turn, and charge across the balloon to Zayed.

"Go back down! We must go back for him!"

"Lady, it is full sun. We cannot go down in daylight."

Alexia gripped his arm desperately. "But you must! Please, you must."

He shook her off. "Sorry, lady, there is only up now. He is dead anyway."

Alexia staggered back as though physically struck. "Please, don't say such a thing! I beg you."

Zayed only looked at her calmly. "Lady, no one could survive that fall. Find yourself a new man. You are still young. You breed well."

"He isn't just any man! *Please* go back." Alexia tried to grab at his hands. She had no idea how the balloon worked but she was willing to try.

Madame Lefoux came to her, pulling her gently off of Zayed. "Come away, Alexia, please."

Alexia shook Genevieve off and stumbled to the side of the basket, craning her neck to see, but they were rising fast. Soon they would hit the aether currents and then there really would be no going back.

She saw Conall lying in the sand. She saw the gastropod give up chasing the balloon and stop next to her husband. The men in white jumped down and surrounded his broken form.

Alexia opened her parasol. Perhaps it would help if she jumped; perhaps somehow it would catch the air and slow her fall.

She climbed up onto the edge of the basket, parasol open.

Madame Lefoux tackled her and yanked her back inside the basket.

"Don't be an imbecile, Alexia!"

"Someone has to go back for him!" Alexia struggled against her friend.

Zayed left off supervision of the balloon to come and sit on Alexia's legs, immobilizing her. "Lady, don't die. Goldenrod wouldn't like it."

The Frenchwoman grabbed Alexia by the face, one hand to each cheek, forcing her to look deep into her green eyes. "He's dead. Even if the fall didn't get him, he was badly wounded, and there was that shot from the smoothbore elephant gun. No mortal could survive both. It'd be hard for a werewolf to survive such a thing and he's no werewolf anymore."

"But I never told him I loved him. I only yelled at him!" Alexia felt as if there was nothing securing her to reality but Genevieve's green eyes.

Genevieve wrapped her arms about Alexia. "For you two, that *was* loving."

Alexia refused to believe he was gone. Not her big strong mountain of a man. Not her Conall. The desert warmth surrounded her. The sun shone bright and cheerful. The sensation of repulsion had lifted at last. But she was cold; her face felt sunken in against the hollows of her cheeks, and her mind was blank.

A small, soft hand pressed against her freezing cheek. "Mama?" said Prudence.

Alexia stopped thinking that her parasol might allow her to jump out of an air balloon. She stopped feeling like she was splitting in half, like her soul, if she had had one, was being wrenched down through her feet, a tendril, a tether to the man far below.

She stopped feeling anything at all.

The balloon jerked, catching first the southern current that had brought them to Luxor, and then after a few masterful manipulations from Zayed, floated up into a higher western current, one that, Alexia vaguely heard him say to Genevieve, would connect them to the northern route.

Even though they spoke directly above her head, Genevieve still holding her close, Prudence still cuddled up against her, the little girl's eyes huge and dark and worried on her mother's face, it all seemed to be occurring far away.

Alexia let it. She let the numbness take over, immersed herself in the lack of feeling.

Five days later, in the darkness several hours before dawn, they landed in Alexandria.

CHAPTER EIGHTEEN

The Truth Behind the Octopus

Everything was still chaos around her, but Lady Alexia Maccon sailed through it all on a sea of profound numbness. She allowed Madame Lefoux to take charge. The French inventor told the acting troupe about Lord Maccon's death. She explained what had happened using scientifically precise language. She also informed them that they had failed to find Primrose.

For ten days, Ivy and Tunstell had waited, with no contact from the kidnappers, their hopes pinned on Alexia and Conall discovering the whereabouts of their daughter. Now Lady Maccon had returned with the earl dead, and Primrose still missing.

And Lady Maccon? Lady Maccon was also missing. Nothing seemed to reach her. She responded to direct questions but softly, quietly, and with long pauses. She was also uninterested in food. Even Ivy was shaken out of her own worry enough to be upset by this.

But Alexia did cope. Alexia was always one to cope.

She did what needed to be done, once someone pointed it
out to her.

Ivy, between tears, managed to explain that she had
been unable to convince the aethographor to give her
Lady Maccon's messages. So Alexia went to bed, slept
most of the day away with dreams full of Conall's face as
he fell, woke up, dressed automatically, and went to get
the messages herself. There were nine of them from Biffy,
one for every sunset she had missed. The more recent
were merely worried notes of "Where are you?" but the
earlier ones told such a depressing truth that Alexia was
almost glad she was too numb to be affected by it.

Not Floote.

Not *her* Floote.

Not the man who had always been there for her. Always
provided her with the necessary cup of tea and a soothing,
"Yes, madam." Who had changed her nappies as a baby,
who had helped her sneak out of the Loontwills' house as
a young woman. Not Floote. Yet, it made horribly perfect
sense. Who else but Floote would have had all the necessary contacts? Who else but Floote would have the training in how to kill a werewolf? Alexia had seen him take
on vampires firsthand; she knew he had the ability.

Lady Maccon returned to the hotel, clutching her stack
of messages in one hand, moving like an automaton
through the bustling city streets that only a week and a
half earlier she had found more friendly and charming
than any other. In the hotel, she caught sight of Madame
Lefoux and Ivy in one of the private parlors off the reception area. She floated past, not even realizing that she
should extend an evening greeting. There was nothing left
in her for even the social graces. She felt, in fact, very

absent from herself. Adrift, as if nothing might bring her back again. Not even tea.

But at Madame Lefoux's summoning gesture, she wandered into their private boudoir and, in answer to her friend's polite inquiry as to her health, said, "As it turned out, it was Floote."

Genevieve looked confused.

Ivy gasped and said, "But he was *here*. Floote was here, looking for you. We sent him down the Nile after you. I thought…Oh, silly me, he isn't with you? I thought he would have caught up. Oh, I don't know what I thought."

Even that didn't pull Alexia back to the here and now. "Floote was looking for me? He probably wanted to explain himself."

Madame Lefoux pressed for details. "Explain what, exactly, Alexia?"

"Oh, you know, the God-Breaker Plague. Killing Dubh. That kind of thing." Alexia tossed Genevieve the little stack of papyrus papers from the aethographor station. "Biffy says…" Alexia trailed off, standing quietly while Madame Lefoux read over the notes.

Ivy said, "Oh, Alexia, do sit down!"

"Oh, should I?" Alexia sat.

Prudence came running in. "Mama!"

Alexia didn't look up.

The little girl grabbed at her hand. "Mama, bad men! Back."

"Oh, yes? Did you hide under the bed again?"

"Yes!"

The nursemaid came in, clutching Percy to her trembling breast. "They came back, Mrs. Tunstell! They came back!"

Ivy stood, face pale, clutching at her throat with both hands. "Oh, heavens. Percy, is he all right?"

"Yes, madam. Yes." The nursemaid passed over the redheaded infant to Ivy's clutching embrace. Percy, unperturbed, burped contentedly.

"See," said Prudence, still trying to get her mother's attention.

"Yes, dear, very wise. Hiding under the bed, good girl." Alexia was busy staring off into space.

"Mama, see!" Prudence was waving something in front of her mother's face.

Madame Lefoux took it from her gently. It was a roll of heavy papyrus tied with cord. The inventor unwound it and read the missive aloud.

"'Send Lady Maccon for the baby, alone. Tonight, after sunset.'" She added, "And they provide an address."

"Oh, Primrose!" Ivy burst into floods of tears.

Alexia said, "I suppose they were waiting for me to return."

"Do you think they wanted you all along?" Madame Lefoux looked upset.

Alexia blinked. She felt as though her brain were moving like a snail—a real snail, slow and slimy. "That's possible, but then, they kidnapped the wrong infant, didn't they?"

The Frenchwoman frowned in deep thought. "Yes, I suppose they did. What if that's it? What if they were after Prudence? What if they are taking you as a substitute? What if they still think they have Prudence, not Primrose?"

Alexia was already standing and wandering toward the door, her footsteps slow and measured.

"Where are you going?"

"It's after sunset," said Lady Maccon, as though it were perfectly obvious.

"But, Alexia, be sensible. You can't simply trot to their orders!"

"Why not? If it returns Primrose to us?"

Ivy, trembling, could not speak. She looked back and forth between Alexia and the Frenchwoman. Her hat, a mushroom-puff turban affair with a peacock-style fan of feathers out the back, quivered with a surfeit of emotion.

"It could be dangerous!" protested Madame Lefoux.

"It's always dangerous," replied Lady Maccon flatly.

"Alexia, don't be a peewit! You can't *want* to die. You're not one for melodrama. Conall is *gone*. You have to keep on going without him."

"I am going. I'm going right out to find the kidnappers and retrieve Primrose."

"That's not what I meant! What about Prudence? She needs her mother."

"She has Lord Akeldama."

"That's not quite the same thing."

"No, it's better—mother and father all rolled into one attractive package, and he doesn't look to be dying anytime soon."

"Oh, goodness, Alexia, please, wait. We must talk about this, devise a plan."

Alexia paused, not really thinking out her next maneuver.

The hotel clerk came in to the parlor at that moment.

He approached Genevieve. "Mr. Lefoux? There is a gentleman for you. A Mr. Naville. Claims he has some important information to impart."

Genevieve rose and brushed past Lady Maccon. "Just wait a few minutes, please, Alexia?"

Alexia merely stood, unresponsive. She watched as the Frenchwoman strode across the reception room to a small gaggle of gentlemen. One of them was very young. Another was carrying a leather case stamped with the image of an octopus. She watched Madame Lefoux tilt her head, lift up her short hair, and pull down her cravat and collar, exposing the back of her neck. She was showing them her octopus tattoo. Alexia's brain said, *Those are members of the Order of the Brass Octopus.* Her practical side said, *I hope she doesn't tell them about the preternatural mummies. There will be a race to the bodies, to use them in munitions, to shift the balance against immortals.* Her even more practical side remembered that there were men dressed in white willing to defend those mummies to the death. Her husband's death.

The rest of her kept walking, in defiance of Genevieve's request. She had her parasol hanging from its chatelaine at her waist. She had the address of the location on a scrap of paper. She moved across the reception room and out into the street, Genevieve unaware of her movements.

There Alexia hailed a donkey boy and told him the address. The boy nodded eagerly. With very little effort at all, she climbed astride, the boy yelled to his creature in Arabic, and they started forward.

The donkey took her into an unfamiliar sector of the city, a sad and abandoned-looking structure behind the customs house. She slid off the animal and paid the boy generously, sending him away when he would have waited. She climbed the step and pushed through the reed mats of the doorway into what looked to be some kind of warehouse, possibly for bananas, if the sweet smell was to be believed.

"Come in, Lady Maccon," said a polite, slightly accented voice out of the dim echoing interior.

With a flitter of speed customary to the breed, the vampire was right up next to her, almost too close, showing his fangs.

"Good evening, Chancellor Neshi."

"You are alone."

"As you see."

"Good. You will explain to me why the child isn't working."

"First let me see that Primrose is safe."

"You thought I would bring her here? Oh, no, she is left behind, and she is safe. But I thought the abomination's name was Prudence? You English and your many names."

"It is Prudence. Did you want my daughter? You got the wrong child."

The chancellor reeled back and blinked at her. "I did?"

"You did. You got my friend's baby. She has not been happy about that."

"Not the abomination?"

"Not the abomination."

There was a long pause.

"So might we have her back, then?" Alexia asked.

The vampire went from confused, to angry, to resolved. "No. If I cannot use the abomination, I will use you. She cannot be let to suffer any longer."

"Is this about Queen Matakara?"

"Of course."

"Or should I say Queen Hatshepsut?"

"To use that name, you should say *King* Hatshepsut."

"What does *your* queen want with *my* daughter?"

"She wants a solution. An easy solution. One that could be smuggled in and then back out with none of the others noticing. But, no, this had to be difficult. There had to be two black-haired English babies, and we got the wrong one. Now I am stuck with you."

"I am not easy to smuggle."

"You most certainly are not, Lady Maccon."

"Yes, but why?"

"Come with me and you will learn why."

"And Primrose?"

"And we will return to you the useless baby."

He led her from the building and together they walked toward the hive.

It was a long, quiet walk through the city. Lady Maccon allowed herself to drift on that sea of absence.

Despite this, she found herself eventually thinking about Queen Matakara. Trapped in that chair, her eyes as sad as anything Alexia had ever seen or felt until now. They were the eyes of someone who wanted to die. She could sympathize.

"It's Matakara," she said into the silent night, stopping in her tracks.

Chancellor Neshi stopped as well.

"She set the God-Breaker Plague originally *and* she started it up again. She and my father." Alexia talked out her revelations. "They struck a deal."

The chancellor continued for her. "He broke with the OBO without telling them what he found. He agreed not to tell the Templars either. In return he got to continue the plague's expansion with the certain knowledge that eventually it would take my queen, too."

"Why not just bring a preternatural mummy into the room with her? Wouldn't that work?" Alexia began walking once more.

The vampire said, exasperated, "Do you think I haven't tried? But your father left iron orders. None of my people ever seem to be able to get to a preternatural body fast enough. It's like they are networked. It's like there is someone in charge who keeps an eye on all the preternaturals in the world. He won't let me break the original agreement, even from the grave."

Alexia wondered if Floote had done as he said and had her father's body cremated, or if Alessandro Tarabotti was one of those who lay exposed above Hatshepsut's Temple. "Why not simply ask me to do it? I was right there. I would have been happy to touch her."

"Not in front of the others. They can't know that their queen wants to die. They can't possibly know. Done at the wrong time, they would swarm—swarm without a queen. That is not pretty, Lady Maccon. I could sneak a child in and out easily enough, but you, Lady Maccon, are *not* sneaky. Besides, if Lady Maccon, English, killed Queen Matakara, it would cause an international incident."

"Why not simply stick with the plan and wait for the plague to expand? It's already reached the edge of Alexandria."

"The OBO found out. A concession to excavate at the temple was issued. Our time has run out. When I heard of your child, I thought she would be an easy solution. I could sneak her in and my queen would be free at last. Done quietly, before dawn, and my drone could have her back out again and no one the wiser."

"But why you, Chancellor?"

"The queen trusts me. I am almost as old as she. I, too, am ready to die. But the others, they are young yet."

Alexia paused again in her walking. "Is that what would happen? I didn't know. When a queen dies, all her hive goes with her?"

"And go quietly if it is timed correctly."

"You were willing to do that to your hive?"

"It is the pharaoh's way. To travel with servants into the afterlife. Why shouldn't we all die together?"

Alexia could understand what came next. He would get her in to the queen, he would arrange for her to touch Matakara, and she would die. So, too, would Alexia, as the other vampires in their pain and loss would kill her outright, and baby Primrose as well.

"Have you thought this through, Chancellor?"

"Yes."

"You are cursing me to die with this last desperate gambit."

"Yes."

"You know, you could still borrow Prudence? She's small enough to sneak in and out."

"Too late, Lady Maccon."

"I thought things were never too late for an immortal. Isn't that the point? All you creatures have is time."

Chancellor Neshi only led the way into the hive house.

Alexia followed. She couldn't think of anything better to do.

It was much the same as before. A crowd of servants descended upon them to remove their shoes, and the chancellor went off to alert his queen as to Lady Maccon's presence.

However, Alexia was much less welcome without her

actor escort. She couldn't understand what the other drones and vampires said to Chancellor Neshi when she appeared at the throne room entrance, but it was said very loudly and angrily.

Above them, Queen Matakara sat on and in and within her throne of blood and watched everything with tortured eyes.

Alexia inched toward her.

Chancellor Neshi went and retrieved Primrose from some hidden sanctum. The baby seemed perfectly unharmed. She waved chubby arms at Alexia, in one fist clutching a large necklace of gold and turquoise.

One of the drones noticed that Lady Maccon was moving toward his queen and launched himself at her. He was a slender fellow, but wiry and muscled, plenty strong enough to hold her.

Alexia thought of going for her parasol. She thought of diving at the queen, getting her bare hand to the woman's exposed forehead. She thought of grabbing Primrose and running away from them all. She thought of struggling against her captor. She could probably break free; she'd had enough experience with *that* by now. For a proper Englishwoman, she was adept at the application of elbows and feet to delicate anatomy. She thought of doing many things, but she actually did none of them. She pushed herself back into the numbness and let it wash over her, for the first time in her life inclined to do nothing at all, to wait and see.

The arguing continued.

Then there was a tumult in the hallway and two drones brought in a struggling Madame Lefoux.

"Alexia! I thought you would be here."

"You did? Oh."

"It was the only logical explanation. Once I removed the idea that a vampire wants to live forever, I was left with the answer. Matakara started the plague, both times. First against the werewolves and later against the vampires and herself. And if she wanted to die that badly, she'd try to get either you or Prudence to touch her."

"And how could you blundering in here now possibly help?" Alexia was confused but not angry. She didn't have enough emotion left to be angry.

"I brought reinforcements."

At which juncture a mechanical ladybug trundled into the room with Prudence riding atop it. "Mama!"

At that, Alexia did get angry. "Genevieve, what were you thinking! To bring my daughter into a hive of vampires, one of them a kidnapper who wanted her in the first place? A hive whose queen wants to die. A hive that will go mad if that happens."

The Frenchwoman smiled. "Oh, I didn't bring *only* her."

Bustling in after Prudence came the acting troupe. The thespians wore identical expressions of seriousness and were armed with the stage swords and props of their trade. They were led by Ivy Tunstell and her husband. Ivy wore an undersized admiralty hat in white and black with a particularly large ostrich feather out the top, and Tunstell's trousers, while tight, were made of leather for battle.

The practical part of Alexia thought that an acting troupe was hardly reinforcements against a hive of vampires.

The advent of this crowd of theatrical invaders caused a tizzy. There were colorful fabrics and people flying everywhere, as the actors employed stage fighting, tumbling, and, in the case of one young lady, ballet to dodge their opponents. There was a good deal of shouting and one operatic war cry from Mr. Tumtrinkle.

Tunstell began quoting Shakespeare. Ivy charged for her daughter, parasol wielded in a manner Alexia felt did her proud. The drone holding the infant stood with mouth slightly open for sufficiently long enough to allow Ivy to bop him hard on the head and yank her daughter away. Alexia half expected her dear friend to then faint at her own audacity, but Ivy Tunstell stood firm, child on hip, parasol at the ready. The tiny part of Alexia that was not numb was outlandishly satisfied.

With uproar continuing and the vampires and drones distracted, Alexia resumed creeping toward the hive queen. Matakara wanted to die. Matakara who had started everything. Matakara who was responsible for *her husband's death*. Well, Lady Alexia Maccon would see her dead. And gladly!

Alexia made it to the base of the platform upon which the gruesome chair stood. She caught Chancellor Neshi's eye and he nodded, encouraging her, before continuing his argument with one of the other vampires. Alexia wondered if anyone else even understood what was going on.

Just as she was about to climb up, a vampire grabbed her around the waist. He lost his strength upon contact but maintained his grip. He yanked her around and bore her down to the floor. As she fell, Alexia could see all was not going well for Madame Lefoux's would-be invasion.

Ivy, clutching Primrose, was fending off two drones with her parasol, but soon enough their surprise at her attire would wear off and she would succumb. Gumption only got a girl so far. Tunstell had Prudence's ladybug held high and was bashing it about. Mr. Tumtrinkle was faced off against a vampire and not doing well, as might be expected. Even all his fancy fencing tricks from *Hamlet and the Overcooked Pork Pie—a Tragedy* were not fast enough nor strong enough, or, quite frankly, deadly enough for an immortal.

A scream diverted Alexia's attention. A vampire launched himself at Ivy, going for her neck. The drone attacking her fell back.

Alexia unhooked her parasol, took aim, and then realized she was out of numbing darts. She turned the middle nodule right and out popped the wooden stake at the tip. She began bashing about with it. She dared not use the lapis solaris; the acid would surely do just as much damage to one of her actor defenders.

Prudence, who had taken initial refuge from the kerfuffle under a small table, emerged at Ivy's terrified scream. She charged the vampire attacking Mrs. Tunstell and beat at his ankle with her tiny fists. It was enough contact to turn her vampire, and him not. He was left gnawing uselessly on Ivy's bloodied neck, and Prudence turned into a bouncing blur of excited infant with supernatural abilities. She was of very little help as she merely bucketed about, not knowing her own strength, hurling everyone aside whether vampire, drone, or actor. Behind her, Ivy crumpled to the floor, still managing to support Primrose but suffering from shock or loss of blood, or both.

And then, leaping up to the balcony from the street below and charging into the room via the open window came a massive beast. And atop the wolf, looking as dig-

nified and butlerlike as might be possible for a man riding
a werewolf, was Floote.

Alexia stopped trying to touch Queen Matakara and
turned in a slow, ponderous manner. She felt as though
she were seeing and experiencing everything underwater.

"Conall Maccon, I thought you were dead!"

Lord Maccon looked up at his wife from where he had
his jaws about a vampire's leg, let go, and barked at her.

"Do you know how I've been suffering for the last
week? How could you? Where have you been?"

He barked again.

Alexia wanted to throw herself at him and wrap both
arms and legs about him. She also wanted to whack him
over the head with her parasol. But he was there and he
was alive and everything was suddenly working again.
The numbness vanished and Alexia took in the world
around her. Her brain, somewhat absent for the better part
of a week, returned to full capacity.

She looked to her butler. "Floote, what have you
done?"

Floote only pulled out a gun and began shooting
vampires.

"Prudence," Alexia called sharply, "come to Mama!"

Prudence, who had been, until that moment, busy trying to suck the blood out of the arm of a very surprised
drone, stopped and looked over at her mother. "No!"

Alexia used *that* tone of voice. The voice that Prudence
rarely heard but knew meant trouble. "Right this very
moment, young lady!"

For Prudence, currently a vampire, *right this very
moment* was very fast indeed. In a veritable flash, she was
at Alexia's side. Alexia grabbed her daughter, turning her

human once more, and then, without any kind of compunction at all, lifted her up and set her in the lap of Queen Matakara of Alexandria.

Prudence said, "Oh, Dama," in a very somber voice and looked deep into the tormented eyes of the ancient vampire. Her little face was as grave and gentle as any nurse ministering to the wounded on a battlefield. She stood up on the frail woman's lap and reached for her face.

Madame Lefoux, having somehow determined what was happening, even through the chaos, appeared on the other side of the aged queen. The inventor assessed the situation. In a few quick movements, she flipped several toggles and snaps at the bottom of Queen Matakara's mask. The awful thing fell away, exposing the vampire's face fully to Prudence's metanatural touch.

Under the mask, Matakara's skin was sunken against the bones of her chin, but it was clear she had once been quite beautiful. Her face was heart shaped with an aquiline nose, broadly spaced eyes, and small mouth.

Prudence, drawn by the newly exposed flesh, placed one small, chubby hand to the vampire's chin. It was a sympathetic, intimate gesture, and Alexia couldn't help but imagine that her daughter somehow knew exactly what she was doing.

Complete and total pandemonium resulted.

All the vampires in the room turned as one, leaving off whoever they had been fighting with or feeding on. They charged. This only frightened Prudence who, now a vampire once more, leaped nimbly out of the way and dashed about the room pell-mell.

Matakara, mortal and still attached to her chair, jerked

against the straps and tubes, letting out a silent scream of agony.

One of the vampires turned to Alexia. "You! Soulless. Make it stop!"

Lord Maccon, still a wolf, mouth dripping with old dark vampire blood, leaped to his wife's defense. His hackles were up, his teeth bared in a snarl.

"She cannot die," cried out one of the vampires. Clearly more of them spoke English than Alexia had previously supposed. "We have *no new queen*!"

"So you, too, will die." Lady Maccon was unsympathetic.

"More than that, we will go mad. We will take Alexandria with us. Just think of the damage even six vampires can do to one city."

Alexia looked around. Madame Lefoux had lost her hat but otherwise stood strong. She was tussling with the beautiful female drone on the opposite side of the throne. Mr. Tumtrinkle lay fallen in one corner. Alexia wasn't certain he still breathed. Several of the other thespians were looking worse for the wear. One of the younger, prettier actresses bled copiously from multiple neck bites. Floote stood in the midst of the melee, wooden knife in one hand, an expression of utterly unbutlerlike ferocity on his face. When he caught Alexia's eye, his customary impassivity immediately returned. Then, coming from the far side of the room, Alexia heard a strangled choking sound and saw Tunstell sobbing, his red head bent over the crumpled form of Ivy.

Alexia's friend lay broken and bloodied, her neck a ruin of torn flesh. Baby Primrose, unharmed, lay squalling in the crook of Ivy's flaccid arm. Tunstell scooped the child up and clutched her to his breast, still sobbing.

A shout distracted Alexia from the tragic scene—one of the other vampires managed to capture Prudence. He ran toward Alexia with the toddler's struggling form held out at arm's length, as if in an egg-and-spoon race. Alexia knew he would try to hand her the child. She dodged away. Not that she didn't love her daughter, but right then she certainly didn't want to touch her.

Lord Maccon snarled and intercepted the attack, perfectly understanding Alexia's predicament.

"Wait!" yelled Alexia. "I have an idea. Chancellor, what if we could get you a new queen?"

The vampire stepped forward. "That is an acceptable proposal, if Matakara has the strength to try and we have a volunteer? Who do you suggest?"

Alexia looked thoughtfully at Madame Lefoux.

Even in the middle of grappling intimately with the beautiful drone, the Frenchwoman shook her head madly. The inventor had never sought immortality.

"Don't worry, Genevieve, I had someone else in mind."

Around her everything stilled as Alexia walked across the room to where Ivy Tunstell lay. Her bosom companion's breathing was shallow, her face unnaturally pale. She did not look long for this world. Alexia was familiar enough with death to know when it stalked a friend. She swallowed down hard on her own unhappiness and looked to Ivy's beloved husband. "Well, Tunstell, how would you like to be married to a queen?"

Tunstell's eyes were red but it took him no time at all to make the decision. He had once been a claviger and had spent his life on the fringe of immortal society. He had sacrificed his own bid for metamorphosis to marry Miss Ivy Hisselpenny. He had no compunctions or reservations. If Ivy were to be dead or a vampire, he would rather her be a vampire. Tunstell was the most progressive man Alexia had ever met.

"Try it, Lady Maccon, I entreat you."

So Alexia signaled to one of the vampires in that utterly autocratic way of hers. The vampire came to do her bidding, when only a few minutes earlier he might have killed her where she stood. He carried Ivy over to drape her on Matakara, setting the actress on the queen's lap like a ventriloquist's doll and arranging her to lie back so Ivy's neck was near Matakara's mouth. Ivy's head lolled back.

Chancellor Neshi pulled a set of leather belts with chain links attached and strapped them over Ivy, lashing her tightly against his queen. Then he turned and nodded at Lady Maccon.

Alexia took Prudence into her arms.

Queen Matakara turned back to a vampire.

She began spouting a string of words, ancient-sounding words, not Arabic at all but some other language. Her voice was commanding, melodic, and very direct. Chancellor Neshi leaped to her side and bent to her ear, whispering frantically. The other vampires stilled, waiting.

Alexia wasn't quite certain what they thought was happening. Would they know that their queen was still destined to die? Did they know the bargain the chancellor was striking? Did they understand the ancient tongue, or did they still think there was a chance?

Chancellor Neshi leaped back down and approached Alexia. When Conall growled and would not let him near, Alexia said, "All is well, husband. I do believe I know what he wants."

Chancellor Neshi sidled past the still-bristling wolf. "She desires your assurance, Soulless, that you will see the deed done, whether this metamorphosis is successful or not."

"You have my word," said Alexia. She was thinking of Countess Nadasdy, a younger and stronger queen. The countess had *failed* to metamorphose a new queen. Yet here Alexia was wagering all their lives on Ivy Tunstell having excess soul and Queen Matakara enough strength to draw it out of her.

CHAPTER NINETEEN

How to Retire to the Countryside

Chancellor Neshi nodded, once, to the ancient queen. At his signal, Matakara bent forward, opening her mouth wide. Unlike Countess Nadasdy, she didn't appear to need any kind of drinking cup for preparation. Her fangs, Alexia noted, were particularly long—her makers even longer than her feeders. Perhaps it was a factor of her age. Perhaps when queens got too old, all they could do was try to make a replacement queen. Perhaps that was the problem: Matakara needed to breed more than she needed to eat. She had been kept alive long past that time. *Her hive should have been doing nothing but giving her girls to try to change over,* thought Alexia. Then again, she probably would have gone through a large number of girls that way. Local authorities wouldn't have been too chuffed.

The ancient vampire sank both sets of fangs deep into the flesh of Ivy's already-lacerated neck. Matakara could not move her arms to hold Ivy. She kept herself attached by the strength of her jaw and with the aid of the straps that held Ivy against her. The queen's dark eyes, visible over the fall of Ivy's black hair, had lost a little of their eternal sorrow and looked almost contemplative. She moved not one muscle as she sucked, except that like Countess Nadasdy, there was a strange up-and-down fluttering in her emaciated neck.

Ivy Tunstell remained limp for a very long time. Everyone in that room held their breath, waiting. Except Conall, of course, who paced around growling at people. The earl had very little sense of gravity in any given situation.

Then Ivy's whole body jerked and her eyes popped open, wide, startled, looking directly at Alexia. She began to scream. Tunstell made a lunge toward her but one of the other vampires grabbed him and held him back. Ivy's pupils dilated, darkening and extending outward until both her eyeballs were a deep bloodred.

Alexia knew what came next. Ivy's eyes would begin to bleed, and she would continue to scream until those screams became garbled by the blood pouring from her mouth. *Of course Ivy doesn't have excess soul! Stupid of me to even think it.*

Except that Ivy's eyes did not start to drip blood. Instead, the darkness in them began to recede, until eventually they were the velvety brown of her true self. Ivy stopped screaming, closed her eyes, and began to jerk violently from side to side as though undergoing a kind of fit. Her copious dark ringlets bobbed about her face and her tiny admiral's cap gave up its grip upon her hair—after enduring so much during the battle—and tumbled to the floor, its white plume sagging sadly.

Ivy opened her mouth once more, but not to scream

this time. Oh, there was blood dripping out, but it was blood from the fangs, four of them, as they broke through her gums and extended forth, shining in the candlelight. Ivy's face, already fashionably pale, became ashen white. Her hair took on an even bouncier and glossier sheen, and she opened her eyes once more. With a tiny shrug, she threw off the thick leather and metal straps, snapping them easily as if they were no more than gossamer silk. She leaped down from the throne to land, light and easy on the floor of the chamber.

She lisped around her new teeth, "What an odd sethathion. Tunny dathling, did I faint? Oh, my hath!" Bending, she retrieved her admiral's hat and popped it firmly back upon her head.

Behind her, Queen Matakara looked even more sunken and bloodless than ever before. She slumped forward, only the artifice of the chair keeping her upright.

Chancellor Neshi said to Alexia, "Your promise, Soulless?"

Alexia nodded and moved forward, this time unhindered by any vampires. She climbed upon the dais and pressed her hand to the ancient vampire's arm in one small spot where the skin was free of straps and tubes.

Queen Matakara, King Hatshepsut, last of the Great Pharaohs, Oldest Vampire, died right then and there at Alexia's touch. There was no fanfare, no screaming in pain. She let out a tiny sigh and slipped out of her immortal cage at last. It was both the worst thing Alexia's preternatural state had forced her to do and the best, for the expression in those dark eyes was, for the very first time, one of absolute peace.

In the silent stillness of wonder that followed, while

drones and vampires adjusted themselves and their teth-
ers to a new queen, Chancellor Neshi picked up Prudence.
Prudence turned, yet again, into a vampire, and before
anyone could stop him, the chancellor dashed on chubby
legs out the window to the balcony and jumped over the
edge, falling to his death in the street below.

The moment he died, Prudence turned back into a normal baby. Or as normal as she got. Alexia filed that little
fact away; apparently something else canceled out her
daughter's powers besides her mother, sunlight, and
distance—death.

There was a good deal of cleanup to be done, a number of
explanations and arrangements to be made, and discussions
to be had. Not to mention several formal introductions and
a few broken bones and bloody necks to medicate. The five
remaining vampires looked at one another and then, as a
body, rushed to surround their new queen, chattering at her
in Arabic and gesticulating excitedly.

Ivy, confused—head bobbling back and forth between
them, white feather puffing about—finally raised her
voice in a most un-Ivy-like way and ordered silence. She
looked to her husband—who was standing, crying, clutching Primrose to his breast—and then turned to Lady
Maccon for assistance.

"Alexia, pleath ethplain whath ith going on?"

Lady Maccon did, to the best of her ability. The pretty
female drone who spoke English translated the explanation for the benefit of the vampires. Soon it became clear
to everyone that Ivy had both a husband and children,
which caused much consternation, as such a thing was
taboo among those seeking metamorphosis. At which Ivy

protested she hadn't sought it, so she couldn't possibly be blamed. Alexia stated categorically that what was changed was changed, and like spilled blood, there was no point going on about it. Mrs. Tunstell was a vampire queen now and they had all better make the best of the husband and twins that came with the package.

Ivy said she felt remarkably restless and wanted to know if she had to stay in Alexandria for the rest of her life.

Alexia remembered Lord Akeldama once mentioning something about new queens having several months to resettle. *How else would vampires have spread over the world?* Ivy said, good, in that case she wished to return to London *immediately*.

The Egyptian vampires protested. Alexandria was their home, had been for hundreds of years! Ivy would have none of it. London was *her* home, and if she had to spend eternity anywhere, it was going to be in the place where one could get a decent hat! She batted her eyelashes and lisped out girlish pleas, her character clearly not so much metamorphosed as her soul. Yet her tactic worked despite her lack of autocratic tendencies. In remarkably short order, everyone was dispersing. Those drones who wished to ally with a new queen and relocate were to pack and meet at the departure dock for the steamer the next morning. The vampires, looking slightly panicked, dashed off to gather belongings and then, sticking close to Ivy, escorted her, her husband, her daughter, and her acting troupe back to the hotel.

Alexia was left in the hive house with Matakara's dead body, Madame Lefoux, Prudence, and Lord Maccon. Her daughter was exhausted beyond her childish capacities and was sitting in a sobbing heap. Her husband was still a wolf. During Ivy's metamorphosis, Floote had disappeared.

Madame Lefoux gave Alexia a long look and then climbed up to examine the vampire queen's body and chair with studied interest, pointedly leaving Alexia to work out her family affairs on her own.

Alexia went over and scooped up Prudence, cuddling the sobbing baby close. She simply stood like that, glaring at her husband, tapping one foot.

Finally, Lord Maccon shifted form.

"Explain yourself," said his lady wife in a very decided tone of voice.

"Floote found me badly injured and imprisoned among his men and tended to me until he could get me out of the plague zone," Lord Maccon explained.

Alexia thought about her former butler. "His men? Ah. While I am very grateful to him for seeing to you, wayward husband, it does seem to me that it was his men who caused all the fuss in the first place."

Lord Maccon said, "According to Floote, they didn't know who you were. He has given them new instructions."

"I should hope so." Alexia paused, considering her next move. "Do you think we'll ever find him?"

Lord Maccon shook his head. "Not if he doesn't want to be found. Floote has a whole network here, and familiarity with the terrain, and no werewolves to track him in the God-Breaker Zone."

"I suppose that saves us from determining what to do with a butler who goes around killing people. It certainly reflects badly upon our domestic staff. Still, I shall miss him. There was a man who knew how to brew a good cup of tea." Alexia was sad to lose her dear old companion, but she also knew it was for the best. She should hate to have to put him on trial or turn him over to Lady Kingair.

"Did Floote tell you it was all based on a deal my father made with Matakara?"

"He did."

Alexia asked her husband, "What are we to do about it?"

Lord Maccon came over to her tentatively, unsure whether she forgave him yet for dying on her, unsure whether he forgave her yet for lying to him.

Alexia could sense his uncertainty. She was having none of any such silliness anymore. She closed the gap between them and curled herself against his nakedness, bracketing Prudence against his large form so that the baby was in close contact with both her parents.

Prudence gave a little murmur of approval.

Conall sighed, giving over his resentment, and wrapped his family tight in his strong arms. He pressed small kisses against Alexia's temple and against his daughter's head.

The earl cleared his throat, still holding Alexia tight against him. The words rumbled in the massive chest so close to her ear. "I have been giving some thought to my retirement."

"Indeed, how very unusual of you. From BUR, or from the pack?"

"Both. I purchased property, in Cairo, shortly after we arrived."

Alexia tilted her head back and looked to her husband in confusion. "Conall, what is this?"

"A strategic retreat, my love. I thought, when Prudence

has grown, we might return here, together. Take long walks, eat pastries, play, uh, backgammon or whatnot."

"In the God-Breaker Zone...but you'll grow old and die!"

"As will you." Conall began stroking her back in a soothing manner.

"Yes, but I was *always* going to grow old and die!"

"Now we can do it together."

"My love, that's a very chivalric thought, but there is no need to be nonsensical in matters of the heart."

The earl stopped petting his wife and leaned a little away from her so he could look down into her upturned face. His tawny eyes were serious. "My dear, I am getting old. Older than you think. I will not allow myself to become one of *those* Alphas. Two Betas have already betrayed me—I must be losing some measure of control. In another decade or so, it will be time to let go gracefully. Can you think of a better way than relocating here?"

Alexia, practical to the last, actually considered this. "Well, no. But, dear, are you quite certain?"

"You like it here, don't you, my love?"

Alexia tilted her head. "Well, it's warm, and the food is tasty."

"That's settled, then."

Lady Maccon was not one to give in so easily as that. "We will have to bring a great deal of tea with us when we relocate." She was quite firm on *that* point.

"We could start a tea-import business," suggested her husband. "Something to keep you entertained in your old age."

"Trade! Really, I don't know..." Alexia trailed off thoughtfully.

Madame Lefoux, all forgotten until that moment, jumped down off the throne platform to join them. "It's very romantic, his wanting to die with you."

"*You* would say that."

"Can I come and join you as well?" She sidled up to Alexia and winked at her.

"Genevieve, you don't know when to give up, do you?" Conall wore a very amused expression.

"Can you imagine the things I could build without supernatural or governmental interference?"

"Good gracious me, what a terrifying thought. You may visit us, Genevieve, but that is all."

"Spoilsport."

"Shall we?" suggested Conall, gesturing at the exit.

The four of them filed out of the now-abandoned hive house. Alexia paused to turn and look at it thoughtfully. They might make use of it as well. After all, Alexandria was a port city. If they were going to import tea... "Oh, dear, Prudence, I'm already thinking like a tradeswoman."

"No," said Prudence.

Conall stepped out into the street. Alexia considered reminding her husband he was naked and then gave up. In Alexandria, they were bound to be a spectacle whatever they did.

She shifted her daughter to her other hip. The baby's eyes were half closed and she was nodding off, the victim of an exciting night. "Come along, then, Prudence, my dear."

"No," muttered Prudence softly.

Madame Lefoux said, "Have you ever considered that she might be saying no because she doesn't like her name? She never says no when you use an endearment."

Alexia stopped, floored by the idea. "Do you think? Is that true, my little puggle?" She used Lord Akeldama's favorite moniker for Prudence.

"Yes," said Prudence.

"Prudence?"

"No!" said Prudence.

"Goodness, Genevieve, you may be on to something. What should we call her, do you think?"

"Well, she has an excessive number of names. Why not wait until she's a little older? She can choose for herself. Can't you, sweetheart?"

"Yes!" said Prudence, most categorically.

"There, you see? Takes after her mother already."

"What could you mean by that?" queried Alexia archly.

"Likes her own way, doesn't she?" suggested the Frenchwoman with a dimpled smile.

"I don't know what you're talking about," replied Lady Maccon with a great deal of dignity. With which she took off at a brisk pace, keeping an eye to her husband's rather distinguished backside as it wandered down the street under the waning Egyptian moon.

CHAPTER TWENTY

In Which Times Shift

After a sea journey only slightly less exciting than the first, Lord and Lady Maccon, their daughter, the Tunstells and their twins, the acting troupe, one nurse-maid, five vampires, and seven drones arrived at the port of Southampton on a blustery day in late April of 1876. Such a crowd had mostly taken over the ship and pro-ceeded, in remarkably fine fettle after such an extensive journey, to take over the train to London.

London was ill prepared for such an invasion. It was also not quite the same London as when they had departed.

Lord Maccon, for one, returned to his pack to find that his previous Beta had emigrated to Scotland for an un-specified indenture and that a young dandy of an Alpha waited tentatively in his place.

Biffy handed him a letter from Professor Lyall, tears in his eyes. Alexia, unabashed, read it over her husband's arm.

"My dear sir. I have no means of making amends.

Even an apology would be more an insult, of that I am well aware. I have trained young Biffy to the best of my abilities. He will make a fine Beta, even though, as you may now already have smelled, he has manifested Anubis form. I thought, perhaps, you might take over training him for his next role—your replacement—contingent upon such a time as you leave us for Egypt and a well-earned retirement."

Upon reading that, Alexia asked, "How did he know your plans? You didn't discuss it with him ahead of time, did you?"

"No, but that's Randolph for you."

They continued with the letter.

"Our Biffy is part of this modern age. Shifting times require a London dandy for a London Pack. Try not, my dear lord, to see him in light of your own abilities as Alpha. He will never be that kind of wolf. I believe he is what our pack will need in the future, regardless."

Alexia looked up at Biffy. The young werewolf seemed to be feeling a more intense emotion over Professor Lyall's abandonment than she might have predicted. What had happened while they were in Egypt?

"Biffy," asked Alexia, because she had no subtlety, "did something significant occur between you and Lyall while we were away?"

Biffy hung his head. "He promised he would come back to me eventually. When we were all ready. Ten, twenty years, he said. Not so long for an immortal. Shifting times, he said."

Alexia nodded, feeling old. "But it feels like a very long time?" *Ah, young love.*

Biffy nodded sadly.

The earl, sensitive to his pack member's feelings, drew Alexia's attention back to Lyall's letter before she could continue interrogating the young dandy.

The letter continued.

"Don't tell Biffy yet. He isn't ready to know his future. Not the one that I envision for him. But he is ready to learn how to lead a pack, and you, my lord, will be an excellent teacher. Despite everything, I remain faithfully your friend, Professor Randolph Lyall."

"Ah, so," said Alexia, looking back and forth between the two gentlemen, their eyes down-turned. "It is an elegant solution," she said at last.

"He was always verra good at elegant solutions," said Lord Maccon softly. Then he bucked up. "Well, young Biffy, I suspect with you as my Beta, I'll never again be allowed out without a cravat."

Biffy was aghast. "Certainly not, my lord!"

"Good to know where I stand from the start." Conall grinned amiably at the boy.

Rumpet stuck his head in. Rumpet had been brought out of retirement to take over for Floote as pack butler. He'd set up as an innkeeper in Pickering after the vampires took over Woolsey but jumped at the chance to return to his old position. Pickering and innkeeping, as it turned out, were not all he had hoped.

"Lady Maccon, there's a gentleman to see you." The butler had a certain curl to his lip that in Alexia's experience could only mean one man.

"Ah, show him into the front parlor. If you will excuse me, husband, Biffy, I'm certain you have much to discuss. There is Channing to consider, if nothing else."

"Oh, blast it. Channing," muttered Lord Maccon.

Alexia let herself out.

Lord Akeldama sat waiting for her in the front parlor, one silken leg crossed over the other, blue eyes bright and slightly accusatory. He was wearing pea green and salmon this evening, a pleasant swirl of spring colors to counteract the gray weather they'd been experiencing of late.

"Alexia, my *darling* toggle button!"

"My lord, how are you?"

"I am here to reclaim my dearest little daughter."

"Of course, of course. Rumpet, fetch Prudence for his lordship, would you? She's sleeping in the back parlor. Did you miss her, my lord?"

"Like a hat misses a feather, darling! The droney poos and I have been bereft, quite bereft I tell you!"

"Well, she was very useful, in her way."

"Of course she was. And Matakara—are the rumors true?"

"Where do you think Ivy acquired her new hive?"

"Yes, Alexia, pigeon, I mean to discuss that little incident with you. Did you have to bring them *all*?"

"A new queen, plus five Egyptian vampires and assorted drones? You object to my bringing souvenirs back from Egypt? Everyone brings back souvenirs from their travels abroad, my lord. It is the *done thing*."

"Well, dewdrop, I don't object *as such*, but . . ."

Alexia smiled craftily. "Ivy has chosen somewhere in Wimbledon for her hive's location. A little too close for comfort, my lord?"

The vampire arched a blond eyebrow at her haughtily. "Countess Nadasdy is *not* amused."

"She wouldn't be. Someone is essentially taking on her old role in society."

"*Ivy Tunstell*, no less." Lord Akeldama frowned, one perfect crease marring the white smoothness of his forehead. "She is terribly interested in fashion, isn't she?"

"Oh, dear." Alexia hid a smile. "That, too, is your territory. I see."

"An *actress*, my little blueberry. I mean, really. Have you *seen* her hats?"

"You paid a call?"

"Of course I paid a call! She is a new queen, after all. Etiquette *must* be observed. But really"—he shuddered delicately—"those hats."

Alexia thought of Professor Lyall's letter. "It is the modern age, my dear Lord Akeldama. I think we must learn to accept such things as a consequence of shifting times."

"*Shifting times*, indeed. What a very werewolf way of putting it."

Rumpet opened the door and Prudence toddled sleepily into the room.

"Ah, *puggle precious*, how is my darling girl?"

Alexia grabbed her daughter's arm before she could launch herself at the vampire. "Dama!"

At Lady Maccon's nod, the vampire bent to embrace his adopted child, Alexia maintaining a firm grip the entire time.

"Welcome home, *poppet*!"

"Dama, Dama!"

Alexia looked on affectionately. "We've learned a few things about our girl here, haven't we, Prudence dear?"

"No," said Prudence.

"One of them is that she doesn't like her name."

"No?" Lord Akeldama looked very thoughtful. "Well,

there you have it. I couldn't sympathize more, puggle. I don't *approve* of most people's names either."

Alexia laughed.

Prudence took sudden interest in Alexia's parasol, sitting next to her on the settee.

"Mine?" suggested Prudence.

"Perhaps someday," said her mother.

Looking at his adopted daughter thoughtfully, Lord Akeldama said, "Shifting times, my dear *Ruffled Parasol*?"

Alexia did not bother to ask how he might know her secret code name. She only looked him straight on, forthright as always. "Shifting times, *Goldenrod*."

extras

orbit

meet the author

Ms. Carriger began writing to cope with being raised in obscurity by an expatriate Brit and an incurable curmudgeon. She escaped small-town life and inadvertently acquired several degrees in higher learning. Ms. Carriger then traveled the historic cities of Europe, subsisting entirely on biscuits secreted in her handbag. She now resides in the Colonies, surrounded by fantastic shoes, where she insists on tea imported directly from London and cats that pee into toilets. She is fond of teeny-tiny hats and tropical fruit. Find out more about Ms. Carriger at www.gailcarriger.com.

introducing

If you enjoyed
TIMELESS,
look out for

BLOOD RIGHTS

Book 1 of The House of Comarré

by Kristen Painter

Born into a life of secrets and service, Chrysabelle's body bears the telltale marks of a comarré—a special race of humans bred to feed vampire nobility. When her patron is murdered, she becomes the prime suspect, which sends her running into the mortal world… and into the arms of Malkolm, an outcast vampire cursed to kill every being from whom he drinks.

Now, Chrysabelle and Malkolm must work together to stop a plot to merge the mortal and supernatural worlds. If they fail, a chaos unlike anything anyone has ever seen will threaten to reign.

Paradise City, New Florida, 2067

The cheap lace and single-sewn seams pressed into Chrysabelle's flesh, weighed down by the uncomfortable tapestry jacket that finished her disguise. Her training kept her from fidgeting with the shirt's tag even as it bit into her skin. She studied those around her. How curious that the kine perceived her world this way. No, *this* was her world, not the one she'd left behind. And she had to stop thinking of humans as kine. She was one of them now. Free. Independent. Owned by no one.

She forced a weak smile as the club's heavy electronic beat ricocheted through her bones. Lights flickered and strobed, casting shadows and angles that paid no compliments to the faces around her. She cringed as a few bodies collided with her in the surrounding crush. Nothing in her years of training had prepared her for immersion in a crowd of mortals. She recognized the warm, earthy smell of them from the human servants her patron and the other nobles had kept, but acclimating to their noise and their boisterous behavior was going to take time. Perhaps humans lived so hard because they had so little of that very thing.

Something she was coming to understand.

The names on the slip of paper in her pocket were memorized, but she pulled it out and read them again. *Jonas Sweets,* and beneath it, *Nyssa,* both written in her aunt's flowery script. Just the sight of the handwriting calmed her a little. She folded the note and tucked it away. If Aunt Maris said Jonas could connect her with help, Chrysabelle would trust that he could, even though the idea of trusting a kine—no, a human—seemed untenable.

She pushed through to the bar, failing in her attempt to avoid more contact but happy at how little attention she attracted. The foundation Maris had applied to her hands, face and neck, the only skin left visible by her clothing, covered her signum perfectly. No longer did the multitude of gold markings she bore identify her as an object to be possessed. She was her own person now, passing easily as human.

The feat split her in two. While part of her thrilled to be free of the stifling propriety that governed her every move and rejoiced that she was no longer property, another part of her felt wholly unprepared for this existence. There was no denying life in Algernon's manor had been one of shelter and privilege.

Enough wallowing. She hadn't the time and there was no going back, even if she could. Which she wouldn't. And it wasn't as if Aunt Maris hadn't provided for her and wouldn't continue to do so, if Chrysabelle could just take care of this one small problem. Finding a space between two bodies, she squeezed in and waited for the bartender's attention.

He nodded at her. "What can I get you?"

She slid the first plastic fifty across the bar as Maris had instructed. "I need to find Jonas Sweets."

He took the bill, smiling enough to display canines capped into points. Ridiculous. "Haven't seen him in a few days, but he'll show up eventually."

Eventually was too late. She added a second bill. "What time does he usually come in?"

The bartender removed the empty glasses in front of her, snatched up the money, and leaned in. "Midnight. Sometimes sooner. Sometimes later."

It was nearly 1 a.m. now. "How about his assistant, Nyssa? The mute girl?"

"She won't show without him." He tapped the bar with damp fingers. "I can give Jonas a message for you, if he turns up. What's your name?"

She shook her head. No names. No clues. No trail. The bartender shrugged and hustled away. She slumped against the bar and rested her hand over her eyes. At least she could get out of here now. Or maybe she should stay. The Nothos wouldn't attempt anything in so public a place, would they?

A bitter laugh stalled in her throat. She knew better. The hellhounds could kill her in a single pass, without a noise or a struggle or her even knowing what had happened until the pain lit every nerve in her body or her heart shuddered to a stop. She'd never seen one of the horrible creatures, but she didn't need to in order to understand what one was capable of.

They could walk among this crowd without detection, hidden by the covenant that protected humans from the othernaturals, the vampires, varcolai, fae, and such that coexisted with them. She would be the only one to see them coming.

The certainty of her death echoed in her marrow. She shoved the thought away and lifted her head, scanning the crowd, inhaling the earthy human aroma in search of the signature reek of brimstone. Were they already here? Had they tracked her this far, this fast? She wouldn't go back to her aunt's if they had. Couldn't risk bringing that danger to her only family. Maris was not the strong young woman she'd once been.

Her gaze skipped from face to face. So many powdered

cheeks and blood red lips. Mouths full of false fangs. Cultivated widow's peaks. All in an attempt to what? Replicate the very beings who would drain the lifeblood from their mortal bodies before they could utter a single word of sycophantic praise? Poor, misguided fools. She felt sorry for them, really. They worshipped their own deaths, lulled into thinking beauty and perfection were just a bite away. She would never think that. Never fall under the spell of those manufactured lies. No matter how long or how short her new life was.

She knew too much.

Malkolm hated Puncture with every undead fiber of his being. If it weren't for the bloodlust crazing his brain—which kicked the ever-present voices into a frenzy—he'd be home, sipping the single malt he could no longer afford, maybe listening to Fauré or Tchaikovsky while searching his books for a way to empty his head of all thoughts but his own.

Damn Jonas for disappearing without setting up another reliable source. Mal cracked his knuckles, thinking about the beating that idiot was in for when he showed up again. It wasn't like the local Quik-E-Mart carried pints of fresh, clean, human blood. Unfortunately.

The warm, delicious scent of the very thing he craved hit full force as he pushed through the heavy velvet drapes curtaining the VIP section. In here, his real face, the face of the monster he'd been turned into, made him the very best of their pretenders and got him access to any area of the nightclub he wanted. Ironic, considering how showing his real face anywhere else would probably get him locked up as a mental patient. He shuddered and inhaled without thinking. His body tensed with the seductive aroma of thriving, vibrating life. The voices went mad, pounding against his skull. A multitude of heartbeats filled his ears, pulses around him calling out like siren songs. *Bite me, drink me, swallow me whole.*

Damn Sweets.

A petite redhead with a jeweled cross dangling between her breasts stopped dead in front of him. Like an actual vampire could ever tolerate the touch of that sacred symbol. Dumb git. But then how was she to know the origins of creatures she only hoped were real? She appraised him from head to toe, running her tongue over a set of resin fangs. "You're new here, huh? I love your look. Are those contacts? I haven't seen any metallic ones like that. Kinda different, but totally hot."

She reached out to touch the hard ridge of his cheekbone and he snapped back, baring his teeth and growling softly. *Eat her.* She scowled. "Chill, dude." Pouting, she skulked away, muttering "freak" under her breath.

Fine. Let her think what she wanted. A human's touch might push him over the edge. No, he reassured himself, it wouldn't. *Yes.* He wouldn't let it. *Do.* He wouldn't get that far gone. *Go.* But in truth, he balanced on the edge. *Fall.* He needed to feed. *To kill.* To shut the voices up.

With that thought he shoved his way to the bar, disgusted things had gotten this dire. He got the bartender's attention, then pushed some persuasion into his voice. "Hey." It was one of the few powers that hadn't blinked out on him yet. Good old family genes.

His head turned in Mal's direction, eyes slightly glazed. Mal eased off. Humans were so suggestible. "What'll it be?"

"Give me a Vlad." Inwardly, he died a little. Metaphorically speaking. The whole idea of doing this here, in full view of a human audience, made him sick. But not as sick as going without. How fortunate that humans wanted to mimic his kind to the full extent.

"A shot?"

"A pint."

The bartender's brows lifted. "Looking to get laid, huh? A pint should keep you busy all night. These chicks get seriously damp over that action. Not that anyone's managed to drink the pint and keep it down." He hesitated. "You gotta puke, you head for the john, you got me?"

"Not going to happen."

"Yeah, right." The bartender opened a small black fridge and took out a plastic bag fat with red liquid.

Mal swallowed the saliva coating his tongue, unable to focus his gaze elsewhere, despite the fact he preferred his sustenance body temperature and not chilled. A few of the voices wept softly. "That's human, right? And fresh?"

The bartender laughed. "Chickening out?"

"No. Just making sure."

"Yeah, it's fresh and it's human. That's why it's $250 a pop." He squirted the liquid into a pilsner. It oozed down the glass thick and viscous, sending a bittersweet aroma into the air. Even here in the VIP lounge, heads turned. Several women and at least one man radiated hard lust in his direction. The scent of human desire was like dying roses, and right now, Puncture's VIP lounge smelled like a funeral parlor. He hadn't anticipated such a rapt audience, but the ache in his gut stuck up a big middle finger to caring what the humans around him thought. At least there weren't any fringe vamps here tonight. Despite his status as an outcast anathema, the lesser-class vampires only saw him as nobility. He wasn't in the mood to be sucked up to. Ever.

The bartender slid the glass his way. "There you go. Will that be cash?"

"Start a tab."

"I don't think so, buddy."

Mal refocused his power. "I've already paid you."

The man's jaw loosened and the tension lines in his forehead disappeared. "You've already paid."

"That's a good little human," Mal muttered. He grabbed the pilsner and walked toward an empty stretch of railing for a little privacy. The air behind him heated up. He glanced over his shoulder. A set of twins with blue-black hair, jet lips, and matching leather corsets stood waiting.

"Hi," they said in unison.

Eat them. Drain them.

"No." He filled his voice with power, hoping that would be enough.

They stepped forward. Behind them, the bartender watched with obvious interest.

Damn Sweets.

The blood warmed in his grasp, its tang filling his nose, but feeding would have to wait a moment longer. Using charm this time, he spoke. "I am not the one you seek. Pleasure awaits you elsewhere. Leave me now."

They nodded sleepily and moved away.

The effort exhausted him. He was too weak to use so much power in such a short span of time. He gripped the railing, waiting for the dizziness in his head to abate. He stared into the crowd below. Scanned for Nyssa, but he knew better. She only left Sweets's side when she had a delivery. The moving bodies blurred until they were an undulating mass, each one undistinguishable from the next until a muted flash of gold stopped his gaze. His entire being froze. Not here. Couldn't be.

He blinked, then stared harder. The flickering glow remained. It reminded him of a dying firefly. Instinct kicked in. Sparks of need exploded in his gut. His gums ached, causing him to pop his jaw. The small hairs on the back of his neck lifted and the voices went oddly quiet, save an occasional whimper. His world converged down to the soft light emanating from the crowd near the downstairs bar.

He had to find the source, see if it really was what he thought. If it was, he had to get to it before anyone else did. The urge drove him inexplicably forward.

All traces of exhaustion disappeared. The glass in his hand fell to the floor, splattering blood that no longer called to him. He vaulted over the railing and dropped effortlessly to the dance floor below. The crush parted to let him through as he strode toward the gentle beacon.

She stood at the bar, her back to him. The generous fall of sunlight-blond hair stopped him, but the fabled luminescence brought him back to reality. So beautiful this close. He rubbed at his aching jaw. *You'll scare her like this, you fool. You're all fang and hunger. Show some respect.*

He assumed his human face, then approached. "Looking for someone?"

She tensed, going statue still. Even with the heavy bass, he felt her heartbeat shoot up a notch. He moved closer and leaned forward to speak without human ears hearing. Bad move. Her scent plunged into him dagger sharp, its honeyed perfume nearly doubling him with hunger pains. The whimpering in his head increased. Catching himself, he staggered for the bar behind her and reached out for support.

His hand closed over her wrist. Her pulse thrummed beneath his fingertips. Welcoming heat blazed up his arm. A chorus of fearful voices sang out in his head. *Get away, get away, get away...*

She spun, eyes fear-wide, heart thudding. "You're..." She hesitated then mouthed the words "not human."

Beneath his grip, she trembled. He pulled his hand away and stared. Had he been wrong? No marks adorned her face or hands. Maybe...but no. She had the blond hair, the glow, the carmine lips. She hid the marks somehow. He wasn't wrong. He knew enough of the history, the lore, the traditions. Besides, he'd seen her kind before. Just the once, but it wasn't something you ever forgot no matter how long you lived. Only one thing caused that glow.

She bent her head. "Master," she whispered.

"Don't. Don't call me that. It's not necessary." She thought him nobility? Why not assume he was fringe? Or worse, anathema? But she'd addressed him with the respect due her better. A noble with all rights and privileges. Which he wasn't. And she'd surely guessed he was here to feed. Which he was.

She nodded. "As you wish, mast—" Visibly flustered, she cut herself off. "As you wish."

He gestured toward the exit. "Outside. You don't belong here." Anyone could get to her here. Like Preacher. It wasn't safe. How she'd ended up here, he couldn't fathom. Finding a live rabbit in a den of lions would have been less surprising.

"I'm sure my patron will be back in just a—"

"We both know I'm the only real vampire here." For now. "Let's go."

Her gaze wandered to the surrounding crowd, then past him. She sucked her lower lip between her teeth and twisted her hands together. Hesitantly, she brushed past, painting a line of hunger across his chest with the curve of her shoulder. *Get away, get away, get away...*

She was not for him. He knew that, and not just because of the voices, but getting his body to agree was a different matter. Her scent numbed him like good whiskey. Made him feel needy. Reckless. Finding some shred of control, he shadowed her out of the club, away from the mob awaiting entrance, and herded her deep into the alley. He scanned in both directions. Nothing. They hadn't been followed. He could get her somewhere safe. Not that he knew where that might be.

"No one saw us leave."

She backed away, hugging herself beneath her coat. Her chest rose and fell as though she'd run a marathon. Fear soured her sweet perfume. She had to be in some kind of trouble. Why else would she be here without an escort? Without her patron?

"Trust me, we're completely alone." He reached awkwardly to put his arm around her, the first attempt at comfort he'd made in years.

Quicker than a human eye could track, her arm snapped from under the coat, something dark and slim clutched in her hand. The side of her fist slammed into his chest. Whatever she held pierced him, missing his heart by inches. The voices shrieked, deafening him. Corrosive pain erupted where she made contact.

He froze, immobilized by hellfire scorching his insides. He fell to his knees and collapsed against the damp pavement. Foul water soaked his clothing as he lay there, her fading footfalls drowned out by the howling in his head.